Teacher's Pet

Acknowledgements

I started writing this on a whim some time back in October 2018. I wrote the first chapter and it stayed in a folder for years. Then, in the Spring of 2020 when the whole word was in isolation because of COVID, my eldest daughter was diagnosed with Lymphoma, so we sat in a hospital for weeks and months at a time.

Writing kept me sane when the whole world was falling apart around me, and now 3 years later, I'm finally putting it out there. I'm eternally grateful for writing always allowing me to return to it, whichever mood I might be in, and for giving me an escape from a reality that was sometimes too much to bear.

So, to all three of my beloved babies and partner in crime - Thank you for giving me a reason to get up every morning when what we've endured was enough to make me give up.

And to my small army of friends who have read every word and hounded me to publish, Dem, Nic and Shahla, thanks for being my biggest hype men.

Copyright © 2023 K.P Gray

All rights reserved.

Contents:

Contents

Teacher's Pet	1
Acknowledgements	2
Contents:	4
Prologue	7
2.	21
3.	26
4.	33
5.	38
6.	45
7.	52
8	59
9.	69
10.	74
11.	87
12.	94
13.	101
14.	111
15.	120
16.	126
17.	131
18.	135
19.	142
20.	146
21.	151
22.	157
23.	161

24. 167
25. 172
26. 174
27. 179
28. 184
29. 189
30. 194
31. 201
32. 206
33. 210
34. 217
35. 225
36. 232
37. 240
38. 242
39. 249
40. 256
41. 259
42. 263
43. 266
44. 268
45. 272
46. 277
47. 283
48. 285
49. 291
50. 297
51 301
52. 304
53. 312

54.	318
55.	323
56.	326
57.	333
58.	338
59.	340
60.	344
61.	349
62.	356
63.	361

Prologue

He'd been waiting at the bar for far too long and was getting impatient. It seemed like every other person with a pair of tits was getting served before him, and he'd had enough of women annoying him in the past 24 hours to last a lifetime. All he wanted was another pint and another round of Jaeger bombs to drown out the relentless moaning he'd had to put up with for the day. If it wasn't one thing, it was another, and he was drinking to forget about it all. He didn't need the hassle she brought along with her temperamental moods, and as good looking as she might have been, it didn't make up for her attitude – although, it's not like he didn't know that going into their situation. He was done for good this time and, come the morning, he was going to let her know, he thought to himself as he waved his card at the barman again trying to get his attention. Finally, he seemed to take notice, and swanned over, looking as though he'd had enough for one night as well. Jackson cleared his throat as he approached and gave a sigh of relief. He'd been waiting over 10 minutes for a drink which was valuable drinking time he had now wasted doing nothing.

'What can I get you?' the guy behind the bar shouted over the noise of the Saturday night crowd, but just as he went to list off what he wanted, a little brunette wormed her way in front of him and started reeling off her own drinks order.

'Are you fucking kidding me?!' he shouted, looking at her with frustration. She might have been pretty, in a weird sort of way, but she'd managed to annoy him in less than 2 seconds which led him to conclude it was quite obviously 'piss off Jackson' day for every woman he bumped into.

'-and 4 jaeger bombs please' Jackson heard her finish. He groaned in annoyance before she turned on him and shrugged,

"You snooze, you lose, Hun" she grinned, throwing him a wink, and that was it, he'd most definitely had enough.

"You do realise, any pretty girl with a pair of tits is going to get served first because he's a man, you ain't anything special darling, trust me. More to the point, I wasn't talking to you, I was speaking out loud, so how about you keep your shit opinions to yourself?" he snapped, gritting his teeth. Women were slowly becoming the bane of his life and this one had just gone to the top of his shit list, which, given the day he'd had, was impressive.

'ANY *pretty girl?*' she asked, cocking her head to the side sarcastically, 'well, luckily for me, I just so happen to fit the brief, so I'll enjoy my drinks whilst you stand here and continue to look like a dickhead, which you have been for the last 20 minutes' she finished loudly, before handing over her card to the barman who was smirking.

'If you don't mind' she said leaning over, 'can you serve this obnoxious twat next, so he doesn't have to abuse any other pretty women who get their drinks first please?'

She threw him another wink and mimed a 'you're welcome' whilst the barman laughed at Jackson stood there with his jaw and his fists clenched. He couldn't stay in the bar any longer. Not only did he want to punch the barman, he also wanted to tell the woman in front of him to go fuck herself.

Despite his temper flaring, Jackson decided he'd already said too much, and he didn't usually make a habit of being rude to women. He hadn't been raised that way, and he certainly knew better. He knew he should apologise for being rude in the first place but as far as he was concerned, she was getting a kick out of it more than anything, so the apology was unnecessary.

"We're going" he said, as he got back to the table where the others were sat and grabbed his jacket.

"We thought you'd fucking disappeared!" Marley shouted, grabbing him and putting him into a headlock before kissing him on the head, "what's the matter?!"

"I'm pissed off, I can't get a drink because everyone with a pair of tits gets served before me, and the bird over there has wound me up, so can we go and get drunk somewhere else?" Jackson said, pulling Marley's bicep from around his neck and rolling his shoulders.

'Jesus Christ, you aren't having much luck with the ladies today are you Jax?" Harry chimed in before downing the rest of his pint and grabbing his own coat.

"Who needs them anyway?" he grunted, before they left the bar and headed to the nearest place that served alcohol.

"Why do I always bump into assholes?" Liv asked as she balanced the tray of drinks on the table and the girls each grabbed a jaeger bomb.

'Why? What happened?' George said as she smelt each drink in turn to see which one was hers and placed her Jaeger down, ready to neck it.

"Some nob head at the bar was upset that I got served before him because apparently 'any pretty girl with a pair of tits' will get drinks and I'm 'nothing special'" she explained as she handed out the other drinks to Jade and Sophie.

'Ah well. You're drowning your sorrows anyway, and your own fella is a nob, so you're used to it" Jade shrugged, raising her glass and laughing.

Olivia rolled her eyes and shook her head. Jade had always been the outspoken one with no filter, but she wasn't wrong. Tommy wasn't the greatest boyfriend, but she loved him, so she put up with it. He wasn't the worst, but he could certainly improve. He was out every weekend with his friends, and when they were together, he was more interested in his phone than anything she had to say. Every time she planned something for the two of them, he was too tired or had other things to do, and worst of all, they didn't even sleep together anymore. He didn't even ask her.

She raised her glass and clinked it with the other girls before they all drowned their jaegerbombs and screwed their face up in grimace. She loved nights like these when she could let her hair down and didn't have to worry about anything. No work, no Tommy and no care in the world.

It was almost the end of the summer holidays, so she only had a week before she'd have to start preparing herself to return to school and to the classroom with a whole new bunch of kids. She didn't mind her job, but sometimes it really did test her patience. It seemed like every year, the kids were getting harder to teach and less willing to learn, but she tried anyway. She was lucky she'd been gifted with the patience of a saint because if she hadn't, she didn't know how she would have coped.

"Nope" Jade said shaking her head.

"Never again" Georgia agreed putting her glass down and grabbing her wine to rid her of the taste of the shot she just took.

"You both said that last time" Liv laughed, grabbing her own spritzer and taking a sip as well, "shall we just finish these and find somewhere else?"

The girls agreed and finished their drinks whilst chatting away loudly in the bar. Jade kept on about how her new boyfriend was amazing and she had definitely found the one, even though they all reminded her that she had said that 3 times already this year. George told everyone how her and Karl were still trying for a baby, and Sophie was going on about wedding plans again, which she'd been doing for the past 8 months since Mike had proposed to her. It seemed like everyone had something to look forward to and Liv just had to sit there and be happy for everyone else, which she was. She was always happy to see her friends happy, she just wished that something would go right for her for once.

...

If there was one thing Jackson hated, other than the women he'd had to deal with today, it was the end of a night out. All he wanted was a kebab and a taxi back home so he could sleep for the next 24 hours, turn his phone off and not have to deal with anyone. Instead, he was in the middle of crowds of people shouting and laughing, with the lads heckling every other person they saw. He didn't know why he did it to himself every time, he knew as soon as the boys got drunk, they became too much and he would have to end up dragging them home.

Now, after they'd been kicked out of the last 2 bars for Marley getting too rowdy, he was on his way to find a taxi, with no food, and no patience either. He'd left them halfway down the road when they'd decided they wanted to try and find somewhere else to drink, and he decided he couldn't be bothered with the consequences that would come with even more alcohol.

He walked along the taxi rank and fished in his pocket for his wallet before opening the door and jumping in the front seat sighing. As the passenger door closed, the rear door opened, and 2 girls stumbled into the back giggling and singing at the top of their lungs.

'14 Arundel Road please!' one of them called while the other one continued to climb over the seats on all fours and find her seatbelt.

'You've got to be joking?!' Jackson muttered, rolling his eyes and looking at the driver, who shrugged.

'Sorry girls,' he said, 'I've already got a passenger, so you'll have to get in the one behind?'

'OH!' Liv cried out, laughing, 'IT'S YOU AGAIN! Why don't YOU get in the taxi behind and be a gentleman for once!'

'I was here first?!" he shot back at her whilst she stared at him and pathetically poked out her tongue.

'Well, I'm not moving, so suck it up buttercup!' she said folding her arms across the same chest that had got her served before him earlier and raising her eyebrows.

She looked prettier now, but he was sure it was the beer goggles working their magic. She had a long brown bob that framed her little round face, with big brown eyes, olive coloured skin and freckles covering her nose and cheeks. Her body was covered from head to toe in a tight black jumpsuit which stretched across her chest and her hips, which he suddenly noticed were both amazing as he studied her from the back seat under the dim lights.

'Well, I ain't moving either!' he shrugged finally taking his eyes off her and turning back around whilst her friend laughed from behind the driver. She could get fucked (again) if she thought she was winning this one.

'Well, looks like neither of us are going anywhere then!" she laughed, shrugging her shoulders too and glaring at him from the back seat.

He really had had enough of women, and if he didn't hate them all already, he definitely did now.

…

How dare he, Liv thought, glaring at him from the back seat whilst he sat there with his perfect hair and perfect face and perfect smell. She hadn't noticed it earlier, but he was very, very attractive which made the fact he was an idiot even more depressing. He hadn't even attempted to apologise to her for earlier at the bar so if he thought she was going to move, he could keep thinking.

'You're not very nice, are you?" she said leaning between the chairs beside him and turning to the driver, 'Can you please just drop us off and then drop him wherever he wants after? Like, off a cliff or something' she asked sweetly, smiling.

'Wow, Pot, Kettle?' He muttered rolling his eyes again and looking at her, 'just drop them wherever they're going' he said to the taxi driver, then made himself comfortable in the front seat.

'thatta boy!' she said patting him on the shoulder before relaxing back into her own seat and buckling her belt.

The night had been a disaster really, but she'd had fun. Jade had seen her 'boyfriend' out, but he happened to be all over another woman. He'd gone from being 'the one' to the scum of the earth in about 0.3 seconds and Jade had gone on a rampage. As lovely as she was, when she saw red, there was no stopping her and despite trying to talk sense into her, she wasn't having any of it. She left early after hurling her drink in Ben's face, and Soph had been picked up by Mike when she'd had one too many and fell asleep on the toilet. Georgia and Liv had stayed out a while longer but, in the end, they agreed that it wasn't as fun with just the two of them.

As the taxi rounded the corner to Georgia's address, Liv leaned in for a kiss to say goodbye. 'I'll call you in the morning,' she said as Georgia tumbled out of the car wishing her and the driver good luck, laughing as she shut the door.

"Where now?" the driver asked in the rear-view mirror, whilst Liv rested her head in her hands.

'3 Furgar Avenue:' she slurred.

The fresh air had hit her, and she suddenly felt like she probably should have stopped drinking 3 vodkas ago. All she had to do was make it 10 minutes down the road. She would be fine, she thought as she rested her head on the window praying the 10 minutes went quick.

...

"Fuck. Right. Off." He said quietly when he heard snoring from the back of the taxi as it pulled up outside the address she had given. He shut his eyes, took a breath, and got out the car to open her door for her, but even that didn't wake her up.

"HEY!" he shouted nudging her softly, "we're here!"

She mumbled a little bit, stirring, but it seemed like she wasn't moving anywhere, and Jackson inhaled deeply in frustration as he watched her trying to unbuckle her seatbelt pathetically. If she didn't hurry the fuck up, he was going to lose his shit. He still hadn't got a kebab and all he wanted was to get in bed, have a wank, and sleep, which wasn't going to happen any time soon if she didn't move her fucking ass.

"Do you need help?!" he asked through gritted teeth as she finally managed to undo her seatbelt, but fell on to him in the process, narrowly missing his balls, and aggravating him even more.

'I, am, fine" she said taking her heels off and attempting to get out of the car, to no avail. She was taking the piss, he just wanted to get home, and if that meant helping her to the house, he would have to, unwillingly.

With that in mind, he lifted her from the seat and threw her over his shoulder whilst she giggled, but he'd only got a few steps forward before she started punching him in the back and shouting.

"'YOU'VE FORGOT MY BAG, YOU FAT IDIOT!" she screamed, earning an eye roll from him that she didn't see and a silent prayer that this whole ordeal would be over soon.

He span on his heels and headed back to the car whilst she attempted to push herself up on his shoulder, and grabbed her bag from the driver who was watching the two of them with an amused look on his face. He handed it to her before heading back up the path and felt her slump back over his shoulder where she muttered to herself something about him being really strong.

'Get the keys' he demanded, marching her up the path and waiting outside the front door. He had totally underestimated just *how nice her ass was as it bounced on top of his shoulder whilst she rummaged in her bag. She smelt good too, he thought, smirking to himself when she cheered behind him. If he didn't hate her so much, she really could have been his type. It was just a shame that she was a bitch.*

He placed her down on the floor carefully and watched whilst she attempted to put her key in the lock, but after 30 seconds he'd had enough of the painful ordeal and took the keys off of her so he could do it himself.

'Honestly' he said, rolling his eyes as he slotted the key in the lock and opened the door with a click.

'Sorry' she muttered, blushing as she turned on the light. 'I haven't been out in a while and...'

'Bye,' he cut her off, walking back down the path to the taxi. He really did need to get home. He could have easily stood and listened to her whine on for a while just to stare at her body, but he knew better than to do anything of the sort when he'd been drinking. He was going to go home, forget all about her, and fucking sleep, he thought as he slammed the door of the taxi and rounded the corner towards his own house.

...

Liv stood watching as he walked down the path and slumped her shoulders as the taxi pulled away. She really didn't know why she insisted on making an idiot of herself every time she had a drink and didn't know if she was more pissed off or embarrassed that he'd cut her off and left her standing there like a loser.

She threw down her heels and made her way up the stairs to her bedroom where an empty bed waited for her. Tommy obviously wouldn't be home, again, but she was used to it now and she certainly wasn't going to lose sleep over it. She just wished he'd have the decency to let her know once in a while. Liv pushed it to the back of her mind and unzipped her jumpsuit, before she hit the lights, jumped into bed, and began regretting the amount of Vodka she'd had whilst she drifted off to sleep.

1.

Last one, Liv thought to herself as she rubbed her temples and checked the time on her watch. It was almost 9:00pm and she'd been at the school since first thing trying to get everything ready. Why they thought it was acceptable to have parent's evenings this late was beyond her, but at least all of her appointments had showed up, which was something. All of the kids she taught were in their final year, and so all of their parents felt like they *had* to make an appointment to discuss whether or not their child was actually going to get a GCSE in her subject.

Parents had flooded her with questions all night about why it was so bloody important that their son or daughter learned how to work out the circumference of a circle? or what was the use of algebra that they would never use anyway? And each time she'd had to avoid rolling her eyes and plaster a fake smile on her face before explaining that she realised it was frustrating, but that was the curriculum, and she couldn't change it unfortunately.

Not that she would anyway. Maths seemed like the easiest thing in the world to her and it was frustrating sometimes when she would have to spend a weeks' worth of lessons going over the same, fucking, topic.

She checked the time on her watch again and exhaled loudly before taking off her glasses and cleaning them on the bottom of her dress. Obviously, her last appointment would be late, she thought, getting up and grabbing a can of Coke from the mini fridge in her classroom. It's not like she had to get home, catch up with Celebrity Great British Bake Off and actually eat for the first time today, she went on in her head, cracking open the can and returning to her seat feeling a little better after a large gulp and another huff.

'*Just 15 minutes left*', she muttered under her breath as she grabbed her phone from the drawer and checked that she hadn't missed anything remotely interesting in the past 30 minutes. There wasn't a single message she wanted to reply to, so she threw it back on her desk and went back to her cold can of coke. Her and the girls hadn't seen each other in weeks, and they were desperately trying to arrange a night together which she couldn't be bothered with right now. She didn't want to hear about weddings or babies or Jade's new fling or have them grill her about Tommy, which she knew they would after the month she'd had.

She decided not to dwell on it and started clearing her desk of everything but the last books she needed, realising that she really, really hated this part of her job. Dealing with parents, who always knew best, and who all believed that their son or daughter deserved A's across the board, regardless of whether or not they refused to apply themselves or listen every once in a while. Just as she began venting in her head again, a knock at her door brought her back to reality and she plastered her fake smile on, ready for the lecture that was bound to come.

'Miss Turnell?' he asked peering around the door and locking eyes with her at her desk, immediately sending her a shade of crimson as she got to her feet.

'C-come in?' she stuttered avoiding eye contact, "Erm, you must be Clayton's dad?' she asked, noting the striking resemblance between the two, and praying that he hadn't recognised her.

"Call me Jackson" he said joining her at the desk, "I'm so sorry I'm late. One of his other teachers had a hell of a lot to say and..." he trailed off, studying her as he pulled out his seat and they both sat down, noting that she looked familiar.

She joined him on the opposite side of the desk and glanced at his face for a split second taking in his features before turning away. He was very striking in close proximity, with dark chestnut eyes and a short, trimmed beard. He had dark curls on top of his head and a friendly smile which she briefly returned before she started, desperate to get the whole thing over with.

'Oh, please don't apologise, I think we all have a habit of doing it" she said, pulling over Clayton's books and
placing them in front of him neatly, "is there anything you want to ask me before we start?" she said, meeting his gaze.

"I don't think so, you know better than me" he shrugged, smiling again and leaning towards the desk to look over his work.

"Well," she said pointing out his workbooks in front of them "these are his workbooks so far over this year, we've covered topics from number, algebra and geometry and we are just beginning to touch on statistics" she began, but then she hesitated…

"Can I be honest?" she asked, taking a deep breath and removing her glasses, earning an eyebrow raise from Jackson which led her to continue.

"Clayton is very, very intelligent however, he refuses to apply himself and to be perfectly honest it's
annoying. He is naturally talented in this subject, but at the rate he's going, I'll be surprised if he reaches a 5, or a C" she shrugged forcing a smile as she waited for him to reply.

"I see" he said thoughtfully, staring at her so intensely that she shifted uncomfortably in her seat.

"I'm sorry," she said, regretting being so blunt about the situation. Clayton was both the best and the worst student in the classroom and spent every day making her life a living hell, although not intentionally. All the boys in the class wanted to be him, and all of the girls in the class loved everything about him which meant he held the attention of almost everyone in the room and thus, she didn't.

"He's your typical 'popular' kid, but he is *so* intelligent" she continued after using her fingers for quotation marks, "he has a natural gift for numbers and picks up things so quickly, when he's bothering to listen. He's just always distracted, and if it isn't his friends, it's the girls" she said shrugging.

"I see," he said again raising his eyebrows, "anything else?"

"Erm, I think that's it?" she said, feeling hot, and acutely aware that her cheeks were definitely red, "the point is, nothing that he knows for his exams has been learnt during his normal lessons with me and his classmates. It's all come from when he's been in detention and honestly, I couldn't fault him then. When he's taught on a 1 to 1 basis, he can do it all, but it means he's only benefitting from 1, maybe 2 hours a week instead of the 6 that are on his timetable and he's very behind as a result. He's more than capable of catching up, but he needs to work hard over the next 4 months to have a chance really".

Jackson continued to look at her and take it all in before he replied. He knew her face, but he couldn't quite put his finger on where he knew her from, all he knew was, she looked good. She had her hair pulled back neatly behind her ears and big dark rimmed glasses framing her eyes. As she spoke, he noticed how full her lips were and he had to make a conscious effort to keep his eyes from wandering down the rest her body and checking her out completely.

"So, where do we go from here?" he asked, concentrating on the matter at hand, "I don't want him pissing talent up the wall if he's got it, but I also don't want to push him if he's just not good at maths? If you know what I mean?"

"I understand," she replied pushing her glasses back up her nose and collecting his workbooks back up. "I can assure you that he really is capable of at least a 7, if not higher? He just needs to get his head down a bit more".

"So, what about extra tuition?" he asked, already deciding that he was going to go home and read Clayton the riot act. He was a good kid, but he was also fucking frustrating. People naturally gravitated towards him because he had something in common with everyone and treated everyone the same. He might've been the popular sports kid, but he also enjoyed watching documentaries, loved drawing and spent hours gaming as all teenage boys did. All of his teachers had said similar things tonight in a roundabout way, but she had been the only one who put it bluntly and he appreciated that.

"That would be ideal! I can put you in touch with some tutors who know the curriculum well and might have space?" she said happily.

"What about you?" he asked, wondering why she hadn't suggested herself.

She cleared her throat, and her cheeks began to redden as she fumbled with her words again, 'Well, I don't really do tutoring, I don't know if I can or whether it would be unethical because of my role as his teacher and…" she trailed off, silently cursing the fact that her face was red hot again and there for red, period.

"And?" he smirked, watching her fiddle with her hands nervously on the desk.

"Well to be honest with you, I just figured it might be a bit awkward after the last time we met" she laughed.

He raised his eyebrows and tried recall what she was talking about, because she wasn't someone you'd easily forget. As he scanned his memories for something, anything, she brought it all back and he couldn't help but kick himself for not realising.

"Well, if it wasn't awkward already, it is now" she muttered, pushing her glasses up her nose again, "I hijacked your taxi? Back in summer" she said sheepishly, with a small smile.

"Oh fuck," he said, eyes bulging, "Oh, sorry, for swearing. I'm so sorry. I was a prick that night and I never should have spoken to you like that. I was having a terrible day, which isn't an excuse, but everything was going wrong, and I took it out on you so…"

"Honestly, you don't have to apologise," she said, shaking her head, "I was quite clearly being a nightmare so, I'm sorry, and thanks for making sure I got home safe, I'm sorry you had to do that"

Jackson was taken back to the night he'd carried her to her door whilst she was flung over his shoulder. He'd made sure she was home safe, got back in the taxi, and wished like hell that she hadn't fucked him off earlier in the bar. Whilst she'd fumbled with her door keys, he'd admired her little waist and every inch of her thick legs. She was insane, but he knew better than to try his luck when she was drunk. Instead, he'd gone home pissed, pissed off and frustrated with the memory of her ass fresh in his mind.

"No really, I'm not usually like that and I'm sorry. I felt so bad the next day, I was going to send you flowers to apologise but I forgot the address and I didn't want to turn up on the door and look like a crazy stalker, plus I didn't know if I should be worried about a boyfriend, or... " he trailed off, shaking his head.

"Can we do over?" he asked, making her smile.

When she nodded, Jackson offered her his hand and Liv extended hers too,

"I'm Jackson" he said, staring at her intensely again.

"It's nice to meet you Jackson, I'm Olivia"

2.

It was just after 10:00pm when Liv finally got home. She bypassed the lounge and went straight to the kitchen where she grabbed a pack of biscuits and then went to bed. It had been a ridiculously long day and she couldn't wait to wind down. She shed her clothes and climbed under the blankets, then scrolled through the messages she'd ignored earlier, sighing heavily. There were 52 in the group chat from the girls, and 2 from Tommy that she had absolutely no interest in.

The girls were discussing dinner plans at Sophie's for a well-deserved girl's night, as well as asking how she was feeling and whether she needed anything, but she didn't. Tommy had text to beg her to answer her phone, but she wasn't ready to open that can of worms either. She hadn't purposely avoided the girls, but she also hadn't gone out of her way to see them. It had been 6 weeks since Tommy had finished things, and she'd walked out of the house leaving everything behind other than a suitcase full of clothes and her stuff for work. She'd left the house without looking back, and without a tear in sight.

Now, she was curled up in bed, in her brother's spare room wondering when life would get better. She couldn't bear to see the girls and celebrate all of their good news, whilst her life was falling apart. She loved them, and she was happy for them, but she had just needed time to feel sorry for herself and get her own life on track. Tommy had been her life for 8 years and she'd put up with everything. All the late nights and the nights he didn't come home, the lying, the manipulating and apparently the cheating too, she had finally discovered. The girls had been telling her that he was a scumbag for years, and she had been avoiding the "I told you so's" since. The relationship may have officially ended, but it was over long before she left.

Liv had always assumed he'd been too scared to commit, and that was the reason he'd never wanted kids, or spoke about getting engaged or getting married, but as it turned out, he was just not interested in pursuing any of that stuff with her. He'd always liked his freedom, would rather go out with his mates than take her on a date, and in the end, she expected it. No grand gestures of love, no special celebrations and quite frankly no affection whatsoever. They hadn't even had sex for almost a year before he'd called it off, and now it was done she kept asking herself over and over, why she had stayed so long?

Liv had been going over it in her mind daily trying to work out why she hadn't realised it was over so long ago, but she always came back to the same answer. She didn't care. She hadn't cried when she left, or felt upset, or angry, she just felt a bit 'lost', like, what was her purpose now?

She was just in a rut.

She hated being in it, but at the same time, she wasn't ready to do anything about it. Instead, she'd spent every night for the last 6 weeks looking for somewhere new to live, binge watching Netflix, and making up excuses as to why she couldn't go out or do anything fun. That was until tonight anyway.

After the parents evening had finished, Jackson and her had exchanged numbers and both apologised again for their confrontation with one another the last time they met. On the way home she'd thought about how fun that night had been, how she'd loved getting dressed up and how she'd been carried to her door like a damsel in distress after one too many. She remembered it had been the first physical contact she'd had with a man in months, and she'd decided she was more than ready to do it all over again.

She opened up WhatsApp to scroll through the messages the girls had sent earlier properly. They were all trying desperately to convince her that she needed to let her hair down so without another thought she replied:

22:06: Saturday sounds good! I'm buying! Let's start early

Just before she put her phone away, she opened up a new message to Jackson and toyed with the idea of messaging him too. After staring at his photo for much longer than she should have, Liv thought better of it and put her phone on to charge before she drifted off for the night, buzzing for a weekend of margaritas and martinis.

...

Clayton was in bed watching Stranger Things by the time Jackson had finished parents evening, stopped at the shop and got back to the house. He knocked on his door and poked his head around to find him engrossed in his TV and phone simultaneously. Jackson leant against the door frame with his arms crossed over his chest and waited as Clayton finished his text and rummaged around under the duvet for the TV remote.

"How did it go?" He asked, when he finally found the controller and managed to pause the television.

"Common theme is that you're bright, but also a twat" he shrugged, sitting himself at the end of his bed.

"Well, I could have told you that" he said, rolling his eyes "I just don't like school. It's boring, and easy, but I can't exactly tell all of the teachers that can I? It would make them look stupid"

Jackson laughed at his son who reminded him so much of himself. He'd always been bright too, but when he was at school, he'd also got into fights almost every day which meant that most of his time was spent in isolation or at home after being excluded. If it hadn't been for his natural talent in most subjects he would definitely have been permanently expelled. Well, that and the fact that the headteacher was also dating his mum whilst he was there.

"Most subjects say you're fine and that you're on track for your grades, apart from maths?" He asked cocking an eyebrow.

Clayton went red and shrugged his shoulders.

"What did Miss. Turnell say?" He asked, looking embarrassed.

"That you're an asshole," Jackson replied with a stern tone to his voice, "she said you have all the potential in the world but you're too busy having a jolly with your mates, or eyeing up the girls to do any real work, and that's the reason she puts you in detention so much, because when you're there, you don't seem to struggle with anything?"

Clayton shrugged again and looked at his Dad.

"I suppose" he laughed, "not that detention with her is a bad thing. She's a rocket, and she's a decent teacher to be fair".

Jackson scowled at him although he couldn't agree more. She was attractive, and stern, but most importantly, she seemed to want the best for his son, which was all he cared about. He shook her from his thoughts and continued with his grilling, despite the fact that his mind kept wandering back to how she looked at him earlier that night.

"Well, that's why she's coming to tutor you here" he said getting up from the bed and heading towards the door. "Now, get some sleep"

"What do you mean, tutor me here?!" He shouted as Jackson left the room and went downstairs to wind down for the night. He knew Clayton would hate extra tuition, but at least he knew he liked her, which was good, he thought as he settled down on the sofa. He quickly found something to watch on TV before he fished out his phone from his pocket and opened the Facebook app, typing her name into the search bar..

Olivia Turnell

~ No matches ~

Of course not, he thought, knowing full well it would be stupid for a teacher to have their real name attached to their social media. Kicking himself for even trying, he started to scroll through his newsfeed leisurely instead. Why the hell did he search her on her Facebook anyway? He had her number, and he would just text her to arrange what dates she was free to tutor Clayton, no big deal. It wasn't like he could add her as a friend an hour after he'd met her, that was weird, and they weren't friends. But the thought of scrolling through her photos to see what she looked like when she let her hair down, or in that skin-tight jumpsuit again, was still playing on his mind. A lot.

With thoughts of Liv leaving him frustrated, he picked himself up off the sofa and decided to call it a night. As he went up the stairs, he typed out a message to her on WhatsApp apologising again and thanking her for her honesty, before climbing into bed and falling asleep the minute his head hit the pillow.

3.

Liv snoozed her alarm and rolled back over in bed, throwing the quilt over her head and begging for another 10 minutes. She'd often wondered why she had taken the career path of a teacher which meant getting up early every day, knowing full well she was not a morning person. Realising that she would snooze her alarm another 3 or 4 times and be late if she didn't get up right away, Liv reluctantly threw the covers back and stretched aggressively.

She jumped out of bed and headed for the kitchen, made herself a coffee that she left to cool in her room, then went for a shower to wake herself up.

Liv let the hot water wash away the sleep and wrapped herself up in a towel reminding herself it was only 2 days until the weekend. She still had to find something to wear, make a plan of action with the girls and inform her brother Owen that she would be home late on Saturday night. Not that he'd care, he'd probably end up going out too knowing him.

Liv returned to her room and grabbed her coffee and phone from the bedside table, a little more awake after having to step out of the hot shower into the cold air. She sipped the hot liquor, thanking God for caffeine, and opened up her the new notifications on her phone, including a message from Jackson.

> 23:25
> "Sorry it's late. I just wanted to say thanks again for being so honest and to apologise (again) for before. Clayton seems happy you're going to teach him. Let me know what days are good for you and how much the sessions are.
> Jax x"

She read it again and smiled before she typed out her reply.

> 06:23
> Don't mention it, I tend to push my luck when I've had a few. You're more than welcome, I'm so glad he's up for it! Mondays and Thursdays are probably my best days so let me know if this works for you both, if not, I can juggle some things around. Liv.
>
> P.S Sorry it's early."

She toyed with the idea of putting a "x" but felt it was best to keep it professional since he was her student's dad, and she didn't know if that would suggest she was interested, or if it suggested he was interested!?

It's a 'x', he probably didn't even mean to do it. She thought to herself pulling on her underwear and finding some clothes. It didn't take long to convince herself that it had been an accident on his part and was probably a force of habit like she had. Instead of dwelling, she stopped thinking too much into it and put it to the back of her mind before she tackled her hair in the mirror, singing along to the radio as she did.

Nothing to it.

...

Jackson grabbed his towel from the bars and wrapped it around his neck before he picked up his phone and bottle and headed to the shower. She'd replied. Last night after he'd sent the message, he'd kicked himself. He didn't want to come across eager, but he'd wanted to message her, badly. He'd thought he'd play it cool when she messaged, leave it a while before he replied, but instead he decided that life was too short to play silly games and started to type as soon as he'd read what she said. Besides, she was just coming over to teach Clayton, he didn't have to worry about what impression he made because it was all for his son's benefit.

Where his kid was concerned it was perfectly normal to be supportive. He should be excited that she was giving his son the opportunity to learn, and that deserved a text back immediately he thought thumbing his phone. If she was going out of her way to help his son, the least he could do was not to keep her waiting, that would be rude.

Jackson realised it was Wednesday which meant she could potentially start tomorrow, and he'd get to see her again. It was strictly for Clayton's sake anyway, he convinced himself as he reread her text, typed his reply and inwardly groaned that she hadn't put a 'x'.

'Too eager', he thought, when he finished his text and added 2 of his own at the end. He deleted the second and pressed send, then threw his phone in his gym bag before he jumped in the showers.

...

Liv was awful at checking her phone and inwardly scolded herself for missing the reply he had sent almost 2 hours ago!

06:45
Not a problem, already at the gym. The early bird catches the worm, as they say. Mondays and Thursdays are good for us, could you come start tomorrow? If so, what time is good for you? Is it better if I'm not there? Do I need to get him anything? Do you need

anything? Let me know how much the sessions are too, and I'll grab the cash out for you. x"

She'd read the text on her way into school but got side-tracked by one of her kids asking her about chess club and whether it was on, which it was. By the time she'd got inside, it was time for her morning briefing, then she had form and then she started lessons straight away after that. It wasn't until lunchtime that she finally got 5 minutes to herself and remembered she'd never replied. She grabbed her lunch and can of coke from the fridge, then grinned when she saw 23 notifications from the girls and another from Jackson.

She ignored the group chat deciding she would go through them later and opened up her WhatsApp to Jackson.

09:42
"Sorry. I don't have a clue how this works."

He had replied an hour after she'd inadvertently ignored his message, making her laugh and she replied quickly feeling guilty for ignoring him all day:

12:23
I'm so sorry, I've been caught up with lessons all morning. I wasn't ignoring you! Don't apologise, it's lovely that you're doing all this for Clayton. I think it's great! Tomorrow sounds good to me, I will just need your address. Clayton should have everything he needs, if not we can sort it at a later date. Lol. You being there is fine, we will see how he works with Dad around and if he struggles, we can talk about

what will be best for him. Erm, just coffee or anything highly caffeinated is fine, thank you for asking. Look forward to seeing you x

'Look forward to seeing you?!' She muttered going crimson when she hit send. What the hell Olivia?!

Liv ate her lunch and quickly fumbled through the settings in her phone for a new display picture. It was about time she changed it because it had been the same for months now, but she was also quite aware that she looked like a twat and thought that if Jackson wanted to take a look, the least she could do was give him something to look at.

No harm done.

...

He'd come across as too strong, he thought as he typed out the second text apologising for the million questions he had asked. Why was it this hard? And what the hell was wrong with him?

He thought back to the night he'd first met her and remembered carrying her to her door. Despite him being in a foul mood, she'd made him laugh and he'd kicked himself when he got home that he'd been too stubborn to talk to her, despite the fact she looked incredible that night. Had it been another day, he would have suggested a night cap, but he'd been rowing all day and women had been the cause of all his stress.

Jackson had kept his phone nearby throughout the day whilst he worked on his latest project and checked it far more than usual.

As a kid and as he grew up, he'd always had a talent for art and technology, so he'd naturally gravitated towards his role as a graphic designer and web designer when he was young. He'd worked at companies under others for years but now, he owned his own firm which catered for small businesses around the local area, as well as some sizeable well-known companies that were nationwide. Jackson did well for himself, but was humble, or so he liked to think.

He'd been working on a design for a restaurant all morning and been pinging emails back and forth with ideas. In graphic design, the customer was not always right and sometimes, it came to the point where he had to refuse work if they wouldn't agree with what he had in mind because he didn't want to be associated with a design that wasn't reflective of his talents. That was the worst part of the job, everyone thought they were an expert, most weren't even in the right ballpark.

He rubbed his temples as he read the last email he was sent and was glad the client had finally agreed on the logo he'd put forward. He was an up-and-coming chef in the country after reaching the final of MasterChef, and this was his first real venture. He wanted things to be perfect, so the whole process had been extremely time consuming. Jackson appreciated his vision, but it had been a ball ache trying to take all of his ideas and whittle them down to one design. Finally, after 16 attempts, he agreed on the 17th logo that Jackson had proposed and other than some minor tweaks, he was happy. Once it was complete, he could start designing everything else using the logo as his inspiration including the menus, the uniforms and the website. Jackson loved jobs like this, that started with a single idea and ended up being recognised all over the world, it was also extremely good for business to have such high-profile clientele.

As he doodled on the drawing pad with his stylus and made the final changes to the logo, his phone buzzed across the desk, and he dropped everything to answer.

"Jesus Jackson, you almost pissed your pants with excitement," Harry laughed as he leant back on his chair opposite. "Got something you want to spill?"

"Nothing at all mate" he said, shrugging his shoulders and trying desperately to keep a straight face. "Just an acquaintance"

"Yeah, alright," he replied rolling his eyes "we'll see"

4.

Caffeine. Caffeine. Caffeine.

He wandered up the aisle and stared at the Nespresso pods for the machine he'd just bought. Melozio, Elvazio, Bianco Leggero... espresso, without milk, latte, with milk, decaffeinated? Definitely not decaffeinated, at least.

He had no fucking clue what he was looking for but grabbed 4 different types and chucked them in the trolley along with his new toy. He'd already picked up some iced coffees and a few cans of cokes since he remembered she'd been drinking one the night of the parents evening. He'd covered all basis and still had enough time to learn how the machine worked tonight so he didn't embarrass himself tomorrow.

By the time Jackson got home, Clayton was back from school and was already watching Deadliest Catch on the TV in the lounge. He shouted hello on his way to the kitchen and asked what he fancied for dinner whilst he unpacked the bags and loaded the fridge. Clayton stood in the doorway and cocked an eyebrow at the box Jackson was holding and wondered what he was doing with a coffee machine.

"What's that?" He asked, reaching in the fridge and grabbing out a sausage roll whilst Jackson fumbled around with the cardboard and polystyrene looking for the instructions.

"What does it look like?" he said with his head in the box looking where they had got to. Clayton grabbed the plastic sleeve of instructions from the back of the coffee machine his dad had put on the side and handed them to him.

"Obviously I know what it is, what I mean is, why is it here?" he asked more specifically.

"Why not?" Jackson shrugged reading through the instructions on how to set it up and ignoring his son's confused stare.

"Erm, because you said, and I quote *"coffee tastes like dog shit and I don't drink it, so I don't need it in the house"*, when I asked why we didn't have a coffee pot next to the tea and sugar? You also said that you are British so tea is the only hot drink you appreciate, unless it's winter, when mulled wine or hot chocolate you can stomach depending on the occasion?"

Jackson rolled his eyes as he plugged in the machine and ran a sink of soapy water. "Are you a savant or something?"

Clayton wasn't wrong, Jackson hated coffee. He'd always liked the smell of it, but everything else made him want to vomit. It was bitter, and it didn't matter how much sugar or milk you added, it tasted vile.

"If you must know, I thought it would be nice to have? Is that okay?" he asked as he washed up the water tank, filled it and placed it on the machine.

"You're such a liar. How convenient that we suddenly have every caffeinated drink to ever exist in the house and Miss Turnell has a mug literally stating that she couldn't live without coffee, and a mini fridge with cans of coke in her classroom?"

"What a coincidence," Jackson said as he continued to mess around with the machine in front of him, ignoring his son.

"Dad....?" he asked, leaning against the side casually, "do you fancy my teacher?"

Jackson laughed as he opened the box of pods and read the instructions again, "No Clayton, I just want you to do well and if I'm going to have coffee in this house to bribe her, it's going to be the best coffee, ok?"

"Aww ok. That's nice of you Dad, I really appreciate it" he said walking out of the kitchen, "shame though, my step-mum would've been a MILF"

"CLAYTON!" Jackson shouted as his son ducked out of the way, narrowly missing getting hit by the box he'd just thrown at him. He laughed at his dad's grim expression and ducked out of the way of another box as he ran.

"Ooooooh, you're a bit touchy Dad. Must be the pheromones in the air" Clayton laughed as he was rugby tackled to the sofa and put in a headlock.

"I'm not gonna tell her!" he cried, tapping out on the arm wrapped around his neck playfully. Jackson let go and pushed Clayton back onto the sofa scowling as he watched his son cry with laughter.

"I'm a gentleman, and what the lady wants, the lady gets. You' could learn a lot from me" he winked returning to his new toy in the kitchen, "besides, she probably has a boyfriend, and she's your teacher. Even if I did fancy her, which I don't, it wouldn't be fair on you"

Clayton acknowledged his dad but didn't say anything else on the matter, just carried on laughing in the lounge. Jackson ignored him and practiced on the machine with different pods and milk, although he had no idea whether his efforts were any good. Now that he thought about it, what was to say that she wasn't taken? She definitely didn't have a ring on her finger, but that wasn't proof that she wasn't seeing someone. Jackson wanted desperately to do some digging before he got his hopes up too far but he thought better of it. It had nothing to do with him really, and he'd already told Clayton it wouldn't be fair, even if she was preoccupying his dreams at night again.

...

Liv couldn't remember the last time she'd smiled so much and kept reminding herself to keep a level head. She promised she was going to keep it professional, and not read too much into anything, which was hard since he text her back almost immediately each time she replied. She agreed to start Clayton's tuition at 5pm so she'd have enough time to finish up school and find the address, she'd also had to tell him that anything to drink was fine when he asked for specifics of what kind of caffeine she liked and decline dinner as he was worried that 6pm was 'dinner time' and he didn't want to interfere with that either if she left late. Liv knew he was just being nice, but it was such a change from what Tommy had been like that she found herself wanting to check her phone all the time. She wasn't used to this kind of feeling, of being excited at speaking to someone and laughing so much.

Throughout the evening their conversation had flown back and forth. Liv hadn't wanted to ask anything too personal, but both of them shared memories of the night they'd first met and the hangovers they had the next day. She asked if he went out local often, but he said he didn't, and neither did she. She said that she was heading out on the weekend for the first time in months.

She'd finally made a plan with the girls and decided to have pre-drinks at Jade's since her flat mate would be at work all day. They'd decided to get ready there too, like the old days, and then go for dinner in town, before heading down to the new cocktail bar that had opened up and served giant porn star martini's, which she had every intention of drinking all to herself. She'd told them all that she couldn't wait to see them and promised that she'd discuss the Tommy situation on Saturday, even though she wasn't ready to.

Despite him calling multiple times and messaging her, Olivia had ignored it. She didn't care what he wanted or what he wanted to say, she wouldn't entertain his ego anymore. As far as she was concerned, he'd made his bed, now he could lie in. The only thing she wanted was her half of the money from the mortgage she was still having to pay. She wanted to find somewhere new to start a fresh and she needed the money behind her before she could afford to.

By the time she had finished making plans with the girls and found something online to wear it was almost midnight. Liv decided she needed the beauty sleep if she was going to get anything done in the morning and tucked her phone under her pillow. After tossing and turning for what seemed like forever, she finally managed to drift off, already excited to wake up.

5.

Liv must have checked the clock 100 times throughout the day and was distracted. Her lessons had been fine, but she'd never wanted the day to end quicker than today. She was impatient, and very much in denial. She was trying to convince herself that she didn't care, but that was definitely a lie. She couldn't wait to check her phone after every lesson and seemed to have reverted back to a giggly teenager every time she'd got a message.

The one time that he hadn't text back, she'd been annoyed and quickly had to tell herself to grow up. She reminded herself that her visit to his house wasn't to see him and the most she'd probably get was a hello before she sat down and got to work with Clayton. She really needed to calm her tits, she thought as the clock neared 1 o'clock. She had even debated letting all the kids finish early for lunch so she could get back to her phone but managed to see the lesson out and set them their homework just in time for the bell to go,

Finally free, she grabbed a can of coke and her bag before heading to the staff room.
"Miss?" she heard behind her as she walked down the corridor.

It was Marcus. He was one of the kids in her form and was known for being one of the brightest in the school. He was naturally gifted with numbers and had an almost photographic memory, which she adored. Unfortunately for her, she wasn't his maths teacher and he had been assigned to Mr. Evans instead who also taught top set students and A-Level maths. He had already aced his GCSE's and was in advanced A-level maths at just 15 years old, which was incredible, but sometimes he needed a bit of a confidence boost. He was amazing, when he was given information in a way that he could process it. Sometimes this meant getting a bit creative, and when he needed help, he always found Liv.

More importantly, he found her when he was having a bad day. Being the smartest in the school didn't make it easy to make friends and made him an easy target for some of the older boys. As far as Liv knew he only had one friend, and that was Lizzie, who was also a bit of a Wizkid.

"Hiya Marc, is everything okay?" she asked, as he caught up and walked beside her.

"I'm okay" he shrugged, matching her step as she crossed the corridor avoiding the groups of children congregating in the corridors.

"What's up?"

"Well, I was wondering if you could talk to Mr. Evans for me to see if I can change my exams?" he asked sheepishly.

Evans was the head of maths and considered Marcus his prodigy. Liv didn't feel the need to tell him that half the reason he was able and ready for his exams was because she'd spent extra time with him, not because he'd done a good job teaching him in lessons. Despite his memory, it was hard for him to concentrate when his peers were taunting him for being smarter than them.

"I don't want to drop my A-Level, but I have been looking into it, and I really want to sit decision maths, instead of mechanics?" he asked, sounding excited, "I mean, mechanics is fine, but I love computers, and if there's anything that's going to help me improve my coding and stuff, it's decision. It seems easy enough to learn, and I like puzzles too… and I figured that if I could teach myself, I wouldn't have to be in so many lessons with everyone else" he shrugged, trailing off.

Liv put a reassuring hand on his shoulder and gave it a squeeze. He might have towered above her, but his personality was so small, if it wasn't for his sheer size he would've easily faded into the background at school.

"Is there anything else going on?" she asked, worried that he wasn't telling her something, but he shook his head with conviction.

"Ok, I'll see what I can do, but I'm not making any promises! What about mechanics? Are you sure you want to drop it altogether, because you will need at least one of the two to get the A level?" she said.

Liv had only asked to make sure he was certain, not because she didn't think he was more than capable, and he nodded in agreement. Decision maths had always been her favourite too, but she knew that Mr. Evans wasn't a fan. He said it was for games and puzzles, neither of which he was interested in in his maths classes. He said that if someone wanted to get a maths A-level in this school they would be doing 'proper' maths, which meant mechanics or statistics along with the core maths modules they had to complete. Liv had agreed to have a word with Evans for Marcus' sake and knew that it was going to take some persuading. If it had been any other kid that had asked, she wouldn't have bothered, knowing that she was going to have a fight on her hand, but Marcus was different, and she really cared about what was best for him.

He thanked her and grinned widely before taking long strides down the hallway and Liv found her way to the staffroom. Usually, she would eat in her classroom but there was a staff meeting after school, so she thought she'd better show her face rather than get pulled for being anti-social later by her prick of a boss or any of the other senior staff team. She found a seat and pulled out her phone where she was finally able to check her messages which didn't disappoint when a message flashed up from Jackson.

```
12:20
"Are you sure there is nothing
you want me to pick up for you
tonight? I don't mind x'
```

She smiled inwardly to herself as she replied. He'd asked her multiple times now about whether he could get her anything despite her assuring him that she was fine, and if she had to guess she'd say he was nervous. As she tapped away excitedly on her phone, Diane came and sat beside her, smiling softly.

"Hiya Liv! How comes you're coming to mingle with the commoners today?" she joked, knowing that Liv hated the dreary discussions of the staff room. She was in her late 50's and taught English to every year group. Kids either loved her or hated her, depending on whether she liked them, and she made it quite clear to them who was and wasn't on her radar. She was old school, and she was very similar to Liv in the way that she would call things as they were. The difference was, Diane had age and wisdom on her side and people respected her, unlike Olivia. All her life she had been told that she was always "too", so now she tried not to be.

TOO opinionated, TOO confident, TOO sure of herself, TOO loud. Liv was used to it now and consciously chose to avoid situations where she would have to mute her bubbly personality to spare people's feelings. Instead, she kept herself to herself at school, unless she had to. That way she was less likely to end up getting herself in trouble. It was a personality trait that she had tried working on repeatedly but now, at 29 years old, she couldn't be bothered to try anymore, it was who she was.
"Oh Di, you know me," Liv laughed, "I'm just here for the drama and to look like I've made an effort, so Mr. Turd doesn't try digging me out again. How are you?"
Diane laughed and patted Liv's leg reassuringly, "Don't let him get to you darling, he's a chauvinistic pig. He doesn't like the fact that a young pretty woman will put him in his place and not run to his beckon call. I'm just as right as rain my darling, worried about you as always! You look like you've lost some weight. I hope you're eating?" she exclaimed, looking disapprovingly at the can of coke in front of Liv.

Liv pulled out her Tupperware pot of noodles and shook it at Diane who nodded her approval before she got stuck in and caught her up on everything that was going on in her life, including how excited she was to see Jackson and how wrong it was because Clayton was his son.

...

Jackson finished early and rushed home to make sure that the house was clean and tidy. He'd asked his cleaner if she could pop in and give the house a once over, but she'd been fully booked all day, which was just his luck. Luckily the house wasn't a mess, but naturally he wanted to make sure it was extra clean since he had company over. He'd popped into M&S on the way home and picked up some snacks for Clayton's first tuition session with Liv, just in case, and a couple of beers for himself for Dutch courage.

She hadn't messaged him back in hours, but he didn't want to come across as needy so hadn't text her since either. She was obviously busy, he thought as he stocked the fridge and checked the time noting had about 4 hours before she was due to arrive but only a couple before Clayton got back. He didn't want to make it look like he was trying to impress his teacher so he wanted it done before he was home, then he could just say that Claire did it anyway and Clayton wouldn't be suspicious.

Jackson asked the Alexa to play some ACDC and got started on getting the house straight, although his thoughts were elsewhere. Whilst he cleaned the kitchen and emptied the dishwasher, he found himself checking his phone on the side every 5 minutes until eventually it pinged. He convinced himself to finish hoovering in the dining room first noting that he was too eager, then grabbed his phone to check it.

15:15
"Sorry, been manic at work. I'll still be over at 5ish but we have a staff meeting about something so hopefully it doesn't

run on for too long. How's your day been? Yes, I'm sure there's nothing I need, just a LOT of coffee, I had a late night remember! x"

15:18
"Ha. Sorry about that. Must have got carried away. I promise to be more mindful and won't text you too late ever again. Hope the staff meeting goes well, you don't sound too impressed! I made sure we have plenty of coffee xx"

15:20
"I wasn't complaining xx"
Typing...

15:21
"Good! Because I enjoyed our late-night chat xx"

15:23
"My boss can't stand me. Have recently been told that it's because he doesn't like the idea of a woman being able to prove him wrong, but still undecided. Hopefully it's to tell us he's leaving, then will be celebrating! Lol xx"

15:23:
"Me too xx"

15:24
"Well, if there's a cause for celebration, you let me know. I could use a glass or two xx"

15:24
"You and me both!"

15:25
"Could be arranged xx"

Jackson was hoping that she didn't think he was coming off too strong and that she was open to the idea of getting to know him. He knew he shouldn't because of Clayton, but she intrigued him, and she didn't have to do much to make him smile. Usually when he started speaking to someone, he didn't mind keeping them waiting, wasn't bothered when they decided to give him a taste of his own medicine and leave him for hours before replying and didn't care when it fizzled out and went nowhere, which it always did. But Liv was different, and he found himself waiting for her reply every time he text her.

6.

Liv found the address just before 5:00 and plucked up the courage to knock on the door. She'd wanted the staff meeting to end the minute it started and found herself looking at the time every 5 minutes. By 4:15 she'd had enough, but the head had continued to rabbit on about the GCSE timetable, revision for year 11 students and the faculty working together for "the good of the students" which meant doing overtime without the benefit of getting paid.

She checked her phone when she reached the driveway and figured that 4:50 was as good a time as any to arrive, so knocked on the door and waited. As she did, she could feel the blush creeping up her cheeks and the nerves start to set in which was new for her. She really should have found another tutor, she thought to herself, as she nervously drummed her fingers on her bag and waited impatiently for someone to answer the door.

Finally, after what seemed like forever, Clayton arrived and opened it with a friendly grin on his face.

"Hi Miss!" he said, as he gestured for her to come in and she stepped into the porch after him, kicking off her heels to add to the line of footwear. "I'm just going to get my stuff, but Dad's through there" he said, pointing to the doorway at the end of the hall which looked like the kitchen. She thanked him before he bounded up the stairs and she stood nervously fiddling with her belt. Before she'd left the school, she'd given herself a PEP talk on how to behave and she had reminded herself that she had no need to be nervous because this was strictly a professional visit.

Apparently however, that had all gone out the window and she was very conscious of the fact that she was sweating. This wasn't Liv. Liv was outspoken, outgoing and didn't care what people thought, but right now, she wasn't any of those things, and that was bad. Liv thought better of her decision to head to the kitchen and decided to stay put until Clayton returned down the stairs so he could show her the way and she didn't have to walk in their alone, which was pathetic.

As she waited, she took in the surroundings of the house. The walls were a stoney-brown colour with thick cream carpets that her feet sunk into. Large, framed posters covered the wall of artists like ACDC, The Rolling Stones and QUEEN, and she could hear Oasis playing quietly in the background where the smell of onion and garlic was filling the air.

"Did you want a drink?" came a voice startling her from behind.

Liv jumped and dropped her bag to the floor, sending stationery scattering all over the place. Jackson quickly apologised through a laugh as he bent down to pick her things up for her and handed her bag back.

"I'm sorry!" She said, sheepishly taking it, "I wasn't expecting you to come up behind me"

Jackson laughed again and apologised as he led her to the kitchen and repeated his offer of a drink.

"I didn't know what to get, so I got everything I could find with caffeine in it" he said, shrugging as he stirred something in the frying pan and wiped his hands with a tea towel.

Liv expected to be nervous after the sweating and the apprehensiveness at the door, but she found herself relaxing the minute she was with him. He seemed so laid back and normal in comparison to the man she met back in summer, but she guessed that the alcohol had played a role in his shitty mood that night. He was dressed in a plain white t-shirt and lounge joggers with grandad slippers on his feet that made her laugh, and she didn't miss his impressive biceps or the way they twitched whilst he dried his hands, which had Liv making a real effort to concentrate on his face without inspecting the rest of his body.

"Everything eh, I'm intrigued?" She said, as she found a seat at the island in the centre of the kitchen and watched him potter around her comfortably. It was a beautiful room, and it was obvious that he spent a lot of time in there. The stone colour continued from the hallway through to the kitchen walls as did the large, framed posters. The worktops and the island in the centre of the room were topped with white marble and everything seemed to have a place. At the end of the room a table that matched the island and worktops stood in front of a wall of glass that led out to the garden, but it was already too dark to see out and Liv wondered what that looked like too.

"Well, there's coffee, lots of coffee? Hot coffee, or iced coffee, or espresso, latte, or cappuccino?" He said shrugging his shoulders and grabbing a bottle of beer from the fridge. "Or coke? What do you fancy?"

"Well, it's a bit cold out there," she said, "so maybe a hot coffee?"

"Coffee it is, and how do you like it?" He asked, opening his beer and getting the milk from the fridge.

"Strong and milky, very sweet" she said watching as he filled the milk frother and changed the water in the nespresso machine. She wasn't surprised that he had a café worthy coffee machine to make coffee after seeing the size of the kitchen, and she was under the impression that he made himself a barista style espresso every morning before the gym, the show-off. There wasn't a lot of fancy gadgets or gizmos scattered around though, and as he got to work, Clayton came hurtling down the stairs armed with his textbooks and pencil case.

"Ready?" Liv asked, hopping down from the chair.

"Ready as I'll ever be" he replied and made his way over to the beautiful white table by the windows where she joined him.

"He only got that coffee machine because you were coming over by the way" Clayton said as he plopped down on a chair on the side of the table and she found a seat at the end, "he hates coffee"

Liv blushed, taken aback, and composed herself quickly. She didn't believe he'd gone above and beyond for her, but she didn't want to let on in front of Clayton that she was embarrassed.

"Show off" she muttered throwing him a wink and sorting her things out, "I don't even like coffee really".

Jackson busied himself in the kitchen with the coffee machine and managed to distract himself enough to tear his eyes from Liv. She'd was wearing a jumper dress with a belt that pulled her in at the waist and had him remembering how good she'd looked back in summer when he'd thrown her over his shoulder.

After finishing what he thought was a decent looking latte, based on his Google searches the night before, he took it over to the table with some snacks and left the two of them to it. He listened as she walked Clayton through a mock exam and explained that they would go through it together to see where he needed to improve and decided that he'd definitely made the right decision in asking her to be there.

As the hour passed, Jackson flitted in and out of the kitchen checking on dinner and finding other ways to avoid glancing at the woman sat at his dining table. It was lucky she was engrossed in whatever they were learning, because he lost count of the amount of times he had to pull his eyes away from watching her. By the time they had finished, dinner was about done, and Jackson was glad he didn't have to keep finding reasons to waltz in and out just to see her. Clayton grabbed his things from the table and headed back up the stairs whilst Liv packed up her own and returned her mug.

"Another?" He asked as she placed her mug in the sink and flashed him a smile.

"I shouldn't really, aren't I interrupting dinner?" She said eyeing the dish on the side.

"I'll make an exception" he said reaching into the cupboard for a new mug and showing off his waistband which Liv didn't fail to notice. As he busied himself with the coffee machine again, Clayton returned back down the stairs and into the kitchen dressed in shorts and a t-shirt

"Marv's mum said she will drop us back dad, so I'll be home at 8:00" he said grabbing some water and running for the front door before shouting a thank you to Liv and disappearing.

"NO LATER!" he shouted after him before the door slammed, and he went back to finishing the coffee.

"So, how was the meeting?" he asked casually, making Liv's stomach flip.

"Nothing remotely exciting. They want us to do more work to help the students prepare for their exams, like we don't do it every day anyway. What about you, how was your day at the office?"

"Productive" he lied, remembering how he'd finished work early and not left his phone alone all day, "but still got some work to get through tonight"

Liv was apologetic and naturally made to leave but Jackson assured her he didn't mean it like that and got her to agree to finish her coffee first. As they got talking, Jackson spoke about his job and what he did day to day. He explained his role and how his company began, and Liv listened without interruption. She didn't try and turn the conversation around on to herself, or seem to get bored, she just listened and took everything in, smiling as he spoke, before they realised that time had run away with them. By the time he had finished going on all about himself it was almost 8:00 and he kicked himself for not asking more about her.

"I better get going before Clayton's back!" she said grabbing her phone out. "He'll be wondering why I'm still here!"

Her car was in for its MOT and needed some work doing which wouldn't be ready until after the weekend. Her brother didn't live far and usually it would be fine to walk, but it was far too cold outside, so she attempted to call for a taxi, which Jackson refused to allow.

"I'll just drop you off?" he said as she waited for the operator to answer, and Liv looked at him with her eyebrows creased. Jackson knew that this meant he'd get to spend more time with her, and after convincing her to hang up with some stern looks, he grabbed his keys and a hoody, then threw on a pair of black trainers.

"Are you sure?" Liv asked, finding her shoes and jacket alongside him in the little porch, but Jackson wasn't going to take no for an answer, and before she knew it he was opening the door for her and ushering her out of the house and into his 4x4.

The 5-minute drive home wasn't awkward like Liv expected it to be and she found herself laughing more than she had in months which both thrilled her, and scared her. She was happy for the feeling but confused about how professional she could keep their relationship when she was quite clearly insanely attracted to him. Once they'd said their goodbyes, Liv went to her room and flopped on the bed where she debated what the hell she was supposed to do about whatever it was she was feeling and asked herself repeatedly whether she was reading too much into the whole thing with Jackson anyway. She needed a drink, and at that point she was grateful that she'd planned on a night out with the girls at the weekend.

7.

When Saturday finally arrived, Liv was more than ready to hit the town with the girls. She spent the morning in the bath shaving every inch of her body, exfoliating and moisturising from head to toe, then packed up her bag ready to leave and head over to Jade's to get ready.

When she arrived, Jade was already washed, dried and wrapped in a robe with curlers in her hair. She told Liv that Sophie and Georgia weren't going to make it until later, and as much as she loved the two of them, her and Jade had always been the closest, so it was nice to be able to see her alone for a while after weeks of hibernating away in her room because of the breakup with Tommy. She was a great friend, and Liv considered herself lucky to have her.

Jade was extremely house proud and lived in a large 2 bed apartment that looked as though it had been plucked from an Instagram post, which was fine when you had no kids, no boyfriend, and a job that paid well. Everything was grey or white, which had never been Liv's style, but Jade seemed to love the crisp clean colours and kept it spotless.

"So, what's new?!" She said excitedly, as she handed Liv a prosecco and sat down with her on the sofa.

"Nothing really, plodding along given the circumstances" Liv said grinning, but Jade raised her eyebrows knowingly waiting for Liv to spill whatever it was that she didn't plan on letting up about.

"Honestly, it's nothing really! I've just been speaking to someone... but not like that!" She quickly added growing redder by the second.

"Well, you wouldn't feel the need to say, *'not like that'*, if it wasn't *like that* would you?" She said rolling her eyes, "so, go on?!" she urged her excitedly.

Liv asked if she recalled their night out back in summer and the guy she met at the bar. She reeled off how he'd turned up at parents evening in the week after clashing heads back in August and that he hadn't recognised her. Liv told her that she taught his son who was flunking at the moment, and that he'd asked for her to tutor him and things had kind of spiralled from there.

"He texts me first, he always replies to my messages and he's really easy to talk to. When I went round to tutor Clayton he'd bought a new coffee machine for me, and he's always checking in on me and stuff. It's just nice" she said through a smile, trying not to sound too eager.

"Oh, this is so cute!" Jade said excitedly, bouncing up and down on the cushions, "I'm so happy and excited for you! When are you going on a date?!"

"Slow down," Liv said, throwing her drink back, "he's my students dad, it's really unprofessional and unethical, so it can't go anywhere!"

"So why are you entertaining it?" she said matter-of-factly raising her eyebrows and tilting her head in a show of judgement.

"I don't know" she shrugged "maybe a rebound, maybe because I wish it could"

Jackson's client had brought forward the day of opening so wanted everything finalised ready for production which meant he was working on a Saturday, and he couldn't afford distractions. His phone had been non-stop abuse all morning with Rachael on his case about him blowing her off, and he didn't have the patience to deal with her.

He was fed up with his choice in women always coming back to bite him on the ass and didn't have the time to be worrying or stressing. Instead, he had messaged Liv before he left for work telling her that he hoped she had a great day and apologising in advance if he didn't reply as he was at work trying to meet a deadline. He'd expected a shitty response, but all she did was tell him she hoped it went well and to text her when he wanted to, because she didn't want to be a distraction.

Wanting to text her was an understatement, he was dying to see her again after her session with Clayton and he didn't want to wait the entire weekend either. Their night was nothing special, they'd just sat and chatted, but conversation flowed naturally, and her laugh was so infectious that he wanted to hear it again the minute she stepped out the car. She'd told him she was going out with the girls this weekend for the first time in ages and as much as didn't want to interrupt her letting her hair down, he didn't want to go hours without speaking to her either.

He reluctantly pushed it to the back of his mind, replied to the guys in the group chat telling them he was too busy to meet for drinks, and whacked up the volume on some Led Zeppelin whilst he attempted to work on finalising the project and adding the finishing touches to the website that he had spent the last week designing.

'Attempted' was the operative word. His concentration was out of sorts, and he was distracted, despite muting his phone and not touching it for over an hour. He picked it up from the other side of the desk hoping to see a message from Liv but was gutted when the only notifications that popped up were the news, Rachael and the group chat again. He was grateful that she wasn't hounding him, but this was new to him. Usually, he couldn't get 5 minute peace from the women he spoke to, but she seemed to understand that he was busy and had kept to her word of leaving him to it, which he both appreciated and found annoying. He wanted her to want to talk to him.

> 13:02
> "If I don't speak to you before, hope you have a great time tonight, can't wait to hear about it. Stay safe and let me know if you need anything x"

He typed out the message and put his phone to one side, hoping she'd reply. As he fiddled around with the final draft of the menu's ready to be sent, he tapped his leg impatiently, but he didn't have to wait long.

13:05
"I'm starting early! Maybe if you get all your work done you can come for a drink. My treat? x"

She sent it along with a picture of a cocktail, and he didn't think twice in agreeing to the offer despite knowing that he had a deadline to reach before the end of the day or risk pulling a shift on a Sunday which he hadn't done since he started working for himself.

> 13:07
> "Sounds good! I'll catch up with you later and see what your plans are x"

13:08
"Don't work too hard. I will see you tonight maybe xx"

Now he had something to look forward to, it seemed his work productivity had gone into overdrive, and he managed to get through everything that his client had asked for in record time. It was amazing what a little motivation could do, and by 4:00pm he had the plans confirmed, the products ready for processing and was ready to settle the tidy balance for his services in order for the website to go live on Monday at 12:00pm.

Jackson revoked his earlier messages with the guys in the group chat and agreed to meet for drinks after all. They'd agreed to meet at 6:00pm in town which gave him less than 2 hours to get ready, catch up with Liv and make the dreaded phone call to Rachael to get her off of his back.

"Just send him the fucking picture!" Jade was shouting at her, tipsy from the multiple cocktails she'd drunk whilst spending the past hour and a half doing Olivia's hair and make-up.

Liv was ready to leave for dinner in a tight pair of black leather pants, a white ruffle sleeved shirt left little to the imagination and heeled boots. Her hair had been parted and sleeked behind her ears, then curled under at the ends so her dark bob framed her face. The girls were now desperately trying to convince her to send a photo to Jackson, who she hadn't stopped going on about all afternoon, much to her own annoyance.

"No! That's weird!" Liv said, shaking her head, and draining the rest of her third cocktail "I'm not 15 for fuck's sake!"

"No, but you also haven't been messaging or dating anyone in over 8 years, so maybe listen to this of us who have?" Georgia said throwing her hands in the air and screwing her features up.

Liv rolled her eyes and carried on packing her bits into her clutch bag whilst the girls did their last little touch ups before the obligatory predrinks photo shoot took place.

"Maybe I'll just change my display picture" Liv suggested, coming around to the idea but not wanting to come across as full on. She busied herself tidying up the mess that was left and checked her phone again to see if he'd text, which he hadn't.

"Stop being pathetic Liv. If we got another few drinks down you, you'd be happy to show him your tits, so what's a photo between friends?!" Jade laughed.

Liv laughed along with her and remembered just how much she missed going out with the girls. It didn't matter how much time they spent apart, whenever they got together it felt like nothing had changed at all, even when everything had. Reluctantly she agreed to send a photo and posed for the girls in front of the windows. With plenty to choose from, she picked her favourite, sent it to Jackson, and regretted it instantly.

He was certainly going to need a cold shower before he got ready, because the minute he opened the message he could feel his dick getting hard. It might not have been the skin-tight number she was wearing the day they met, but it was just as flattering on her body.

>17:18
>"Wow."
>
>17:18
>"You look beautiful. Drinks on me tonight. Can't wait x"

He didn't care that he was coming off strong, because all that was running through his mind at that point was how he was meant to stop himself begging her to come home with him after he saw her in person. Jackson waited whilst she typed and peered at the picture again confirming that a cold shower was probably not going to be enough. He was still amazed at the shape of her body, with thick thighs and a tiny waist, and he couldn't help but imagine how his hands would feel wrapped around it whilst she was sat on top of him.

```
17:31
"Me neither x"
```

He took a final look before convincing himself to leave the phone and make his way to the bathroom so he could finally get ready. If this was how he felt when she had clothes on, he couldn't help but wonder what he'd be like if she was without them.

The cold shower didn't help.

And it didn't help that the photo was imprinted in his brain as well as saved on his phone which he happened to look at every 5 minutes whilst he was getting ready. Jackson laid back on the bed with his phone and figured he better deal with the devil itself before it got worse and before he left the house. He scrolled through the 15 messages from Rachael that he'd ignored, and sighed at the thought of giving her the satisfaction of a reply.

The woman was crazy about him, but also crazy, period. He'd called it off, she'd *'given him time to think'*, but nothing was going to make him reconsider, especially not now. He thought about calling her for a second, but he couldn't deal with her screaming down the phone at him and ruining his mood. Instead, he explained everything in a well written message, hit send, and locked up the house ready to meet the boys.

8

Liv and the girls found a table in the corner of the bar and ordered a round of cocktails and shots. It wasn't a place they'd usually spend their time, but it was the place that was closest when the heavens opened outside, and they had to dive to the entrance to keep them safe and dry.

"So, what's next?" Jade asked Georgia continuing the conversation from dinner about the baby planning. She'd been trying for almost a year now with no success, unbeknown to all of the girls who thought this was a recent development, and they were having to look at other options.

"Well, we're going to go to the fertility clinic and both get tested and then go from there. Hopefully if we can suss out where the problem is, it might be fixable or if not, we might have to consider IVF or surrogacy maybe?" she shrugged taking a sip of her drink.

"Oh George," Sophie said rubbing her arm, "you know we are with you every step of the way and if we can help at all you will ask, right?"

"Of course!" she said, shrugging it off as if it was nothing "Other people try for years and maybe it just isn't the right time for us. We're still happy regardless, and if it's not for us then we will cross that bridge when we come to it"

"Well, we are all proud of you" Jade said as she raised her glass, "and here's to the rest of us finding a love as bulletproof as yours!"

The girls clinked the glasses and "cheers"d one another. Jade was right, Georgia and Karl really did seem as though absolutely nothing could phase them, and since the day they'd met they'd been besotted with one another. It was weird they hadn't got together sooner since she was best friends with Karl's brother for years before they dated, but the stars aligned eventually, and 4 years on they were still as in love as ever.

Liv pulled out her phone and read the messages Jackson had sent over dinner. Jade told her to text him back where they were and said that she needed to vet him properly before Liv started falling head over heels, although Liv was adamant this wasn't the case. Jackson was out with the boys, and she didn't want to hound him into meeting her.

> 21:14
> "Started raining so we are in some bar downtown. It's called Lively's? Let me know if you are still up for a drink. Hope you're having a good night! xx"

"Is he coming then?" Jade said peering over her phone at the message, but Liv told her she wasn't sure yet as he was out with his friends too. With that, Jade took her phone and threw it to Sophie before Liv could snatch it back.

"Please type: This is Jade. Olivia's best friend and confidant. We will expect to see you within the next 30 minutes. Any excuses will not be tolerated, and your number shall be deleted permanently. Kind Regards... and send it!"

Olivia rolled her eyes as Sophie quickly typed and refused to give her phone back.
"Oooooooh!!!!! He's typing!!" she squealed as Liv tried to grab the phone back again from Sophie's outstretched arms.

"Soph, come on!" Liv said going red and desperately trying to grab the phone.

"Hi Jade (and Sophie and Georgia), I'll see you in 10. Tell Liv I'll come find her when I'm there and introduce myself. Let me know what you're all drinking. Kind Regards." Sophie read aloud from the phone and handed it back to Liv who was beetroot by this point.

"Well, what an absolutely lovely gentleman," Jade said raising her glass again, "here's to Liv's new man, and him having some fuckable friends for me too"

...

Jackson hadn't left his phone alone all night and the boys hadn't left him alone either. When he first arrived at the bar, they asked what had changed his mind, but he shrugged it off for a while as if he didn't have an ulterior motive. He'd gone to the toilet and came back to find Joe holding his phone and asking who Liv was when messages had popped up.

"What happened to Rachael?" Marley said as they took their drinks off to find a table.
"She was a weapon!"

"Yeah? If by 'weapon' you mean fucking psycho. She wouldn't leave me alone, wanted to be involved with Clayton, and refused to leave my house before he got back which meant they bumped into each other when I told her I didn't want her to meet him" he said as they found a seat.

"So, who's Liv?" Joe asked again, "Surely you haven't moved on that quick, that's a record even for you!"

The rest of the boys laughed including Jackson, but he wasn't fussed.

"I called things off with Rachael months ago, but she won't let up. Constantly on my case. Liv's just a friend"

"A hot friend?"

"Well, least we know the real reason you agreed to come out tonight" Harry winked, "you're trying to get your leg over!!"

The boys cheered around him, and Jackson rolled his eyes and told them it wasn't like that. He told them to calm down and that they were just meeting for a drink later as she was out with friends.

"Single friends?" Joe asked beside him, like that had ever stopped him before. Since they were kids, Joe had a habit of getting whatever and whoever he wanted. It didn't matter whether they were taken, single, married or into the same sex. Women gravitated towards him, and he thrived off of it. He'd only ever had one real relationship, and as far as he was concerned, he never wanted another.

"Well, looks like we are coming too! Show us her then…" Marley said.

Jackson knew that none of them would let up until they'd seen a photo so pulled up the one she had sent him earlier and passed his phone around.

"I would" Harry said.

"Yep, me too" Marley Replied

"Not bad" Joe said raising his eyebrows approvingly and handing the phone back to Jackson who was shaking his head.

"Well, I'm glad you all approve. Not that I give a fuck. It's not like that anyway"

"Bullshit" Joe said, draining his beer. "I've known you your whole life, and you don't entertain things you don't want to go anywhere. When are you meeting her and when?!"

"Later, they're having dinner somewhere and then coming to town. But if you try and pull fucking funny business again, I swear I'll put you in hospital this time Joe"

"Well, let's get you pissed then, ready to embarrass yourself!! Jaeger it is" Marley said getting up from the table and heading to the bar without another word.

The lads were getting rowdy, and Jackson was regretting his decision not to meet her alone. He'd had one too many himself and decided he better pace himself, so he didn't look like an idiot when it came to seeing Liv. The last thing he wanted was her friends to think he was a dick but by 9:00pm he was getting impatient and nervous. Liv had messaged him saying they were leaving the restaurant soon but didn't know where they'd end up.

It wasn't until 10:00 when her message come through, and the boys were about one more drink away from getting thrown out. Jackson said his goodbyes and made to leave without them, but they weren't having any of it and tagged along noisily to the busy bar downtown.

...

10 minutes felt like an hour and Liv felt sick with nerves. So much so, she drained another cocktail, which was one more than she should have. She figured it would give her some Dutch courage and had a skittles bomb just to be sure. She kept peering at the door, but it wasn't until Jade started clapping that she realised he'd arrived and was making his way to the bar.

Jade pushed her to get out of the seat, but Liv was frozen and not willing to move. He looked good, which didn't surprise her, but she felt as though another drink was in order before she wanted to go over there.

"Move your ass now before I climb on the table and call him over!" Jade said glaring at her, "Georgia and Sophie can stay here because they're happily taken, sorry girls. And I will escort you, and introduce myself as your very single friend, okay"

The girls laughed and Liv reluctantly got up and started to make her way through the crowded bar. She didn't even know how Jade had seen him since the place had become packed in the last 20 minutes, and he was struggling to see over the people between them as well.

"Hey!" Jade screamed when they finally arrived at the other side of the room where he stood with his friends, both of whom looked familiar.

"There you are," he said leaning in and planting a kiss on her lips and pulling her in close to him.

"Well, that was unexpected!" Jade said to Marley who was standing there with a look of shock on his face.

"You have no idea," Marley said shaking his head and looking around the bar.

Liv pulled away, going beetroot again and smiled shyly up at Jackson. She definitely hadn't expected that, and it hadn't felt at all like how she thought it would. He didn't seem like the kind of guy to go in all guns blazing, and she was taken aback by how forward he had been, kissing her before he even said a proper hello?

He kept his hand on the small of her back as he introduced her to Marley and Harry who both looked offish when they leaned in and kissed her on the cheek. Liv felt like something was up and couldn't put her finger on it but introduced Jade to the boys too. She'd been so looking forward to seeing him after spending time with him in the week, but he seemed completely different now he'd been drinking, and she wasn't sure she liked it.

"Let's get some drinks!" he shouted, kissing her again, which she didn't return. She felt awkward and said she'd be over in a second, but she just needed to get her bag.

"Don't be an idiot, I'm getting them!" he said urging her forward, and Liv gave Jade a look which she returned. As he approached the bar, Liv took a step back to find Jade and shrugged his behaviour off, Jade asked if she was okay, but Liv was conflicted and wanted to get out of there.

"I'm just popping outside" she said, leaving the boys behind her as she found her way to the door and found the fresh air hit her like a ton of bricks. She walked under the shelter outside she sat down, took some breaths to digest what had happened and prepped herself to go back in. She hadn't been near another man in over 8 years, and she wasn't prepared for him to be so forward in kissing her or touching her.

Pull yourself together! she thought as she found the door again and waved over to where they stood at the bar. Marley was stood chatting to Jackson but didn't look happy, Jade was chatting to Harry, who was laughing, and Liv was ready to try to speak to him again after calming herself down.

"Sorry!" she said as she found her way back to the bar, "I needed fresh air"

"Well, me and Marley were just talking about what the chances were of the 3 of us getting out of here and taking it back to my place for some fun?" he said putting his hands around her waist again. Liv scowled at him and pushed him away whilst Marley assured her it wasn't the case.

"J, mate, don't be a dick," he said getting between the two of them and pushing him away, "you've had your fun and that's uncalled for. Get a cab home before he's back because he's going to go fucking mad alright"

Just then, Liv heard her name being called from behind her and turned around to find Jackson making his way from the men's room towards her at the bar. She turned again to the man Marley was currently rowing with, and back to the other Jackson who looked just as confused as she did.

Jackson leant in and gave her a kiss on the cheek before asking what was going on, and Liv repeated the question back to him whilst scowling at the other Jackson who was laughing uncontrollably at the bar. Marley rolled his eyes and Jackson asked Liv if she was okay.

"Erm, what the fuck is going on?!" she said, fuming and turning red with anger "because you, well, that you!" she continued pointing back at the bar, "just kissed me and then suggested I have a fucking threesome with your mate! Do I look like a mug?!" she screamed, as Jade and Harry turned around to see the commotion.

"WHAT?!" Jackson said throwing daggers at Joe who had decided to take advantage of their identical looks to get at his brother.

Joe laughed whilst Marley kept him and Jackson apart and Liv asked again what was going on. Marley urged Jackson to leave it and take Liv somewhere to talk, whilst Harry and Jade still looked confused about what had happened whilst they'd been chatting.

"Honestly Joe, fucking grow up and get the fuck out of here" Jackson said taking Liv's hand and leading her to the other side of the bar "and why the fuck did you two let him do it again?!" he added, scowling at Harry and Marley who were trying to convince

Joe it was time to leave and stop him from egging Jackson to come back.

...

"I'm really sorry about Joe, Liv" he said, pulling out a chair for her at the table. She was still glaring at him as she sat down, crossed her legs, and her arms over her chest.

"Let me get you a drink and we'll talk, okay?"

Liv raised her eyebrows, and Jackson made his way to the bar where he bought drinks for the two of them and sent drinks over to the table where Jade had returned to with Sophie and Georgia. When he got back, Liv seemed to have relaxed a little and took her drink with a thank you.

"So..." she said taking a sip, "Is there a story as to why I've been sexually assaulted by your clone this evening, because he's lucky I didn't throw a drink in his face"

Jackson laughed, without meaning to, and stopped abruptly when she scowled at him. "That would be my twin brother Joe, he thinks he's untouchable, and loves to piss me off in any way he possibly can. Right now, that happened to be by kissing you, and I'm really sorry it happened"

Liv rolled her eyes and sipped her drink some more swinging her foot back and forth. Jackson didn't say anything but watched her as she processed the information and eventually decided to talk to him again.

"He's a shit kisser" she said, throwing him another dirty look which had him biting back a laugh, "but very ballsy"

"So, can we start over?" he begged, hoping that his brother hadn't ruined his chances of seeing her tonight. He knew it was a bad idea to let them know he was meeting Liv, and it wasn't the first time that Joe had pretended to be Jackson to make him come across as a dick.

"You look nice," she said, refusing to smile as he watched her stir her drink with her straw.

"Well, I thought I'd make an effort since I was meeting you" he winked and Liv rolled her eyes, "How was dinner?"

"Yeah, it was good, but it was small, and I'm fucking starving" she laughed, as he watched her still. Jackson was still in awe of how beautiful she looked, and the photo she sent was nothing in comparison to how she looked in real life. She didn't have her glasses on that she usually wore, and her skin was glowing. Her big brown eyes were frames with big dark lashes, and she looked like she could see right through him.

"How about I say hello to your friends, and then we go and find something for you to eat?" he said finishing his drink and helping her from her chair.

"It's a date" she said as they headed back to the table where the girls sat with Harry and Marley.

"Don't get my hopes up" he whispered following her over with his hand on her waist, and Liv smiled back at him.

9.

After hours at the bar laughing with the girls, and his friends, Jackson and Liv found the only place that was still open in town to sit and eat. She'd definitely had a few too many, but Jackson had stopped drinking when he got to the bar saying he didn't want to embarrass himself and wanted to make sure she got home safe.

"So, what was wrong with you that night anyway?" she asked shovelling chips into her mouth and swigging her coke.

"Women trouble" he shrugged, brushing it off.

Liv raised an eyebrow that beckoned him to go on and he rolled his eyes and stole some of the chips from her plate.

"The woman I was seeing at the time got a bit too attached. We'd agreed that it was a casual thing, but she wanted more, and I didn't. She'd been hounding me all day about leading her on and blah blah blah, even though I made my feelings clear in the beginning and told her I wasn't looking for a relationship"

Jackson gauged Liv's reaction carefully to see whether he'd made a mistake telling her.

"So, you're *that* guy?" She asked through a mouthful of donner meat, "I never pegged you as a playboy, tell me more"

Jackson laughed loudly and was surprised at how easy he found her to talk to. He could have borne every one of his secrets to her there and then if they had all the time in the word, and he really wished they had.

"I'm not *that* guy, I just know what I want. She wasn't a bad girl, but she wasn't the kind of person I wanted to settle down with, and I thought we both saw it like that. I never meant to lead her on, but

I also never wanted to make her feel worthless" he explained as Liv listened.

"Well," she said matter-of-factly, "that's the issue with no strings attached"

"Yeah? What's that then?"

"Somebody always gets attached. They don't work. Somebody, usually us women because we are emotional, naive little souls, always gets hurt"

Jackson watched her as she ate so comfortably in front of him and respected every word she said. It seemed like a common trend that every time there was a good thing going, they'd suddenly want more from him than he was willing to give, then things turned sour, and they became bitter.

"So, are you speaking from experience then?" He said as he got up from the bench and made his way to the kebab counter to order another of what she had.

"I'm sorry, but you have to get me way more drunk than this to tell you that," she said shaking her head playfully.

"Interesting," Jackson muttered as he considered his options. He didn't want to rush things or scare her off. He thought better of how desperately wanted to ask her back to his for a night cap so he could speak to her for hours and sat back down. They sat in silence for a few minutes, but it wasn't awkward, she ate and smiled when she caught him watching, which he seemed to be doing a lot.

"I don't speak from personal experience, I was with my ex for 8 years, but that's a story for another day. I do however have a best friend who is exactly the type of girl who commits to these "no strings attached" situationships and ends up heartbroken on a regular basis. So, I know all about them, and they never end well Mr. ..."

"Well, thank you for the pep talk and words of wisdom, I will most definitely hold out until I've found someone worthy of my strings" he said laughing.

He thanked the server for the kebab he brought over and put it between them in the middle of the table.

"What about Clayton's mum?" She asked licking her fingers before finding another chip.

"Somethings just aren't meant to be," he shrugged, joining her in taking some chips "I worked a lot, building the company, but the more I made, the more she smoked or sniffed. We both dabbled in it before Clayton, but she went back to it on nights out when he was about 6. Soon she was doing it every day, even in the house then one day she called me hysterical" he said swirling a chip round in some sauce.

"She'd left some of her coke on the side that Clayton got hold of and he ended up in intensive care on dialysis. He was lucky to make it, and I told her she wasn't welcome in the house, or near our son ever again. I couldn't forgive her after that, I barely forgave myself for not fixing her sooner, and I never wanted to try and make it work after what she did. She got clean, then relapsed again, and again, but now she seems to have sorted herself out" he said shrugging his shoulders, "Clayton goes to see her at the weekend on a Saturday but that's only been more recently, it took a long time for him to trust her again. So, since then, I've never been interested in settling down. It's hard when you've been through something like that, you just want to protect your kid and I didn't want women flitting in and out of his life like his mum did"

He'd never told any of the women he'd been with the story, no matter how many times they asked but he felt comfortable around Liv, comfortable enough to tell her anything that she wanted to know. Liv listened for the sake of listening and didn't listen to reply. She was quiet whilst he spoke, and interested in everything he had to say, without being judgemental. And she was honest, she spoke her mind, and told him exactly what she thought, not what she thought he needed to hear.

"He's lucky to have you" she said after some time spent eating and processing what he'd said, "and you've done a good job raising him too"

"I appreciate it" he said, watching her again whilst she played with her food.

Liv walked beside him along the street on the way to the taxi office and wondered where she went from here. It was obvious she liked him, and she wanted to get to know him, but she wasn't used to this situation anymore and she'd been out of the dating game for years now.
"You know, you're the first person I've spoken to other than the girls, in almost 10 years" she said laughing as she nudged him towards the road. "You're also my students dad, the best-looking guy I've seen in a while, and well put together"
"Thanks? I guess" he replied walking back in sync with her. "I don't know whether these are pros or cons for me?"
"Time will tell" she shrugged, "there's an infinite number of possibilities in an infinite universe. Who are we to decide what happens based on a few exchanges?"
"Who indeed."
Jackson beckoned a taxi and helped Liv in the back, before he got in after her. They sat quietly on the back seat whilst the driver found his way around the winding roads to her brother's address where she got out.

"This is me," she said, unbuckling and getting the door. Jackson asked the driver to wait and met her outside the car before throwing her over his shoulder again whilst she laughed uncontrollably.

"Déjà vu" he said, watching her drop her keys again and picking them up for her. He put her back down on the floor so she could let herself in, and watched her laugh trying to find the keyhole "This isn't where I dropped you last time?"

"No, it is not, but that's a story for another day too" she said smiling up at him.

"Guess it's a date"

Jackson looked at her and leaned in before thinking better of it. Liv badly wanted to invite him in but didn't want to ruin the night they'd had, instead she tip-toed up towards him steadying herself with her hands on his shoulders and placed a kiss on his cheek.

"See you Monday" she said, and with that, she was gone, and Jackson was left needing a cold shower all over again.

10.

59 new messages.

Liv wasn't ready to read anything that Jade had to say yet, and it was 5:30 by the time she'd finally got into bed after seeing Jackson. Her head was pounding, her stomach was churning, and if she didn't get coffee injected into her veins within the next 30 seconds she was going to die. There was no doubt about it, this was the end. *Goodbye cruel world,* she thought as she crawled out of bed to the door on all fours.

"Owen.. Help.. Me.." she croaked as she laid on the landing and prayed that her brother was at home.

"Morning Dreamboat!" he beamed from above her wearing a towel around his waist and nothing else.

"Shhhhhhhhhhh.. Gross.. Please.. Coffee.. Help.."

Owen laughed and helped Olivia to her feet and down the stairs where she curled up on the sofa. Whilst she laid feeling sorry for herself, he got her a coffee, buttered her some toast and gave her some paracetamol to take the edge off of the hangover from hell.

"How was your night?" he shouted from the kitchen before coming in dressed, "and who was carrying you home at 5:00am"

"5:30" she corrected him, swigging her coffee and swallowing down the paracetamol he'd given her. "It was good. Weird, but good, and Jackson would be the dreamboat carrying me home, it's a long story"

"Lucky it's Sunday then" Owen said, finding the remotes and getting comfortable.

Liv told him about back in summer and about how he turned up at parents evening, then what had happened the night before. She said his twin brother had tried to piss him off by kissing her, and that they' spent the night eating kebab and having a laugh.

Owen was 5 years older than Liv and the only sibling she had. They'd been close since kids and he'd taken her in with open arms the minute she told him she'd finally left Tommy. He'd always hated him, but always supported Liv's decision to stay with him despite his flaws, and never criticised her for it. As her older brother he always looked out for her, and always made sure she was looked after too.

"So, you both like each other?" he asked, as she curled up tighter on the sofa looking at him and shrugged.

"Well, you obviously like him?". She nodded, "And he must like you if he got pissed off with his brother putting it on you, which is a dick move by the way"

"I guess. But it's complicated because of Clayton. It's unprofessional and unethical to start dating his dad. So, I feel like I should cut my losses before I lead him on" she said already hating the thought of not speaking to him.

"Don't be stupid. It's the 21st century Liv, and nobody gives a fuck. His son will be leaving the school within the next year so what's the problem? You deserve to be happy, and if your loud ass laughing this morning was anything to go by, he definitely does that"

Liv smiled. She really did love Owen, and he always had her best interests at heart, but she was also aware of what Jackson had said last night about women flitting in and out of Clayton's life. She didn't want to be the one to complicate things for him, she respected him and herself too much for that. She didn't need to get attached only to be dropped when he got scared of catching feelings, and what made her any different from all of the other woman he'd dated.

"Everything" Jackson said kicking his brother hard under the table.

He'd come for a late breakfast and to apologise for what he'd done the night before kissing Liv and asking for a threesome. He'd asked him what was so special about her anyway, and that's what had led to the pain radiating through his shin.

"Everything? Blimey, she's done a number on you hasn't she? You've only known her a week Jax and you're already losing your mind over. Does she feel the same?"

"Fucked if I know, I don't want to ask" he said rubbing his face in his hands. This was not him. He didn't chase women, he kind of just let them come to him, and treated them respectfully up until the point they started demanding more. But she hadn't demanded anything, she hadn't even suggested anything.

"Well, you don't ask, you don't get" Joe said shovelling some eggs and bacon in his mouth and washing it down with coffee. "What's with the fancy coffee machine anyway?"

At that moment Clayton came into the kitchen and Jackson gave Joe a look to tell him the conversation was over. The last thing he wanted was Clayton involved and getting mixed messages about what was going on.

"Yes Uncle Joe!" he said, grabbing his breakfast off of the side and joining them at the breakfast bar.

"How you doing bud, how's school?"

"Yeah it's good, Dad got me some extra tutoring from my maths teacher which is good. That's also the reason he got the coffee machine by the way" Clayton laughed along with Joe and Jackson rolled his eyes.

"Oh really?! Is your tutor hot?" he asked, raising an eyebrow at Clayton and Jackson stared at him again.

"Yeah, Miss Turnell is a wet dream" Clayton laughed, and Joe laughed along with him, whilst Jackson told Clayton not to be rude.

"She's got these proper big eyes, big boobs, big bum, all the boys at school love her" he said, brushing off his dad's warning.

"She sounds fit, I met a bird like that last night actually…" Joe trailed off after Jackson kicked him in the shin again and stared at him.

"Dad fancies her, tried to make himself busy in the kitchen when she was here, but she called him a show off, so don't think she's interested Dad" he said shrugging his shoulder and laughing uncontrollably with Joe whilst Jackson sat there grinning and shaking his head.

Despite how fucking annoying he was, Joe had an amazing relationship with Clayton, attended every football match he'd ever played and spent hours in the past training with him at the park, or taking him to football games. Jackson had never been any good at sports, but Joe was good at everything. He had played football since he'd been able to walk but never took the leap to going pro.

"She's back tomorrow Dad, I can be your wingman, Uncle Joe can teach me"

They laughed some more, and Jackson told them it wouldn't be necessary as there was nothing going on between them and that she was his teacher. Clayton wasn't convinced but changed the topic to football and started discussing the Premier League with Joe and where Chelsea would end up in the table.

Whilst they chatted, Jackson finished his breakfast and checked his phone again. It had been hours since he messaged Liv, and she still hadn't messaged back. He remembered her telling him that she wasn't a morning person, but it was almost 12 o'clock and he was worrying.

He text her again just to put his mind at ease and then called the boys in for the football which would was due to start.

Liv begged Owen to get her phone for her as she curled up and refused to move other than to use the bathroom. By the time she was ready to look at the screen 74 messages were waiting for her, but the group chat could wait.

Jackson:

05:42
Thank you for tonight and thank you for listening. I'm glad I got to see you. Sweet dreams xx

09:49
Rise and shine. How you feeling this morning?

11:44
Clayton's under the impression you think I'm a show off? And here I was thinking I played things cool when you were here. How's your head?

How he was up so early she didn't know, but she was happy to wake up to messages from him. She thought back to the bar where he'd made an effort to get to know all of her friends, and Marley and Harry had told her all about him. When she remembered how he threw her over his shoulder to get her back to the house she couldn't help but laugh out loud and text him back begging for help.

> 12:13
> SOS.
>
> 12:13
> I'm dying.
>
> 12:14
> Not even coffee is helping.
>
> 12:14
> Why did you let me drink so much?
>
> 12:14
> Why did your brother kiss me?
>
> 12:15
> And how were you awake at 9:00am? I think I'm still drunk! My head feels like it's about to fall off, and I can't stop laughing that you had to carry me to the door (again). Thank you for last night. I really needed to laugh again. Hope your heads okay!? xx

Once she'd finished sending him her onslaught of messages, she scrolled through the girls chat where she was inundated with messages about where they sloped off to together.

Jade wanted to know if Liv slept with him.

Sophie wanted to know if they kissed.

George wanted to know if she got home safe.

And they all wanted to know what happened when they left the bar together and left Harry and Marley behind.

Liv didn't know if she had it in her to give them the full story but tried anyway. She explained that they'd gone to another bar which was quiet, and he spoke about her job and why she got into teaching. Then they got a kebab and spoke again for hours about when they'd met in summer, Clayton's mum, and his past relationships. Then found a taxi back, carried her to the door, and leant in for the kiss but stopped himself at the last minute. Liv said she kissed him on the cheek, but there wasn't a full-on kiss, much to Jade's disgust.

All of the girls loved him, but Jade made it clear that she hated his brother, even though Georgia and Sophie found the funny side of what happened. She could laugh about it now, but last night Liv was mortified and so angry about what had happened that she could have quite easily left and never waited to hear from Jackson. She was glad she didn't though, because it was quite possibly one of the best nights of her life.

Jackson's phone buzzed over and over again, and Clayton and Joe stared at him from across the room.

Liv had finally messaged back, and he laughed as he replied:

```
        12:18
        There   she   is,   sleeping
   beauty, was starting to worry.
```

> Have you taken some pain killers? In my defence, I slowed down because you kept going, and Jade was an extremely bad influence on my friends who are suffering too today!
>
> 12:20
> I spoke to him, he apologised, he said he would apologise to you personally, but I told him the next time he goes near you, it won't end well. He's here now watching the football with Clayton. Early bird catches the worm, I went to the gym, heads fine, thanks for asking xx

Jackson was still kicking himself that he didn't have the balls to kiss her the night before and wished he could go back and do it over again. When he got home in the morning, he couldn't sleep. He tried to shower, he released some frustration, he tried to watch TV, but he couldn't stop thinking about Liv and by 8:00 he had to go to the gym to take his mind off of things.

He was conflicted. He wanted to pursue things, but he didn't want it to be the same as all the other times he'd been involved with women. He didn't want to make it awkward for Clayton at school, or for Liv at work, and he didn't want to rush anything if she didn't feel the same.

Joe had turned up at the gym and ran beside him on the treadmill until he was ready to talk.

"You're a dick you know" Jackson said, throwing his towel on to the treadmill and watching Joe fly 2 metres backwards.

"You know I was joking Jax," he laughed, picking himself up "she's far too good for you anyway"

"Yeah, that's what I'm worried about" Jax said, finding his way to the weights and letting Joe spot him from behind.

After the workout they'd decided on breakfast at his and the football naturally followed. Jackson lounged on the sofa finally ready for sleep after it evaded him that morning, but not ready to sleep on Liv's replies just yet.

12:24
When I called you a show-off I meant it in the most sincere way possible. Didn't want Clayton to think his dad was able to impress me with a coffee machine that he bought especially for the occasion xx

12:25
The fact you've been to the gym has actually made me feel nauseas. What are you? Superman? Xx

                    12:27
                    Haha! He told you that did he? Traitor. Just didn't want to leave you disappointed that I didn't have coffee in the house. Can't stand the stuff and figured you might not come back if there wasn't any xx

                    12:29
                    I couldn't sleep, gym helped. Superman? I don't know about that xx

12:30
Wow. That's a deal breaker. It's been nice knowing you xx

12:32
What's up? Anything I can help with? (Although I'm in no fit state to physically help you right now in any way shape or form I can listen intently to anything you have to say) xx

        12:32
        Deal breaker? Does that mean you don't plan on coming over tomorrow night? I promise to make you a latte xx

12:33
That depends...

        12:33
        On?

12:34
What's on your mind?

        12:37
        Well,

        I got home, and then I was pissed that my brother got to kiss you before I did. Then I was beating myself up about not kissing you goodnight when I dropped you home. Then I was wondering about what you were thinking because you didn't kiss me either. Then I asked myself whether I should have invited you back, but I didn't want Clayton to find out and be annoyed, or you to think I was coming off too strong. I could have spoken to you for hours. Then I started wondering why I was wondering all this stuff. Then I remembered how much I enjoyed being with you last night and was thinking about how I could ask you out again, but by that point it was 8am so I went to the gym to try to stop thinking about you, but it wasn't very successful, and Joe turned up which pissed me off again xx

Typing...

Jackson bit the bullet and knew that he wasn't going to fuck around. He'd shared more in one night with her than he had in the past 10 years of on/off relationships with other women, and he'd be damned if he didn't give it a shot. He hadn't even struggled to write out exactly what he wanted to say but was petrified of her answer. In the back of his mind, he considered the possibility that she might not have been interested in him, and that she may have just been being friendly, but he hoped it was more. She hadn't given him the impression that she wasn't interested but he didn't dwell on it long before she text back.

12:47
Sounds like you've been doing a lot of thinking. You should get some sleep. If it's any consolation, he really was a shit kisser, and I didn't

enjoy one second of it. I can't say I wasn't disappointed you pulled away, but I understand why you did, and I appreciate it. You really are a gentleman and it's not that I didn't want to kiss you, I just didn't know if you wanted me too.

I really don't know how to do all this stuff Jax. I don't know how to text, or date, or anything like that. I was in a relationship for 8 years and this is all new to me, not to mention I'm clayton's teacher. I listened and respected every single thing you said last night, and I don't want to be blind sided with expectations that aren't mutual. I really loved last night too, probably a bit too much.

I'm sorry it made you lose sleep, if I hadn't laughed so much, or been so drunk, I think I would have too xx

12:52
Trust me it's not like that, I'm not trying to get you in to bed Liv, it's the last thing on my mind. But I told you more last night than I've ever told anyone. How about dinner? Next weekend? Then you've got all week to change your mind? Xx

13:06
I'll allow it. Get some sleep (so I can go get some too without feeling guilty) xx

13:08
Haha okay it's a date. I'll try, sweet dreams xx

11.

Sunday came and went in the blink of an eye and Liv was not ready to confront school. Her hangover may have subsided, but the lack of sleep was still heavily influencing her ability to move, think, or stay awake. She mentally prepared herself for the morning briefing and remembered that she still had to speak to Evans about Marc's exams and wasn't in any mood for his advances towards her which were bound to come if she asked him for a favour.

He was a kind of 'I scratch your back, you scratch mine' guy, and she wasn't in the mood for him to piss her off. It was either going to go one of two ways, he'd do as she asked, or she would finally go to HR with the long list of issues she had with his professional conduct the sleazeball.

Liv knew that men could be weird, but it didn't make it acceptable, and the only reason she hadn't spoken to HR before was because she'd always handled her own, told him straight, and brushed it off like it was nothing. Today though, she had a fire in her that meant he had no other choice than to listen, and to accept what she was telling him.

Much to her disgust, she was early for the briefing and only a few of the staff had arrived, none of whom she wished to speak to. She found a seat in the corner and swigged down some coffee whilst she poured through her emails and notifications. She waited for the room to fill with others, and willed the meeting to be over and done with already so she could get back to her classroom.

After about 10 minutes, Evans walked in behind another teacher from the department and they both headed towards her. She forced a smile but inwardly rolled her eyes as they pulled out the chairs beside her and started to make small talk about their weekend and how Liv's was.

"I saw you went out," Evans said in his sleezy voice, smirking at her, "Did you have a nice time?"

"Yeah, was needed after the year I've had" she said, hating the fact that she'd accepted his friend request on Facebook.

"Well maybe you'll come to the end of term get together with everyone this year. I mean, now you're not with Tommy and haven't got commitments".

Liv smiled and said she'd consider it, already knowing that she wasn't going. It was a night where the staff got together at a local bar, and slated the people that didn't attend, or the kids that they taught, which didn't interest her at all. Luckily, the head entered the room, and she didn't have to entertain the notion anymore, just pretend she was listening to whatever the nobhead in front was talking about.

Jackson had been up since 5:00am and in the office since 6:00. He wanted to make sure every detail of the website was good to go before it went live and felt like he might have rushed it through on Saturday so he could see Liv.

To his surprise, it was actually pretty spot on, with only minor tweaks needed on some of the images and a better font throughout. He navigated through, ensuring that it all worked properly and was easily manageable, then sent out an email to his client telling him that he'd double-checked, and he was at the office if he had any issues or wanted any alterations.

As he typed, his phone rang for the fourth time. He had already told her it was over, and he hoped she found someone else, but that wasn't good enough. He figured if he ignored her long enough, she'd get the hint and leave him alone, which also didn't happen.

"Rachael,…"

"Jax, what is going on? Why have you been ignoring me for weeks? We're both adults and you haven't even got the decency to sit down and speak to me face to face about all of this?"

"I did speak to you, I told you when I saw you last, I told you when you refused to leave my house, I text you, I even avoided you so that you'd get the hint, and you're still harassing me at 7:00am on a Monday. What do you want?"

"I want you to stop pretending like I mean nothing to you, that's what. I do mean something to you, even if you don't want to admit it, and I'm not willing to let you throw this away because your ego won't let you get close to anyone Jax. I know you. I know you better than you know yourself, and I know that you'll regret this. Just come and see me tonight and we can talk about things? Please?

"Wow, better than I know myself? That's a new one. Look Rach, tonight isn't good. I've got stuff planned tonight and to be honest, I don't want to talk about it. I told you from the get-go that this wasn't a relationship we were never going to run off into the sunset with one another. It was just one of those things, and it happened too many times. That's it! Now, can I get back to work?"

"DO YOU KNOW WHAT JACKSON; YOU HAVE NO FUCKING IDEA HOW MUCH I CARE ABOUT YOU AND HOW MUCH I'VE SACRIFICED SO I CAN BE THERE WHENEVER AND WHEREVER YOU WANT ME TO BE. WHY ARE YOU ACTING LIKE SUCH A DICK AND LIKE YOU DON'T FUCKING CARE AT ALL, WHAT IS THIS TO YOU?! A FUCKING GAME?!"

"Rach, you're saying it like I didn't tell you from the very beginning. We never agreed to a relationship, and let's be honest we aren't the kind of people that can settle down with each other. You always have to be centre of attention and this isn't about you. This is about me, I don't need someone like you dictating what's best for me, when you don't even know what's best for yourself!"

"So, you've found somebody else?!"

"I didn't say that did I?"

"But have you?!"

Jackson didn't know how to answer what she was asking because in his head, he'd found the woman of his dreams, but in reality, he didn't know whether it was going anywhere or not. The pause did enough to send her steaming off again though, and she continued shouting down the phone at him.

"YOU PIECE OF SHIT! YOU COULDN'T EVEN WAIT FOR IT TO BE OVER BEFORE YOU FOUND SOMEONE ELSE TO FUCK?! DIDN'T EVEN GIVE ME THE COUTESY OF TELLING ME THAT THE REAL REASON YOU ENDED IT WAS BECAUSE YOU'RE SEEING SOMEONE ELSE? I'LL TELL YOU WHAT, I HOPE YOU'RE FUCKING HAPPY AT WHAT YOU'VE DONE, YOU ARE LITERALLY THE SCUM OF THE EARTH"

"Right. You're obviously pissed off, but I'm not seeing anyone, not that it's any of your fucking business. I told you from the get-go that this wasn't a relationship, you made it into something that it wasn't and that's not my fault. I'm done with this conversation Rach, have a nice life" he seethed, hanging up the phone.

The phone rang over and over and he ignored it not wanting to unsettle the dust any more than it was. Rachael was fine to waste time with, but he couldn't commit to someone like her. She wanted marriage, and kids, and to be involved with Clayton, which he didn't want any of. Not with her anyway. She'd become upset and angry over the tiniest things, constantly hound him at work or at home if he told her he was busy and showed up out of the blue demanding why he hadn't seen her or answered her.

He'd asked her time and time again what she thought this thing was, and then she'd get emotional and tell him how she knew it was just fun and that she was sorry, and it wouldn't happen again. She was happy with the arrangement to be friends until she wasn't, and that had been one too many times. But he'd made a rod for his own back, always being the one to pick up the pieces every time things failed for her with someone else.

Even before he met Liv he'd called it quits on the relationship, or whatever they were doing, and it was the last straw when she'd spent the night and refused to leave before Clayton came home. He'd been confronted in his own house by a woman he'd never met who was telling him how amazing his dad was, and how lovely it was to meet him.

Jackson had demanded she get her coat and dropped her home saying he didn't want to see her again, but she hadn't taken him seriously.

"I was bound to meet him one day Jax, and if it was up to you it would've never happened. I'm sorry, I just wanted to be a proper part of your life" she'd said as he waited for her to leave *"I'll give you some time to think about it"*

But all the time in the world wasn't going to make him change his mind. As far as he was concerned, she'd burned her bridges and he wasn't interested in rekindling anything with her. He hated being

THAT guy, but where Rach was concerned, he had to be cruel to be kind, and he guessed he hadn't heard the last of her yet.

Jackson busied himself replying to emails and ignored his phone buzzing next to him for over an hour. He wasn't prepared to speak to her again and hoped that their last conversation would make it clear that they were over. By 08:30, Harry was in the building and sat down at the desk opposite Jackson's whilst his phone buzzed over and over again for the 18th time.

"So…" he asked kicking his feet up on the desk and putting his arms behind is head, "Did you?"

"Nope" Jackson said, not looking up from his screen.

"Not even…"

"Nope" Jackson cut him off. He knew the questions were coming, and even if he had gone all the way with Liv, he certainly wouldn't be sharing the information. He didn't mind when it was about a woman that he wasn't really interested in, but he was genuinely trying to win Liv over, despite opening up to her about his relationship history which consisted of nothing more than a mutual agreement of dating, fucking, and never settling down.

"Wow. That's different" he said raising his eyebrows and grabbing out his laptop.

"She's different" he shrugged, ignoring his phone again which was buzzing across the table.

"Are you gonna answer that?" Harry asked.

"Nope" He replied, making Harry aware that it was about to be an extremely long day. If Jackson was in a mood, there was nobody getting a conversation out of him no matter how important. If it was a client, he delegated it to someone else, if it was an employee, they knew better than to approach him on his bad days, and just went to Harry instead. Jax was still pissed off and angry at everything Rachael had said. He wanted her out of his life for good, and the last thing he wanted was her fucking up his chances with Liv, which she would definitely try if she found out.

12.

"Luke!" Liv called as the meeting finished and he made to leave the room to get to class, "Can I have a word?"

"Course?" Evan's was tall and relatively good looking in a preppy sort of way. If he wasn't such as asshole, Liv could imagine other people being attracted to him, but he just made her feel sick. He was always a little too sleazy for her liking, a little too frivolous with his physical contact.

"So, Marc found me the other day and is a bit worried about his maths subjects. He's really interested in completing decision maths, rather than statistics, and he wanted me to speak to you to see if we could swap them over"

"Why on earth would he want to do that? Decision maths is awful, and it's not a subject that we teach on the syllabus. He's great at statistics, he'll do just fine" he said rubbing her arm and making to leave. Liv inwardly shuddered before she chased after him, blocking his path and earning herself a raised eyebrow as a reward.

"I'm not saying he's not great at statistics, we both know he's a child prodigy, I'm saying that he wants to do decision maths, because he feels it will be more beneficial to what he wants to do after school. You know as well as I do his heart is with computing, can't you just make an exception this once"

"Miss Turnell, I don't appreciate you chasing me down and questioning my authority when it comes to what subjects my students will and will not be studying for their qualifications. As I said, decision maths is not on the syllabus and that isn't about to change anytime soon"

Liv smiled politely, leaned in close and pulled on his tie before she whispered into his ear. His immediate reaction was to touch her hip, as much as it made her skin crawl, she wasn't about to take no for an answer.

"And I'm telling you, that if you don't allow *my* student, to change his option from statistics to decision maths in the next few seconds. I'll be ensuring that I have a written complaint by the end of the day about your inappropriate behaviour around each and every female member of staff in this establishment…"

He started to contest but Liv cut him off short pulling his tie harder.

".. are we clear?"

"Crystal." He spat out through gritted teeth, "but just so you know Olivia. I don't do well to threats"

With that, he stomped off out of the staff room and down the hallway straightening his tie as he did. Olivia rolled her eyes and composed herself before she followed suit and headed off to her own classroom ready for form. If she was never that close to him again it would be too soon, but as long as he made good on her demands she'd live.

She set her bag down and dug around for her phone before texting Jackson who hadn't messaged her yet, hoping that she hadn't said anything to upset him, and caring more than she should have.

> 09:02
> Did you manage to get some sleep? Hope work goes okay today. Will be with you around 4:30/5:00 for Clayton's session xx

As the class started to fill with students from her form, Liv kept an eye out for Marcus ready to tell him the good news. She signed the kids in, shared the latest on new rules in the school including the phone ban, and then wished them a lovely day before they left. As the students funnelled out, Liv called Marc to the side and told him she had spoken to Evans about allowing him to sit the decision maths exams and Marc leant down and hugged her.

"Thank you Miss!" he said excitedly smiling down at her.

"You let me know if you need help, won't you?" she said smiling back, glad that she'd been able to help a little, "Instead of attending the statistics lessons with Mr. Evans, you can either set up in the library, or come into the back of my classroom if it won't be too much of a distraction. Okay?"

"I will" he said happily, and with that he went about his day with a new spring in his step and a smile on his face.

Little things like that always made Liv happy, but she was still pissed at Evans for his shit attitude towards her. She really did hate him, but since he was technically her boss, she had to tolerate him, at least for now. This year had really opened up her eyes, and as much as she loved her job, she didn't know if it was something that she wanted to be doing for the rest of her life. She had toyed with the idea of packing it in, but until the house was sold, she wouldn't be able to afford not to work. She figured she could always make money on the side from tutoring GCSE and A-level students, but for now she was going to have to plod along and continue keeping herself to herself.

Jackson couldn't concentrate at work. He was angry at Rachael, and angry about how vindictive she could be. The last thing he wanted was for her to find out about Liv and to ruin the possibility of it going somewhere, he wasn't willing to let that happen. He didn't want to give her the satisfaction of seeing him face-to-face, but he also didn't think she would leave him alone if he didn't.

Liv had text him as normal, and he was angry at himself that he hadn't messaged her sooner. With his head going back and forth about how to deal with Rachael all morning and how to prevent the impending meltdown, he'd completely forgotten to check in. More to the point, he didn't want to take his bad mood out on her, which he had a habit of doing, but figured he should tell her what was going on. The last thing he wanted was for her to be pulled into a drama that she didn't deserve.

> 12:13
> Sorry I haven't got back to you Liv, been loads going on this morning. I slept but was up early. I'll be home about 5:00 so see you there xx

He felt like he was blowing her off with the blunt text.

> 12:13
> I'm sorry, hope you're okay? Just distracted today, but can't wait to see you xx

With that, Jackson put his phone away in his drawer and got his head down with planning new commissions and delegating them to others in the office. Ultimately, Jackson had the final say on everything, but those he hired were as particular as him when it came to their work, so he very rarely worried that things wouldn't be done to a good enough standard.

Some of the commissions he got through were uninteresting, but he prided himself on helping out anyone. He didn't see the difference between the shop down the street and the high-end boutiques and large-scale companies that requested his services, and that's why he was so well known. He was a people person and helped wherever he could. Over the past year him and Harry had discussed expanding the business and it was only now that they were exploring the possibility.

As the day drew on, he'd accepted another 4 jobs for the coming weeks. 2 boutique shops wanted websites designing, a photography company was looking for a full package of logos, websites, and business cards, and a local band was looking for some new gig posters to be designed too.

Jackson had taken on each of them, liaised with the customer to find out their initial ideas, and put them through to various employees to discuss them further. A lot of the work could be done on the phone or through email, and then the client would be invited in to look through the project and give their opinions or the employee would travel there.

As he scrawled through his emails, he pulled up one from Chef Vine who was ecstatic about all of the design work and products that Jackson had completed over the weekend. As well as the payment for the work, and a monthly commission for maintaining the website, he'd invited him to eat at the restaurant on opening night at a black-tie event with a plus one. Automatically Jackson's thoughts went to Liv, and after a morning of stewing about Rachael, he finally started to calm down.

"So, what did you lot end up doing Saturday?" Jackson said to Harry after hours of them working in silence opposite one another.

"Oh, you over your mood now?" He replied, clicking away at his screen, and sorting out calendars for the next 2 months.

"Yep" Jackson said, retrieving his phone.

"What's up with you?"

"Had Rach on my case all morning," he said showing him the 54 missed calls on his phone and 22 message notifications. Harry raised his eyebrows and Jackson told him the conversation that he'd had with her earlier in the day.

"Well, rather you than me" he said, knowing full well that Rachael could be psychotic since she'd turned up at the office on more than one occasion and had to be ushered out. "So, what about Liv?"

"What about her?" Jax said, ignoring the messages from Rachael and pulling up the one that had come through from Liv almost 3 hours ago.

"You obviously like her?"

"Is that a question or a statement?" he said, raising his eyebrow and typing out a reply.

"Take your pick. But the real question is, how much do you like her? Is it going to be another one to have on your arm until she wants more, and you don't, or is she actually someone you can see yourself settling down with and doing more than just dating?"

Harry had stopped what he was doing by this point and was looking at Jackson, they'd been friends since they were kids, and he was more than aware of the rocky periods of Jackson's life. He'd watched his best friend give up his shot of happiness time and time again because it was never the right time, and he was always putting Clayton first, but he wanted him to be happy.

"If Saturday is anything to go by, then you definitely like her enough to blame me and Marley for Joe being his usual dickhead self, and that's saying something"

Jackson exhaled and shrugged his shoulders whilst he considered his answer. He did like her, and it had never been the case where he pictured the future with any of the women he'd been with. Not even Liv, up until he'd read the email inviting him to dinner. She was the first person he thought of, and he was already imagining what it would be like with her in a long black dress on his arm.

"Yeah, I think I like her, like her" he laughed, and Harry smiled, finally happy that it looked like Jackson had come to his senses.

13

Liv had called the garage, but her car wouldn't be ready until Thursday, which meant she probably wouldn't be able to pick it up until the weekend. That meant she'd be walking or taking taxis everywhere for the rest of the week, which was a chore, especially when she had to be at work before 08:00am. On the plus side, it meant she might get another lift home from Jackson, but it also meant walking to Clayton's tuition from school in the freezing cold.

She packed up her desk and headed to the staff room where she made herself a coffee for the journey and typed out a message to Jackson.

> 16:24
> My car's still in garage but I'm leaving school now so should still be with you for 5:00. If I'm not, tell Clayton to go to pg. 37 of his textbook and read through it, and try the questions. You'd better have my latte on the go, it's freezing outside xx"

With that, Liv pocketed her phone, threw her bag over her shoulder and headed out the door to Jackson's. She'd worked out that she could hopefully get there within 30 minutes, but it was already getting dark so she wanted to hurry if she could.

As she walked, Liv thought back to the weekend and kept asking herself whether she should have agreed to the date. Spending time with Jackson had been just what she needed to lift her spirits, but she found herself thinking about him all the time. Even though she felt like she liked him, she would be lying to herself if she said she wasn't worried about his track record.

He'd opened up to her about the women in his past and how he hadn't wanted to get too close or tied down, but if that was all he was looking for, was she okay with that? She wasn't up for getting her hopes up only to be let down, when he decided she wasn't what he wanted. If there was a chance of just being friends with benefits, would she take it?

Olivia was tired of being last on the list of priorities and she would make that clear to Jackson before it went any further. She'd tell him about her relationship with Tommy and why they weren't together, and that she didn't want to settle for less than what she felt she deserved. She figured if they both had their cards on the table and agreed that they were both open to getting to know each other, then there could be a chance, even if it was a slim chance.

She just didn't want to get her hopes up for nothing and in the grand scheme of things, they'd only been talking a week. She just found it crazy that she felt happier after one week of talking to Jackson than she did in the whole 8 years she was with Tommy, and if that was the case, she'd be stupid not to pursue it. Life was too short for ifs and buts, and if it went nowhere, it went nowhere. She had nothing to lose right now, literally.

For the first time in her adult life, she was single, with no commitments, no worries and no stress. She wasn't even committed to her job anymore and other than turning up for work she was able to do whatever, whenever she wanted, which was liberating.

Jackson had only messaged Liv a handful of times and he was scared she'd think he was blowing her off. He'd told her he'd had a stressful morning and he'd speak to her about it later, but he didn't want to burden her with issues of his past and the women in it, even though he was going to have to. With Rachael back in the picture, he didn't want to blind side her and have her think that she was the "other woman". Again, she'd been understanding and hadn't hounded him all day, but it wasn't behaviour he was used to, and he didn't know whether she was genuinely too good to be true or whether she was secretly pissed off at him.

He'd clocked off early so he'd be home by the time she got there but as he drove her message come through and he called her.

"Hey? Everything okay?" she said as she answered the phone sounding happy.

"Of course, just a long day. Where are you? I'll swing by and get you on my way home"

"Well, aren't you the gentleman! I'm just about to take the shortcut through the park, so I'll meet you on the other side"

"To fuck you are, wait there and I'll be there in 5, it's dark!"

"Erm, I'm a big girl Jax, just stay on the phone to me if you must"

"Yes, I must. But can you please just wait for me. I'm coming out of Dumpton, so I'll literally be 2 minutes"

"Hmm. What's it worth?" She said perching herself on the bench outside the entrance to the green.

"I'll let you pay for dinner"

"So much for taking me on a date, sounds like the other way around now? Don't be choosing anywhere too posh because I'm not made of money"

> "You should consider yourself lucky, I've never let a lady take me out, you'd be the first.."

Jackson went on to make small talk about what her favourite foods were and found his way to the park in record time since traffic was on his side. He pulled up alongside Olivia who checked her phone as she got in the passenger seat and raised her eyebrows.

"Well, aren't you a regular Vin Diesel?" she said buckling up and placing her bag between her legs whilst Jackson pulled out on to the road and headed to the house.

"No traffic" he shrugged, throwing her a lopsided smile.

"Uh huh, in rush hour? Lies, lies" she said, winking.

When they arrived, Jackson helped her out of the car and opened the front door. He helped her with her bag whilst she ditched her shoes in the porch and carried on their conversations about what was up with her car in the garage. Liv wasn't very tech savvy so she couldn't explain in detail, but Jackson politely nodded anyway. Once they were both in, Jackson told her to go on without him as he was going to get changed. Liv watched him head upstairs and strolled towards the kitchen. As she did, he shouted back down that she could use the coffee machine, and then headed for the shower, happier than he had been all day.

Liv smiled as she headed to the kitchen and over to the table to wait for Clayton. She didn't know how to use the fancy coffee machine so decided to wait for Jackson instead, and text him to tell him just that. As she smiled down at her phone and scrolled through some of their messages, she reconvinced herself that she definitely wanted him, and didn't care about the conflict of being

Claytons teacher. As far as she was concerned, he was leaving the school in the summer, and so until then, she could see where things went.

As she daydreamed, a figure caught her eye from across the kitchen and she sat frozen in her chair whilst a woman glared at her. She was tall and slim, with thick dark curls framing her face. Her lips well full and her eyes bore into her with her brows pulled into a frown.

"And you are?" she said curtly, taking Liv by surprise. She didn't know who the fuck the woman was, but she could tell already that she didn't like her. Other women didn't intimidate her, and she'd be damned if she'd be intimidated when she'd done nothing wrong.

"Hi" she said getting to her feet and walking towards her, "I'm Olivia, I teach Clayton and I'm doing some private tutoring for his GCSE's"

Liv extended her hand and the woman in front of her glared at it before she shook it.

"Rachael," she said forcing a smile, "how comes you came in with Jackson?"

"Oh? He saw me walking to the house and offered me a lift as my cars in the garage" she said, already knowing where this was going.

"Ah okay," she said forcing a smile again, "well it was nice to meet you"

With that, she left the kitchen and trotted off down the hallway towards the stairs where Jackson had gone minutes earlier and Liv returned to the table, angry. She didn't know who she was, but she'd hazard a guess that this was an ex, or a current girlfriend. Either way, she was fuming.

How dare he suggest that they go on a date when there was still someone obviously involved in his life, involved enough to be at his house and demanding answers from her?

Liv messaged Jade asking her to pick her up at 6:00 and waited for Clayton to come down to the kitchen which felt like forever. She busied herself getting out textbooks and paper and by the time she was done, Clayton was coming in from the hallway looking upset.

"Hi Miss," he said, plopping into the chair next to her.

"Hey! What's up?" she asked.

"Dad's gonna be pissed at me for letting that woman in the house," he shrugged.

"Don't be silly, why would he be pissed?" she asked, closing her books again. Now wasn't the time to be angry, or *'pissed'* about Jackson or the woman she'd just met, and her frustration immediately eased when she noticed Clayton was upset.

"I met her before, but dad was pissed off then and made her leave the house. He was proper angry that she wasn't leaving. But she turned up and I said he wasn't here so she said she would wait, and I didn't want to leave her outside because it was cold?" I don't know who she actually is, but I know he's gonna be mad" he said tapping his pen on the table.

"Oh Clayt, don't be silly. I don't think he will be mad at you. Shall we go out and work somewhere else? We can get a hot chocolate in the café down the street instead?"

"It's okay Miss, you don't have to do that" he said, but Liv insisted and made him go and get his jacket before leaving the house. Whilst he got himself ready, Liv typed out a message to Jackson so he wouldn't think she'd kidnapped his son, and packed up her bag as quickly as she could. Clayton wasn't the only one who didn't want to see Jackson at the moment, and Liv needed time to calm down.

```
17:06
We're going to the café for
Clayt's maths session, he's a
bit worried about letting your
friend in the house. She seems
nice. I'll drop him home after
then Jade is going to pick me
up x
```

Liv knew that the comment was petty, but she was pissed off and wanted him to know about it. She didn't know if she had a right to be pissed off, but she was. Regardless of whether it was right or wrong, having another woman question her about who she was to Jackson made her blood boil, and she was glad to be leaving the house.

Jackson had run straight upstairs, stripped and got in the shower, ready to chuck some lounge clothes on and start dinner. He had already convinced himself to pluck up the courage to ask Liv to the black-tie event but was at war with himself as to whether or not he was being too forward. After her session with Clayton, he'd offer to drive her home and he would ask her on the way. It wasn't for another few weeks, but at least she'd know that he was serious about pursuing something real and wasn't after a one-night stand with her.

Jackson turned off the shower and towel dried his hair as he left his bathroom, only to be greeted by Rachael sat on his bed, legs crossed, drumming her fingers.

"What the fuck are you doing in my house?!" he demanded, wrapping the towel around his waist and grabbing his phone from beside her on the bed. He quickly opened his notifications from Liv and swore under his breath before darting for the chest of drawers for some boxers.

"What do you think I'm doing here?" she said glaring as he manoeuvred around the room, "you wouldn't answer my calls or texts, and I'd had enough. You don't just get to decide that this is over and not have the decency to talk to me face to face Jax?!"

"I don't?" he said shoving his legs through his boxers and finding a t-shirt and joggers.

"No, we are going to sit down and talk this out and get back on track. I'm not just giving up when we've already been through so much"

"Rachael, there is nothing to "give up"! We were never in a relationship?! We dated, we fucked, we rowed, we ended. That's it. I told you I never wanted a relationship, and this is over, now get out"

"No" she said walking over to him and taking his waist, "Jax, can we please just.."

"Seriously Rach, get the fuck off of me and out of my house, now" he said shrugging her off and finding his phone again.

> 17:12
> Liv, I'm sorry. Tell Clayton I'm not pissed off at all. Please let me take you home after so we can talk and I can explain about Rachel, it's honestly not what you think!

"Are you joking? You can't even have an adult conversation with me without looking at your phone, who's so important that you can have a conversation with them whilst I'm here trying to get you to open up for once?!"

"RACH! YOU'VE FORCED YOUR WAY INTO MY HOUSE, WHILST MY SON WAS HERE, FOR WHAT?! WE ARE OVER. DONE. THAT'S IT. THERE'S NOTHING TO TALK ABOUT. I DON'T NEED TO OPEN UP. I WANT NOTHING TO DO WITH YOU EVER AGAIN, AND TRUST ME IF YOU AIN'T OUT OF MY HOUSE IN THE NEXT 30 FUCKING SECONDS, I WILL MAKE YOUR LIFE A FUCKING LIVING HELL!"

"Is that meant to be a threat?" she asked backing up and staring at him.

"I DON'T FUCKING CARE HOW YOU TAKE IT, GO AND FIND SOMEONE ELSE AND MAKE THEIR LIFE A MISERY"

Jackson tried to call Liv, but it went straight to answerphone. He tried Clayton's phone too and that was the same. Rachael was still muttering something in front of him and he walked straight past her without another word, found his keys, some trainers and left the house with her in toe.

When the door shut, he hopped in his car and reversed out of the driveway without another word, whilst Rachael screamed at him to be a man and talk to her. Jackson kicked himself for ever thinking it was a good idea to get into bed with her in the first place, and for messing things up with Liv before they'd even begun as he peeled off down the road.

Jackson found the café around the corner and parked across the road whilst he waited for Liv and Clayton to finish. He could see them through the window and was besotted at how happy she looked whilst teaching. He didn't have a clue what he was meant to say to her after her run in with Rachael. He didn't know what was said, but he knew how belittling Rachael could be. He was dreading Liv calling things off, he'd never been that invested in women before, but now, now he'd fucked up again.

Without even thinking, he called Harry.

He didn't know what else to do and Harry was always the one with his head on straight. He told him what happened and asked him where he was meant to go from here. He was scared that he'd fucked his chances with Liv before he'd even managed to take her on a date. First Joe kissed her, then Rachael belittled her, and now she was even avoiding his house.

Harry calmed him down and told him to stop panicking but said that if he was open and honest with Rachael and told her there was someone else, she'd move on a lot quicker. Jackson wasn't convinced though. If she had already met Liv, and then found out she was the one he wanted to date, she'd go to drastic measures to make her life hell, and Jackson wasn't willing to risk that. He checked the time and pulled off around the corner to try and sort things out before they finished, and he insisted on dropping her home.

Knowing full well he'd have to speak to Rachael again at some point and get things sorted once and for all. He dialled her number and bit the bullet.

14

Liv clocked Jackson pull up and pull off again and was thankful he wasn't there watching her anymore. She still had half an hour left of Clayton's session and was going through solving and simplifying algebraic equations which was something that all of the kids hated.

"Only way is up from here," Liv said when Clayton rolled his eyes at the suggestion, and without the distraction of his classmates, he picked it up relatively easy. As he worked his way through the questions in the textbook, Liv asked if he was okay now.

"I suppose," he said answering the equations as he spoke, and avoiding eye contact. "Dad does everything for me, but he doesn't ever tell me about his girlfriends and stuff which I know he's had. That woman earlier was there one day when I got back from Mum's, but they were arguing about her leaving before I was back and then Dad was really angry so now I just think he's gonna be a bit pissed off at me as well for letting her in again"

"Honestly Clayton, I wouldn't worry. He was probably pissed off at her and not at you. Parents just want to protect their kids, and he obviously wants what's best for you, or I wouldn't be here teaching you now, would I?" she said, giving him a reassuring pat on the arm.

"I think that's only half of the reason" he laughed, raising his eyebrows, "I think a lot of it had to do with the fact he fancies you"

Liv went red and shyly brushed the comment off before getting back to work. Clayton was so similar to his dad and his uncle in the way he looked, and the way he spoke. She could tell how close they were not only from what Jackson had been saying over the weekend, but by how highly Clayton always spoke about him. Even in class sometimes she'd overhear him speaking about him to his friends, and she really admired the lengths he went to make sure they had a good relationship.

Liv pulled her phone to see if Jade had replied, only to find missed calls and messages from Jackson that had been sent not long after she must have left the house. She'd already told Jade to pick her up from his, so the ride home was going to have to wait and so was he. She waited whilst Clayton finished up, and cleared the table whilst he got his bag and coat on, but Jackson was already back outside by the time they'd finished.

Liv wanted the ground to swallow her up when she walked outside and he offered her a lift, but politely declined saying that Jade would be there any minute and she would wait for her. Clayton climbed in after saying goodbye and sat toying with his phone whilst Jackson got out the car and spoke to Liv who was waiting in the cold.

"Will you let me explain?" he said quietly, avoiding Clayton listening in behind him in the passenger seat.

"Explain what? Your personal business is nothing to do with me, you don't owe me an explanation" she said, pulling her coat more tightly round her waist.

"Okay, it's not about *owing* you anything Liv. I don't want you to think I'm not serious about everything I said yesterday because of what happened today?"

"I don't think that"

"Well, you could have fooled me" he said smirking as she crossed her arms over her chest and tried desperately to look for Jade's car. "She's not coming by the way"

"Sorry?"

"I text Jade, I told her I was going to drive you home as I needed to speak to you. She said that if I make you cry, she'll kill me. I told her I appreciate the vote of confidence, and that was that. So, can you please get in the car now before we both freeze to death?"

With that, Jackson knocked on the window and beckoned Clayton to climb in the back, whilst Liv got in the passenger seat, buckled up, and plastered a smile on her face in front of Clayton.

Jackson watched Liv get into the car and was thankful that Harry had worked his charms on Jade and landed her number. When he called her and explained what had happened, he asked what he could do to fix it, but she said that wasn't her place to say, and if he was serious about Liv, he'd have to think of something. This was shortly after she'd threated to 'do his kneecaps' and 'kill him' if he made her cry.

He made small talk in the car about the work that Clayton had been doing, but it was less than a 5-minute drive back to the house, so it was only short. Clayton hopped out and said bye, whilst Jackson told him he'd be home soon, and to order something for dinner as he hadn't cooked yet.

As he pulled back out of the driveway, Liv was quiet, and Jackson was nervous. He didn't push a conversation, and neither did she, they just sat quietly in the car whilst he drove.

"Where are you going?" she asked, noting that he was going in the opposite direction to her brother's house.

"*We* are going to talk," he said looking over and smiling at her, "and before we talk, I promised you a latte, which is exactly what you will get"

Liv rolled her eyes, bit back a smile and returned to gazing out of the window, whilst Jackson pulled into the COSTA drive-thru, ordered himself a hot chocolate, and Liv an extra-large latte, with plenty of sugar.

"Caramel syrup" she muttered next to him as he gave the order, and he repeated it into the speaker whilst laughing.

"So..." she said, when she'd taken a sip of her coffee and Jackson was driving again, "who's your friend?"

"That would be Rachael," he said, looking left and right at the junction and heading towards the seafront so he could park up and talk to her properly. Jackson knew this was going to go one of two ways but was hoping like mad it was in his favour. He'd been open and honest with Rachael, who wasn't happy, and now he was going to be open and honest with Liv too.

"She seems nice," Liv said sarcastically, as Jackson got himself comfy in his seat and faced her with his drink.

"You think?" he laughed.

"Oh, absolutely" she drawled.

"I don't blame you. Rach is a bitch" he said gauging her reaction, which was like stone "We've known each other for years, and we fooled around together on and off. We both had relationships in the past, but we just naturally gravitated back to each other for a bit of fun when we weren't seeing someone else. Then one of us would settle down again, or start seeing someone in my case, and then it would die down, until we were both single again. Anyway, it was like that for years, and it was always just casual, always has been, until last year both of us had been single a while, then we got to talking again. She was never someone I wanted to be romantically involved with, she's not always level-headed, but it was easy for when I was bored or lonely and it was familiar. It wasn't the case of finding someone new who I'd eventually end up letting down again it was just Rachael, and she knew as well as I did, that it was never going to a case of being together properly. But in the end, that's what she wanted. She begged me to let her meet Clayton and get to know him, she wanted to make it official and wanted a family, and I didn't. Well, I didn't with her anyway. So, one day we went home pissed and ended up falling asleep, which never happens. She refused to leave, and Clayton came home, and she was trying to start conversations with him, but he just went to his room. I was fuming, and ended it there and then, dropped her home and told her we were done"

Jackson took a sip of his drink and watched Liv as she waited for him to continue. He was always surprised at how much she listened instead of interrupting or answering, and he wanted her to know that he wasn't trying to play her.

"She called me earlier, in fact she calls me a lot, and I told her again that I wasn't interested, not in the slightest, but when I ignored her calls, over 50 of them, I guess she wanted to know what was going on and so she turned up at the house. I got out the shower and she was there, and I wanted to run down and speak to you straight away and tell you that it's not what it looks like, but I grabbed my phone and you'd already gone. Then she wouldn't shut up, so I just walked out and came straight to find you and Clayton, but then I didn't know what to say to you, so I called Harry, and then I called Jade, and now we're here" he finished, taking a breath.

"I see" she said sipping her latte and inhaling, "look, I appreciate you telling me, but as I said, you don't owe me anything Jackson. Whatever is going on in your life is nothing to do with me. We aren't together, it's not like we are sleeping together or anything, so you really don't have to explain yourself to me"

"I get that, but I don't want you to think I'm playing you, when I'm not?" he said getting frustrated at how easy going she was about the whole situation.

"Playing me how? You've already told me you're not interested in settling down and I'd be a bit of a mug to expect anything different, wouldn't I? I'm not that girl Jackson. I was in a shit relationship for 8 years, and to be perfectly honest, I haven't got a clue what I want or need. Do I just need a good shag? Do I need someone who's going to worship the ground I walk on? Do I need to just have a year away from men who haven't got a fucking clue what they want? All of the above? I don't know. But I know I don't want to be dragged into drama with your psycho ex, because I don't deserve it. I have laughed and smiled more in one weekend with you, than I did in the last 8 years with Tommy, and I don't want that all to be for nothing, by getting my hopes up only to be dropped when it's no longer convenient for you"

Jackson couldn't help but smile as she ranted because despite all of the negative things she had to say, all he was focused on was everything that fell in line with what he wanted. She was beautiful, feisty, honest, considerate and outspoken and he loved that.

"Liv, I told you I wasn't interested in settling down with women I didn't want to meet my son, but haven't you been teaching him for almost 5 years?"

"Yes, I have, but that doesn't change your opinion on relationships Jax"

"That doesn't. But you do"

Liv was taken aback and was trying her best not to get distracted from the situation in hand because of the way he looked. It annoyed her that he looked good in anything and even with a fitted black tracksuit on, he looked dressed up. She rubbed her temples and swigged her coffee a bit more before she decided to take her leave. Without saying bye, she got out of the car, slammed the door and walked off into the dark, knowing that if she stayed, she'd do or say something she'd regret.

The temperature was almost freezing, and water was spraying over the sea wall as she walked. *What a fucking stupid place to park* she muttered, stomping off towards the town where she'd catch a cab home.

She couldn't believe he would stoop as low as to say that she was the reason he was reconsidering a proper relationship just to get her in bed. She stormed across the car park, angry that he'd spoke to Jade, and angry that Jade had taken his side, she just wanted to go home, binge on Masterchef, eat chocolate and forget today ever happened.

Everything was fine yesterday, she'd agreed to the date, she was even looking forward to the date, and she'd enjoyed speaking to him every minute of every day but now? She was kidding herself if she thought she was special in comparison to the other women he'd been with, and soon enough he'd get bored of her as well and she'd be left in the same position as the woman she met earlier.

"LIV! It's fucking freezing, get in the car!" Jackson called from behind her.

"Well, you shouldn't have parked in such a stupid fucking spot then should you?!" she flung back over her shoulder, cradling her coffee in both hands.

She heard him grunt with frustration and before she knew it, she was in the familiar position of being draped over his shoulder again and desperate to keep her coffee upright. Jackson did a 180 degree turn and headed back towards the car whilst Liv screamed at him to put her down.

"Seriously Jackson, I want to go home!"

"Excellent, I'll drive" he said laughing at her half ass attempts to get him off her. "You know you will fall if I let you go right?"

"Good!" she said elbowing him in the back and succumbing to the fireman's carry which there was apparently no way of getting out of.

"I hate you" she seethed.

"Hate you more" he said unphased as he lowered her to the ground next to the passenger side door. Liv crossed her arms, and Jackson placed his either side of her shoulders on the window.

"What is your problem?" he asked as she stared at him in disgust, "you don't trust me?"

"Would you trust you? With everything you've told me, would you genuinely be ready to just forget about all of that and put yourself on the line? Without hesitation, and without being scared or worried or-"

"- oh, fuck this" he said cutting her off, and with that he leaned in and kissed her.

Liv's arms reacted instantly, and she draped them around his neck pulling him in closer to her. She fucking knew she should have walked quicker, but at that moment, she didn't care. It felt right, more right than it should have, and as he kissed her, she forgot about everything she was worrying about before.

Liv pulled away before Jackson did, and stared up at him with big brown eyes, knowing she was going to get her heart broken. *The higher you climb, the harder you fall* she thought, but she would climb mountains to get a feeling like that again. Both of them were silent, but the silence wasn't awkward. Jackson looked as happy as Liv felt, and both of them were too distracted to notice the wave that crashed over the wall and drenched them both from head to toe.

"OH MY GOD! JACKSON!" Liv screamed, but he was laughing so hard he was crying. Liv stood with her arms outstretched as water dripped from her sleeves. Her hair was stuck to her face, and eyes were scrunched tightly shut, stinging with sea water and her feet were already starting to go numb.

Liv started to laugh as Jax removed her glasses and attempted to clean them unsuccessfully. She wiped off her eyes, more than aware there was mascara everywhere, before she tip-toed up to kiss him again, and with that, she knew he had her.

15.

Jackson put the heaters on full blast in the car and both of them took off their jackets. Fortunately, Liv was wearing black, but that didn't stop him from staring at the way her sopping clothes now clung to her body. She was still laughing as she cleaned off her glasses and Jackson pulled out of the carpark to take her home, despite not wanting the night to end.

"So, are you still going to go on a date with me?" he asked as she pulled her hair up into a bun next to him and shivered.

"We'll see" she smiled, scrunching up her face as she huddled closer to the heater.

As they drove, Jackson told her that he'd spoken to Rachael. He'd told her that he was interested in someone else, and that she hadn't taken the news well. He left out the part where she'd threatened to ruin her life, and his too, figuring Liv had had enough of those kind of dramas for one day and they fell into a comfortable silence for a few minutes.

"You know I only told you all that stuff because I want to be honest with you right?" he said as they neared her house and he realised he didn't have a lot of time left.

Liv nodded and gave him a half smile whilst she continued to rub her hands together for warmth.

"And I've never told anyone stuff like that before?" he went on.

"So why me?" she replied, genuinely curious.

"Why not you?" he said, cocking an eyebrow at her whilst she put her hands back up to the heater. Liv shrugged, but Jackson was curious and urged her to answer.

"I don't know. I'm just me, aren't I? I'm nothing special, and in my defence, the first time you met me, you looked like you wanted to kill me"

"I did" he said, "you were pissing me off, and then I took you home, and then I didn't stop thinking about you. Because even though you're obviously fucking annoying..."

"*Bit harsh*" she muttered.

"...You're honest, funny, and you tell me what you think, not what you think I need to hear. I don't feel bored when I'm with you and you might see yourself as 'nothing special' but you'd be surprised". Jackson reeled off everything to her without having to think for a second, as if talking to her was the easiest thing he'd ever done.

"Then I walked into the classroom, and I knew I knew from somewhere. Then when you told me, I kicked myself for not remembering, and I pretty much decided then that I was going to ask you out".

Jackson paused and looked over to Liv who was still staring out the window at the raindrops trickling down, but she didn't reply. They just drove in silence for a while until he finally heard her beside him.

"Can't believe you think I'm annoying" Liv said, as Jackson rounded the corner to Owen's house and slowed down.

"That's all you took from that entire conversation?" he laughed, pulling the car to a stop and unbuckling again so he could face her.

"Pretty much" she smiled, before grabbing her bag and making to leave. Liv leaned over and kissed him again and he instinctively pulled her towards him, feeling her smile against his lips. When she finished the kiss, he was left wanting more, but watched her leave instead, thankful he'd taken the leap of faith to kiss her in the first place. She looked back and waved to him before she went through the door, and Jackson left, feeling better than he had in a long time.

Liv closed the door behind her, took off her shoes and went straight to put the shower on.

"What the fuck happened to you?" Owen said as she climbed the stairs and walked past him on the landing still dripping wet.

"Met Jackson's ex"

"And she waterboarded you?" he laughed.

"No, no. Jackson kidnapped me instead. Then took me to talk at the seafront, but he annoyed me, so I got out of the car, then the sea attacked me. Then I came home" she said closing the door behind her.

Liv decided against the shower and categorised her current situation as a bath job. She turned on the taps and let the water start to fill whilst she grabbed her Kindle from her bedroom and found some PJs to sling on once she got out.

She dug out her phone, returned to the bathroom, and sunk herself into the bubbles whilst the bath continued to fill up, replaying the last hour over in her head. Kissing Jackson hadn't been how she had imagined it would be, but it didn't feel forced. It felt natural, but she'd imagined it building up into some romantic first kiss that would envy the movies. Instead, they'd argued, he'd kissed her, and then she almost drowned.

At least it was memorable, she thought as she pulled up the new Romcom novel she was reading, she lowered herself further into the bath but struggled to get back into her book whilst she was distracted about thoughts of Jackson, and everything he had said to her.

Liv dropped her kindle on the floor and reached for her phone instead to call Jade who answered almost instantly.

"There you are?! Took you long enough! Was starting to think you'd been tied up and held captive!" Jade said.

"Well, I may have well of been! Why did you tell Jackson you weren't going to come and get me?"

"He told me he wanted to apologise to you? Who was I to stand in the way of a regular guy and a regular gal having a lovers quarrel"

"Hardly lovers Jade"

"Well, I'm an optimist, what can I say! So, what happened?"

"Erm, you first missy? How the fuck did Jackson get your number so quick eh?"

"You know me Liv, I'm a social butterfly. Plus, Harry is hot, so I gave him my number. He gave it to Jackson, Jackson called me, told me the gist of what had happened.. so, what did happen?"

"Well, his ex is LOVELY!" she laughed, "she reminds me of Lauren Poeman we went to school with. Came in, looked me up and down and asked me why I came in the house with Jackson. Excuse me Hun? Who are you the *police? Anyway, I said he picked me up on the way through and I was Clayton's tutor, but she waltzed upstairs, and I left the house as Clayton was upset. Was just a bit of a kick in the teeth because he asked me out on a date yesterday and then I have some random woman looking at me like I've fucked him on the table in front of her... Oh, and then Jackson told me she's psycho, so that's great"*

"Ah, fuck her. She just hates the fact that he doesn't want her, and by the sounds of it he wants Miss Turnell" Jade laughed down the phone and Liv joined her knowing full well she wouldn't be able to keep tonight to herself.

"Apparently so.."

"Go on, you're obviously dying to tell me something"

"We kissed!"

"OMG YAY!!" Liv heard Jade clapping in the background and screaming excitedly, *"I'm getting Thai and coming over and you can tell me everything and then we can go on double dates YAY! Send me your order and I'm going to get some clothes on and be over. Ask your ugly brother too. Love you!"*

With that, Liv hung up and messaged Owen asking what he wanted. She spent another 15 minutes soaking in the tub before she finally succumbed to the fact the water was getting cold, and her fingertips were going wrinkly. By the time she'd got back to the room, her phone was going again and notifications from Owen and Jackson popped up on screen. Liv forwarded Owen's order to Jade, and then laid on her bed whilst she read and replied to Jackson.

19:37

"I'm sorry I parked in such a stupid place, and I'm sorry you got wet, and I'm also sorry for Rachael. Hope you're dry now, and I do appreciate you hearing me out Liv xx"

19:48

"Well let's be honest, you didn't give me a choice? But thank you for tonight, other than being kidnapped, almost drowning and being told horror stories of your ex, I had fun xx

16.

Jackson had ignored his phone buzzing the whole time he'd been with Liv but knew Rachael wouldn't let up until he'd spoken to her again. On his way back to the house he listened to the onslaught of voicemails she had left before finally answering her call on the driveway.

"Were you with her?!"

"Her has a name, but yes. Rach seriously what do you want?"

"Jackson, I'm just giving you a chance to make up your mind properly. You know as well as I do that we are good together, and if you just for one second thought about it then you'd see it too"

"Rach, we had this discussion earlier and I told you then, we aren't good together. You thought we were something more than we were, and that was never the case. I appreciate that we have history, but that's all it is. It's never been like this before when either of us found someone else, so why are you making a massive deal out of it now?"

"Because Jackson this time was different?"

"Maybe for you, but it wasn't for me. Just leave it now and stop ringing me!"

"You watch Jackson, you'll come running back when she realises how fucked up you really are! Do you think she'll tolerate your bullshit like I have all these years? We will see, and you want to hope I don't see you together because I'll be telling her everything there is to know about you Jackson!"

"*Fuck off Rach*" he spat and with that he hung up the phone and threw it across the passenger seat.

She'd always been a nasty piece of work, but he'd always ignored it because firstly, it was never aimed at him, and secondly, she was easy to waste time with and always felt the same as him, up until now. She had agreed that their arrangement was nothing more than sex. Something was different this time, but he didn't have a clue why she was overreacting and making out like he had done something wrong.

Jackson calmed himself down in the car before he went back to the house and knew he was going to have to tell Liv at some point. The last thing he wanted was Rachael fucking up his chances with her, and despite all his flaws, he wasn't trying to take advantage of Liv or use her. He was genuinely interested in pursuing something with her that he didn't want Rachael involved in.

Clayton was sprawled out across the sofa in joggers and a t-shirt when Jackson got in and propped himself against the door frame. He wasn't concentrating much on what was on TV, but felt he owed Clayton an apology for earlier, and for dropping him home to speak to Liv. This was the exact reason he'd never wanted a relationship because he didn't want to feel like he was ever abandoning his son.

Jackson thought better of sitting on the beige sofas, soaking wet, and told Clayton he was heading for a shower. When Clayton turned to see him, he looked puzzled, then laughed and returned to the TV without another word.

Jackson let the hot water run over his body for the third time that day and thought about the last week. In hindsight he was glad that he hadn't kissed her over the weekend, but he couldn't help himself when she was stood there glaring at him, and he couldn't imagine ever getting bored of that feeling.

This wasn't normal for him, he never felt like he was ready to date properly. Over the past 10 years, women hadn't been anything more than something to pass the time with, and he'd had his fair share, but he'd never been seen in public in a relationship, his family had never met the women he slept with, and other than Rachael, even his friends didn't have much clue about who he spent time with. He didn't know how these things worked anymore, but he knew he was more than ready to give it a go.

He got himself changed, returned downstairs, found Clayton in the same position he had left him in, and flopped down on the sofa in the window.

"How was it today bud?" he said, as Clayton stared at the football highlights from over the weekend, not phased that Jackson had even entered the room.

"Yeah was good, Miss Turnell is a good teacher" he shrugged, "Did you sort things out with your friend?"

"Yeah kind of.." Jackson said, glad that Clayton was the one to address the elephant in the room.

"I didn't mean to let her in, but didn't think I should leave her out in the freezing cold" he said looking over to his dad, "who is she?"

"Just an old flame I suppose" Jackson shrugged. He'd never discussed his relationships with Clayton before, and even though he was big enough and ugly enough to know that his dad had a sex life as well as a home life, he didn't want Clayton to feel like he wasn't at the top of his list of priorities, because he always would be.

"I see, but not going on anymore?"

"Nope?"

"Any reason?"

"Nope?"

"It wasn't because I met her that day? Because you looked pissed when you left, and even more pissed when you got home as well?" he said sitting up on the sofa, "You know I don't care if you have a girlfriend, right?"

Jackson got up and sat next to Clayton on the other side of the room whilst he got comfy again. Despite being young he was old for his years, and Jackson was always proud of how mature he could be when he needed to be.

"Yeah I know, but you're my priority Clayt, you know that. Besides, I've just never found the right one. I wouldn't just introduce you to anyone, and that's how I knew it wasn't going to work with Rachael, but she doesn't see it like that".

"And now?"

"Now what?"

"Well, you're obviously after my teacher?" he laughed, making Jackson's face turn red and become defensive.

"What? I just dropped her home because it was freezing and didn't want her waiting in the cold either? Why would I be dating your teacher? Not that she isn't pretty and stuff, but still?"

Clayton was laughing as Jackson tripped up over his words and denied the statement over and over again, without sounding very convincing.

"Okay Dad, whatever you say" he said getting up to answer the door, "but just so you know, next time you come in you should wipe the lipstick from your face before saying you're not seeing her *like that*"

17.

Rachael was pacing, and it didn't matter how many times he ignored her, she'd call him until he spoke to her. How dare he just drop her like she was every other girl, their relationship wasn't the same as that, and it was far more than just sex. They'd been to and fro for years, but now they were both a bit older she figured they'd both agreed that it was time to settle down.

He'd even said it himself! *'Be nice to settle down and not be doing this all the time wouldn't it'* he'd said after they spent the night together at a hotel one night. That's all she needed to know, she just needed to hear him say the words that he was ready, and she would drop anything to be with him.

What she failed to comprehend was that he never meant settle down with her. She had her flaws like everybody else, but she had a good heart, or so she thought. In the past she'd been a bit off of the rails, but she wasn't like that now, she was stable, and she was desperate for him to reconsider. He was good for her, he always brought her back down after the others had sent her psycho, but now he was doing the same.

He knew what this would do to her, and she wasn't going to let him get away with it. She would give him one more chance, and if he couldn't speak to her like an adult, accept that this wasn't over, and commit to her like he'd promised, she didn't know what she would do.

Rachael grabbed her meds from the side and swallowed them down with wine. Right now, she was okay, she was still in control, but she could feel herself losing her patience and was petrified of another psychotic break. In her head, she was doing the right thing, and it was just a case of making Jackson see sense, but if that failed... *it's not going to fail,* she chastised herself.

Jade was like a kid in a sweetshop when Liv told her about Jackson and didn't feel it necessary to hide her excitement, despite Liv telling her she didn't want Owen to hear.

"Okay, okay but seriously Liv. He does sound genuine. And I know I don't have a good track record, and I'm a shit judge of character, but you seem so happy and excited every time you talk about him. It's nice" she shrugged.

"Yeah, I know, just hard isn't it"

"Hard why?" Jade asked, shoving noodles in her mouth and furrowing her eyebrows, puzzled.

"It's not that I'm not over Tommy, that was over a long time ago, but I actually haven't spoken to him. I need to sort out the house and I don't want him asking if I've moved on and whatever and being difficult about it, if I say that I have… plus, he's Clayton's dad" she shrugged.

She'd been putting off the conversation about the house since she walked out with nothing, and she really needed to come to an agreement about selling so that she could move out of Owen's and get a space of her own. She knew that Tommy didn't have any right to dictate what she did and did not do now, given the fact that he moved on before she even left, but that didn't ease her mind.

"Fuck him, the cheating bastard" Jade spat. "In fact, ring him right now!"

"No Jade" she sighed.

"Get it over with and see what he's got to say?!"

Liv shot her a look, but Jade kept on about how it was better to get it out of the way sooner rather than later and how he didn't deserve to keep the house after all he'd put her through. Despite her valid arguments though, Liv didn't feel up to it, and she certainly didn't want to ruin how she was feeling by having to face speaking to Tommy.

"I will call this week at some point, I promise. Plus, it's half term after this week, I'll have loads of time on my hands to go and pack up my stuff, and I'll have my car back" she said, but Jade wasn't convinced, and Liv was more than aware that she didn't want to have to see him at all. She'd told him when she left to pack her things up and she'd collect them at some point, but she still hadn't been back. She just couldn't be bothered to hear him out and wanted to be as far away from him as possible.

"Look, forget about him. He was a prick anyway, and now you've moved on, and I can almost guarantee that Jackson is 100x better in bed" she winked.

"Jade! I don't even remember the last time I had sex" she laughed, "I've probably forgotten what to do!"

"Trust me, it's like riding a bike, it all comes back to you!"

"Well, we might not even get that far, who knows" Liv said, shaking her head and hiding a blush.

"Uh huh, I give it until the end of the month.. at a push" Jade countered, wiggling her eyebrows suggestively.

Both of them laughed, but Liv considered the possibility that she actually would be sleeping with someone new. 8 years was a long time with somebody, and it's not like their sex was exciting, or very often. Before him, she'd only been with one other person, and that was a scary realisation since she had no doubt Jackson had been with plenty of women. With that thought looming over her, a knot formed in her stomach and the thought of finishing her meal quickly evaporated. Liv was hardly skilled when it came to bedroom antics, and now she was nervous that whatever happened would be a forgettable experience and she'd be forgotten soon after.

18.

Work went slow through the week, and by the time it got to Thursday, Jackson was desperate to see Liv, and for more than the hour he could catch her for after Clayton's tuition. Instead, he'd encouraged Clayton to stay at his mums for a few nights after so he could do just that, and it meant he'd be able to organise their date on Saturday too. Clayton wasn't fussed, but Jackson was already feeling guilty for getting him out of the house despite him saying it was fine and knowing the exact reason why he had suggested it.

He was due to have a consultation at midday with a new client who was rebranding their entire company, which was a mammoth job, but he wasn't in the mood. It meant going over every detail of what they already had and making sure that the transition into new image was as smooth as possible, but that was Jackson's area of expertise. Harry was in the office too and was spending his time pouring through applications for a new receptionist and administrator, since the business was expanding. Both Harry and Jackson had been discussing branching out the company to include interior design, which was due to take effect within the next 3 months, with clientele already enquiring for their services.

"What's going on with you and Jade then?" Jackson asked, breaking the silence as he fiddled about with a new design he was working on that wasn't quite right yet.

"Not much to be honest, been texting a bit, but haven't arranged to see her or anything" he shrugged, "she seems alright, fit, but don't think it's something I'm going to pursue, she hasn't hinted at anything like that, and I'm cool with it. What about Liv?"

"Seeing her again tonight, then taking her out on Saturday just trying to debate where? Plus got invited to a black-tie event so I'm going to see if she wants to go" he said nonplussed.

"Blimey, you feeling alright?" Harry asked, cocking his brow in question.

"What's that mean?"

"Well firstly, when do you ever put thought into where you take any woman you date, and secondly, how many times in the past 10 years have you been making forward plans with women?"

"I always put thought into where I take women, what you going on about?"

"No, you don't, you always take them somewhere nice, but you don't usually have to debate where?"

"She don't like all that stuff H, I've already seen her stuff her face with a kebab, and she isn't high maintenance, from what I gather anyway" he shrugged.

"Okay... so where you thinking?"

"The Ballontine?" Jackson said questioningly.

"You fucking tosspot" he laughed, "you just said she weren't high maintenance, and you want to take her to a Michelin star gaff where portion sizes are tiny?"

"Yeah, maybe not" he said rubbing his temples. He'd been thinking for days about where to take her but couldn't decide on anywhere. He'd even messaged Jade to ask her what her favourite food was, but all she replied was *'anything edible',* like that was any help. He had to book it by tomorrow and he still had no clue. The last thing he wanted to do was ask Liv, he wanted it to be a surprise, but he was running out of options.

"Why you stressing for? Women are happy with anything, it's the thought that counts. You could make her a picnic and she'd be happy with it mate, and if she feels anything like you feel, I'm sure you'll have an absolute whale of a time" Harry said, smiling and giving him an encouraging nod.

"Cheers H, I'll see what I can come up with. I need to get ready for this meeting" Jax replied, rolling the kinks out of his shoulders.

"Erm, you might want to delegate that meeting over this way" Harry said peering out through the glass wall and down to reception where the woman Jackson had been trying his hardest to avoid stood with her older brother glaring up at the two of them. The meeting had been booked in weeks ago and not once did he make the connection in surnames, which now seemed obvious. She hadn't called since Monday and he figured she'd gotten over the drama, but apparently not.

"You can definitely take that one" Jackson sighed, seething at the idea of being in the same building as her. Harry laughed, patted him on the back and went down to reception to meet them. Glad for the opportunity to miss engaging with her, Jax kept his gaze on his monitor reshuffling his design, only to sigh when Harry returned a few minutes later.

"What now?!" he said impatiently as Harry walked back in.

"Careful Jax, don't flip out because she ain't taken her eyes off of you, but they've asked specifically for you to do the consult. I told them you were busy and had other stuff to do, but they said they'd wait or reschedule"

Jackson took a deep breath and rolled his eyes. She wasn't going to let this drop, and now it was evident that she was going to get in the way of his business, as well as his personal life. He dialled down to Alice on reception who answered immediately and tried to keep his cool.

"Alice, can you please tell Mr. Stone that I'll be down within the next 15 minutes, but I can only give him half an hour of my time as I have prior arrangements today that need seeing to"

"Straight away Jax" she said, acknowledging the tone of his voice, and glad she wouldn't be in the room, "anything else?

"Just offer them a drink, or the exit, your choice"

Jackson heard Alice laugh before she hung up the phone and geared himself up for the onslaught of filthy looks he was about to receive from Rachael. He'd only met her brother in passing but knew they had always been close. He was usually overly protective of her, which didn't bode well for the next hour of his life, but he didn't care at that moment in time, because as far as he was concerned, the quicker she was out of it, the better.

At lunch, Liv planned on spending time marking some homework, but Evans had demanded that she take the canteen duty instead, which bugged her. It had only been a few days since she had asked him to allow Marc to change his subjects, but he was making her life hell in the most passive aggressive way. Thankful that it was the last week of term, Liv packed up her desk, dismissed her class, and walked the halls to the canteen to monitor the first half of lunch.

Working in a secondary school really was mentally draining at times, and Olivia wondered how her generation ever coped without smart phones. By 13:10, the canteen was almost filled and the group divides between the kids she looked after were plainly obvious.

At the back of the hall sat the gossip girls; the older girls who contoured their face every day and waltzed around with their river island handbags which weren't nearly big enough to fit the items they needed in there. They always sat next to the T-Birds. If they weren't on the field playing football, they were huddled around one dining table with the gossip girls crooning over them, sitting on their laps, or practicing TikTok dances close by.

Then there were the 'emo' kids, or that's what they were called when she was at school. Now, they referred to themselves as the 'scene' kids or e-boys and e-girls, which absolutely baffled Liv. They'd always have their phones up loud listening to punk music of some description, half of which she had never heard in her life and would tirelessly try putting colour through their dark hair, despite the school policy stating this was unacceptable.

You had your B-side kids which were the same as all of the others, just less popular, and then the clever kids, who would rarely be found in the canteen and usually packed a lunch so they could spend time in one of the maths or science corridors to eat instead.

Liv considered herself to be one of the more liked teachers in the school, but there were still a handful of students who didn't like her at all, which she was fine with. She felt as though there was a common misconception that teachers were supposed to like their students and do anything to help them because they were young, and still evolving, but it turned out that regardless of age, some people were always going to be assholes. Especially those who were unwilling to accept help, which was usually those who thought they were destined to be the next influencer or YouTube sensation.

As she roamed the canteen, interacting with the kids casually and making sure none of them were getting into trouble she found herself crossing paths with Clayton who'd just left the T-birds table on his way out to the field.

"Hi Miss!" he said, encouraging his friends to walk off ahead whilst they jokingly raised their eyebrows up and down suggestively. Liv ignored it since she'd become used to this behaviour from pubertal boys over the years and focused on Clayton who evidently wanted to speak to her.

"Hey, you okay?" she asked stopping her 5th lap of the canteen to stand and chat to him.

"I'm good, you?"

"Fine thank you" she smiled "What's up?"

Clayton lowered his voice as he spoke to her and looked awkward enough for her to know exactly what he was about to talk about before he spoke. "I think my dad really likes you, and I just wanted to say that he is a really good guy, and I don't want him to be single forever and I really think you should give him a chance, even though it's weird you're my teacher, but yeah" he trailed off.

Liv kept her blush at bay and watched as Jackson's mini me fiddled with the straps of his bag awkwardly. He had obviously spoken to Jackson at some point, and it was a relief to know that he wasn't against the idea which was something she knew they'd both been worrying about.

"Thank you" she smiled, genuinely meaning it "I think he's a good guy too"

With that Clayton smiled and nodded his agreement before he ran off after his friends telling her that he would see her later. Liv watched him go as she smiled at the revelation, only to have it drop instantly when she caught Evans scowling at her from across the room. She turned her back to him and rolled her eyes walking in the opposite direction. The last thing she needed was him getting wind of whatever was going on between her and Jackson and using it against her.

19.

Jackson swanned down the stairs 20 minutes after Rachael and Ben arrived, put his game face on and greeted them both with Rachael leaning straight in for the kiss which he didn't acknowledge. He led them to a room behind the reception desk and offered them drinks before giving over the order to Alice and finding a seat.

"So, how can we help?" he said, as professionally as he possibly could.

"Well, Racheal tells me your familiar with my business, but we are now looking to expand the gym and offer merchandise. Gym wear, accessories, a new website, it's a big job, and Rachael says you're the best in the business"

"I'm sure she did," he muttered, "so what would you like from me?"

"Well," Rachael began, leading Jackson to grit his teeth in anger, "Ben has put me in charge of marketing and so I'll be leading the project. We have our standard logo, as you know but we want something a bit more refined to use throughout the products"

"Well, in that case, I feel there would be a great conflict of interest with me running point on the project given our current circumstances, and would recommend another member of my team to take on the project, or find another company"

Jackson wasn't playing around with her shitty games and wasn't going to let her worm her way back in using the guise of working together. It not only annoyed him, but it wasn't fair on Liv either, to have his ex sniffing around him and making excuses to still be involved because it was work related.

Rachael was speechless and her brother sat with his eyebrows raised. He was your typical gym bunny, with broad shoulders and a tight-fitting shirt spread across his muscular pecks and bulging at the biceps. To others, he would probably come across as intimidating, but Jackson didn't care, there was no way he was crazier than the woman sat next to him, and Jackson was more than willing to test the theory if it came to it.

"I don't understand?" Ben said, but Rachael spoke before he could reply.

"I'm sorry, but if you're referring to you dumping me for another woman, that has nothing to do with business does it?"

"So, you two aren't together?" Ben asked, looking confused, "Rach, what the fuck are you going on about, why would we come here if you weren't together?"

"Because I told you, he's the best in the business"

"As I said, we are happy to cater to your needs Ben, but I personally don't feel it would be good for your business, or mine, if I were to work alongside Rachael. I'll happily do you a good deal, and allocate another, more than qualified person to run point with her leading your campaign, but I'm not muddying waters at work and don't want the backlash in my personal life either" he said matter-of-factly.

"What's that supposed to mean?" she scowled at him, but Ben was already shushing her before Jackson could reply.

"Look, I'm sorry this is awkward" Ben said, shutting Rachael down when she tried to speak. If Jackson knew anything it was that Rachael liked to spin a story and she was less than honest most of the time, because she would do anything to benefit herself. "We're going to discuss it moving forward, but I would love the company on board whether it's your input, or one of your colleagues. My business is my life, and regardless of your history, I want the best for the new merchandise and website, which I hear is you"

"I appreciate that" Jackson said, thankful that at least one of them had their head screwed on straight, but Rachael was pissed.

"I'm sorry? But he has sat there and blatantly disrespected me and you're fine with it?" she screamed at him.

Jackson had predicted this would happen and wasn't surprised when her voice took on a high pitched shrill, he'd been on the receiving end of it already this week and was in no way ready for a repeat. He knew as soon as he came down the stairs that he would be laying his cards out on the table, because he knew Rachael, and how sly and vindictive she could be. He knew full well that she would try and get close to him again if he gave her even the slightest opportunity, and he didn't want that for either of them.

"Rach, just shut up for 5 minutes" Ben said, rolling his eyes and throwing a stern look her way, "you're a grown ass woman, stop dragging me into your petty break ups. I wouldn't have brought you if I knew that was the case, so either be quiet, or get out"

Rachael stared at the two of them for a second before grabbing her bag and walking from the room. Jackson followed her with his eyes as she left, flipped him the bird, and stormed out of building muttering under her breath.

Ben apologised but Jackson shrugged it off. He wasn't completely oblivious to the history between the two of them, but Jackson explained that whilst their relationship had been around for a while, they'd always agreed that it was never going to progress as she now wanted it too. Her brother he wasn't surprised. He knew of her track record and said that he was fed up with always having to play the big bad brother when her illness got in the way and ruined every relationship she'd ever had.

After an hour of chatting, Ben and Jackson had agreed on a plan for the site and he listened to some ideas about the new logo. He apologised again for how things were left with Rachael, but Ben brushed it off as if he completely understood, and Jackson was relieved that he didn't have to worry about her for now.

It might have been a small win, but he wasn't holding out hope that she was done for good. If there was one thing he knew, it was that she was relentless, and he didn't know what else to do or what else to expect.

All he knew was that he felt obliged to tell Liv, but he didn't want Rachael's behaviour to scare her off before he even got the chance to take her out. Ben left and he returned to his office toying with the idea in his mind for a while, before deciding that he had to be honest. He would have to tell her when he saw her, and pray that she didn't run the other way, because he wanted this, badly, and he didn't

20.

What. A. Prick.

Liv was fuming. Evans decided to tell her period 5 that she now had to take on the maths detentions after school since he was busy trying to apply for Marc to sit his new A-level, that she so wanted. Liv had smiled through gritted teeth but knew full well that he could have done this in any 5 minute break he had and was just trying to get her back up. As long as it got Marc the exam he wanted, she would grin and bear it. Besides, she had seeing Jackson to look forward to, and that was enough to get her through.

Liv tapped out a message after her final class had finished as she had to make her way Evans' classroom. She knew he was still angry at her for showing him up, but she wasn't going to put up with him continuously putting her out, and if it carried on she knew she would lose her patience, which wouldn't bode well as she wasn't well liked as it was.

```
15:17
"Hey,  hope  work  went  okay
today.  My  dickhead  supervisor
has  decided  to  delegate  me  to
take  detention  duty  tonight,
and  my  car  is  still  in  the
garage  so  I  might  be  late.
Sorry  to  be  a  pain,  but  can
you let Clayton know? xx"
```

She watched as he started typing and wandered down the corridor ready to spend the next hour listening to the 7 students in detention talk about how much of a prick Evans was, and she sure as hell wouldn't be disagreeing.

15:24

```
   I'll pick you up. I wanted
to speak to you anyway. 4:30?
xx
```

        15:34
        4:30 is good, should I be worried?
   xx

```
15:35
Course not beautiful. See you then xx
```

But Liv was worried, and that meant that she was going to spend the next 45 minutes distracted, overthinking and overanalysing what he could possibly want to talk about. She figured it wouldn't help to stew over things, but *'we need to talk',* never sat well with her.

What if he thought Monday was a mistake and he wanted to call it quits? Obviously she would be glad that he had the guts to tell her and not lead her on, but she'd be lying to herself if she said she wouldn't be heartbroken. Upset? She wasn't in love with him, but she wanted him, and she didn't want to face rejection before they'd even got to know each other.

Liv brushed it off. She figured there was no point in worrying until she knew what he wanted to talk about, but by the time 4:30 rolled around, she was so nervous to see him she felt sick.

Jackson had everything planned. He'd booked everything for the weekend down to the taxi home and was confident that he'd decided on something she would like and something that was fun, not pretentious. He was excited, but he wanted to surprise her which meant keeping it secret, instead of blurting it out. He'd also taken it upon himself to cook for her after she finished tutoring Clayton, he'd bought the ingredients and a bottle of wine, hopeful that since she didn't have work the following day she'd take him up on his offer.

He pulled up at the school with plenty of time to spare and as he waited eagerly for her to finish he tried to figure out how to brooch the subject of Rachael. He knew he didn't want her to find out down the line, and he didn't want her to think this was some sort of love triangle because it wasn't. A few moments later he watched her leave the main foyer and search around for his car in the rain. He laughed when she spotted him, threw him a glare and beckoned him over so she could stay under the shelter as much as possible. He pulled off slowly heading towards her and watched her jog over to the door and hop in quickly cursing about the weather.

"Hey" she said bluntly, although he wasn't sure whether her mood was aimed at him or the rain that had started.

"You okay?" he said as she faffed with her hair and her bag looking anxious. He pulled away and out of the car park throwing her a curious glance and noticing how she bopped her leg up and down impatiently. Something was clearly the matter with her, but he was damned if he knew what.

"Pull over" she sighed, when they'd made it 30 seconds down the road.

Jackson did as he was told and undone his seatbelt before turning to face her.

"Liv? What's up?" he asked anxiously.

"Well, you said you wanted to talk, and so I've spent the last hour overthinking and I've figured that you regret what happened Monday, which is fine, but I just thought it would be better to speak about it now and get it out the way so that I'm not distracted when I'm teaching Clayton. If you don't want things to go any further I understand, but I just want to know because I hate not knowing and being left to stew on things and it's making me frustrated and angry and…"

Jackson kissed her. Partly to shut her up, partly to show her that there wasn't a single thing he regretted about the time they'd spent together on Monday, but mainly because he wanted to, and she was even more attractive when she was frustrated, much to his surprise.

"Can I talk now?" he said as he pulled away, and Liv was left red faced nodding at him.

"Thanks" he winked, loving the way she continued to scowl at him abashed, "The reason I wanted to talk to you wasn't because I regretted Monday, and it certainly wasn't because I was thinking of calling things off. It's the complete opposite, so if you could keep that feisty little attitude, which is hot I might add, in check for 5 minutes and let me explain, you'll know that you're panicking about nothing. Do you want to talk here? Or do you want me to drive?"

Liv shrugged, continuing with her frown, albeit coupled with a smile, and Jackson pulled away again towards home.

"I wanted to talk because I wanted to be honest with you. Rachael came to my office today and wanted me to work with her and her brother on a project" Jackson clocked Liv raising her eyebrows next to him and went on taking it as an invitation to go on, "I obviously told her straight that I wasn't interested in having anything to do with her, even if it was just business, and that I felt they'd be better going elsewhere so she basically told me to fuck off. Her brother continued with the deal"

"Uh huh? And?" she asked, watching him as he drove

"And… That's it? I just didn't want you to think I was still seeing her behind your back, and I didn't want her to be a reason for you to want to stop before we started" he added sheepishly.

"Well, that's a fucking relief then" she said exhaling, "I thought you were going to tell me you changed your mind, and our date was cancelled!"

Jackson laughed as she screwed up her face at him from the passenger seat and shook her head. They drove home chatting some more. Liv told her about his issues with her supervisor, and how her whole detention had been spent with the kids coming up with different nicknames for him. She spoke a little about school and Jackson was more than aware that he could listen to her talk for hours, even about nothing.

21.

Jackson had busied himself in the kitchen cooking whilst Liv sat with Clayton at the table. For the first time since she'd been teaching him, the garden lights were on, and she could see out over the lawn and the patio. She noticed a summerhouse over to one side and a rattan table and chair set positioned close to the window under a wooden pagoda. It looked like somewhere you could spend the whole of summer, and Liv's mind wandered to what she planned on doing about her own house. She'd promised Jade she would speak to Tommy next week, but she didn't know what she was supposed to say. She knew she shouldn't have left it so long, but she didn't want to have to face him again. Not because she was hurt, but because she was embarrassed that she'd been blind for so long.

"How's it coming?" she asked pulling herself away from that train of thought and back to the present. Clayton was working his way through geometric questions on the volumes of shapes with relative ease and he'd barely needed her guidance at all.

"Getting there" he shrugged, as he made quick work of calculating the equation in front of him.

"You know, you have you're pretty good at maths? And to be fair, if you listened in class before I started teaching you here, you'd have no problems sitting these GCSE's?" she added, raising an eyebrow.

"Yeah I know, I just get distracted Miss. Besides, if it wasn't for that, you wouldn't have met my dad" he smirked, looking up from his textbook. Liv scowled at him playfully and rolled her eyes when he laughed at her and waggled his eyebrows.

"Funny story, but we'd already met months before, and he was horrible to me" she whispered.

"This true dad?!" he called across the room whilst Jackson put something in the oven.

"Is what true?" he asked, propping himself up against the kitchen island and stared at the two of them. Liv's cheeks started to burn as she drank in the sight of him over Clayton's shoulder and his intense gaze landed on her.

"Miss was just telling me that you were horrible to her the first time you met, but obviously *I* can't imagine you being like that" he laughed, knowing full well his dad was an asshole at times.

Jackson cleared his throat looking a little abashed before he replied, "I wasn't horrible, I was in a bad mood, and your teacher has a habit of being particularly annoying when she wants to be. Plus, she tried to steal my taxi too" he shrugged casually, smirking at the two of them.

"Lies" she whispered as Jackson returned to whatever he was doing in the kitchen and Clayton laughed at his revelation. Liv spend the remainder of the hour trying desperately not to sneak glances at Jackson each time he moved, or hummed along to the music, or just breathed. At one point he caught her and winked, which had her belly doing summersaults and by the time the lesson was finished, she was chastising herself and him for having some sort of chokehold on her attention.

Liv packed her bag up when all was finished and found her usual seat at the island whilst Clayton ran upstairs with his books. The weather outside was still awful, and she was pissed she didn't have her car back yet. Although she was grateful that she didn't have work in the morning and wouldn't have to get to school without it again, she was in a dilemma as to whether she should bother to ring a taxi, which Jackson wouldn't allow, or just ask him for a ride.

"Want a drink?" he asked as he grabbed two glasses out of the cupboard and opened the fridge, "I've got wine, bubbly, spirits? I can attempt a cocktail if you want to be fancy?"

"Very presumptuous of you to assume I would say yes?" she said, nodding towards the two glasses he set aside. When Jackson simply shrugged and smiled, she shook her head and smiled back at him, "Surprise me"

Jackson took the wine from the fridge and poured it into both the glasses in front of him whilst she watched. He had just set the bottle aside when Clayton returned to the kitchen to thank Liv and grab a bottle of water out of the fridge with his bag in tow.

"Love you dad, I'll see you Sunday" he said hugging him briefly before heading for the front door, "have a nice night!" he called back.

Liv looked at Jackson who was holding out a glass for her and took it hesitantly. "What's going on?" she asked, taking a sip, and noting that the wine wasn't as disgusting as she thought it would be. It may have been because she was used to drinking echo falls as a predrink instead of whatever he had served, but wine never sat right with her, until now.

"Well, I figured I'd surprise you with dinner" he said, sipping his own drink and watching her as she smiled excitedly.

"Are you actually cooking me dinner?!" she asked, almost fit to burst with excitement in that moment. It was without a doubt the most romantic thing anyone had ever done for her, which was saying a lot, but she couldn't believe he'd surprised her. It also helped that food was truly the way to her heart, and whatever she was about to eat smelt so good she was already salivating.

Jackson set the table as Liv watched him from the kitchen. He had now learnt that she was awful at surprises, and wanted to know everything, which he wasn't planning on telling her despite her persistence. He'd told her she had to wait, and apparently, she didn't like that either.

Whilst Jackson flitted around the kitchen, declining her offers of help, she sipped on her wine. He chatted about the business and about the expansion whilst she listened and took it all in. She'd ask questions now and then and it seemed like she always found ways to make him question how he could do better or do more. He liked that she challenged him, and it was a welcome change from when women would fall over themselves agreeing with him just to make him happy.

When he was just about ready, Jackson told her to make herself comfortable at the table so he could bring her dinner over, and Liv happily obliged. He was glad he'd gone ahead with the idea, and happy that it seemed to be going well. He didn't feel like he had to force anything with her, everything seemed natural, but he'd be lying if he wasn't worried that she'd think he was trying too hard.

"Do you mind if I text? Just to let Owen know I'll be home late so he doesn't worry?" she asked as she topped up his glass and took the bottle to the table.

"Course not, do what you want" he responded as he pulled a joint of meat out the oven and left it to rest on the side. Liv peered back over her shoulder, but he instructed her to stop looking, which earned him a huff before she found her seat looking out over the garden. Liv avoided looking back over to the kitchen by firing off a text to Owen, and another to Jade telling her that Jackson had surprised her with dinner. Seconds after the blue ticks flashed up, Jade was calling her. Liv shook her head and laughed before declining the call hoping Jade would get the hint. She was obviously going to tell her everything, but now was not the time to have that conversation.

Instead, she went back to staring at Jackson. It was clear that he liked to spend time in the kitchen, he seemed to be in his element grabbing plates and utensils from here and there, dishing up food methodically. She suddenly grew nervous, and then realised quickly that she'd already drunk two glasses of wine. If she didn't slow down, she was likely to make an idiot of herself. She tapped her foot anxiously as she watched him wipe up, before travelling to and from the kitchen to bring the food to the table.

"This looks amazing" she said, eyeing up the spread he'd put on, with steak and chips, salad, charred asparagus, mushrooms and onion rings spread out across the table with a sauce to top it all off.

"Well, I didn't know what to cook, but I figured I've seen you shovel a kebab in your mouth so steak was definitely a winner. How do you like your meat?" he asked, grabbing a knife and carving away at the joint in front of them.

"I'm easy" she smiled, as he plated rare slices of steak on her plate and she sipped her wine again, trying to tear her eyes away from the way his biceps twitched each time he carved through the meat. When he was satisfied he had put enough on her plate. He took his seat again and lifted his glass to hers.

"To first dates" he said, sending her a wink. Liv raised an eyebrow and blushed as she repeated his sentiment, then tucked into the food in front of her.

They ate, and they spoke, and they laughed the whole time. Liv didn't know if it was the drink, or the company, but she felt happy around Jackson. She loved listening to him talk, and she loved that he asked her genuine questions about what she liked, and her friends, and her life. In the whole 8 years she'd been with Tommy, he'd never once bothered to ask how her friends were. He'd barely even bothered to ask her how she was. Liv found herself wondering if this whole situation was too good to be true and whether reality was going to come and bite her in the ass soon, but for now, she was happy to just let things be.

22.

Liv helped Jackson to clear the table and load the dishwasher before he prepared for making more drinks. They'd somehow made their way through 2 bottles of wine whilst they were chatting over dinner, which left him completely out. Instead, they agreed to make cocktails in the kitchen and laid out spirits over the island, playing a guessing game of what they could make with what they had. Liv however had failed to mention that she'd worked in cocktail bars all through uni, and reeled off recipes whilst he stood there and quizzed her.

"What about a long island tea?" he said, trying to trip her up for the third time. He wanted to know what they had the ingredients for, but he was coming up empty so far, and it looked as though they were going to have to come up with their own concoction.

Jackson scrolled through the hub sat on the windowsill checking what they needed whilst Liv listed them off behind him,

"Vodka, Gin, Rum, Tequila and Triple Sec, with lime" she reeled off, "But, we have no tequila"

"Fuck sake. So, what are we going to have?" he said laughing.

"I'll tell you what, since you cooked, I'll make the drinks, and you can tell me if you like them. Deal?" she asked, hopping down from the stool tipsily.

Jackson agreed and sat across the island from her whilst she dug in the freezer for ice. He watched as she tiptoed across the kitchen and measured out shots of this and that chatting to him freely as she did. He watched as she would screw her face up and ponder what else the drink needed every few seconds, and stifled a laugh each time she had a little eureka moment. After 5 minutes of mixing, Liv presented him with an orange concoction in a long glass filled with ice and with fruit she'd found in the fridge. She encouraged him to take a sip which he did apprehensively. Much to his surprise, he was impressed by her work. Although he wasn't one for fruity drinks, it tasted good.

"Interesting," he said, drinking it down quickly. It was apparently far too easy to drink, and he'd almost finished his by the time she poured her own and started drinking it, but Jackson didn't care that he was well on his way to being drunk, because this was the most fun he'd had in a long time.

"So, are you drunk enough to tell me about your ex yet?" he asked, remembering back to their conversation at the weekend.

"Depends, what do you want to know?"

Jackson gazed at her as she stirred her drink and busied herself looking anxious. He didn't want to push her if she wasn't ready, but he did want to know what kind of man walked out on a woman like her. As far as he was concerned, she was the full package, and he couldn't imagine anyone not seeing that.

"Well, we don't have to talk about it" he said, noting she was uncomfortable, and regretting asking her. He just wanted to know everything there was to know about her and that included knowing why she was single.

"It's fine" Liv picked up her drink, drunk it, and poured another before she pulled up a chair. "Let's play a game. I'll give you a statement, you have to guess whether it is true, or it's a lie. If you get it right, I drink, if you get it wrong, you drink, got it?"

"Okay, think so?"

"I am 28 years old"

"Fact", she drunk.

"Your turn"

"I am 34 years old"

"Lie. Clayton's 15, and you had him in your 20's you said" and he drank.

"Correct. I'm 37 in a couple of months, so you better start planning something special for me" he said.

"Ha, I'll think about it. Right, next one.. I've never had a one night stand" she said looking him dead in the eye. Jackson didn't know what to think, he'd had plenty when he was younger, and some up until a few years ago, but he wasn't like that anymore. He thought about it for a few seconds before he made up his mind, called it a lie, and was quickly told to drink when she told him it wasn't.

"Never?" he asked, worried that he'd offended her, but she didn't seem to mind.

"Never ever. I was with my first boyfriend when I was 18, and then I got with Tommy, and that's it"

"Sorry? You're telling me you've slept with two people? In your life?"

"Why is that a surprise?" she laughed, filling her cup up again, and Jackson's. He figured she'd picked this game as a way to get to know one another but he was concerned that the more she learnt about him, the more likely it was that she was going to go running for the hills.

"I just don't understand how you haven't had men lining up to take you out?" he said, and his confusion was genuine.

"Well, what can I say? Maybe I'm just picky" she shrugged and encouraged him to go on with another statement.

"You're the first woman I've cooked a romantic dinner for" he said, sipping his drink before she'd even answered.

"Lie" she laughed, Jackson already knew she thought he was a womanizer, but it was the truth. He'd barely even had women in his house because he never wanted Clayton to know, so Liv really was the only woman he'd gone out of his way for.

"Drink"

"Really?" she asked raising an eyebrow.

"Hand on heart, you're the only woman I've really had here, or I've invited and made dinner for" he said, "so, you need to drink"

Liv blushed and smiled before she drank, or she attempted to, before the glass slipped from her hand and fell on the floor around her feet.

"Shit! I'm sorry" she apologised attempting to step over it so she could clear up. She took a step back but misjudged how far the glass had travelled over the tiles until a searing pain shot through her foot making her scream, look down and almost pass out at the sight of blood coming from her foot.

23.

By the time she'd realised what was going on, Jackson was carrying her up the stairs apologising for not getting to her quicker, and telling her she would be fine, despite the fact she felt like she was going to pass out.

"Jackson! There's blood on the carpet!" she said looking down the stairs behind them.

"Fuck the carpet, I'll clean it. You're getting in the shower and then I'll see if you need to go hospital"

"It's fine, I think I just overreacted from alcohol and shock" she winced, as the pain in her foot continued to throb. He'd carried her like a child keeping her feet elevated, through what she figured was his bedroom, and into a large bathroom with a giant shower.

Jackson turned the taps on, waited a few seconds, and sat her down on the floor of the shower fully clothed. "Jackson I have clothes on!"

"I don't care, I'll give you something to wear after. I didn't exactly do this as a ploy to get you naked Liv, but I want to check your foot and I couldn't exactly hoick you up over the sink"

This was true, the glass had shattered all over the floor in front of the sink so it wouldn't have been beneficial for either of them to be in the kitchen. Jackson was wearing slippers, but Liv had left her shoes at the door and was in just a thin pair of tights.

"We need to take your tights off" he said, looking at her.

"We?" she said raising an eyebrow suggestively. If she couldn't joke at a time like this, she'd only cry and she didn't want to be a cry-baby.

"Not the time," he laughed, as water fell over him and his t-shirt clung to his shoulders. "Do you want to do it or should I?"

"Are you trying to get me out of my clothes Mr. Cotts?"

"Liv" he laughed, "Seriously. Put your arms around my neck and lift your ass up a bit so I can get them off"

She did as she was told and felt Jackson's hands run up her thighs to her waistband, manoeuvre her tights over her underwear and pull them down to her knees. It wasn't how she imagined her night ending, but it hadn't been for the fact that her foot felt as though it had been sliced open, she would've enjoyed it.

"You can let go now," he said, waiting for her to manoeuvre back so he could finish stripping her tights. But Liv didn't want to, she was quite happy where she was, and was pissed that her foot was hurting so much because she wanted to stay like she was.

"Do I have to?" she asked

"I promise once I've sorted your foot, you can stay wherever you like" he said, sounding sincere, "but please sit back so I can have a look"

"Promise?" she asked.

"Promise" he said, and with that she unwrapped herself from round his shoulders, sat herself back against the tiled wall, and watch as he pulled her tights down the rest of the way and off completely, scrunching her eyes shut so she didn't have to see.

Jackson was trying to keep his mind focused on the issue at hand and not on how good it felt to run his hands over her ass and legs. He needed to check out her foot, but that meant avoiding checking out her body as her flowy dress now clung to every curve of her body, and if that wasn't enough, all she'd wanted to do was stay wrapped around him, which had killed him not to let her.

He threw her tights to one side and lifted her foot high under the running water to assess the damage which was surprisingly better than he thought. She had a gash on the left side of her left foot which looked deep, but her right was a different story which he already suspected when he initially noticed the gaping hole in her tights.

A shard of glass was embedded in her heel which was slowing the blood, but he worried how bad it would be if he removed it. He didn't want to scare her and told her to wait whilst he grabbed bandages from downstairs, but she was reluctant to let him leave. He promised he'd be back, and kissed her head before running back to the kitchen to grab whatever he could. By the time he was back, Liv was shivering in the shower, and he turned up the heat to help.

"There's glass in your foot I need to get out Liv, but we need to dry it off before I can bandage it"

"Okay," she whimpered, keeping her eyes closed,

"I'll take it out, and clean it, then wrap it in a towel, okay? I'm going to need to put pressure on it too?"

"Okay" she said. Still not opening them.

"Can you take your dress off? So that once I've sorted your foot I can find you something dry to put on?"

"You do it," she said still scared to look.

Jackson got up and unbuttoned her dress before lifting it over her head. He met her gaze once it was off, leant in and kissed her, apologising for everything that had happened. Liv told him she was fine, and he returned to her foot with tweezers.

"Ready?" he asked, ignoring the fact that she was sat in front of him dripping wet in nothing but a bra and panties, and Liv nodded whilst clenching her fist around the dress balled up at her side.

Jackson pulled the glass from her foot which had Liv cursing in pain and rinsed it quickly before turning off the water and wrapping both feet in a towel. He scooped her up from the floor, took her back to the room, and placed her on the bed before wrapping his dressing gown around her. Liv sat with her knees pulled up against her chest whilst Jackson pulled items out of the first aid box and placed them on the bed beside her.

Jackson stood up and stripped off his wet clothes before wrapping a towel around his waist and getting back to looking at her foot. Liv stared at him as he did, watching him as he crouched next to the side of the bed and undid the towel on her left foot.

"Is it bad?" she sniffled, drawing his attention back.

"It's not great, but I don't think you need proper stitches. I've got butterfly stitches here anyway which should be fine. So, I'll stitch it and wrap them both and then we will see what they are like in the morning. You're staying the night by the way"

"Am I?" she questioned.

"Yes" Liv didn't argue, and Jackson wouldn't have cared if she did. He couldn't believe this had happened, and he wanted to keep an eye on her and make sure she was okay. It wasn't because he wanted anything to happen between them, not that he would say no, but he didn't want to be up all night worrying if he sent her home.

He pinched the gash closed and applied the butterfly stitches along the side of her foot before applying gauze and wrapping it tightly in a bandage. He then took the towel off her right foot, assessed the hole in her heel and was glad that it looked better than he wrapped it in a bandage to match the first foot.

"How does it feel?" he said, standing up and packing everything strewn across the bed away.

"Painful" she laughed.

"You want some painkillers?" Liv raised her eyebrows like this was the most stupid question in the world, and Jackson laughed in response.

"Yes to the painkillers, and yes to some drinks too, but can I... have something to wear?" she asked, blushing. In all the commotion she'd forgotten that she'd stripped half naked in front of Jackson and was currently sat in wet underwear that was making her cold. She was also more than aware that he was half naked, and if her feet weren't throbbing in pain at that point, she would have happily returned to her earlier position wrapped around his shoulders.

Jackson rummaged in the drawers and pulled out a t-shirt and some boxers that he put on the bed for Liv. He gave her a dry dressing gown then disappeared into the bathroom to get changed himself before returning.

"You okay? Or you need help?" he said grabbing the towels from the floor and putting them in the laundry basket.

"I'll manage" she said, stripping the dressing gown on the bed and reaching for the t-shirt he'd left for her as Jackson threw her the remote.

"Find something to watch whilst I clean up your mess," he said playfully, climbing on the bed "I'll get some drinks, the painkillers and then we will watch a movie and you can sleep here. I'll sleep in the guest room"

He kissed her and she wrapped her arms around him again, pulling him in.

"I'm sorry I ruined your first effort at a romantic dinner" she said against his lips as he kissed her back.

"You'll make it up to me one day" he smiled, then left Liv to herself whilst he made his way downstairs and she got herself changed, regretting her decision to decline his help.

24.

Jackson was conflicted. He'd already said he'd stay in the guest room, but that meant walking out of the same room where he'd just seen the most beautiful woman in the world sat in nothing but underwear and missing his chance to sleep next to her. He readjusted the bulge in his boxers again as he got to the kitchen and found the broom to sweep up the glass. She was right, there was blood on the carpet, and on the sides, and on the tiles, and if anyone walked in, they'd have thought there'd have been a massacre in his house.

As he cleaned, he considered his options. He wanted to be respectful, and that meant respecting her privacy, but he also wanted her, and everything she had to offer. It's not like he planned on this being a one-time thing, he was certain she was as interested in him as he was her, and he didn't need to rush things. Just because they wouldn't be sharing a bed that night, didn't meant they wouldn't be sharing a bed indefinitely, that's all he needed to know.

By the time he'd cleaned up, he'd convinced himself he was doing the right thing, and that it was for the best. He didn't want to come on too strong, on scare her off, so even though he wanted her, more than anything in the world that moment, he'd take the guest room and leave her in his bed.

Jackson grabbed some ibuprofen from the cabinet, a couple of the spirit bottles from the side, glasses and some mixers from the fridge before heading back to his room, and back to Liv.

When he walked in, juggling an armful of stuff, Liv was laid flat on her front across the bed, scrolling through Amazon Prime on the telly.

"Decided?" he asked, finding a home for the drinks, glasses, tablets and phones he'd brought up too.

"No. I'm notorious for being indecisive, so figured I'd let you pick" she said propping herself back up so she could sit against the headboard.

"I've been downstairs for 20 minutes, and you couldn't decide on one film?" he asked, handing her her phone, the tablets and a bottle of water to take them with. Liv shrugged and Jackson rolled his eyes before asking her to pick a genre.

"Comedy or action" she said, swallowing down the ibuprofen and making herself comfortable. Jackson poured the drinks, decided on Bad Boys which was a bit of both and got into the bed next to her. He thought it would feel weird, settling in to just watch a movie with a woman, but it didn't, and they both raised a glass to the mockery that was their first romantic date.

"Your phones been buzzing by the way" he said after sinking half of his drink.

Liv busied herself replying to the messages on her phone and telling Owen she wouldn't be home, whilst Jackson checked his diary to see what he had scheduled for the following day. If he could, he'd take the day off so he could get Liv home and change the plans for Saturday, if he couldn't, he would be going to work in a foul mood knowing that he could have spent the morning waiting on Liv instead of being in some godforsaken meeting instead.

If he'd have known the night would go as it had, he would have booked it off anyway, but after scrolling through the diary he realised there was no way he was able to get out of it. Him and Harry were conducting the first round of interviews for the new interior design team, and they had 12 candidates on the books. He wondered if Harry would do them by himself, and sent him an email, only to receive a phone call a few seconds later catching him completely off guard. He looked at Liv apologetically, but she encouraged him to take it and Jackson jumped out of bed and went to the bathroom.

"*That email was a joke right?*" Harry shouted down the phone, *"We've had this booked in for months? How did you forget?"*

Harry was laughing, so Jackson figured he wasn't completely in the bad books, but he was being genuinely serious with his email.

"Been distracted" he said, leaning against the shower and watching Liv as she typed on her phone.

"By what? What could possibly distract you from the fact you're expanding our business into a million pound company almost overnight? You know we've already got clients lining up to make use of the interior design sector, or did you forget that as well?"

"You know I don't care about the money H, and I didn't forget, I just didn't want to come in"

"What could you possibly be doing tomorrow that holds more weight than interviewing candidates for the company?"

"It's not what" He sighed

"Sorry?"

"Liv's here. She's staying the night?"

"Come again?"

"You heard"

"As in staying the night, at your house, where you live?" Harry questioned, but when he was met with silence he simply sighed. *"Fuck me. Erm, look. As much as I love you, and I really want this to work out for you, and I mean that, tomorrow just can't be done. If I have to message Liv myself and tell her I will, but you will make it up to her. We NEED to do this tomorrow Jax, you've been planning this for years and we've got people travelling from up and down the country for the opportunity"*

"Yeah I know, she'll understand" he said.

"Course she will, I'll see you in the morning. 8:00 sharp, and I know you're drinking because I can hear it in your voice, so take some pills before you go to bed, you aren't young anymore, and I can't be dealing with you hungover"

With that Harry hung up and Jackson got back in to bed, already annoyed that he had to get up in the morning and spend the day at work.

"You okay?" she asked, wincing as she turned to face him.

"I'm fine. I wanted the day off tomorrow so I could look after you, but we've got interviews for the expansion and Harry won't do them by himself" he said realising he had genuinely been willing to sacrifice something he'd worked so hard for just so he could spend time with her.

"Well, that's cute!" she said drinking again, "I'll finish this and then I'll call a cab. I'm not offended Jax"

"I'm not kicking you out Liv" he laughed, "I just can't stay with you tomorrow because I have to work. You're still staying here so I can keep an eye, I've just got to be at work at 8:00"

"You sure?" she asked sheepishly?

"Yes," he said leaning in to kiss her, "I'm sure."

With that they spent the rest of the night drinking in bed, laughing and sharing stories. By the time it hit midnight, Liv was curled up in a ball next to him lightly snoring, and it took every ounce of his willpower to get himself up, and walk away, leaving her sleeping peacefully under the covers whilst he found his way to the guest room.

25.

Liv hadn't been asleep long, but she woke up desperate for the toilet, which she hadn't planned on. She shuffled her way to the end of the bed, mindful of the bandages wrapped round her feet, and limped over to the ensuite painfully. Jackson was nowhere to be seen and must have snuck out when she fell asleep, but she wanted him back. She found her phone plugged in on the bed beside her and looked at the time. She'd only been asleep an hour, but she'd fallen asleep curled up next to Jackson and she didn't want to get back into bed alone.

Liv shuffled her way out of the room and down the hallway where she could see the light from the TV flashing. She peered round the door to find Jackson sprawled out on his back with one arm behind his head, and one resting on his boxers sleeping peacefully. She admired the view for a second, whilst she debated whether she'd be welcome next to him or not, then limped towards the bed anyway.

She didn't care whether he liked it or not, she was scared in that big room all by herself, so he was going to have to suck it up and deal with it, she thought as she made the short distance over to the bed and crawled over next to him where he stirred.

"What are you doing?" He asked, not moving when the bed buckled beside him.

"Can I sleep with you? I don't want to sleep by myself" she asked hesitantly

"Thank the fucking lord, I fucking hate this bed" he said, climbing over the top of her and picking her up from the duvet. Liv wrapped her legs around him whilst he carried her back to the room she'd left and placed her back down on the bed. He climbed over her again and laid down, before Liv made herself comfortable with her head on his chest, and her leg draped across his.

"I'm apologising in advance" he said, as his cock twitched on her thigh, and Liv laughed. Jackson cuddled her in and kissed her whilst she readjusted her leg and found comfort for the night. "Let me sleep woman" he muttered, whilst she fidgeted a bit more, and then they drifted off, with him already dreading having to wake up.

26.

... ...

Nope. There was no fucking way he was going to work he thought as he heard the alarm go off and his phone vibrate on top of the chest of drawers. Instead, he ignored it. Pulled Liv closer to him and pretended it didn't exist.

"Jackson. If you don't turn that alarm off in the next 0.2 seconds, I swear to *GOD* this is *OVER!*" Liv spat out through gritted teeth grabbing a pillow and rolling over so she could place it over her head.

Jackson was fuming. He threw back the covers, got out of bed and walked over to the chest of drawers where he stopped the alarm and threw it back where it was before climbing back in next to Liv.

"Nuh uh" she said as he pulled her into a spoon, not caring about the fact his dick was hard. He wasn't planning on using it, but he wasn't planning on getting out of bed either.

"You have to go to work".

"I'm not going" he grunted.

"There's something poking my back?" she chuckled.

"Don't care"

"Uh Huh?"

"Uh huh"

"Jackson?"

"Olivia"

"Get up"

"Don't wanna".

"You've got to".

"I'm my own boss".

"..and I really fucking hate mornings" she muttered falling back to sleep.

FUCK! Jackson jumped up when he heard his phone alarming again, thankful he'd put a second one on for when to leave the gym. He had less 20 minutes to get ready, and get to work, and that was a task in itself. He tapped out a message to Harry telling him he was running 10 minutes late and quickly turned on the shower.

Jackson was never late. He hadn't planned on falling back to sleep when he got back in to bed with Liv, but she felt so fucking good. He couldn't help it, and even the erection hadn't stopped him from falling asleep within minutes. Liv was muttering curse words at him about how she was never sleeping over again, and it was meant to be her day off, but Jackson needed to move his ass. He kissed her and apologised, before jumping in the shower and mentally planning what he was going to wear.

Liv peered in at him from the bed, but apparently, she really did hate mornings, because she only had the energy to use one eye.

"I've changed my mind" she said, eyeing him up through the steamy shower screen.

"About?" he called back.

"About you going to work"

Jackson groaned as his cock twitched at the thoughts that began running through his mind. Part of him wished she hadn't stayed because it was taking everything ounce of self-control he had not to crawl back in behind her again just to feel her ass against him.

"You told me I had to" he said, washing the suds out of his hair and off of his body in a hurry.

"Well, I just told you I changed my mind?"

"You did" he said, opening the shower door to grab a towel.

"And?"

"And.." he said, wrapping it round his waist and climbing on top of her in bed, "I've got an important day, so I *have* to".

"You're getting me wet." She said, biting her bottom lip as she looked up at him.

Jackson laughed and kissed her before leaving the room. He needed something suitable for the interviews and didn't have time to iron anything. He grabbed some tweed trousers, a matching waistcoat and the only white ironed shirt he had then rushed back to the bedroom to chuck them on.

"What are you doing?" he asked when he walked in to find his t-shirt on the floor, and Liv curled up topless, with the quilt gathered up against her chest just about covering her nipples, but her bare back was still on show. She was still wearing his boxers, but she had one leg curled around the duvet, showing off her little bandaged foot.

"Sleeping" she murmured.

"Uh huh, and you're half naked because?"

"You got me wet. I can put it back on if it makes you uncomfortable" she said sleepily.

"You have no idea" he muttered through gritted teeth, praying his erection would fit in the trousers he was about to put on. He stuffed his feet through the trouser sleeves aggressively, threw his shirt on, and buttoned it whilst he stared at Liv's perfect body wrapped up in his bed sheets. By the time he'd finished, his dick was hurting, and he was regretting ever setting the second alarm.

Jackson buttoned his waistcoat, and spruced up his hair in the bathroom before he brushed his teeth and sprayed his aftershave.

Liv apparently really did hate mornings, because he could hear her starting to snore quietly again when he left to find shoes, and he was in two minds whether to wake her or not to say goodbye.

When he got back, she'd rolled on to her back, and Jackson was faced with the most amazing pair of breasts he'd ever seen in his life. Tanned, with large brown nipples stiff and inviting. He couldn't believe that this was happening to him. The one day he couldn't take off work, the woman of his dreams was sprawled half naked across his bed, snoring softly with her chest rising and falling each time she did.

Jackson covered her over begrudgingly and kissed her once.

"I've got to go" he said, kissing her again. Liv grunted, but wrapped her arms around him and met his tongue with hers.

"Are you sure?"

"Honestly? No. I'm fucking not. Do not move from this spot, because when I'm back, we're going back to bed".

Liv laughed and he kissed her again before grabbing his phone and heading for the stairs, fuming and frustrated at the thought of leaving her in bed without giving her the wake up she deserved.

27.

Jackson made it to the office with 2 minutes to spare, but Harry was already there pacing the floor.

"I've text you 6 times and tried ringing you twice!" He said, looking relieved at the sight of Jackson strolling through the door looking as put together as ever.

"I missed my first alarm" he said, dropping his bag and flicking the kettle on. He needed tea. His head wasn't 100% and his mind was still rerunning the images of Liv sprawled out on the bed.

"How was last night?" Harry asked bringing him back to reality.

"A disaster. Dinner went well, then we had a few drinks, Liv smashed a glass, cut both of her feet open and I ended up having to clean them up. There are blood stains on my carpet, and I can feel a hangover brewing".

"Shit! Is she okay?" he asked, brows crumpled with concern.

"She's fine. She's still sparko in bed".

"And how are you feeling? Other than the hangover"

"Well H, I'm feeling like I'd still rather be in bed" he laughed.

The first candidate arrived at 8:10 and the others soon followed. For the interviews, they'd planned a 2-part process where they were first given a scenario to build a mood board with, and then a face-to-face interview where they had to present it, as well as answering a series of questions Harry had put together. Whilst they were instructed to complete their mood boards, Harry and Jackson were going to look over their previous work and portfolios and narrow it down from there.

"Good morning everyone and thank you for coming" Harry said when the final candidate arrived and found a seat. "As you may or may not know, for the past few months we have been expanding Cotts & Perkins to include all areas of design, which includes interior design for some high-profile clients currently planning new business ventures. We have 3 positions available with a well-paid salary alongside commission, but are keen to establish who, if any of you, would be right for the role and what you can bring to the table"

Jackson looked around the room at the people in front of him and put a smile on his face before her spoke, "For the first part of your interview each one of you will have to pick a client from the pile on the table. It will detail an idea the client has had, what they are looking for and their budget. From there, you are to create a mood board, and a pitch, as to how you would make these ideas a reality. You have until 1pm to create your mood boards, and in the meantime, we will look over the portfolio of work that you've all brought with you"

He held the attention of everyone in the room naturally. He was an immediate presence, and it was evident that there were a few nervous faces as he spoke. He waited while they took in the information, jotted down notes and then left it to Harry to finish updating them.

"There are 20 scenarios and clients to choose from, so there's plenty for you to think about. Some of them are our personal favourites and some of them, we weren't too convinced about. Some contain more information than others, but it's your job to distinguish how you can use the information to your advantage. Cotts and Perkins pride themselves on helping customers from all walks of life, so bare this in mind when you pick, and push yourself. We will be around all day for you to ask us any questions you need, so whenever you're ready, grab a tablet and find the scenario you want"

The candidates got up and walked to the table at the back of the room to make their selections. Some were quick, and Jackson guessed that they'd looked at the ones with the highest budget, but some took their time to look in depth at what they were working with. One guy in particular caught Jackson's eye who was at the bench a lot longer than others. He couldn't have been older than 20 and he was toying between two scenarios for a while before Jackson approached him.

He was tall and slim, wearing a cheap shirt, and trousers with a pair of loafers. His hair was long and dark, pulled up into a messy bun, with thin framed circle glasses resting on the bridge of his nose and a puzzled look across his face.

"Nobody said you had to pick just one" Jackson muttered noticing the two he had in his hand couldn't have been anymore different from one another. One client wanted to turn their garden summer house into a studio, stroke office, for their photography business, with a low budget, but high expectations. The next was a full-scale revamp of a high-end restaurant, with an almost limitless budget, very specific aesthetic, and very particular client.

"Th- thanks" he said, taking them both and offering his hand out to Jackson who shook it firmly, "B-brad Walker"

"Jackson Cotts" he replied, "Good luck, and I hope you haven't bitten off more than you can chew" he said, before Brad nodded his thanks and walked off towards a table in the back.

Once everyone had picked their client, or *clients* in Brad's case, they set down to work on their presentation. Some had huddled together, sharing ideas and advice, and others had isolated themselves away, focused on their own project. Brad was sat at the far end of the room with headphones in his ears, tapping his foot rhythmically on the floor while he worked away on paper. Jackson was intrigued by him, but he didn't know why, he seemed basic, but you could almost hear his brain ticking away.

"Find me Brad Walkers portfolio please H" Jax said to Harry.

"Who's he?" He asked sifting through the table in front of them. Jackson tilted his head towards the boy sat in the corner and finally checked his phone hoping that Liv had text now it was gone 9:00. He knew if she had her way, she'd still be asleep, but he was happily surprised to find messages from her and opened them whilst Harry dug out a large black file.

08:32:
"Come back. This bed isn't as comfortable without you in it xx"

08:56:
"I can't get back to sleep now, and it's far too early to be up. You owe me a lie in! I hope the interviews go well today and someone catches your eye. Text me if you get time. Thank you for last night, I'm sorry I ruined it, and thank you for looking after me, I really appreciate everything xx"

Jackson smiled down at his phone as he tapped out a reply and Harry started flicking through Brads work.

"How you feeling and how are your feet? Trust me, leaving you in bed like that this morning took literally every ounce of my will power and I've been distracted all morning thinking about it. You didn't ruin anything, consider myself lucky that you spent the night, and I'm glad you came and found me. Best sleep I've had in ages"

"I meant what I said this morning, you are more than welcome to stay today until I'm home later. I'll pick up dinner? xx"

Jackson pocketed his phone and took the iPad from Harry showing the portfolio he'd asked for. Brad's folder was extraordinary. Not only did he have a talent for interior design, but he also had a passion. The only thing he was lacking, was real world experience. Everything on paper looked good, but his CV showed that the only experience he had was volunteering with companies. His work had obviously been commended and used in various projects, but he'd never been able to take the credit since he was just doing work experience. Jackson doubted he'd ever seen a cent of the profit made and he didn't seem to have any experience of a paying job.

Secretly he hoped that he pulled something spectacular out of the bag with his mood boards, because he really wanted to give him the opportunity to explore his creativity and make a name for himself. Harry was just as impressed as Jackson looking through the file, but he shared the same concerns, it would be risky to take on someone with no experience when they had such a reputation, but everyone had to start somewhere, and as Jackson watched him work in the corner, he had a suspicion that they would get more than they bargained for with the young man in front of them.

28.

After Liv had messaged Jackson in the morning, she'd taken more ibuprofen and curled up in bed. She'd tried to get back to sleep, but it became impossible after he left, and she was still daydreaming about him all dressed up for work. She'd never seen him in a suit, but she could definitely get used to it. He looked like he'd been plucked from the pages of a men's magazine, and she was fuming herself that he had to leave for work.

Liv winced as she got out of bed and went to use the bathroom, wondering whether or not a shower was a good idea considering the state of her feet. She still wasn't sure how last night had ended so badly and after struggling to make it to the toilet she figured that she had no choice but to stay at Jacksons house for the day. Jade was at work, and so was Owen, so she was stuck whether she liked it or not.

Not that she minded, she couldn't wait to see him after their night together and she knew she wanted him even more than she had before. When he'd got back into bed this morning and pulled her back towards him, she could have happily gone all the way. She didn't want to make the first move, or read more into it than she should, and she certainly didn't want their situation to end in a one-night stand, but she'd be lying if she wasn't tempted when she felt him pressed against her under the covers.

Liv grabbed a t-shirt, then shuffled her way along the corridor and down the stairs. As she did, she had a sudden dreaded thought that Clayton would come back and find her sat in a pair of boxers and t-shirt which was completely inappropriate, but now she was sat on the bottom step she didn't know how she was going to get back up. Liv then noticed the blood on the cream carpet and couldn't believe it. She was going to have to try and get it out, but she was also scared of making it worse. She hobbled to the kitchen to assess the damage there, only to be surprised when she found none. She figured that Jackson must have cleaned it up when he was cleaning the glass last night but was still embarrassed about the whole fiasco in the first place.

    After making herself a coffee Liv sat at the island and had a think. She wanted to see Jackson, that much was sure, but she didn't want to come across as too strong, lingering in the house all day. She needed to do something about the carpet first and foremost, because she didn't want to let it sit, but she also didn't want to spread it everywhere. Before any of that, she needed to message Jackson again and make sure Clayton wouldn't be round anytime soon, because that would be extremely embarrassing, and she would definitely have to quit her job.

    Liv grabbed her coffee and half hobbled, half crawled back up the stairs to the bedroom where she had stupidly left her phone, climbed back into the bundle of blankets and flicked on the TV before she found comfort. She unlocked her screen where there were messages from Jackson and the group was chat waiting, missed calls from Owen and Jade, and she tried to make a mental note of everyone she had to reply to. She also had to ring the garage about her car, which she was in no fit state to drive at the moment, and she wanted to get a carpet cleaner round before Jackson got back too.

    Liv started with the most important task at hand and messaged Jackson, she didn't want to interrupt him, but she also didn't want to make things awkward by bumping into Clayton half dressed, lounging in his dad's bed. Not to mention having to explain the blood over the carpet.

```
                    09:50
                    "I don't want to bother you
                    while you're working. My feet
                    are holding up okay, bit sore
                    but  I'm  back  in  bed  with
                    coffee. Is Clayton due back
                    today? Because  I  don't  want
```

> to make things awkward if he comes in and I'm here!!"

Liv figured that he must have had his phone in his hand because his reply came instantly, and Liv laughed.

> 09:51:
> "Lucky you, know where I'd rather be. How's your head? Don't panic, Clayton isn't due home until Sunday evening, so you're more than welcome to stay. You don't have to, but I'd really like to come home to you later. I'll pick up some food? Xx"

> 09:51:
> "Well, that's a relief! Get back to work then, I'll be here when you get back"

> 09:52:
> "I'm the boss, I do what I want"

> 09:52:
> "And yet, you went to work, and left me in bed. Somebody sounds like they're getting a bit above their station"

> 09:53:
> "...very true. Still very pissed off"

> 09:53:
> "I'm just kidding, I just don't want to distract you. You've got a busy day and I have a busy day watching Netflix in bed. See you later xx"

> 09:54:
> "Let me know what you want to eat xx"

09:54:
"In fact, scratch that, I've seen how indecisive you are. I'll figure out something to eat xx"

> 09:54:
> "Well, that's rude"

09:55:
"You know what you want then?"

> 09:55:
> "You to hurry up and get back in bed with me"

09:56:
"I'll see what I can do"

Liv smiled and dialled Jade's number, hoping that she'd have time to answer and wasn't with a client. When it forwarded her to answerphone she hung up and rang Owen who answered almost immediately.

"Well, well, well. Good morning you dirty stop out" he said.
"Good morning"
"Are you alive"
"Apparently so! I need a favour though"
"You want me to pick you up? Because I can't until I finish work at 3"
"No, I'm fine, but I might need you to pick my car up?"
"Why can't you do it?"
"Dropped a glass last night and I ended up cutting my foot open so I can't drive for a few days"
"What?! You okay?!"
"Yeah, I'm fine. Jackson put the butterfly stitches on and cleaned it up and stuff. Just fucking

hurts but I'm gonna take some more painkillers and go back to bed"

"He sounds like a hero, whilst you sound like a lazy shit. Are your spare keys still in the drawer at home?"

"Yeah think so, if not Mum has it"
"Okay, I'll sort it, but you owe me one"
I'll knock it off of the list of things you owe me.
"Fair point, you home tonight?"

Liv hesitated, she didn't know if she was pushing her luck staying for a second night, but she wanted to, and Owen laughed.

"I'll take that as a no. Just be safe and I'll see you tonight or tomorrow and you can fill me in"
"Love you O"
"Yeah love you too. Call me if you need me"

With that, he hung up and Liv found the ibuprofen on the bedside cabinet which she washed down with coffee and curled into bed again. She wasn't used to running on broken sleep or being woken up at stupid o'clock when she had been drinking the night before. She figured she'd get a few hours in and then tackle the carpet and Jade's questions, but for now she needed some shut eye.

29.

After browsing through all of the portfolios and jotting down notes ready for the interviews at 2:00pm, Jackson was bored. It was only 10:30am and he still had 3 hours to spend pottering around the candidates and browsing where they had got so far. He would usually engage with them throughout the day when they held these kinds of interviews, but his mind was somewhere else. Most of them had stayed in one spot, but Brad had been alternating between two different desks throughout the morning, intriguing him further.

Jackson approached the desk he wasn't working at and was surprised to see how far he'd got with sketches on paper for both the restaurant and studio. He clearly had a high productivity rate, and Jackson was impressed that he'd managed to get a rough idea in just over an hour.

"Wh-what do you think?" Brad asked, joining him from the second desk.

"You work quick" he said.

"I l-l-listen to music, it means I'm not d-distracted" he shrugged, "I have a q-question though"

"Go on.." Jackson cocked an eyebrow.

"I-I-I'm a bit of a perfectionist, and I kn-n-now this is just a draft to pitch to you both, but I want it to reflect what the client w-w-wants, so I was wondering if there was any way that I c-c-could contact them?" he said "I know you have high profile clientele and I d-d-don't want to overstep the mark, b-b-but I don't think I can give you my best b-b-based on the information I've got. I c-c-can give you something, don't get me wrong, but it m-m-might not be what they want"

Jackson had noticed his stutter earlier, but it seemed more prominent now that he was having a proper conversation with Brad. He was shaking his leg up and down on the spot as he spoke and Jackson could see he was uncomfortable, not that he had any reason to be. He was impressed again, in all of his years carrying out interviews at the company, he had been the first person to ask to talk to the client, which Jackson though was one of the most important things to do.

"S-s-sorry, I s-stutter when I'm nervous" he shrugged.

"Don't apologise, I'm impressed. I can get you the contact details, or I can call them on your behalf if there's specific questions you have?" he asked.

"D-don't worry, I d-don't stutter this m-much on the phone" he laughed, "it's when people are in f-f-front of me"

"So how do you think your pitch is going to go?" Jackson asked.

"P-p-eople don't pay for me, the p-p-pay for my designs" he stuttered, and Jackson laughed.

"I agree," he said "I'll get you the numbers and find you a side room to use? That okay?"

"Amazing, th-thank you"

Jackson pulled his phone out of his pocket, pissed that it was only 11:00am, and wrote down the numbers for Brad.

"tell them that you work at Cotts & Perkins and you are working alongside me to get a pitch together. If you tell them you're in an interview, they might be difficult. Get whatever information you need but remember you've only got another few hours to get the pitch drafted"

"N-no worries" he said grabbing the paper and wandering off to the office that Jackson directed him too.

Jackson found Harry deep in conversation with 3 of the candidates who were huddled together for their pitch, all of which happened to be all females. Jackson was keen to prevent a sexual harassment complaint being filed, so called him over without another word.

"I've hired Brad" he said, typing out an email on his phone once they got out of earshot of the candidates.

"Sorry, what?! He hasn't even done his pitch yet and you've seen how little experience he has as well. There's people here that are much more qualified AND experienced Jax?"

"Uh huh"

"I'm not playing Jackson, the reason we do the interviews like this is so we get to see all of their skill sets, how they plan, how they pitch, what their aesthetic is like. You can't base it on one conversation you have had with the kid, and a flick through a portfolio, which, whilst impressive, isn't even as extensive as other candidates in this room?!"

"And you can't base a decision based on how short a woman's skirt is and yet here I am having to drag you away from a sexual harassment lawsuit"

"Ha. Funny joke" Harry dead panned.

"If you must know, Brad couldn't decide between two of the scenarios, one low budget, one high budget, so he took both. If you look on his bench, he's already drafted an idea for each, which is more developed than half of the ones I've seen on other people's benches. More importantly, he just asked for permission to contact the clients directly to liaise with them about what they want, despite the designs I've seen being miles better than what I imagine they are about to tell him. How many candidates do you know that have asked to reach out to the clients themselves when we've done this type of interview before?"

"Okay, you've made your point, but we can't exactly tell people he's got the job without conducting the interview" Harry said, working a crick out of his neck.

"We won't, he can do his pitch last, and we can tell him then. I've already emailed Alice to draft up a contract" he shrugged, pocketing his phone and grinning over at his best friend who was frowning.

"Thanks for allowing my input"

"You make dumb decisions" he said grabbing his keys and heading to the door.

"Where are you going?!" Harry asked him.

"There's still 3 hours until interviews? I'm going to go and get some lunch platters made up at Marco's for everyone" he winked.

"Yeah, course you are. You better be back by 1:00 Jackson, I mean it"

"Yes Dad, back by 1:00"

Jackson jumped in the car and called the deli. It was going to take them a while to complete the order so if he got it in early enough, he'd be able to get back to the office by 1:00 no problem. He reeled off what he wanted and had to beg Marco to do it on short notice, but he agreed in the end after telling Jackson that he owed him one.

Jackson made his way into town to pick up some bits and set an alarm on his phone for when to pick up the lunch platters, then made his way home where he fully planned on giving Liv the wake-up she should've got this morning.

30.

Liv could smell coffee, but to open her eyes and see Jackson carrying it still dressed in the suit he left in, made it smell that much sweeter. She propped herself up, accepted the mug and took a sip whilst Jackson unbuttoned his waistcoat and shirt and hung them up.

"Put your coffee down" he said, as she watched him toe off his shoes and unbuckle his trousers too. She did as she was told, and wondered where this was going, but didn't feel the need to tell him to stop. She'd been thinking about him ever since he left, and now he was here, she wanted him. Bad.

"How are your feet?" he asked, throwing his phone and wallet on the side before taking his trousers off and draping them over the chair.

"Erm, fine?" she asked cocking an eyebrow as Jackson leaned against the drawers at the end of the bed, hands gripping the ledge either side of him. She eyed up his biceps, and the hair on his chest that trailed down to his boxers, which she was trying to avoid staring at. He wasn't hard, but he was getting there, and Liv's heart was racing.

"Why are you just standing there?" she laughed nervously.

"Because I'm nervous" he muttered, watching her as she squirmed a little.

"Well, you're making me nervous, so if you could just decide whether you want to get back in bed with me or not, it would be greatly appreciated"

"I want you" he said without hesitation, drumming his fingers on the drawers behind him.

"So, what are you waiting for?"

Liv didn't know if she was ready, but she knew she didn't want to wait. Every time she'd stirred in the night, she'd felt his dick getting hard, but he readjusted himself each time, pulled her closer and gone back to sleep without pushing for more. This morning, she could feel how hard he was again, and couldn't help but imagine how good it would feel for him to slide inside her from behind and fuck her back to sleep.

Liv pulled the covers back and beckoned him closer with a finger seductively.

"Are you sure?" he asked, climbing on to the bed in front of her. Liv didn't gratify him with an answer just parted her legs to acknowledge his questioned and watched him move closer. Jackson reached behind her knees and pulled her down the bed towards him. As he did, her top rose up her body showing off her stomach. Jackson's hands traced her inner thighs, and he watched her as she closed her eyes and leaned her head back.

"You'll tell me if you want to stop?" he asked, lowering his mouth to her stomach and kissing his way up towards her neck. Liv looked down at him and nodded before she closed her eyes again, enjoying every second of him touching her.

"Promise?" he asked, lifting the t-shirt of his she was wearing over her head and admiring her body as he did.

"Promise" she moaned as he moved between her leg and rest his hard cock against her. Jackson lowered himself again to kiss her, and Liv wrapped her arms around his shoulders, hungry for more of him. He pushed himself hard between her legs, pissed that there was still fabric separating them, and she moaned against his lips as his cock pressed against her.

"You're so beautiful" he said, cupping her breasts and taking her nipples in his mouth, one after the other. Liv was breathing heavy, and he watched her as she bit her lip and stretched her arms up towards the headboard.

Jackson readjusted his cock in his pants and pushed against her again, earning a moan that had him wanting to skip the foreplay and slide inside of her. Her back arched as he went back to trailing kisses all over her body, savouring every one. He knew he couldn't go all the way now, not when he had to get back to work, but the thought that he couldn't was killing him. He wanted to fuck her for hours, and once he started, he knew he wouldn't be able to leave.

Jackson shuffled down the bed and found her ankles. He lifted one high, and kissed his way down the length of her calf before draping it over his shoulder as he kissed her inner thigh. He could tell she was wet for him; he could smell she was wet, and all he wanted was to feel her wrapped around his cock immediately.

Jackson inhaled deeply and run his hands up the outside of her thigh as she squirmed beneath him. Liv fisted his hair whilst she moaned profanities and curled her toes, begging him not to stop. He wanted to fuck her. He needed to. Be he wanted to take his time, and time was the one thing he didn't have today.

Jackson felt her over the underwear she was wearing and massaged up and down her slit. He could feel her toes squirming on his back and watched as her breathing got heavier. Liv propped herself up on her elbows looking flushed and stared at him looking up at her. Her eyes fluttered shut, and she moaned again as lifted himself up and kissed her neck, stretching her legs wider and leaving her wanting more.

"You want me to stop?" He asked when he heard her whimper.

"Fucking god no!" She moaned, lowering her leg and removing his hand from between her legs. She hooked her fingers over the band of his boxers and eased them over his ass before letting his cock spring free and eyeing it up, looking worried.

"Erm, there's not a chance that is going to fit in any part of me" she said nervously, causing Jackson to burst into fits of laughter. He may have found it funny, but she was genuinely anxious, and didn't know if it was time to change her mind.

"I'm not going to do anything you don't want me to Liv, but you'd be surprised by where I can fit" he said kissing her back down on to the pillow and resting his cock against her slit again. She wrapped one arm around his shoulder whilst the other reached for the boxers she was wearing. She wanted them off, wanted to feel him skin to skin, but Jackson took her wrist and pinned it behind her head, stopping her. Liv was moaning in frustration. He'd teased her enough, and if she didn't feel some part of him inside of her soon, she was going to scream.

"Liv," he said exhaling loudly and kissing her again "I can't fuck you"

Liv grabbed either side of his head and looked at him with her brows furrowed. When he didn't tell her he was joking, she lifted her leg back between them and sat up on the bed whilst Jackson pulled his boxers up again and leant in towards her for a kiss which she avoided

"What the fuck are we doing then?" She asked reaching for his t-shirt angrily, hating herself for giving it up to him so easily. Jackson glared at his phone which was buzzing on the side behind him and reached the t-shirt before she did, throwing it to the other side of the room.

"Liv," he said taking her hands and pinning them beside her as she tried to push him away from kissing her.

"Jackson, get off me" she said, and he did without hesitation. Liv was mortified that he didn't want her, she felt like an idiot for egging him on when he clearly had no intention of finishing what he started. She didn't understand, but she wasn't waiting around for him to explain. She stepped out of the bed completely forgetting about the state of her foot and swore loudly before limping off to the bathroom and slamming the door behind with Jackson quickly in tow.

"What's wrong?!" He demanded swinging the door open and standing in front of her. Her feet were hurting, and she winced a little when she shifted her weight to stand taller to face him. Jackson must have noticed, because within seconds her legs were taken from under her, and she was over his shoulder again.

"YOU DONT GET TO THROW ME OVER YOUR SHOULDER EVERY TIME I SAY SOMETHING YOU DONT LIKE JACKSON!" she said kicking her legs. Jackson let her drop down his torso and wrapped her legs around him.

"Yeah, I do, when you're kicking off for no reason. If you'd have let me explain I would have!" He said sounding frustrated.

"Explain what?! Why you now don't want to fuck me after I literally laid myself out on a silver platter for you?!" She shouted as he sat her back down on the bed and pinned her arms behind her head again, looming over her.

"Liv, all I've thought about since they day I met you is how much I want to fuck you. I come home the very same night I met yet and couldn't get you out of my fucking mind, because you fucking annoyed me so much, but you looked so fucking sexy. In fact, I wanked over you that night, remembering the way your ass bounced on my shoulder, how nice your tits looked, and how good you smelt. But right now, my alarm has been going off for 10 minutes which means I'm late for work again, and if you think I'm going to rush being inside of you for the very first time, you are fucking crazy. *When* I fuck you, and trust me, I'm going to... it's not going to be some fucking 5 minute quickie because of other commitments that I *have* to get to, I'm going to fuck you for fucking hours, until you beg me to stop! Okay?!" he said, staring at her so intensely that she thought she might cum there and then.

Liv pouted. She may have overreacted, but she hadn't been touched in so fucking long that she was desperate for him. She wanted him now, and she didn't want to have to wait, especially after he'd already made her feel so good.

"I didn't mean it to come across like that Liv" he said, releasing her wrists and leaning in when she wrapped them around him and kissed him.

"I really like you, and it's making me nervous, and I really don't want to fuck things up or push you away like I've always done before. I don't want you to be a quickie in the day, or a one-night stand, I genuinely want you. Every hour of everyday" he said as he kissed her over and over, "Please stay tonight? I promise you I'll do everything you want and more. I just don't want to ruin it and I know if I start something right now, I physically won't be able to stop myself Liv and I *need* to go back to work this afternoon or Harry will have my balls in a vice"

"I like you too," she muttered, embarrassed that she'd overreacted when all he'd wanted to do was make their first time together memorable.

"Good, now can you please behave and let me put some clothes on, I've got interviews to get to" he winked, kissing her again and matching her tongue stroke for stroke.

Liv watched as he dressed again in his shirt and waistcoat, then tidied up his hair in the mirror. She finished her lukewarm coffee whilst she stared at him clearing the notifications on his phone. She felt guilty again for making him late, she'd never considered herself high maintenance before, but maybe she was.

"I'll be back by 6:00 with dinner, there's a bath in the bathroom if you want one because of your feet" he said kissing her.

"You saying I smell?" she asked, raising an eyebrow.

"Well, I could smell that you were ready to take my cock if that counts" he said pocketing his phone and wallet as he sent her a smug grin and winked at her.

"Jackson! That's gross and embarrassing" she said turning red and pulling the covers up over her face which Jackson quickly removed.

"It's sexy" he replied, inhaling deeply, before he kissed her "I'll see you at 6:00 Olivia"

31.

Harry rolled his eyes as Jackson strolled in at 1:04, looking empty handed.

"Where's the lunches?!" He asked, sounding annoyed.

"I needed your help getting them in" he said returning to the door with Harry not far behind.

"So?"

"So, what" Jackson asked as he picked up and piled platters up on top of Harry's outstretched arms.

"Did you?"

Jackson cocked an eyebrow at Harry like he had no clue what he was talking about and kept piling up the food before grabbing the bags. "Did I what?"

"Did you fuck? Obviously"

"Nope. Just went in and checked on how she was with her feet and stuff," he lied, convincing himself not to reminisce about watching her body react to his every touch and hearing her moan.

"How the mighty have fallen" Harry muttered returning to the office with his trays piled high, "are you genuinely feeling her this much?" He asked.

Jackson nodded, and shrugged like it was nothing, but it was a big deal for everyone around him. He'd never had to put thought or effort into what he did with the women he dated, he just went with it, but with Liv he felt like he wanted to go above and beyond. He'd never skived off work for a woman, because his job had always come first, but now, he was even more distracted than he was in the morning, wanting to leave all over again. Seeing her tits this morning was one thing, but feeling them, holding them, tasting them was something else.

He was desperate for the next 5 hours to pass quickly, so he could get back to her, and back between her legs, but he knew all too well how the time was going to drag.

Jackson helped Harry lay out all the platters, and grabbed the last few bits from the car, including his phone and wallet. He made to leave to head back to the office again but a call from behind had him spinning in his tracks and cursing. Jackson rolled his eyes as Rachael approached him wearing a thick fur coat with bare legs and ankle boots.

"Missed me?" She asked leaning in for a kiss which Jackson avoided.

"Are you joking? What do you want?!"

"I figured that actions speak louder than words, and so I wanted to show you what you were missing" she said opening her coat to show her in nothing but lacey underwear which had Jackson rolling his eyes. He'd seen it all before, plenty of times, and he didn't know how to make her see sense.

"Rach, please. I've said we're done. Have you stopped taking your meds again or are you just completely oblivious to what I'm saying" he said matter-of-factly.

"I've always taken my meds, but have you?" She spat.

"We're completely different people Rach, I'm not psychotic, with or without my meds, unlike you"

"No? You just chase anything in a fucking skirt instead. Have you told her that you fucked your therapist? Or that you are an addict?"

She said through gritted teeth, "because I'm sure she will be running for the mountains if she uncovered all your dirty little secrets, and maybe I'll make sure she does!"

"Don't fucking threaten me Rachael, everyone has a fucking past and I'll tell her when I'm ready to! Go home and put a fucking pin in it" he said, turning around and heading back for the door quickly followed by Rachael who blocked his path.

"I know you Jackson and you're incapable of love. Giving it or receiving it, the sooner you realise that the sooner you'll be asking for me back. I know you will. Whether you like it or not, I know you miss the way I make you feel, you know we're meant to be together, because you know you can be yourself. It's just the meds making your brain feel fuzzy" she pleaded with him placing her hands on his chest and looking up at him, "please don't do this Jackson, we're good together? And I can't do this without you. You keep me grounded and I don't want to spiral again"

"Rach, I'm sorry, but nothing about us was real. We fucked, and we spent time together, but I don't want to be with you. You were fine to waste time with, but I don't love you -"

"AND YOU DO HER?!" she screamed, cutting him off "You barely even know her Jackson and she definitely doesn't know you otherwise she'd be running for the hills you fucking idiot. You might look nice, dress nice, and treat them nice, but that's only until you get bored, and they don't serve your purpose anymore, as nothing more than a fuck!!"

"SHE'S DIFFERENT!" He shouted, losing his temper. He needed to leave because he could feel the rage building up and he needed to stay professional.

"So, you do love her? She's 'the one' is she?!"

"I fucking hope so!" he said through gritted teeth.

And with that Rachael's whole aggressive demeanour dropped. Her shoulders slumped, her eyes shut, and she looked broken. Jackson watched as she walked off down the street, wiping her face as she did, but even that didn't calm him. She was manipulative and she didn't like it when things didn't go her way. Deep down he knew he had hurt her, and that she was going to try and get back at him somehow, but he didn't care, he just wanted to keep Liv out of it. He needed to tell her everything before she agreed to go all the way, and he wanted to give her the opportunity to walk away if she wanted to without the sex complicating things.

Harry eyed Jackson as he walked in, noticing the look on his face and took the bags from him without question.

"Basement?" He asked, when Jackson strode past him.

"Basement"

Jackson learnt early on with his diagnosis that his mood could change in an instant, especially when it came to work. He'd had a gym installed in the basement years ago for times when it did and planned to take full advantage of it right now. He hung up his shirt and waistcoat for the second time today, swapped his trousers for some shorts that he kept to hand, and planned on 5 rounds with the boxing bag before going back for the interviews.

He played the conversation with Rachael out over and over again in his mind whist he wrapped his hands, hating that she knew so much. In a way it's what had drawn them together, but now it was also the thing that made it impossible for her to leave him alone. They weren't the same, no matter what she said, and his condition was under control, which is more than he could say for her.

Or at least that's what he thought.

32.

Liv found the bathroom and let the bath run whilst she searched for towels. She'd dug out another t-shirt and some boxers from the drawers in Jackson's room, then awkwardly lifted herself in, avoiding submerging the bandages on her feet. She washed quickly, since laying sideways was less than comfortable, then attempted to get out a few times without hurting herself.

In the end, she had no other choice than to swallow down the shooting pains going through her feet and get out properly. Liv checked the time again, only to sigh with frustration that she still had 4 hours to wait for Jackson to get home. 4 whole hours to kill, and feet that wouldn't work.

She returned to the bedroom slowly and called Jade which went to answerphone again. She rolled her eyes and went to throw it on the bed, but when it started vibrating quickly afterwards, she answered it. She'd assumed it was Jade returning her call, but instead was greeted by the one voice in the world she didn't want to hear.

"Liv"

"Tommy"

"How are you?" he asked sheepishly.

"Absolutely fantastic, you?" She said sarcastically.

"Yeah good actually, but can we talk"

"About?"

"Well can you meet me?"

"Not really, whatever it is I'm sure you can tell me on the phone"

"I just figured it would be better in person, it's about the house and stuff"

"Unless it's a date as to when you plan on giving me my half of the money, I don't really care Tommy"

"Well, that's the thing. Sarah is pregnant and I can't sell the house anymore, or not anytime soon anyway. The baby is due in June, so it's come as a bit of a surprise"

Liv didn't need to do the maths it was evident that she fallen pregnant whilst they were still together, and she didn't know how to feel. She stayed silent for a bit only to be pulled back to reality, when Tommy spoke again.

"Liv?"

"Okay, whatever. I'll come and pick up my stuff tomorrow with Jade, and I'll speak to my solicitor about where I stand"

"I'm sorry"

"No, you're not. I'll see you tomorrow"

Liv threw her phone on the bed and didn't know what to do with herself. Instead, she sat on the floor and sobbed. Not because she was upset, or that she missed him. But because she'd spent so many years wasting her time with him. Her phone rang again behind her, and she ignored it. She couldn't bear to speak to anyone feeling as she did, she felt worthless, and couldn't help but wonder why she hadn't been good enough.

It took some time, but Liv pulled herself together, wiped her tears and got herself up. She grabbed her phone, hobbled down the stairs for coffee and called Jade who finally answered. Liv broke down again and told her everything, convinced that the tiredness wasn't helping things. She started with Tommy, and Jade cursed down the phone about how he was a pig and she was entitled to the house since she put forward the deposit, but Liv wasn't interested in the stress. She would deal with it at some point, but for now she didn't want it to ruin everything else.

Then she took a breath and told her about Jackson, their night together, the accident, the misunderstanding that he didn't want to sleep with her, and that she was spending the night with him again. Jade squealed as she explained and sounded more excited than Liv was.

"I told you! I said you'd fuck him before the end of the month!" she said excitedly

"We'll see Jade, it might not happen!" she laughed, glad her best friend was able to take her mind off of things

"Well, sounds like that's what's on the agenda tonight" she laughed, "just be careful, and USE PROTECTION!"

"I didn't even think of that!" She gasped. Liv hadn't been on birth control for almost a year. The hormones made her miserable and depressed and in the end she'd decided to stop. It wasn't like she was having sex, so there wasn't a chance of her getting pregnant, but now it was something she really had to think about.

"Lucky I did! I'm sure he has condoms! You'll be fine!" She laughed, "I'm so excited for you!"

"I'm not. I'm scared! It's really big Jade" she mumbled, but all she could do was laugh. Jade told her she'd ring her in the morning and that she wanted to know everything. Liv told her she would be having a lay in after her early start, and Jade said that if she hadn't heard from her by midday, she was sending the police and coming to find her herself. They exchanged goodbyes, and Liv was left feeling nervous all over again, which she would take over feeling worthless any day.

33.

Jackson buttoned his shirt as he took the stairs back up to the floor. He nodded to the group of women that were huddled together at the table eyeing him hungrily when he reappeared and found Harry in conversation with Alice at the desk.

"Better?" She asked, as he approached and took a look at the order of interviews they'd arranged.

"Much" he replied shortly.

"You wanna talk about it," Harry asked, running down another list filled with meetings they had scheduled next week.

"Rach being petty again. She won't leave me alone, and I don't want it to ruin things with Liv. It's frustrating"

"Want me to chin her?" Alice said completely straight faced, and Jackson laughed.

"She's psycho, literally, so maybe avoid that" he replied.

"Offers there" she shrugged, getting back to her work on the computer.

"Shall we get the interviews started then?" Jackson said, straightening his collar and grabbing his pen.

"Why not"

"Alice, send up the first candidate and let the others know their time slots. If they want to stay, they're more than welcome to, but if not, they can go out and about. Tell Brad Walker that we've put him as last, so he has extra time to display the 2 scenarios he picked, and then make sure his draft contract is ready too please"

"Starting salary?"

"£27,000 + commission. 6-month probationary period, then up to £32,000"

"Anything else?"

"Can you call Flo's and get her to do me up some flowers for Liv" he winked and made his way up to the meeting room with Alice telling him she was right on it.

Harry had decided on the order of the candidates and started with the gaggle of women he'd been chatting to before Jackson left earlier in the day.

The first was petite and blonde with blue eyes. She wore a smart black dress and black heels, with tights and a red belt. Her pitch was a beauty salon. Modern and sleek with a hint of 60's nostalgia. It hit the brief with its monochromatic tones, but it wasn't special. He'd seen it before, and he wasn't impressed. Jackson asked her some questions about her previous work and what she was hoping for, then sent for the next candidate after crossing her off the shortlist.

"Not impressed?" Harry asked, peering over at Jackson's notes.

"Nothing new" he shrugged "client specified she wanted it to be unique, but I reckon if I walked down a high street in Essex I'd see plenty the same"

"Agreed"

The next two women pitched their idea in a similar fashion. Stylish and sleek with a modern flare, but nothing quirky that he hadn't seen before. If he was going to expand the business, he wanted it to be new and exciting. He didn't want something that had been done before, he wanted something original or at least some original touches.

As the candidates came and went, he felt like he was going to have to lower his standards. A couple showed promise with their pitches, in particular a flamboyant middle-aged guy who designed a new hotel lobby to include unique and detailed chandeliers from the ceiling to the floor encased in glass, and a futuristic lobby reception desk. Two women came with great ideas, one for a retro themed bar, which she based around the back to the future franchise, and another for a new boutique which took its influence from Parisian patisserie.

By the time Brad's pitch was up, Harry and Jackson had shortlisted the other 3 for the roles. Each of the candidates were told they could leave following their pitch and that somebody would be in touch by the end of the day to tell them if they were successful or not, so Brad was the last one left in the building with Harry and Jackson by 5:15. Jackson had been clock watching all day, and was counting down the seconds until he could get back home to Liv, but he still had to get dinner and pick up another few bottles of wine. Jackson checked his phone and found a message that Liv had sent him hours ago, cursing himself for not checking it sooner. With all the commotion of Rachael, and the interviews he hadn't had a minute to check his messages or reply to her.

14:50
"I'm sorry I overreacted, and I'm sorry for kicking off. I think I'm just nervous. Shall we order dinner in tonight? Then you can come home sooner, and I don't have to wait for you forever? Don't worry about replying if you're busy. See you later xx"

17:17:

> "Sorry I haven't replied, the interviews have been non-stop. Don't apologise Liv, I'm sorry I wasn't clearer. I'll be home just after 6:00. I'm just finishing up at work. Do you want me to get anything from the shop? I'll grab some wine and bits? Can't wait to see you xx"

Brad walked in and Jackson invited him to sit and take a seat in front of them. In his hands he had sketches, and the tablet he'd used for his mood boards which Harry projected on to the screen.

"You want to stand up front, or behind?" Jackson asked pocketing his phone, remembering how Brad didn't like to speak directly to people.

"B-b-behind if that's okay?" he stammered.

"The floor is yours"

Brad got up and walked to the back of the room with his tablet after laying out his sketches and notes in front of Harry and Jackson.

"I started with their p-pitches, and the basic design elements they m-mentioned to come up with a rough idea of how I thought they wanted it to look, but I wasn't h-h-happy with either of them" he began, showing images of a first draft of both the photography studio, and the restaurant.

"I called Miss Clancy, about her studio. Asked what she photographed, how often she used it, whether it was a natural light or soft box lights so that we could delegate space if we needed to. I asked what her interests were, f-favourite colours, design types and aesthetics, and I came up with this." Brad pressed for the next slide and 4 images popped up beside each other showing each angle of the studio.

"She specialises in newborn photography, so I figured they'd need space for parents, prams, photography equipment, and the set up. There's built in units for props and an axis for backdrops. A small desk area for editing, but most of it is about comfort. I went for neutral colours that weren't gender specific so creams and browns with a splash of black to break it up a little. Soft furnishings and rug as well as some added extras for décor and that are pleasing to the eye. It's simple, but that's what she asked for and I predicted that it come in under budget too"

As he spoke about his work, his stutter disappeared, and you could hear how passionate he was about what he did. The drafts were beautiful, and Jackson didn't feel like they needed tweaking in the slightest. Not only was he impressed, he could see that Harry was too.

"The restaurant was slightly harder, I couldn't get in touch with the right person for ages, but when I finally did, he didn't have long to speak. He said he wanted it industrial/modern style, which is being done left right and centre now, so I wanted to put a twist on it. I incorporated black marble into aspects of the design as well as the weathered wood and cast iron being used throughout. These are just snippets of some of the ideas I had, but without the dimensions, I struggled to accurately depict it"

Harry and Jackson browsed through some of his sketches, and both of them could see his vision instantly. He'd taken everyday items and used them in a new way to bring some character. A copper bath that had been turned into a sofa, a bicycle that had a sink for a seat, and a plant pot for a basket, then a singer sewing machine table that had been turned into a lamp.

Brad continued to explain his vision, about the hardwood floor with a marble arc, where the bar was placed. Wrought iron and wood shelving. Rope, clocks, and upcycled items left, right and centre. There were a few things that he had yet to complete, but Jackson and Harry were both impressed at how the plans looked, and how thorough he had been with both of his scenarios.

"I really like it" Harry said, raising his eyebrows as Brad rejoined them at the table.

"Told you so" Jackson said, nodding down to Alice who brought up the contract she'd been drafting and handed it to Jackson who flicked through it briefly.

"I've seen you live relatively local, so I've taken the liberty of getting Alice to draft up a contract for you to have a read over. If you're happy with the terms, we can set up a formal induction meeting on Tuesday?"

"F-f-for a second interview?" he asked, sounding hopeful.

"No, for a job. You're hired" Jackson said offering his hand out, which Brad shook energetically. "I really like how you work, and how focused you are. You're passionate, and it shows in the way you design. I think you'd be an asset to Cotts and Perkins and it looks like you've convinced Harry too"

Harry held out his hand and shook Brad's who looked overjoyed at the news. They encouraged him to read through the contract carefully and to write down anything that he was concerned about for his meeting on Tuesday, but in the meantime they would seek out his references and get the ball rolling for a start date.

Brad thanked them both and left the room smiling whilst Jackson and Harry packed up their bits.

"So, who else are you interested in?" Harry asked as he put Brad's tablet on the charging dock and gathered up his sketches to one side.

"I like Lacey and Ria, and Michael had a bit of flare about him too. So, it's your call?" he shrugged.

"We can go over them again on Monday and see what you think, I'll finish up here as you've got stuff to be doing tonight" Harry said.

"It's fine, I said I'd be home by 6 anyway"

"Uh huh, that's why you haven't stopped looking at your watch since 3. Just go home Jax, and don't do anything I wouldn't do".

"Well then, my options are limitless aren't they" he laughed, and Harry smiled. Jackson took the stairs, and thanked Alice for the flowers before heading to the car, ready to get back to Liv and finish where he left off earlier.

34.

By 5:30, Liv's stomach was in knots. She was nervous about seeing Jackson after earlier, even though she'd enjoyed every second of it. She felt like it was more the waiting that was getting to her than anything else, and she couldn't even pace because her feet were hurting.

Jade had messaged her again telling her she wanted all the details as soon as she opened her eyes, and Owen had messaged her to say that he'd got her car home safe and sound. She heard Jackson pull up on the drive outside and felt her stomach drop again. She wasn't used to any of this, and she didn't really know how these things played out.

Jackson got in and found her on the sofa curled up in one of the blankets watching TV. He was carrying flowers and wine and placed them on the side before he kissed her. Liv kissed back, and her stomach knots melted away before picked her up and placed her on his lap with her legs draped either side of him.

"How was work?" she said as he kissed her neck and stroked his thumb up and down her ass cheeks.

"Eventful" he said, sounding deflated. Liv lifted his chin, and silently encouraged him to go on, but he was hesitant.

"What's happened?" she asked, when the knots in her stomach started balling up again and Jackson avoided looking at her.

"I need to tell you something, because I know if I don't tell you now, it's going to end up pushing you away and I don't want that. I want you to know before anything happens between us" he said, looking scared.

"Let's get some drinks, and order some dinner, and you can tell me whatever you want" she said, kissing him softly and hobbling off of him. Liv grabbed the wine from the sideboard and limped towards the kitchen before Jackson picked her up and finished the journey.

"I'm sorry I left you all day with your feet in that state" he said, putting her down on the island and heading for the glass cabinet. He poured them both a drink whilst Liv flicked through her take away apps to find something she fancied but after 10 minutes of back and forthing with Jackson, she agreed on the first thing she saw and ordered Thai. They had 30 minutes to kill until it arrived, so Jackson made himself comfortable on the stool between her legs as she sat on the Island top and started talking.

"So, Rachael turned up at work again today" he said stroking her calves up and down. Liv rolled her eyes and took a large swig of her drink already dreading where this conversation was going, but Jackson chuckled.

"Well, she's persistent isn't she" she said, forcing a smile.

"Apparently so"

"What did she want?" Liv said exhaling. It wasn't Jackson's fault that she wouldn't leave him alone, and she appreciated him being honest with her, but it also wasn't something she wanted to complete with indefinitely.

"She told me I was making a mistake leaving her, and didn't like it when I said we were dating..." Jackson paused and drained his drink before he continued, "I really want to be honest with you Liv but it's really hard for me to explain everything. Rachael only knows because it's how we met"

Liv was getting anxious. She could see he was nervous, but he looked hurt, and worried about whatever it was he was about to tell her. She didn't say anything, she just topped up his glass and waited until he was ready, which didn't take long, but felt like a lifetime.

Jackson knocked back another glass and breathed deeply, steadying himself before he started.

"Obviously I've already told you that I haven't been in relationships since Clayton's Mum. Never been in love, never looked for a relationship, and never really wanted one up until now either. About 9 years ago, I went through a bad stage, and that's when I first met Rachael. I'd completely gone off the rails, my mum was looking after Clayton constantly and I was drinking and partying a lot. I never touched drugs, I wouldn't after what happened with Clayt, but I woke up with a different woman every day, and sometimes multiple women. I know it's not nice to hear, but I wasn't well. I was on a high most of the time, reckless and dangerous, but when I wasn't fucking, or drinking, I was a mess. Joe would have to come and find me wherever I ended up, peel me off the floor and stop me from doing something stupid. I hated everything about life, I'd go AWOL for days and contemplate suicide, and in the end, Mum told me that if I ever wanted to see Clayton again then I needed to go to rehab. It wasn't until I was there that they diagnosed me, and I've been on meds ever since"

Liv listened whilst he spoke the way she always did, she wasn't judging him or making assumptions, she was just listening to what he had to say, and Jackson appreciated that.

"I was in for alcohol and sex dependency, but I got myself sorted and the meds seemed to help. I wasn't an alcoholic, but I drank in excess without any thought as to why but they said that was because I didn't have meds to balance me out. I can drink now, but I know my limits. It was all just weird. It was like my head was always fuzzy, all of the time when I weren't on the meds. I needed to feel needed, even though Clayton needed me more than anything. Rach was in at the same time, for similar reasons and we both seemed to sort our heads out, she was a lot more extrovert than I was though. When I had my drops, I pulled away from people, but when Rachael had hers, she was fucking psycho. She had to be sedated plenty of times, and now she's on antipsychotics too. When we were in there, we joked about always having each other if things didn't work out with other people, which always seemed to be the case. She's flitted in and out of relationships, but usually she fucks them up by having one of her break downs that they can't handle. Then I'd go and pick up the pieces because I understood how shit it felt. But I was lucky, I had Clayton to keep me grounded. I stopped drinking every night for the sake of it, stopped bedding different women, and threw myself into work as something to focus on. I've got an addictive personality, but I swapped my unhealthy ones with healthy ones. I still craved the sex, but I wasn't desperate enough to sleep with multiple women anymore, I'd get it when I could, but not if it meant sacrificing work, or time with my son" he shrugged trailing off. Liv stayed silent and listened whilst he reeled off his past to her, and he hoped more than anything that she wasn't going to leave him for it. He watched as she smiled and held up her glass to cheers him.

"That's it?" he asked, clinking glasses and watching whilst she sipped her drink, "you don't have any questions?"

"Nope"

"Really?" he asked confused.

"I saw your meds in the cabinet earlier when I was being nosey" she shrugged, topping her glass up again. "My dad has bipolar"

Jackson breathed a sigh of relief and wondered what he'd been so nervous about. She'd never given him any reason to think that she'd think less of him but opening up wasn't in his nature.

"So, were you going to ask me about them?" he said, kissing her inner thigh as she made herself comfier on the countertop.

"Nope" she said, popping the P.

"Why not?"

"I figured you'd tell me when you were ready? I don't care that you have it, as long as you promise you'll keep managing it and you'll tell me when you're not. I've seen my dad go off the rails more than once and it's not nice watching someone you love ruining their life", Liv went red, "I mean like, my dad, I'm not saying you or that I love you or anything, I just meant someone you care about. You know what I mean!"

Liv laughed nervously whilst Jackson watched her trip over her words, he knew what she meant, but watching the blush rush across her cheeks and hearing her try to correct herself made him laugh as well.

"Well, whilst we're on the subject, it must have been a day for exes" she shrugged, making Jackson cock a brow.

"Tommy called me earlier" she said, and Jackson watched her make herself noticeably smaller when she spoke about him.

"and?"

"and.. he's still an asshole" she said, avoiding Jackson's gaze. He lifted her chin and watched as her eyes glassed over and tears began to pool.

"You want to talk about it?" he said, drying her cheek.

"I don't know"

"You can tell me", he said, kissing her forehead, and standing in front of her, "You've listened to everything I've told you, it's the least I can do"

"It's just shit. He's still in my house, I left with nothing, under the agreement that we would sell it, split the money, and I could find somewhere else. Now, it turns out that the woman he left me for, and don't get me wrong, I don't care that he left, but she's pregnant and now he's not willing to move. I just feel like an idiot, that I spent 8 years of my life in a loveless, sexless relationship where there was no intention of commitment. No, 'I love you's', no proposals, no talk of kids. Just him doing whatever the fuck he wanted, day in, day out, which included fucking multiple women, and deciding to start a family with one. I just feel like there's something wrong with me and ..."

"Woah. I appreciate what you're saying Liv, and I get it, but this has nothing to do with there being something wrong with you. Sometimes, we can't see what's right in front of our eyes. Not all men are meant for commitment, and you clearly deserved better than him. Sometimes, we settle for what we know, and not what we want" he said kissing her forehead.

The door rang behind them, and Jackson saw to it before he returned to the kitchen with the food. Liv had pulled herself together again, deciding that now wasn't the time to talk about the person she'd like to forget about most in the world, so she welcomed Jackson between her legs again whilst she perched on the edge of the countertop.

"You okay?" He asked, as his hands run up her thighs and rested on her sexy little thigh brows. He didn't think he'd ever get tired of seeing the crease of her thigh, or any part of her body in fact.

"I'm okay, I was just admiring how good you look in a suit" she said as she unbuttoned his waistcoat and started on his shirt buttons. "You're usually in jogging bottoms when I come round, I feel like I've been missing out"

"Oh really? I look that good that you're trying to get me out of it?" He said running his hands further up her body until they were resting on her hips.

"Precisely, don't want to ruin it with dinner"

"I forgot" he said, as she worked on the buttons.

"Well, I haven't because as much as I would like to resume our earlier position, I haven't eaten all day and I'm starving"

"Well, I better feed you then" he winked at her before finishing the rest of his shirt buttons and tossing it to one side.

Jackson lowered Liv off of the side and onto the stool, then grabbed some plates whilst Liv opened all of the containers and got stuck in.

"So, how was work after Rachael appearing" she asked around a mouthful of noodles.

"I was angry, so I went down to the gym in the basement"

"You have your own gym?!" She asked surprised, shoving a dumpling in her mouth. Jackson loved how comfortable she was eating in front of him and topped up their glasses again.

"It's not a proper gym, just somewhere to go when something at work has pissed me off. Harry knows everything that happened, so he suggested it when I got out of rehab"

"That was nice of him" she said, smiling.

"Yeah, he's a nice guy" he agreed.

Jackson watched as Liv poked her food around her plate a little, picking here and there, whilst she watched him eat.

"You not hungry now?" he asked, and she smiled again, a blush rising up her cheeks..

"Not for food -"

And no sooner had she finished her sentence; did she find her legs wrapped around Jackson's waist again as he carried her out of the kitchen and up the stairs..

35.

By the time they reached the bedroom, Jackson was hard. Liv had kissed him all the way up the stairs whilst he groped her ass tightly, and he knew if he didn't get his dick out of his pants soon it was going to become painful. Jackson laid her back on the bed whilst he undid his trousers and took them off, and Liv made herself comfortable against the headboard, with her legs parted in front of him.

He climbed on the bed between her legs, kissing his way up her body as he did, taking her in. When he reached the bottoms she was wearing he ran his fingers lazily up and down her thighs and Liv watched him, beckoning him further up her body with her index finger. He moved at her command tracing the curves of her hips, her waist, and her breasts and lifted his shirt over her head for the second time that day, watching as her perky tits fell out and onto her chest. All he wanted was to make her feel good, but the thought of having her wrapped around his cock was almost too much.

He'd played this situation out in his head over and over again. He'd planned to take his time worshipping every, single, inch of her, but now she was in front of him, he didn't want to wait. He wanted to feel what it was like to be deep inside of her, and what it was like to watch her body react to him, react to how he fucked her.

Jackson kissed her hungrily, whilst Liv found the waistband of his boxers again trying to free his cock. He helped it out and finished taking them off, whilst Liv wrapped her little hand around it and stroked him back and forth, taking him by surprise and almost making his knees buckle. Jackson let out a growl of approval and kissed her again. With her free hand, she held his jaw tight, and forced him to kiss her properly while the other continued to move up and down over his length. Jackson hadn't expected it, he'd expected her to be timid and reserved, but she was giving him everything he wanted and more. He guessed the wine had a lot to do with it, but he certainly wasn't complaining by any means.

He pulled away and encouraged her back down the bed so she was lying flat, then traced his hands down her body again, pausing when he reached the waistband of the boxers she was wearing.

"Are you sure?" He asked, not knowing what the fuck he was going to do if she said no, knowing a cold shower wasn't going to be enough to fix the state of him right now, but Liv bit her lip and nodded. Jackson exhaled with relief and got to work on undressing her completely, getting his first look at what he'd been thinking about since the moment they met.

If he thought it was hard to keep some form of control when she was just topless, it was going to be almost impossible once he saw her naked. Jesus, fucking, wept at the sight of her pussy, and so did he. He couldn't remember ever seeing one as beautiful as hers in his life, and before he knew what he was even doing he'd lowered his mouth and started running his tongue up and down the length of her slit, over and over.

He felt Liv's back arch off the bed and heard her moaning loudly as she tried to pull away from him. He wrapped one hand around her hip pulling her towards him, and the other one reached up to cup her breast where he stroked his thumb over her hard nipples again. Jackson could hear her begging for him to stop, but he knew why. He could read her body already, knew the signs and knew that she was on the brink of an orgasm.

"10 seconds and I'll stop" he begged, running his hands back down her body so he could slide fingers inside her soft, tight, pussy. He wanted to feel her drip for him, needed to.

"Oh fuck" she panted, fisting the sheets whilst Jacksons fingers slid in and out of her and his tongue traced circles around her clit over and over. He watched her breathing get heavy, listened as she moaned, and felt her tense up as she finally succumb to the orgasm that was radiating through her body, calling his name loudly as she did, but he didn't stop. He wanted more.

"What the fuck just happened" Liv panted when she'd come down from the high she was riding and propped herself up on her elbows so she could see him better. "Was that an orgasm?!" She said, sounding surprised, but Jackson couldn't help but laugh.

"Well, yeah, a little one, but I plan on doing better. If you hadn't kept telling me to stop, I would have done better then as well" he said as kissed her inner thigh.

"Oh my god" she panted, not knowing what else to say, and Jackson laughed again.

"Are you trying to tell me that as well as never having a one-night stand, you've never had an orgasm?!" he asked, confused.

"Well not like that! I thought I had, but apparently, I definitely haven't. I can fully comprehend why people become addicted to sex right now" she breathed heavily, running her fingers through his hair as she did.

"Trust me, it gets better" he said kissing her belly and finding his way up to her neck.

Liv was still breathless, when Jackson laid her back down, and she opened her legs wide to him. She thought she'd be nervous, but she wasn't, she wanted every part of him, and she wanted it now.

"Lay down", Liv said, taking Jackson by surprise.

"Why?"

"Because I want you to"

Jackson did as he was told and watched as Liv straddled him. She pressed kisses to his neck, and down his body, and could feel his cock, resting between her ass cheeks as she bent over him.

Liv slid herself down his body, kissing as she went, until she reached his dick. She was still intimidated by the size of it, but wanted to give him everything she had, even if it wasn't the best. Liv looked up at him as she took it in her hand and ran her tongue over his helmet.

Jackson inhaled sharply and propped himself up on his elbows so he could watch her work. As he did, Liv's back arched whilst she stretched her lips around the tip and took him in her mouth slowly. She grabbed the base with her hand, squeezing gently as she worked her tongue up and down his length earning a moan each time she did..

"Liv," he said watching her ass spread wide in the air, "I want to fuck you, now"

"Right now?" she said, releasing his cock with a popping sound, but keeping her hand firmly wrapped around him.

"Right now," he growled.

Liv got to her knees and straddled him again teasing his cock between the folds of her pussy. He moaned as she balanced herself and stroked his cock up and down the length of her slit, over and over, teasing him and pleasing herself as she did. He watched her for a few seconds longer, as she smiled down at him, then without warning she was flipped on to her back with Jackson between her legs again.

"I do the teasing here" he said sliding his fingers inside her again, happy with how wet she was.

"I thought you wanted to fuck me?" She panted, rubbing his cock.

"I do" he said, moving his fingers slowly whilst she moaned quietly beneath him.

"What are you waiting for then?" she whispered, staring up at him.

"You're sure?"

"I'm sure," she nodded, biting her lip. Liv took her hand from his cock as he removed his own from between her legs. He watched her face, and watched her chest rise and fall as he leaned down to kiss her and lowered his body over hers. Liv wrapped an arm around his shoulder whilst the other touched his chest. He watched her, asking for permission one more time, and when she nodded, he slowly eased his way inside of her.

Jackson had known she'd be tight as soon as he slid his fingers inside her, but not so tight that he would struggle to even get the tip in. He pulled back a little and tried again managing a bit more each time he did, and each time he'd ease another inch in, he'd hear her hiss with pleasure and pain. When Jackson finally managed to slide the length of his cock inside her, he groaned almost ready to cum before he'd started.

She was making it impossible for him to last long, but he wanted to. He wanted it to be the best she'd ever had. Wanted her to want him over and over again and planned on doing just that through the night. Jackson began to move slowly and watched as her body relaxed and grew comfortable with him being inside her. She'd been nervous and tense when he started, but soon her body moved with him, and she wanted more.

Jackson lifted her leg up over his shoulder and ran his hand down her thigh reaching for her clit again which she swatted away with her hand.

"I can't do both" she panted as he pumped inside of her again over and over.

"You can" he said, running his hand back between them and using the other to hold hers out of the way. Liv thrashed around as he focused on giving her maximum pleasure touching every inch of her, he could. He continued to thrust inside of her, ran his tongue over her body, and traced circles around her clit with his thumb whilst Liv moaned loudly into his shoulder. He eventually released her hands so he could adjust her hips and she dug her nails into his back hard as she fought back another orgasm.

Jackson felt her tense again, and leaned in and kissed her. As he teased her tongue with his own, he felt her start to relax. When her pussy began to tighten around his cock, Jackson thought he was going to lose it. He didn't want it to end yet, but he could feel how close she was.

"Liv, stop moaning, or I'm gonna cum" he growled into her ear, but as he did, he felt her back arch and another orgasm ripple through her. He didn't think she could get much tighter, but she did, and Jackson had to slow his strokes to stop him from ending far too soon.

"I'm sorry, I can't help it!" She screamed as he hoisted her other leg up and reared up on to his knees. He couldn't wait any longer, he wanted to give her more, but it was just too good.

"Fucking hell," he moaned as the change of position had her pussy feeling even nicer "what are you doing to me?"

He watched as she grabbed for anything she could to hold on to and her tits bounced each time he slid in and out of her. Liv panted over and over again, enjoying every second of what Jackson was giving her and Jackson felt the same. This was different to the other times; he didn't think he'd get tired of being inside her and watching her body react every time he touched her.

"Jax" she moaned, making his dick twitch again, and he leaned down to kiss her. She met his tongue with hers, and he wasn't willing to wait any longer. Jackson took his time fucking her with long hard strokes and before he knew it, he was moaning her name and experiencing the most intense orgasm of his life whilst she bit on his lip and screamed through another orgasm. His legs tensed when he gave her the last few strokes he had, and Liv rode out her own orgasm with his still inside her.

"Fucking hell" he said, leaning down to kiss her head as he removed himself from between her legs and laid beside her. "You're gonna be the death of me," he laughed, as she made herself comfortable on his chest.

36.

Liv lay lifeless with her leg draped over Jackson, still unable to catch her breath and couldn't believe she'd fucked up. She didn't want to ruin the moment, but she knew they hadn't used protection, and she was starting to panic.

"You okay?" He asked stroking her leg.

"I need to tell you something" she muttered.

"Okay?" He asked as she sat up to face him.

"I'm not on anything.." she said, and Jackson looked at her confused, "like contraception wise"

"Fuck. I'm sorry, Liv I didn't even think" he said getting up and finding his boxers. He thrust his legs through them in a panic which wasn't helping Liv keep calm, but the most worrying thing was the look on his face.

"It's my fault, I can go to the chemist tomorrow and get the morning after pill, I should've said but I got caught up in the moment and..." she was too embarrassed to finish what she was going to say and knew how bad she'd fucked up. Condoms should have been the first thing she'd asked about, but after the first orgasm she could barely think straight.

"It's fine" he smiled, kissing her, but it hurt worse when he left the room without saying anything else.

She pulled the covers up over her whilst the room sat empty and dark. She couldn't believe she'd fucked things up already by being so stupid. She'd wanted to know whether contraception was something she needed to think about if this was going to be a regular thing, but judging by the look of Jackson's face, it looked like it was over before it began.

Liv refused to cry and decided it was time to leave instead. She found the boxers somewhere in the quilt and hoisted them on before finding the t-shirt she'd been wearing and heading to the bathroom. She didn't understand how she'd gone from feeling on top of the world to feeling like nothing in a matter of seconds, and the tears came even though she didn't want them to.

She heard the door open and wiped her face quickly before Jackson come towards her. "I'm really sorry Jax, I'll go home and I'll go to the chemist tomorrow and fix it" she said quietly.

Jackson wiped her cheek and lifted her up again and heading back towards the bed.

"Why are you crying, and why do you want to leave?" He said, sitting down and straddling her on top of him before rubbing his thumb over her cheek.

"I just feel like I've fucked it all up and I don't want you to be mad about it"

"What? I'm not mad, Liv, I'm the one who should be sorry, I should have asked, or better yet, I should've used a condom, but I got carried away. This is my fault"

"You looked really mad and then you left the room" she mumbled, pouting.

"I'm sorry. Look, shit happens, we will deal with it" he shrugged lifting her chin up, "besides we'd have good looking kids anyway".

Liv laughed and shook her head. If he fucked her that good again, then she'd probably agree to kids in all fairness, she thought, but she was definitely getting ahead of herself. She kissed him again, and felt his dick twitch beneath her, earning an eye roll and him muttering something about his dick not behaving.

"I got you something" he said nodding towards the drawers and lifting her off his lap, "that's why I left the room" Jackson picked up the flowers he'd bought her, and handed them to her with a glass of champagne with strawberries in it, before grabbing his own.

"To first times" he winked lifting his glass, and Liv joined him before taking a sip and blushing at the memory of her first orgasm.

The night became a blur of sex, food and alcohol in the end. Jackson had agreed to take Liv to the chemist the next day so they figured while they had the opportunity, they may as well fuck as much as they possibly could. He had her in the shower, on the sofa, and in his bed multiple times through the night, and by the morning he was aching.

When he finally woke up it was 10:00 in the morning but he knew better than to even try and stir Liv. She'd already warned him that she didn't plan on moving all day, so he left her in his bed, found some boxers and some lounge pants and went downstairs to assess the damage from the night before. There were still glasses on the kitchen side, and plates of food they'd half eaten. Clothes were on the floor as were cushions in the lounge, and he couldn't remember a time when the house had ever looked so messy, even with a teenager.

Jackson put Soccer AM on in the background and got to work on tidying, whilst his mind drifted back to the night before. He still couldn't believe he hadn't been careful with her. He'd never been reckless with the women he slept with, he'd always used protection or at least come to an agreement that they were on contraception and that he didn't have to worry about unplanned pregnancies. But what he really didn't understand was, why he didn't care?

If somebody else had told them that they weren't on contraception, he would have hit the roof. He'd never even considered the idea of having more kids, but when Liv told him last night, he didn't care. He wasn't scared of committing to her on any level. There was no way that he wanted to jump straight in and have kids, but he wasn't put off by the idea, and it was the first time he'd ever imagined his future with a woman in it. He didn't want to scare her off, but he also wanted her to know that he wanted her completely.

Jackson was still tidying up when the door went, and Joe walked in not long after, obviously using the spare key he had.

"What the fuck went on here?" he asked raising his eyebrows at the mess in the kitchen and the lounge as he peered in.

"What are you doing here?" Jackson asked grabbing himself some water out the fridge and leaning against the counter.

"You weren't answering my texts, and when I called your phone was off so I figured I would come and check on you. You're never AWOL?"

"I've been busy"

"I can see. Is everything okay?" he asked pulling up a stool and sitting at the island.

"Yeah, fine?"

"So why does your house look like a pigsty and why is there blood on your carpet in the hallway?"

"Because I haven't tidied it yet? And I accidentally cut myself. Why are you interrogating me?"

"I just worry about you" he shrugged, "I am your older brother, it's my job"

"You are literally 6 minutes older than me Joe, and honestly I'm fine, but if you don't need me for anything, can you leave?"

"Why are you trying to get rid of me? And where's Clayton?"

"I'm not, I'm trying to tidy up because I've got stuff to do today, and Clayton stayed at Holly's last night. He's coming back tomorrow?"

Liv must have woken up at the noise, because the toilet flushed and Joe looked at Jackson accusingly before darting for the stairs.

"DON'T BE A DICK!" Jax shouted chasing him out of the kitchen, but Joe was already halfway up the stairs before he caught up and swiped his foot making him fall face first.

"OW!" Joe shouted, kicking behind him and crawling up the rest of the way whilst Jackson clung to his legs, trying to drag him off whilst he laughed hysterically.

Liv heard the commotion as soon as she'd got back in bed and jumped out to see what was going on, wincing at the pain that shot through her foot again. She quickly threw a t-shirt on, and the boxers that were on the floor and hobbled to the stairs where she saw two versions of Jackson scrapping with each other. Both of them stopped when they saw her and Liv raised her eyebrows.

"Jackson was being secretive!" Joe blurted out, nudging his brother in the side.

"No, I wasn't!" he said "I just didn't feel the need to tell you that Liv was here as I knew you'd do something stupid, like this!"

Liv looked at them both whilst they got to their feet, rolled her eyes and went back to the bedroom. She had no intention of being up before midday, but now she had no choice due to the fucking morons and they're childish nature. She heard them bickering down the stairs and grabbed her phone before following after them slowly still pissed that she ever cut her foot open.

"Morning," she said, joining Joe at the island and smiling over to Jackson who already had the coffee machine on the go.

"Morn-" Joe started, but Jackson and Liv both looked at him disapprovingly.

"Look, I'm sorry for kissing you the other night. If I knew Jackson liked you, liked you I wouldn't have" Joe shrugged.

"Liked me, liked me?" Liv asked raising an eyebrow again whilst Jackson stirred her coffee and sniggered in the background.

"You know what I mean. I'm sorry"

"Uh huh, apology accepted" she said, "to be fair, you should apologise for that kiss even if he didn't 'like me, like me' because it was fucking awful"

"Excuse me?" Joe gasped whilst Jackson laughed so hard, he pulled a muscle. Joe sat gobsmacked next to Liv who accepted her coffee gratefully acutely aware she was going to need extra caffeine after the night she'd had.

"You heard the lady" Jackson shrugged and Joe threw him a look of disgust.

"Well, she was quite obviously pissed and doesn't remember, but I can show you agai-"

"I swear to God, if you touch me again, I will actually cut you" Liv laughed as Joe edged in closer on the stool. She could already tell that they were going to get on. He seemed like a wind-up merchant like her, and she would definitely have to find a way to get her own back on him.

"So, you making breakfast then?" Joe asked, as Jackson pottered around the kitchen, still trying to tidy the mess from the night before, "and what kind of kinky shit did you two get up to that left blood all up the stairs and bandages on your feet?"

Liv almost choked on her coffee, but Jackson just rolled his eyes and refused to even acknowledge the question. Liv started turning red and shied away whilst Joe sat and stared at her.

"There was no kinky business. I told him he needed to make an honest woman out of me first and so we called it a day and went to sleep".

"Uh huh" Joe pondered, "and the claw marks down his back came from one of Carol Baskin's pets yeah?"

Liv went red again and heard Jackson sniggering again as he loaded the dishwasher.

"On that note, I'll leave you two to get back to consummating the marriage, and wait for you to tell me all about it Jax" he said getting to his feet and leaning over Liv's shoulder, "in detail"

Liv elbowed him in the stomach playfully before he left, and Jackson saw him out. She ignored their brief exchange, and Joe's jibes about her at the door, and scrolled through her phone and the

15 messages from Jade asking what happened, if she was up, why she hadn't called yet and what time she could see her.

She tapped out a message quickly saying that she would call her soon and Jackson returned to the kitchen where he kissed her neck and joined her at the island. Now Joe was gone, Liv could enjoy him all over again and planned to take advantage of the fact that she was awake.

"How'd you sleep?" he said as she climbed on to his lap and kissed his neck.

"Like a log" she muttered, "why are we up?"

"I was tidying, and I was going to bring you breakfast in bed" he said, tilting his head so she could work her way down.

"Well, unless breakfast consists of what's currently pressing against my ass" she said, teasing him with her tongue, "I'm not interested"

Jackson laughed and picked her up before heading back to the stairs to bed where she devoured everything he had to offer for breakfast.

37.

Rachael still hadn't slept and could feel herself slipping into a bad place again. Since she was young, she'd never been able to fit in properly, and had always pushed people away. Her family had stayed by her because they were family, but everyone else had always left her in the end. Everyone apart from Jackson.

Jackson had always understood her and understood what it was like. He had always been the one to pick up the pieces when everyone else walked out on her, helped her get back to herself, but now he wasn't there for her either. Now he'd abandoned her too, and she was losing it. He'd promised her from the very beginning that he'd always be there, and now that he wasn't, she didn't know what to do.

She knew that he loved her in a weird kind of way, but it was real to her. She knew that he was the only one who could fix her, keep her sane, and she wasn't about to let that all go. She knew that with him, she could be 'normal' and that is all that she wanted, she just had to make him see.

When she had introduced herself to Clayton, it was because she knew he was scared to take the leap. He didn't want Clayton feeling left out, but she would never have done that. She would have welcomed him with open arms and they could have been a family, Jackson just needed to see that it was possible, and stop closing himself off to the opportunity.

Rachael threw her meds at the wall frustrated because the more she thought, the more she fought with her own emotions. She needed to sort herself out, get dressed and find Jackson to talk this through. He might have thought he loved this other woman, but she didn't know him, and if she couldn't speak sense into Jackson, then she would speak sense into her.

Rachael showered, dressed, and attempted to cover the dark circles under her eyes with make up before finding her car keys. She knew he would protest, but she would make him see that they were meant to be together, she had to, because she had no idea how she was supposed to live without him.

38.

Liv answered her phone in a daze after drifting off again in bed, but Jackson was nowhere to be seen.

"Hello?"

"Is there any adequate reason that you can give me as to why it is midday, and I am only just hearing your voice!" Jade said less than impressed.

"Tired" Liv muttered in response.

"I fucking bet you are! Was it amazing?! Did you do it?!"

"Yes, and yes" she yawned down the phone. She appreciated Jade's enthusiasm but she was too tired to hold the conversation.

"Well, you need to get your ass in gear. I hate to be the bearer of bad news, but we have to go and see your shithead ex and get your stuff"

Liv had completely forgotten about speaking to Tommy the day before and wasn't up for him ruining her state of euphoria plus, she had to get to the chemist ASAP after multiple rounds with Jackson.

"I need to go to the pharmacy" she muttered embarrassed.

"Oh Liv..." and she could envision Jade rolling her eyes as she said it.

"It just happened!" she said defending herself, and she wasn't lying. She couldn't help herself last night when Jackson was on top of her, and she'd do it 100 times over again too.

"I know it happens! But you don't know where he's been or if he's clean! Have you asked?"

But Liv hadn't considered that either and was kicking herself again.

"Look, don't stress, do you want me to come and pick you up?"

"Yeah, let me just go and speak to Jax and then we will go okay? I'll text you the address, but give me an hour"

Liv found some clothes, again, and made her way downstairs where Jackson was sat at the island tapping away at his laptop. She kissed him on the cheek and wrapped her arms around his shoulders whilst he shut down the screen he was on and looked up at her.

"Whatcha doing?" she asked, suspicious of his quick minimisation of tabs.

"Well, I'm planning something that's a surprise, but depends on whether you're up for it, or whether you're dumping me already"

"I'm not dumping you, but what's the surprise?"

"It wouldn't be a surprise if I told you would it"

"Very true" she said kissing him again and sitting down, whilst he got up and went to the coffee machine.

"What's up?" He asked, staring at her from across the kitchen, and she looked at him confused, "you shake your foot when you're thinking. You do it when you're with Clayton, and when we spoke in the car that time, and when I came to parents evening" he shrugged.

"Huh, figures you'd remember something like that" she smiled. "Erm… So, obviously I know we spoke last night about going to the chemist and stuff" she mumbled.

"Yeah?"

"Well, this might sound rude, but do I need to go to the clinic too?" she asked, acutely aware that her face was beetroot. She was embarrassed that she'd even had to ask the question, and embarrassed she hadn't even considered it until Jade said.

"No Liv," he laughed, grabbing the milk out of the fridge, and shaking his head "I'm clean, I promise. I'm usually really careful, and I really am sorry that I wasn't las night. But, if it makes you feel better I will go and get checked?"

"Course not, I trust you, I just don't know how this all works and-"

"And you're worried about the amount of women I've been with?" he finished, bringing her coffee to her and kissing her again, but Liv shook her head. "As far as I know I'm completely clean Liv, but I will get booked in next week to be sure, okay?"

"Honestly Jax, you don't have to do that, I just figured I should ask. I mean, maybe I should be tested? You're the first person I've slept with in almost a year, but it turns out Tommy was cheating on me and so how do I know?" she started ranting.

"Liv, stop panicking" he reassured her, "I'm not planning on sleeping with anyone else, so I'll get tested okay. Let's go get lunch and we will go to the chemist whilst we are out?"

"I told Jade she could pick me up. Tommy called yesterday didn't he?"

"Yeah?"

"Well, the woman he cheated on me with is currently living in my house, which we were supposed to be selling…"

"Okay?"

"Turns out, she's pregnant, well she was pregnant before we split up, and now he doesn't want to sell the house, but wants my stuff out, so I have to go and pick it up"

"What?! It's your house?! He can't just dictate whether or not you can sell it"

"What choice do I have? I can't put her out on the street" she shrugged, fighting back tears again. She wasn't upset, she was frustrated. Frustrated that not being able to sell the home meant limiting her options, not being able to find her own place anytime soon and staying with Owen for even longer.

"Have you got legal advice?" he asked concerned, but Liv shook her head, "I know some people who owe me favours so I'll pull some strings on Monday, don't worry okay?"

Liv nodded, smiled up at him and leaned in to kiss him which seemed to be her new favourite thing to do.

"Ring Jade and tell her to meet you here and I'll drive you both to Tommy's. You two can go get some drinks after whilst I sort some things out?" he suggested, and Liv agreed. She didn't think he was genuinely giving her a choice, but either way she was happy that he'd be with her.

"I assume you told Jade you need to go to the chemist too? Maybe get her to grab some clothes and shoes that you'll be able to wear, or see if she can buy the pill from the chemist before she comes? I don't know how it works"

Liv agreed and called Jade to make arrangements, whilst Jackson busied himself upstairs, then left the kitchen to finally get herself ready for the day, feeling a little lighter than she had before they spoke.

Jade arrived after an hour and Jackson let her in.

"Can I get you a drink or something?" he asked sheepishly when Jade narrowed her eyes at him and looked him up and down.

"Liv's already told me you've told us to go for cocktails, so I'll save myself" she smiled, "where is she?"

"Er, she's upstairs, she just got out the bath. I've got to make some phone calls but let me know when you're ready to go and I'll be ready" he said gesturing towards the stairs and heading back to the kitchen.

Jade followed Liv's voice when she called and found her in the bathroom off of Jackson's room.

"Well, well, well" she said wiggling her eyebrows up and down suggestively, making Liv rolled her eyes "How are you feeling?"

Liv and Jade both laughed before Jade got comfy on the bed and let Liv get changed into the clothes she'd bought over for her. She wasted no time in demanding that she told her everything, so Liv reeled off about the past 2 days whilst Jade 'ooh'd' and 'aww'd' in all the right places.

"So, you've really never orgasmed before?" she laughed, sounding genuinely confused.

"It's not funny! I thought I had?! But it was different with Jackson than it was with Tommy, 1000x different!"

"Well, I've got your pill, however, what are you going to do for contraception? You can't just keep shagging and not be on anything, and if you two are gonna be in a relationship, you don't want to have to root around for a condom every time you want to fuck? Even saying it sounds like a fucking chore!" Jade muttered.

Liv hadn't thought about it. They were going to have to use condoms for now, but if the night before was anything to go by, she couldn't be sure that they'd remember every time. It just happened naturally, and she didn't want it to feel forced. She was going to have to go to the doctor in the week, but she was going to talk to Jackson first. She didn't want to go another hour without sex, let alone however long it was going to take her to get contraception sorted, and she was pretty certain that Jackson would agree too.

Once she was dressed and Jade had stopped reading her the riot act, they went downstairs where Jackson was pacing at the other end of the kitchen on the phone. Liv was still struggling with her feet and didn't know how successful she was going to be carrying anything at the house, but she knew wanted it over and done with so she could get on with her life and move on.

When Jackson saw them both standing there he smiled and ended his phone call. Liv's breath caught as she drank in the sight of him strolling towards them and they locked eyes.

"Ready to go?" he asked, leaning in to kiss her cheek whilst Jade fake gagged beside them. Liv swatted her arm playfully before nodding at Jackson who laughed.

"Let me grab my things and I'll meet you by the car" he said, kissing her again and earning another gag from Jade, who narrowly avoided Liv's second swipe at her.

"Can you stop!" she muttered, as they left the kitchen and Jackson to do whatever he needed to.

"You got it bad girl" she laughed, "so, so bad"

39.

Jackson drove with Liv by his side and Jade behind him who'd been discussing Harry. Apparently they were regularly texting, but Jackson didn't feel the need to get involved until she put it on him.

"So, is Harry as nice as he seems? Or is he just good at blagging over text?" she said leaning between the seats to get a better gauge on his response.

"He's a genuine guy. Out of all the people I know he gives the best advice, and he's frustratingly honest" Jackson said without missing a beat.

"Well Liv, looks like you partnered with the wrong one" she said, but Jackson side eyed her angrily making them both laugh.

"If he's so honest, then why is he single?" Liv asked before Jade even got the chance too. She'd dressed up for the occasion in jeans and a fitted top with her hair in a high bun. Her face was pristine as usual, and Jackson was aware of how easily she found it talking to people.

"He has high standards" he said shrugging.

"Is that an insult?" Jade retorted.

"No. of course not" he laughed, "Harry is a proper gent, but he won't settle down with anyone he doesn't see a future with or that he has to tame. He likes a lady."

"Interesting" she muttered, "Well, that's me fucked"

They all laughed, and Jackson went on to tell her stories of what a good guy he was and how he helped him through a lot through the years. Jade wasn't convinced that she was the kind of girl for him, but Jackson thought he could use someone who was carefree and exciting. He said that most of the women he'd dated fizzled out because he got bored, but he always went for boring women, so it wasn't a surprise. Jackson had met a few over the years and they'd all been nice, but none of them had seemed 'fun'. Jax thought that Jade would keep Harry on his toes, but he didn't know if she was the type he'd go for.

As they neared the house, Jax watched Liv's foot start to shake irritably when they and he could tell she didn't want to be there, and neither did he. Part of him didn't want to intrude on the situation between her and her ex, part of him wanted to thank him for being a prick and giving him the opportunity to pursue her, and part of him wanted to make him hurt for hurting her. He didn't know which part was going to win, but he knew he wanted to support her in any way he could.

He pulled up outside the house, the same house he'd had to carry her too the first time they met and he smiled, although Liv wasn't impressed when she noticed.

"I'm only smiling because I remember having to carry you to that doorstep" he said when she looked at him accusingly. She rolled her eyes and laughed before she got out of the car with Jade and Jackson told her to shout if she needed him. He didn't want to leave her, but he also didn't want her to think that he was overstepping the mark by getting involved.

He watched as she limped down the path and forced herself to stand up tall when she got to the door. She knocked politely, looking nervous, but Jade followed quickly after pounding with her fists and shouting "POLICE, OPEN UP!" whilst Liv tried desperately to stop her and Jackson laughed hysterically. He liked her.

Tommy answered the door quickly wondering what the fuck was going on but rolled his eyes when he saw Jade standing there with a sarcastic smile spread across her face before she let herself in.

"Why you got to be so fucking extra all the time Jade?!" he spat, and she stuck her middle finger up at him and placed it an inch from his face.

"Why you got to be an ugly, cheating bastard for Tommy" she griped, mimicking his tone of voice.

"Hurry up and get your stuff, I can't be fucking dealing with her today and Sarah will be back soon"

"By HER stuff do you mean the TV that's on the wall, the sofa's you've been shagging on and the bed you sleep in every fucking night you vile piece of shit, because if you don't, then we will take as long as we fucking need, fuck you very much" and with that Jade started picking up the sacks in the hallway with Liv's clothes in and headed back out to the car.

"I fucking always hated her" he said to Liv as she left but she wasn't interested.

"Think the feeling has always been mutual Tom. You're gonna have to carry some of this stuff out because I've cut my foot open".

"Let your bodyguard do it then" he said leaning against the doorframe and Liv rolled her eyes in frustration. She couldn't be bothered to argue with him, or even be in the same vicinity as him. The house she'd left wasn't the same as the house she was in. She'd wanted her home to be warm and cosy, and she prided herself on making sure she had warm colours through the house, deep creams and browns, with wood furniture and character, but that had been replaced with cold grey wallpapers and white modern tat. She was angry that he'd changed it without even telling her and frustrated that the more she looked, the more stuff she noticed missing.

"Where's the fuck is my furniture?!" she snapped, as she noticed the new table in the dining room was sleek white and silver, and her old farmhouse style table was missing along with the bench and high back cava chairs she'd spent a fortune on.

"Sarah wanted a change and you ignored all of my calls, so I got rid of it" he shrugged.

Liv inhaled deeply and counted to 10, repeatedly. She picked up a bag and a suitcase and started to wheel it out before she heard Jackson's voice and watch Tommy's body language change.

Tommy was short and stocky, so Jackson towered over him, making him look tiny. Tommy had dark blonde hair, and dark brown eyes but in comparison to Jackson he was nothing to look at. He stared at him confused as he entered the house and then even more so when he leaned down to take the bags from Liv and left again.

"Who's that? Your new shag?" Tommy spat at Jade as she headed for the stairs, but she didn't even look back as she answered unphased.

"Oh, I wish Hun, but he's not mine. He's Liv's"

Tommy looked from Jade to Liv who was blushing again, but not because she was embarrassed, because she'd been put on the spot. She waited for Jackson to come back in and without hesitation, introduced him to Tommy who looked like he'd been slapped across the face. Jade bolted back down the stairs looking furious and shouting again at Tommy.

"YOU BETTER FUCKING TELL ME THAT YOU'VE PUT ALL OF LIV'S STUFF IN STORAGE BECAUSE I CAN'T SEE ONE THING OF HERS UPSTAIRS?!" she demanded, and they all looked at him.

"Tommy?" Liv said, trying to stay calm "where's the rest of my stuff?"

"I told you, you wouldn't answer your phone, so Sarah got rid of it when we were decorating, I tried to call you for weeks and you fucking ignored me?!" he said, raising his voice.

"Let's go" Liv said turning away from him, but Jade hadn't finished.

"How fucking *dare* you have the cheek to 'get rid' of any of her stuff when the house *BELONGS* to her? *SHE* got the fucking mortgage, *SHE* spent thousands doing the house up, *SHE* spent the money getting the extension, all whilst you shovelled shit up your nose, went out every weekend, and fucked other women?! Now you're reaping the benefits with your slutty little mistress because she'd up the duff?! You are a fucking despicable and disgusting human being Tommy, I don't know how you can even look at yourself in the mirror and she's fucking lucky to be rid of you!" she shouted, and every fibre in her body was shaking.

But she wasn't wrong. Liv had saved and saved and saved to get the house exactly how she wanted it. She'd started from scratch, put hours of time and effort in every weekend and school holiday, and now everything she had worked for was gone. She was upset and angry, but she couldn't muster up the energy for an argument. Tommy had never hit her, but he'd belittled and bullied her plenty of times and she didn't think that would go down well in front of Jackson who was currently propped against the front door enjoying "The Jade show".

"Take your scummy mate, and your new fucking fella, and get the fuck out of my house Liv" he said pointing in her face, but before he could utter another word, Jackson was making his presence known and towering over him again.

"You might have felt able to belittle her when you were together, and judging by the way she shrinks when she's near you, I imagine you did, but I am telling you now, if you EVER raise a finger to Liv again, not only will you find yourself in a hospital bed, you'll find yourself and your pregnant girlfriend without this roof over your head too, because I will buy it, and will take great pleasure in forcibly removing you from the property. The ONLY reason you're still here is because Liv won't put a pregnant woman out on the street, but I gladly fucking will. Do we have an understanding?"

Liv watched as Tommy absorbed everything Jackson had to say and his face screwed into a frown. He wanted to argue back, Liv could tell, but he knew it wasn't a fight he was going to win and so he thought better of it.

"Just get out" he said avoiding eye contact with Jackson, but Jackson wasn't happy with the response and leaned in closer.

"Did I stutter? Do you understand?"

"Yes, I understand" he said through gritted teeth "Now can you please leave before Sarah gets back"

With that Jackson held out his hand for Liv's and they all left the house, with Jade purposely knocking over a lamp and some photo frames as she went, smiling as they smashed on the floor.

"Fuck you Tommy" she sang, flipping him the bird as she made her way out of the house, stomping through the flowerbeds as she did.

40.

Jackson dropped Liv and Jade off at the bar and went to the gym. He needed to let off some steam and he didn't know where else to go. He was going to cancel the date he had planned for Liv, but he figured that it would be good for her to have something to look forward to after the shit show at the house. Thoughts of what he wanted to do to Tommy for destroying all of her hard work plagued his thoughts as his feet hit the treadmill, and he was grateful that he didn't have to pretend to be okay in front of Liv when he wasn't.

He'd been content when he was with her, but now he wasn't, all he could think about was how angry he felt when Tommy had tried to belittle her, like she meant nothing. He wanted to hurt him, but he wasn't willing to risk Liv's respect. As he ran, he felt the tension in his body leave, but a voice he didn't want to hear, brought him back to reality, and got his back up again.

"I've been looking for you" Rachael said leaning on the treadmill as he jogged. He didn't have the patience anymore to fuck around with her, and she was really testing the little of it he had left.

"Well, you found me" he panted, not taking his eyes off of the view in front of him. Rachael slowed the treadmill, so he had no other option than to look at her, but he hopped off, grabbed his towel and found the weight bench instead.

"Can we talk?" she asked, following him around like a lost puppy, and earning looks from others in the gym since she was definitely not dressed for working out. Her long dark hair was pulled into a ponytail and she wore a fitted black dress with thigh

high boots. The dress stretched over her generous chest, and she'd chosen not to wear tights despite it being 4 degrees outside.

"Are you giving me a choice?" he asked, adjusting the weight on the bar at each end and lying back flat before he started chest presses.

"Well not really" she shrugged, straddling him in the middle of the gym, and leaning herself forward on to the bar pinning it against his chest.

"Get. Off. Of Me" he spat staring up at her, conscious of the fact that people in the gym were now staring at them even more.

"Not until we talk. Did you tell her?"

"Get off my lap, and I'll talk to you" he said through gritted teeth, as anger bubbled to the surface.

"You used to like me sitting on your lap Jax" she winked.

"CAN YOU GET THE FUCK OFF ME?!" he shouted, and suddenly everyone who wasn't looking at them now was. Rachael smirked, shifted her weight, and climbed off of him, whilst Jackson reset the bar and got up himself. He walked frustratedly over to a corner of the gym and she followed quickly after him, appreciating the glances as she did.

"Seriously Rach, I cannot do this anymore"

"Do what?"

"THIS! YOU?! You can't keep asking for us to work when we are never going to. I'm seeing someone else and I'm not going to let you fuck that up Rach. She knows about me, she knows about me and you, and she knows that I want to make it work with her. Why won't you just let me be happy?"

"Because I used to be the one that made you happy Jax. It wasn't *always* you picking up the pieces. I've been there for you as well!"

"Oh really? When?"

"You know what I mean Jax. She doesn't know you; you might think she does, but she doesn't, not like I do!"

"But she will, if you give me a chance to let her instead of turning up out of the blue whenever you can and trying to ruin it. Look Rach, I'm sorry that you're not happy, and I'm sorry that you haven't found someone to love you and every part of you, but I genuinely think I have, and I'm not throwing it away for something that would never work. You've never been the one for me, and deep down you know that as well as I do. You need to go home, and you need to grow up. I don't know how many times I can tell you that I don't love you, and I never have"

He watched the tears well up in her eyes, but he wasn't staying around to watch them fall. He needed the gym right now, but he couldn't whilst she was there, he needed to get away from her, and the sooner he was back with Liv, the sooner he'd feel calm, which he desperately needed.

41.

By the time Jackson was due to arrive, Liv was 4 cocktails deep and feeling it. She couldn't remember the last time she'd drunk 3 days in a row, but she was happy, and that's all that mattered. Jackson pulled up outside not long after they'd ordered their 5th drink and joined them at the bar shortly after. He leaned in and kissed Liv before taking a seat, but she could tell he wasn't himself.

"Everything o-oh shit" she said, stopping herself mid-sentence when she watched Rachael walk through the door, and figured the night was not going to end the way she thought it was.

"Mind if I join?" she asked rhetorically, pulling up a stool and joining them.

"And you are?" Jade said, raising an eyebrow but Rachael wasn't interested.

"I'm Rachael. You lied to me" she said glaring at Liv who was looking at Jackson begging him not to overreact with her eyes, but she could see he was losing whatever patience he had left.

"What the fuck are you doing here?!" he spat out, and Liv could see his knuckles turning white where he'd balled them up so tight.

"Calm your fucking tits Jax, it's not like I'm going to make a scene, but since we're all together, now we can all uncover where we stand and why you're shagging her but still entertaining me" she smiled. Jackson instinctively went to react put Liv put her hand on his leg under the table and squeezed hard. She didn't want this to tip him over the edge, and she didn't want her to get a rise out of him.

"That's a good question, but why don't we talk somewhere else, and you can stop trying to get a rise out of him and say whatever it is you think I need to hear directly to me?"

"Well, isn't someone a big girl. Off you fuck then" she smiled at Jackson, but he wasn't willing to leave Liv. Liv looked at Jade, and Jade looked at Jax, but it didn't seem like either of them were comfortable letting her sit with Rachael alone.

"I promise if I need you, I'll shout" she said, which earnt an eye roll from Rachael and an exasperated look from Jax. He leaned in and kissed her, which had Rachael scowling then found a table in the window with Jade and refused to take his eyes off of them.

"Trust me Jax, she can hold her own" Jade told him as his hands balled into fists again, before signalling the waiter for some more drinks, "She's only doing this for you, so let her" she smiled, patting his hand and throwing him a sympathetic look.

"So, what is it you so desperately want to tell me" Liv asked, before sipping her drink and watching as Rachael glared at her.

"That it's not going to work between you and him" she smirked.

"And why's that?" Liv asked, raising an eyebrow and leaning back on her chair.

"He might *think* that he loves you, but that's because you're shiny and new. You don't know the real him, the scary him, and

Jackson when he's at his worst, but I do. I've picked up the pieces time and time again, I've peeled him off the floor when he's hit rock bottom and I know when the day comes that you see the worst in him, you'll leave anyway" she shrugged.

"Says who"

"What, you think you won't?"

"Look, you're entitled to your opinion. I've heard the way Jackson talks about you. I know he cares about you, but I also know that he thinks you're getting in the way of his chance at happiness? If you love him, how is that fair?"

"Because it's an illusion, it's not real happiness. He enjoys the chase, enjoys the sex, but he doesn't enjoy everything else that comes with a relationship. You're another fling to him, and you should see that before you get hurt"

"Uh huh, and what were you?" she asked as Rachael ordered from the bartender and returned to their conversation,

"More than he's making out I was I imagine"

"So, you're here because you don't want my feelings to get hurt? You're just looking out for me? Do me a favour. What do you want? Because if you're hoping to get Jackson back, this isn't the way to do it, by getting in the way when he's trying really hard to move on with his life. You think I'll leave because he's gonna have bad days, don't we fucking all? You've had your 5 minutes of fun, you've asked for him back, and he's told you to fuck off.

Intimidating me isn't going to work, or are you just trying to get a rise out of him, so I can see what he's really like?"

Rachael was smirking at her and didn't look like she was phased in the slightest by Liv's onslaught as the waiter brought over shots and proceeded to light them.

"Maybe you're right," she said getting from her stool, and leaning in towards her "but if you think I'm going to watch him be happy with somebody else, you're mistaken Liv" and with that she pushed the tray from the table and multiple flaming tequilas landed in Liv's lap, igniting her clothes and making her scream.

42.

Jackson heard her scream and ran straight towards her, but Rachael was already out the door. Liv was hopping around, trying to get out of her clothes, whilst the barman had taken the soda streamer and aimed it straight at her, drenching her and the floor. Customers had crowded around in an effort to help, blocking Jackson from getting to her as quick as he wanted to but when he did, he inspected every inch of her.

"WHAT THE FUCK?!" Liv shouted making to leave after Rachael, but Jackson stopped her and sat her down. He needed to make sure she was okay, but Liv was too angry to let him.

"Jade! Get him off me! Or go and drag her back here!" she shouted fighting against him as he held her, "Jackson, I'm fine! I'm not burnt, I'm pissed!"

"Liv. Let, me, look!" he screamed. Liv stopped still and stared at him angrily. "Is there somewhere we can go?" he shot at the bartender, and he pointed towards the back which they followed.

Liv was shaking and Jackson didn't know whether it was from the cold, or from the shock, but either way he wasn't happy. He was losing it, but he had to keep it together in front of Liv for now.

"Jackson, seriously I'm okay. My belly and my hands sting a bit but it's not bad, most of it got on my blazer and I got it off quick. Now can we go and fucking find her so I can try and set her on fire too!" she said as Jackson lifted up her top and assessed the damage. She wasn't wrong, she'd been lucky. Compared to what it could have been, Liv had got off lightly and other than some minor red inflammation, she seemed okay. There were no blisters or bleeding, and Jackson was just happy that she was okay.

He got up and made to leave but Liv grabbed him by the wrist, stopping him in his tracks.

"No. You don't get to decide when you leave after this, I do. You're going to take me home because I can't take any more freak accidents happening, especially out in public, and you're going to make me feel better after a shitty fucking day, okay?" she asked, but Jackson's expression was blank.

"Okay?!" she asked again, and he nodded. "You don't get to close off to me because your ex is a psycho bitch. That's what she wants, and we aren't giving it to her. Now, come kiss me better"

But Jackson hesitated, and Liv caught it. He didn't know what to do, he couldn't put her at risk just because he wanted to be with her, and he didn't want Rachael to keep hurting the people he loved either.

"Jackson? Talk to me"

"I just don't want to put you at risk Liv, I need to sort Rachael –"

"No, what you need to do, is take me home. You don't get to decide when it's too much for me! I do" she cried, "I spent 8 years being treated like shit, with someone who never wanted commitment from me, but would happily find it with someone else. 8 years of feeling like I wasn't good enough, of being unhappy, and never doing anything about it! So, if you think I'm going to just let you walk out on me because of something *I* haven't done, when I am happier than I ever have been, then you've got another think coming! Now, take me home!"

Jackson watched tears fall down her face and heard the emotion in her voice. He could tell she was hurt, but not by what Rachael did, by what she knew Jackson was thinking of doing. He wanted her to be happy, and he didn't want that to mean having to worry about Rachael every minute of the day.

"Okay" he said kissing her head and leading her out of the bar where Jade was stood demanding that the incident was reported to the police and the CCTV footage given to them too. Jackson settled the tab, walked them both out to the car, and drove back to the house in silence debating what he was going to do. In his mind, there was only one option, but the thought of giving up a chance with Liv wasn't something he wanted to consider.

43.

Jackson become distant after the incident, and Liv didn't know what she had to do to fix things. Over the next few days, he didn't ask to see her at all, didn't make plans for the weekend and didn't reach out unless she text him first. He'd say that he missed her too, but whenever she asked to see him, he'd say that work was busy, or he was doing something with Clayton, which was fine, she just couldn't help but feel like he was pushing her away because of what happened.

Her feet were feeling better and finally healing up, but the red burns were still sore when she got in the bath or the shower. Liv considered that it might be for the best that they called it off because she couldn't take many more of these injuries leaving her feeling disabled. On Wednesday morning, she woke up to a text from Jackson for the first time in days, but it wasn't what she expected.

He told her that he could feel himself slipping, and so he was going away for a few days to get himself back on track. He didn't say where, but he said that he would see her when he got back and that they would talk. He said he missed her, and he was sorry, but he didn't know what to do. He was scared to lose her, but even more scared about what Rachael would do if he stayed with her, and he couldn't bear the thought of her coming to harm just because of him.

Liv had tried to reply, and had tried to call him, but nothing was going through. She wanted to give him space and respect his decision, but she also didn't want him to think that she didn't care and she was worried about him. He'd promised he'd tell her when he was slipping, but she wanted to be there to help, not just sat on the side-lines waiting for him to come back to her. She wasn't prepared to wait, and she wasn't prepared to put herself through the torment any longer. She was going to find him, and she was going to tell him that she wanted him, with or without Rachael as baggage. They were either going to do it, or they weren't, and she wasn't going to be left on hold guessing whether or not he wanted to try.

44.

As Jackson drove, he considered his options. There was no denying he wanted Liv, she was all he could think about, but he couldn't be with her whilst Rachael was in the state she was in. He knew her well enough to know that she'd stopped taking her meds, and he knew that it wouldn't be long until she was at her worst, he just didn't want Liv to be on the receiving end of that.

He needed time to think, and that meant time away from everything. Time away from work, time away from Liv (begrudgingly), and time away from Clayton too, who he'd sent away with Joe for a few days. There hadn't been many times that he'd needed this so bad, but if he was going to make the right decision, he needed to keep a level head.

Jackson pulled into to the wellness spa and parked up before grabbing his case and heading for the reception. He'd booked in for 3 nights and had no other plans than hitting the gym and chilling out. He'd brought his laptop in case work needed him, but when he'd told Harry what had happened with Rachael, he'd insisted he take time off.

They'd completed the interviews for the new team, so the rest of the week he could afford to go away, and it was what he needed. He needed to find some clarity, but he couldn't help but think he'd rather be there with Liv. After collecting his key card, he found his way to the hotel room and threw down his bags before heading to turn on the shower. The room was big, but he hadn't asked for anything fancy, it was just him after all and he only needed somewhere to sleep. The bed was piled high with pillows in the centre of the room, with a large TV directly opposite, but not much else other than some bedtime cabinets. The windows were floor to ceiling and looked out on the grounds which held a golf course and swimming pool, which didn't look like it was getting utilised very much with the current weather.

The weather was dreary and grey, like his mood, and as the rain drizzled down the window his thoughts turned to Liv again. He should have just asked her to come, should have just spent the few days away with her, but he didn't know what to say. He didn't want to ask her to commit to him, because he was scared of the answer. He didn't want to be putting her in harm's way, and he certainly didn't want Rachael doing anything stupid again. He knew he was going to have to walk away from her, but he couldn't bear the thought of not being with her and missing out on the woman of his dreams because of someone he knew when he was a completely different person.

Jackson finally got in the shower and let the water wash over him whilst he tried to convince himself that what he was doing was right but the more he thought, the worse he felt. He was second guessing whether the retreat was a good idea after all, but something was telling him it wasn't, something was telling him he needed Liv and that this break away was another way of him pulling away and fucking things up.

...

"Liv, he left to get away from everything" Harry said to her as she begged down the phone.

"I get that, but I'm worried about him. He's barely spoken to me in days and now he's unreachable. I'm *begging Harry, just tell me where he's gone because I'm going mad sitting here thinking he hates me and he's going to call things off, I just want to know where I stand"* she pleaded.

"He doesn't hate you Liv, it's the complete opposite and that's why he doesn't know what to do"

"Then let me go and see him! I can't wait for days for him to make some stupid decision because of Rachael, and I won't let her win! Or ruin his life for that matter"

"He's going to kill me" Harry sighed exasperated before reeling off the details to the retreat Jackson had booked the day before, telling her it was her own funeral, *"I hope you can talk some sense into him Liv. But please don't count on it, he's in a bad place, and I haven't seen him like this in a long time"*

"Thank you Harry, I promise I'll fix it"

"I'll call them and ask them to get you a room ready. It's going to be late by the time you get there and at least if it doesn't go 100% with Jax you don't have to worry about driving all the way back" he said, and with that he hung up.

Liv rooted through her wardrobe and packed an overnight bag along with a dress she thought would be suitable for dinner. When it was done, she jumped in her car without even thinking, ready to drive the next 2 hours to the middle of nowhere.

45.

Jackson had spent 4 hours in the gym, but it did nothing to lift the weight from his shoulders. He was just going to go back to the room, check in on Clayton and order room service before he slept, and sleep would come easy given the session he'd just put in. Tomorrow he would book in for a massage and hope that he'd have some idea of what the fuck he was planning on doing with his life.

He got back and showered quickly before grabbing his work phone out of the bag and calling Joe. Him and Clayton had gone into London to watch the football and he wanted to catch them before the match, but Joe's phone went straight through to answerphone. He toyed with the idea of calling Liv, but he told himself that the reason he'd got away was so that she could get some clarity, as well as him. Instead, he chucked his phone back on the bed, turned on the TV and browsed the menu before calling down to reception.

"Can I order room service please?"

"Of course, what's your room number?"

"34"

"Oh, Mr. Cotts?"

"Yes?"

"Your business partner called earlier today and has booked you a table in the restaurant at 6:00. He said to let you know that it's important that you attend. We did try calling a few times, but you weren't in your room".

"Harry?"

"He didn't leave a name Sir; he just booked the table in the a la carte restaurant and asked us to inform you to be there at 6:00 I'm afraid"

"Okay, thanks" he said, rolling his eyes and checking his watch. It was already 5:30, and he hadn't intended on having to dress up for dinner. Jackson called Harry's phone, but it went straight through to answerphone which wasn't surprising since they were in the middle of nowhere. He rummaged through his case and found himself some jeans and a shirt, then spruced up his hair in the bathroom and headed down to the restaurant to grab a drink before he got there and he could ask what the hell was going on.

The head of house showed him to a table of two in the corner of the restaurant and he took a seat before ordering himself a drink and a bottle of wine for the table. He browsed through the a la carte menu and checked his watch again wondering why Harry had bothered booking a table for 6:00 when he was going to be late, and why whatever he had to say couldn't have been put in an email either.

As he waited, he glanced around the room and took in the décor. The restaurant was nice, but Jackson hadn't planned on attending whilst he was at the retreat. He always attracted the wrong attention, even in places like this, and women were a distraction he didn't need or want. Not when the woman of his dreams was waiting at home and he was currently giving her the cold shoulder. Jackson got his phone out and figured he wasn't doing her any favours by ignoring her. It wasn't her fault he was cold and standoffish, but he didn't know another way to be. Being in a serious relationship scared him, especially given his history and the risk of Rachael rearing her ugly head again.

Whilst he toyed with the idea of texting her, he browsed through the photos that he'd taken over the weekend. Some when they were drunk pulling silly faces at the screen, others in bed when they'd just woke up, and some that he'd sneakily taken of her sleeping, sprawled across the bed. She really was beautiful, and he didn't know if he was willing to completely ignore that fact that he loved her, at least he thought that's what it was.

He thought about her constantly and when he wasn't with her, he felt like something was missing. He'd have dinner with Harry, tell him that he realised he'd fucked up, and then drive straight to Liv's and ask her to forgive him, because if she didn't, he didn't know what he was supposed to do. He just wanted to see her, and he didn't want to wait.

He checked his watch again, growing impatient, when the waiter finally pulled out a chair bringing Jackson's attention back to the room, and to Liv's face staring back at him.

Before she'd left Harry had messaged her to say that he'd booked a table so she might want to dress for the occasion. Liv had decided on a silver strappy dress with white heels, drawn in at the waist with a white belt. She'd curled her hair, put some make up on, but still felt like she was underdressed when she walked in. Whilst she waited to be seated, she watched Jackson scroll through his phone, but he looked sad, and it hurt her to watch him. She wanted to run to him, but in the back of her mind, she was worried that this may have been a bad idea after all.

Liv took her seat and Jackson got to his feet to push her in, before he kissed her cheek, and suddenly, all the doubts she had melted away. She didn't know what to say first. She wanted to tell him he was an idiot for pushing her away, but she could see in his eyes that he hated himself more than she did right now.

"I can't believe you're here" he said taking his seat again and smiling over at her.

"I'm sorry" she said, as he poured her a drink and one for himself too, but Jackson didn't look mad, or upset, he looked just the opposite. The sad expression that she'd seen on his face before she got to the table had disappeared, and he was happy again.

"Honestly? I was coming home tonight because all I wanted was to be with you. I'm the one who should be sorry, sorry for pushing you away. I just don't know what else to do when things get hard, and it's not fair, because it isn't even anything you've done" he said, and Liv was glad that turning up hadn't been a mistake.

"Jackson, you don't get to decide what's best for us without talking to me, okay? I get that you're scared, but so am I. Take Rachael out of the picture completely, and ask yourself do you want to be with me?"

"More than anything"

"And do I make you happy? Because I'm always happy when I'm with you, and I've been absolutely miserable these last few days, but if you don't want this then I'll go and I'll leave you to get yourself back togeth-"

"You make me happy Liv" he said cutting her off, "so happy it scares me"

"Then can we just be together? No silly games, no running off when things get a little bit hard, and no pushing each other away. I just need you to tell me when somethings wrong, and we will fix it, together" she said as he held her hand and ran his thumb over her knuckles, "I don't need you to give me the world Jax, I don't care about your past, or money, or Rachael. I just need you to trust me enough to know that I won't run away on your bad days, and promise that you won't on mine either"

Jackson lifted her hand to his lips and kissed it softly, smiling as he did.

"I promise" he said, and she watched a smile break across his face which told her she might have just made the best decision of her life.

46.

Jackson forced himself to sit through dinner and drinks, but all he really wanted was to take Liv back to his room and apologise properly. After the failed date on Saturday, he was glad that they got to spend time together, but he just wanted to fall asleep next to her and actually sleep. He'd been spending hours at the gym in the mornings to try and burn off energy, but he hadn't been able to sleep properly since he spent the night with her on Friday. Every night when he'd tried to get some rest, he'd toss and turn, wanting to reach out, but telling himself it was wrong. Every night he would end up at war with himself, and every night, sleep evaded him.

Now he was with her, he knew it wouldn't be a problem. He knew he'd sleep soundly next to her, and that she'd give him the peace he was craving. He watched as she polished off dessert which he'd insisted she had, even when he declined, and still couldn't get over the fact she'd travelled so far, just to tell him he was wrong. He loved that about her, she always told him straight, and she never felt the need to mince her words to make him feel better.

He marvelled at the woman in front of him, and debated whether or not he'd be able to stop himself, but -

"Okay, I'm officially stuffed" she said, defeated after only half of the tiramisu she ordered, and Jackson laughed.

"So can we go to bed now?" he asked, signalling for the tab.

"Yes, but I have my own room to go back to" she shrugged, "since you worked so hard on avoiding me, Harry figured I better have somewhere to stay in case I was still dumped".

"You were never dumped," he said creasing his eyebrows, "I was just considering my options".

"And how did that go for you?"

"All roads led back to you" he said watching her as a blush crept over her cheeks and she chewed on her bottom lip. Jackson pulled out his chair and held out his hand to help her to her feet, before leading her back to his room.

"You want me to order drinks?" He asked when they arrived, but Liv wasn't interested. By the time he'd dropped the key on the side and drawn the curtains, she'd dropped her dress and was waiting for him.

Jackson looked her up and down hungrily and screwed his face up in frustration.
"Liv, I didn't know you were coming. I've got no condoms or anything with me, but I cannot physically sleep next to you like that and not touch you. Please find something to wear" he begged running his hand over his face watching her as she climbed on to the bed and crawled over to the headboard giving him a perfect view of her ass.

"Liv!" Jackson said, stomping towards his suitcase to find her some clothes.

"Jackson?"

"Seriously?"

"Seriously," she said pulling him by his shirt towards her and on to the bed. "If you don't want to touch me, that's fine, but you're not going to stop me. So, lie down please"

Jackson did as he was told, and Liv got to work on his shirt buttons whilst she straddled his lap. He might have said that he wasn't going to touch her, but the bulge growing beneath her said different. Liv pressed kisses along his chest, and down his stomach before she unbuttoned his jeans and ran her tongue above his boxer shorts.

"You sure you don't want it?" she whispered in his ear, but Jackson's will power had already failed him, and he flipped her onto her back so he could get his dick out quicker. Liv lay with her legs open and ran a finger over her clit whilst she watched him get out of his clothes, and he watched her pleasure herself in front of him.

"We can't keep doing this" he said, climbing on top of her, and kissing her neck.

"You promised you'd take me at my worst earlier" she panted as he teased her with his cock. Liv didn't even want the foreplay, she just wanted to feel him inside her again, but he was hesitating,

"Jackson, if you are not going to fuck me in the next 2 seconds, then get off, lay down, and let me fuck you" she said as he played with her earlobe and held her by her neck softly.

"Don't tempt me" he laughed running his hands down her body and she begged as he eased inch after inch inside of her.

"You want me to fuck you Liv?" he asked, barely moving, but even that was enough to make her moan. She nodded in agreement, but Jackson wasn't ready for that yet. He wanted to enjoy every second of it, and when he fucked her, he wanted her to feel the difference.

He moved inside her slowly and watched as her hands grabbed at what they could. Every time he pulled away and back again, he felt like the next stroke would be enough to make him cum, but he wanted this to last, and he wanted to watch her cum for him over and over again. Liv's legs moved instinctively when he changed position, so when he readjusted her ass, she draped her leg over his shoulder and pulled him down to kiss her. Jackson felt even deeper than before and Liv bit down on a pillow she'd grabbed from somewhere, to try and stifle the screams she was letting out.

Jackson felt the tension in her body come over her quickly and before he knew it, she was desperately trying to hold back an orgasm. He could feel the way her she got tighter around his cock and see her back arch up from the bed. He kissed her again, just like he had done before, knowing she'd give it up, and she did. Jackson watched as her eyes rolled back and she desperately clung to him whilst he moved, but he wanted more.

"Bend over" he said, pulling out and stroking his cock whilst she pulled herself together again.

"Really?" she panted, looking defeated, but Jackson wasn't finished with her yet. He nodded, and Liv rolled herself over and reared up on all fours whilst Jackson got himself in position behind her. Despite spending hours having sex over the weekend, he hadn't bent her over once, because he knew full well it was going to set him off.

He watched her move her hair from her neck and lower her shoulders to the bed so her back was arched down in front of him. Her ass was high in the air and his imagination was running wild with things he wanted to do to her, and for her. He ran one hand over her ass cheek whilst the other reached underneath to circle her clit. Liv moaned again whilst he played, but he needed to be inside of her. He hated himself for skipping on the foreplay, but right now all he wanted was to feel her wrapped tightly around his cock, watch as her ass bounced each and every time his cock slid inside of her, and listen to her beg him to fuck her harder, which she would. He wanted to tease her. Make her want it. And when she begged him to give it to her, he would, over and over again.

Jackson slid inside of her, and any hope he had of being in control evaporated. He moaned louder than her each and every time he drew back and slid inside of her, because being on top of her was nice, but this was something else. It wasn't just how good it felt to fuck her, it was the view he was looking at, the feel of her ass slapping against him over and over, and the look on her face as she turned back to watch him. Jackson thought he could make her wait, but he was wrong. Every single stroke was taking every ounce of his willpower not to lose it, but when she started moaning his name he couldn't hold out.

"Jax I'm gonna cum, don't stop" she begged, but he knew he couldn't stay inside of her. They'd already played it dangerous over the weekend, he couldn't risk it again and make her take another pill.

"Liv" he said, biting back the moan from escaping as her pussy got tighter, "I need to pull out, I've got nothing on"

"I'm begging Jax, harder, I'm so close" but he couldn't give it to her harder without risking another incident.

"Liv, I can't"

"I don't care Jackson, I'll take another pill, I want you to fuck me" she begged, and Jackson wasn't going to argue. He took hold of her waist either side and forced her to take his cock over and over again until she was screaming his name and he felt her orgasm run down his legs. As it did, she leaned herself back onto his lap, and sat there whilst his cock twitched inside of her, and he admitted defeat too. His hands run up her body and over her breasts whilst he waited for it to end, and both of them fell in a heap on the bed, breathless and tired.

47.

"We can't keep doing that" he said, out of breath whilst he ran his fingers up and down her back. Liv laid on his chest enjoying the moment, but they both knew he was right. They weren't naïve teenagers, and she knew better than to risk having unprotected sex, multiple times a night, multiple times a week.

"But when it feels that good, it's really hard to resist" she said looking up at him with big brown eyes, chewing her nail nervously. "Are you mad?"

"I'm not mad" he said furrowing his eyebrows at her, and shrugging "I'd fuck you like that every day for the rest of my life if I could, I just don't want you to get pregnant without wanting it"

"Wanting it?" she asked, propping herself up so she could see him better.

Jackson continued to run circles on the small of her back with his fingers whilst Liv watched his face and waited for his reply.

"Well, I just mean, I don't know if you want kids or not? You've never spoken about it, but I wouldn't want it to be an accident because I didn't have the decency to pull out or say no" he said.

"But you don't sound like you're ruling out kids either" she said, sounding confused. Jackson didn't know why, he had Clayton so it's not like he didn't enjoy being a dad. He'd just never found anyone he looked forward to spending time with, let alone considered raising a child with, but since he met her, he couldn't stop imagining what their future would be like.

"Liv, I want everything with you. That's what I was driving home for tonight to tell you. When you know, you know, and I've spent every single day since I saw you at school thinking about you. Even before that. But not just sex. Don't get me wrong, the sex in unreal, but I just want you. I'd take you even if you never wanted to have sex with me again, because you make me happy, happier than any woman ever has. I wake up and all I want is to see you, I haven't been able to sleep properly without you next to me since you stayed, and even when I tried to convince myself I was wrong, and that we shouldn't be together, you're all I thought about. I love everything about you" he said, cupping her face, and kissing her like she was the only thing in the world that mattered.

48.

Returning to work wasn't fun for Liv, not when she had Luke breathing down her back continuously. He'd had it in for her since she demanded he change Marc's exam subjects, and with only 3 and a half months until he sat the test, he needed all the help he could get. For the past few weeks, Liv had been staying late to help him after school on Tuesday's and helping him during her chess club on a Wednesday too. On Monday's and Thursday's, she was still tutoring Clayton at home, and it felt like her and Jackson didn't have any time for each other.

He was busy with the expansion at work so even on Monday's and Thursday's when she was there, he was working late. Now her car was back there no need for him to drop her home, and with Clayton around they had to act like there was nothing going on, which was hard. They'd discussed whether or not they should tell him, and Jackson was working up to it, but Liv was nervous. She didn't want Clayton to feel awkward about the situation, but she didn't want to deceive him either.

It was the last day before the weekend and Liv was looking forward to 2 days off from Luke who'd made it her mission to make her miserable. Not only had he doubled her marking workload, he'd also put her on canteen duty three times this week alone so she didn't have time to eat or talk to Jackson through the day. In the past 5 days she'd marked 150 workbooks, tutored 4 nights of the week, held chess club, attended a staff meeting, broken up 2 fights and had to cover detention for Evans as well. She was tired of work, and tired of his bullshit.

She was just glad she could leave at a reasonable time tonight, and since Clayton wasn't at home, she could see Jackson too. Liv didn't know how much longer she could take being in her position and felt that it might be the right time to start looking for a new job. As much as she loved her students, she didn't like dreading coming to work every day.

As the pips rung for the final lesson, Liv waited for her students to arrive and read through her messages from Jackson.

2:05:
Liv, I'm not going to be home until 8:00 tonight, we're finalising the last bits for next week and it's been a headache today. Come grab the key after work if you want, and I'll pick us up dinner on the way home. I have a surprise for you tomorrow too xx

All Liv wanted was to go back to Jackson's, eat, drink and sleep. She'd had enough of the stress this week, and she couldn't be bothered to do anything. Even though she was annoyed that it was another night where he was working late, she admired his drive and the passion he had for his job. Liv told him to send over the address and she would see him around half 3, then went back to waiting for her class.

As they filtered in slowly, Liv caught Evans arriving too and wondered what he wanted now.

"Can I help Mr. Evans?" she asked through gritted teeth, wondering why he was in her classroom and not spending his free period perving over the internet or something.

"The head wants to see you, so I volunteered to take your class" he said, and all of the kids moaned to show their disappointment, including Clayton.

"I'll be back by the end of class" she said smiling, but she heard Evans muttering under his breath about how he wouldn't count on it, which suggested that she may not be. Refusing to give him the satisfaction of seeing her annoyed, Liv got to her feet and briefly told the class what they would be covering before heading out of the room and towards the head teacher's office.

Mr. Turn was an intimidating man to most people, but to Liv, he was just like any other grossly overweight and arrogant man with a chip on his shoulder. As she approached his office, she couldn't help but feel pissed off and frustrated about her week ending here, and potentially her career. If Evans had stitched her up, there wasn't a lot that she could do, but she'd be damned if she wouldn't be taking him down with her.

She knocked and entered without waiting for an invitation and found the head sat in his chair with Liz from HR. If she was in the room too then it was bound to be bad, Liv just didn't know how bad it would be, or what to expect.

"Hi Olivia, take a seat" he said in the gravelly tone that she hated, and she could hear his loud breathing from across the room. He was dressed in a cheap shirt that stretched over his big stomach, and a garish blue tie. His grey hair flopped over his forehead and his glasses were resting at the end of his wide nose.

"Thanks, why am I here?" she asked, not wanting to beat around the push.

"I'm afraid that at this time, we cannot disclose much however there has been an incident of misconduct that has been brought to our attention, and we will be suspending you pending further investigation" he said matter of factly.

"I'm sorry? But is this a joke?" she laughed looking from the man sat in front of her, to the woman who looked apologetic.

"As you are aware Olivia, I am not the joking kind, and the matter is in fact very serious. Liz will be your contact during the investigation, but I must ask that you have no further contact with any of the faculty at the school until the issue is resolved. The police will also wish to question you" he said drawing the conversation to a close.

"I'm sorry, the police?" she said, "what the fuck is going on?"

"I'm sorry, but at this time I cannot disclose any further details"

"Well, can I go and collect my stuff?!" she said getting from her chair, not wanting to stay in the room any longer.

"Liz will collect it for you and bring it your vehicle if you'd kindly wait there"

"Is there anything you wish to say for the record?" Liz asked her as she walked out of the room.

"Yeah, I fucking quit" Liv snapped, storming out of the room to wait by her car which she couldn't open since the keys were currently in her bag, in her classroom. Fortunately, it wasn't raining, but it was cold, and Liv didn't have a coat on. She was lucky that the anger burning through her veins was enough to keep her warm, but still couldn't believe what was happening.

Incident of misconduct? She had no idea what on earth they were talking about, and at that point she really didn't care. She'd had enough of the shithole anyway, and it was time to move on to bigger and better things.

She watched as Liz made her way over to the car, still looking apologetic, and carrying her coat and her bag in her hands. Liv snatched them from her angrily and rooted around for her car key which obviously dropped on the floor making her scream profanities.

"I'm really sorry Liv, can I help with anything?" Liz asked as Liv threw her bag in the passenger seat and put her coat on.

"Can you tell me why an earth I've just been suspended when I've done nothing but go above and beyond for all of my students, put in extra hours continuously and never even bit back to a grilling I didn't deserve in this place?"

"Legally, no" she said, squeezing her arm reassuringly, "but I promise that I will get a letter drafted to you by the end of the day and hand post it myself. Do you have a union, or a lawyer?"

"Do I need one?" she asked, growing more frustrated by the second, and Liz advised her to seek advice moving forward.

"I know you've said you quit, but it's not a formal resignation so it won't stick if you want to return. If you want to go for another teaching job when this is all over, your best bet is to make sure you have a union to advocate on your behalf throughout the investigation. For what it's worth, I'm really sorry, and I think you're a brilliant teacher" she said.

"Thanks Liz, keep me updated okay?"

"Of course," and with that, Liv climbed into her car contemplating why nothing seemed to be going right for her at the moment. She dug out her phone and found the address Jackson had sent her, then headed into town to find him. At least she had one thing to feel good about, she thought as she drove, but even then, he came with a whole lot of baggage that she was worried would catch up to her.

49.

"Have the tech guys finished installing the software on the new computers yet?" Jackson said, flicking through the list of jobs that were left before the new expansion opened on Monday. He'd worked his ass off for months, but this week had been non-stop. He'd been at work from 8:00 until late every single day finalising designs for existing clients whilst simultaneously arranging appointments for new clients who were looking for interior designers.

He'd barely seen Liv which was driving him mad, and he hadn't heard from Rachael, which was pleasant, but worrying. Harry had been finalising the contracts and references of all the new employees, as well making sure the website was ready, and finishing commissions he had deadlines for. They had both worked themselves into the ground, and Jackson was glad that this weekend he would get to celebrate properly.

The black tie event at Chef Vine's new restaurant had arrived, and he was going to surprise Liv by taking her out to buy an outfit and booking a hotel for the night. The restaurant was on the outskirts of London, but he wanted to make a weekend of it and do something nice for her, especially as he hadn't seen her all week.

After spending time away in the retreat, Jackson was happier than ever. He'd slept better than he had in days and realised that waking up beside her every morning was what he wanted for the rest of his life. He'd wanted to tell her so many times, but he didn't know if it was possible to feel that way after only a few weeks. He looked at his mum and his stepdad sometimes and remembered how they told him it was love at first sight, and if he had to guess now, he'd say he believed them.

Jackson was chasing up the tech guys down in the back room when Liv arrived. She looked around sheepishly and approached Alice at reception who pointed her over to Jackson in the back. Liv walked towards him whilst Alice mimed her approval over her shoulder as she did, but Jackson ignored her. Alice always had an opinion on the woman he slept with and always made it quite clear which ones she'd steer clear of, not that he listened half the time. She'd been in and out of relationships with women over the years too, but not once had she ever asked him for advice.

"Hey" Liv said, looking around the wide-open space and taking it all in. The office was big and open planned, with large glass windows out the front, and offices walled off with glass too. Jackson prided his business on being able to share beautiful art and designs, and he didn't want that closed off behind solid walls. There were plush sofas in the office rooms, and desks dotted around the open space each with multiple screens and people working with styluses and keyboards simultaneously. There was a buzz in the air, and you could feel how relaxed the atmosphere was as soon as you entered, which Jackson loved.

"You look nice" he said kissing her and gesturing for her to go up to his office. Liv took the stairs and Jackson followed after telling both of the men tapping at the computers he needed them on the server in the next hour and asking Alice to bring Liv up a coffee.

"Hold on? It's only 2:45? Why are you here so early?" he asked, as Liv took her shoes off and made herself comfortable on the sofa in his office. Jackson watched as she curled her legs underneath her and joined her on the sofa.

"I got suspended" she said, resting her head on his lap and staring off at the wall somewhere.

"Why?", but Liv told him she didn't know. He knew well enough that they weren't supposed to discuss the cause of investigation until there was a formal meeting held, but he also knew that in most cases, someone had the decency to give them a heads up. He wanted to help, but she didn't look in the mood to discuss anything at the moment.

"It's just a bump in the road beautiful, we will sort something out" he said as she closed her eyes and sighed, "I've got a surprise for you" he said, hoping that the thought of time away would cheer her up.

"Go on"

"Well, I was hired for a commission for someone a few months back, and we finalised it a few weeks ago. He's a chef and he's opening up a brand-new restaurant next week, but as a thank you he invited me and a plus one to the opening gala he is holding. So, I thought I'd treat you to a weekend in London?" he said, and he watched as a smile spread across her face.

"Are we actually?" she asked, sounding excited, and Jackson explained that he'd been planning it for weeks, he'd just never had the chance to ask.

"I figured that you would look better on my arm than Harry would, and it meant we got to spend some time together, especially after this week" he said, and Liv picked herself up from his lap to kiss him.

"What about Clayton?" she asked, but Jackson explained that his nan and grandad were taking him away for a couple of days, and that she didn't need to worry. He always appreciated how she thought about his feelings whenever Jackson made a decision to put her first, and he was grateful at how understanding she was when it came to him working late or having commitments.

"Who's the chef?" she asked out of curiosity, but Jackson had no idea that she was obsessed with cooking programmes.

"Erm, you probably won't know him, it's his first restaurant, but he's called Tim Vine?"

"As in, MasterChef winner Tim Vine?" she said excitedly, already getting her hopes up, and when Jackson confirmed, she started clapping with excitement.

"I *love* him!" she said, earning a look of disgust from Jackson, who wasn't happy about the 'L' word being thrown around so frivolously, "you know what I mean! I just really loved him on MasterChef last year, did you know I'm OBSESSED with MasterChef?"

"I'm kinda getting that picture now, yeah" he laughed as she continued to clap excitedly and smile from ear to ear. As she did, Harry walked in, and she flashed him a smile too.

"Have you finally showed her that you've learnt to count to 10?" Harry jibed, but Jackson ignored him.

"How you doing Liv?" he asked, leaning against the desk. He was dressed in trousers and a roll neck shirt with loafers on similar to what Jackson hard worn the night she met him out. Liv took in his features noticing his strong jaw line and swept back hair. He had piercing blue eyes behind his square framed glasses, and his teeth overlapped slightly at the front but he was handsome.

"Well, I'm alive which is good considering Jackson's ex tried to set me on fire" she shrugged, "I just lost my job, but I gained a meal at a celeb restaurant, so you know. You win some you lose some".

"Sounds tragic!"

"Thanks for the support, and how are you?" she asked, thankful for him and all he had done to reunite her with Jackson.

"I'm okay thanks, in fact I'm great in comparison to you" he said laughing. "Anyway, I came to steal prince charming away for a bit as I need his expertise and if we don't get everything finished tonight, he won't be going anywhere".

"I hate to be the one to stir the pot, but he told me he was the boss" Liv mock whispered.
"I am!" Jackson said, screwing his face up at her in shock.

"He likes to think he is, and we like to let him feel good so we don't meet The Hulk version of Jackson, but without me, he would be nothing" he said, pushing himself away from the desk. "It was lovely to see you Liv, if I don't catch you before you go, and well done for hunting his stubborn ass down, I was scared he was going to let you go".

Harry left the room, and Jackson unwillingly got to his feet. "You know I would have come back to you, don't you?" he said pressing a kiss to her lips.

"Oh really, and why's that?"

"Because we belong together, and there's no getting rid of me now"

50.

"Rach?" Ben called as he let himself in to the flat. She'd been AWOL for days now, with no contact with the family whatsoever and they were all starting to worry. Obviously, Ben had drawn the short straw, but the rest of the family were losing the will to live with her.

She wasn't answering, but she had obviously been home. There were empty bottles strewn across the kitchen and empty glasses too. Ben wasn't surprised to see empty packets on the side which suggested that not only had she been drink excessively again, but she'd also been taking drugs too, which wasn't good. Ben didn't want to have to beg and plead with her to go back to rehab, but it looked like that was where things were heading.

It wasn't the first time he'd had to be the one to tell her she needed to sort herself out again, but this time seemed different. He called her again and heard movement in the bedroom which led him to investigate. Rachael was strewn across the bed under the quilt whilst a stranger slept naked next to her. Ben rolled his eyes, frustrated that he was having to do this again, and kicked the mattress a few times to stir them both.

"You!" he pointed at the man who woke suddenly and began desperately trying to find some clothes, "Get out!".

"I-I-I'm sorry" he stammered grabbing his boxers from the floor and shoving his legs into them.

"Put some fucking clothes on Rach and get out of bed!" he spat, leaving the bedroom to wait in the lounge for her to get herself sorted. Ben started collecting the empty cans and bottles from the floor and putting them in a bin bag. He knew she wasn't going to come around easy to the idea of rehab, but she didn't have a choice. She was off the rails and anyone could see that.

The man who'd been sharing her bed appeared and headed straight for the door before Rachael came out after him. "I'll call you later" she said as he left, but he didn't seem interested, for which she blamed Ben.

"What do you want?" she said, heading for the back door and lighting up a cigarette.

"You been ignoring everyone for days and they're worried" he said holding up an empty bag he'd found on the side, "what's this?"

"What does it look like? If you're here to read me the riot act Ben, don't bother because I'm not interested. I'm fine, and I don't need you to come in and play the big bad brother, I know I'm a fuck up, you don't have to tell me".

"You're right, you are a fuck up, and you need to go back in and get yourself sorted. You're acting like a child Rach. 100's of people get dumped every single day, and you two weren't even in a relationship!"

"IT WAS DIFFERENT!" she shouted, bursting into tears, "AND NOW I'M JUST MEANT TO WAIT AROUND UNTIL HE COMES CRAWLING BACK, WHICH HE ALWAYS FUCKING DOES!"

"Rach! It's not going to happen, and you need to go back in because you're losing your fucking mind"

"What because I haven't answered you lot in a few days!?"

"We're used to that Rach, what we aren't used to is having to come and collect you from the police station for trying to set somebody on fire? What are you playing at, and what makes you think he's ever going to want anything to do with you now? You've lost your fucking mind!"

"She fucking deserved it, and if I see her again, I promise I'll kill her. If you haven't got anything good to say, get out!"

"Seriously Rach, just get yourself sorted and take your meds. Why don't you get away for a few days and get your head right" he suggested, but he knew she wasn't going to go for it. He had never seen her this upset or fall this far down this quickly.

"Just get out Ben, I ain't going back in, I'm fine" she said, flicking her cigarette and lighting another.

"Clearly! Do you know what Rach, whatever. You can't help somebody that doesn't want to help themselves, and you're a fucking lost cause", and with that, he left the flat, and left Rachael stood at the back door still feeling sorry for herself.

Rachael knew she was slipping, but nobody understood, she couldn't explain what it felt like to anyone other than Jackson. He didn't have to ask because he knew, he knew what it was like to be fine one minute and then fall apart the next. She just couldn't believe he was the cause of it this time.

Deep down she knew that what she'd done to Liv would mean he'd never come back, but she wasn't willing to accept defeat just yet. In her mind, they were made for each other and Jackson knew better than most, that she couldn't always control what she did. She needed to talk to him, make him understand that she needed him, but every time she called his phone it went to voicemail.

She had been warned by the police not to go to his house, but she felt like she had to explain. She owed him an apology, she was sorry she'd pushed him away, but she'd changed, and she needed him to help her get back to herself. If he didn't, she didn't know what she'd do, and she didn't want to know either.

51

"Liv, were going to be late" he called, checking his watch for the 5th time. Fortunately, he'd booked a car to take them to the restaurant because if he'd had to flag down a taxi last minute, they definitely wouldn't be arriving on time.

Jackson waited impatiently on the bed whilst she finished up in the bathroom and busied himself with his cufflinks. He'd already straightened them 3 times, but he had nothing left to do and Liv was taking over the entire sink before she'd forbidden him to go in. She'd wanted to surprise him with the outfit she'd picked out so whilst he'd been fine to potter about whilst she did her hair and make-up, the big reveal had to be a surprise.

"Are you ready?" She called from the bathroom, like he hadn't been asking her the same question for the past 15 minutes.

"Yes, I've been ready for- oh God" Jackson stopped short when he saw the sight of her and ran his eyes up and down the length of her body.

"You look incredible" he said, taking it all in again. Her dress was black and long, with one shoulder strap that draped over her arm, leaving the other bare. Her chest was bare too, and the dress clung to her hips, her waist and her breasts, which looked more inviting than ever tonight. The bottom of the dress flailed out, but her left leg was peeking out of a slit that went from floor to thigh leaving him speechless.

"I'll just get my shoes and we can go, but can you grab my bag" she said pointing to the bathroom she'd just came out of.

Jackson did as he was told, but watched her every move as he did, unable to take his eyes off of her. He watched as she bent over and did up the straps on her heels, as she flattened out her dress again, and as she smoothed back the hair behind her right ear. He was mesmerised, and if he didn't think he was falling before, he was certainly sure of it now.

Liv was thankful that he approved of what she was wearing but got the impression there would never be something he didn't like. She'd watched him dress in his tux whilst she was doing her make up, and if it wasn't for the fact, she would be eating in the poshest restaurant she'd ever been to that night, she would have cancelled there and then to get him out of it.

Not that it was a bad thing that she got to stare at him dressed up all night, she couldn't wait. He'd been to the barbers earlier in the day whilst she went out and found a dress, and his hair and beard looked pristine. He'd worn a black tux, with a velvet jacket and a bow tie that made him look like he'd just stepped out of a Bond film and Liv just hoped that she lived up to the expectations and didn't look out of place.

"You really do look incredible Olivia" he said as they got to the car waiting out front and he helped her in.

"Well, you aren't too bad yourself" she said as he joined her in the back seat, and they headed off to the restaurant. Liv was trying hard to take things steady, but she was besotted by Jackson and the way she felt when she was around him. Even when he hadn't been complimenting her, or they weren't in bed, she found herself relaxed, and happier than she could ever remember. She was looking forward to a night where they spent real time together, as a couple, and something more than stealing time together around their busy lives. She wanted tonight to be about them, and she was thankful that fate had led her to him, even if the road was rocky to begin with.

They arrived at the restaurant as others were getting there too, and Liv held on to Jackson's arm tightly. She wasn't used to the glitz and glamour of a formal event, but it looked like he was. He confirmed who they were with the maître d, whilst she tried to calm her nerves, then led her into the restaurant, resting a reassuring hand on top of hers wrapped around his arm.

It was bigger than she expected, and she was amazed just by the sight of it, let alone the smell. Each table looked as though it had been set to the millimetre, and every item on it had its place. She'd never seen so many different pieces of cutlery before and guessed that they were about to tuck into one hell of a tasting menu. When she'd watched him on TV, Tim Vine had been very well put together, calm and confident, and the aesthetic of the restaurant suited the man she imagined he'd be. She was hoping that she wouldn't fangirl too hard if she saw him, because she really did love MasterChef, and having the chance to eat in one of the contestants' restaurants was making her excited.

Jackson took two drinks from the tray of a waiter and clinked glasses with Liv who returned the gesture.

"To first times" he said again, and Liv sipped down her champagne whilst the blush appeared over her cheeks as usual.

52.

Jackson kept close to Liv all night, although he realised early on that he didn't need to. Her natural confidence shone through, and she drifted in and out of conversation throughout the night without looking to him for help. Not long before they were due to sit to eat, Liv excused herself to find the bathroom. She told him she'd pick up drinks on the way back, and Jackson waited around for her, feeling a bit lost.

"Mr Cotts" came a voice from behind him that made his eyes roll and got his back up immediately. He should have known she would be attending too since she was the one who put his name forward as the best in the business to Tim, but he didn't think he'd have to speak to her.

Gabrielle was a work horse, and she was all about her business and her money. She'd never married, and never had kids, but pursued men for fun, especially men like Jackson. Men who seemed well put together and had all their ducks in a row, whether they were taken or single. Jackson had never entertained the idea because he refused to mix business with pleasure, but she'd been persistent, to the point he still got random emails from her, and she hadn't been a client for almost two years.

She was petite and slim, with a blonde pixie cut and big brown eyes. Her teeth were slightly too large for her mouth, but she was relatively pretty, with high cheek bones and a soft jaw line. She'd worn a short tuxedo dress with bright red lips and red heels, and seemed to have attended alone, which didn't surprise him. If she came alone, it gave her a better chance of leaving with somebody.

"Gabrielle," he smiled, leaning down to kiss her on both cheeks whilst she ran a hand over his shoulder.

"Jackson, darling! How are you?" she purred, smiling up at him suggestively. Part of Jackson was glad that Liv had gone to the toilet because he didn't want her to feel uncomfortable. He also didn't want Gabrielle getting off on the fact that he wasn't alone and that he was now taken.

"Very well thank you, and thank you for putting in a good word for me to Tim. It was an enjoyable project to work on" he said enthusiastically, hoping that by avoiding asking how she was, it might have been the end of the conversation.

"Absolutely any time! You know how amazing I think you are" she winked, and Jackson ignored her, "besides, I've got a new project coming up in the summer that I want to work together on, and I wanted to make sure you hadn't lost your touch"

Gabrielle tilted her head slightly to one side and walked two fingers up his shoulder as she spoke. Jackson was polite, and eager to get back to Liv who he clocked picking up the drinks from the waiter, but it appeared that Gabrielle hadn't finished with him yet, and he didn't think they were talking about work any longer.

"You know Jackson, I've always thought we'd work well together. Both being such dedicated people to our work and all. Maybe we should arrange a time where we can put our heads together and do some brainstorming about all these ideas I've got going on in my head?"

But Jackson wasn't interested, he could see Liv coming back smiling at him sweetly, and he barely even heard what Gabrielle had said. He hadn't had to introduce Liv to anyone since they'd arrived, she'd always been more than happy to introduce herself, but given the circumstances, he wanted to make it clear to Gabrielle that he wasn't interested, and clear to Liv too.

"That sounds like a good idea," he said as Liv approached with drinks in her hand, including one for his guest it appeared. He took the drinks from her and thanked her whilst Gabrielle looked back and forth between them and smiled. "This is Olivia, my partner. This is Gabrielle, another chef who introduced me to Tim".

"I know who you are," she smiled excitedly extending her hand, "I'm a big, big fan of yours. Your food looks stunning! I've followed your journey since Great British Menu, and honestly, wow".

Jackson looked at Liv and at Gabrielle, who was clearly getting off on the fact that someone was interested in her. Liv looked excited to be meeting such a wide range of talented chefs, and Jackson was surprised at how in the know she was about the current world when it came to cuisine. Gabrielle entertained her for a few minutes and invited her for a meal at her restaurant as a gift, before saying her goodbyes and leaving Liv giddy with excitement.

"Honestly, I can't believe how many chefs are here" she smiled, as they found their way to their table, and Jackson tucked her in. They were sat on a table of 6 and although Jackson wasn't familiar with any of the other names that were yet to join them, Liv was having another fangirl moment about seeing one of them. Jackson listened as she reeled off the achievements of the chef that hadn't arrived yet, and wondered if she was going to be able to hold it together throughout the meal.

"So how come you never told me how into food you were?" he said, once she'd stopped to catch her breath.

"It's never come up in conversation" she shrugged as a waiter filled one glass with water and another with a small glug of white wine before moving on to Jackson's, "I religiously watch cooking competitions every year. Great British Menu, MasterChef, Great British Bake Off.. Well, all of them really"

"So, can you cook?" he asked, sipping his wine, and growing even more intrigued with her than he thought was possible.

"I enjoy cooking, but people don't tend to enjoy eating it" she replied sheepishly, making Jackson laugh.

Whilst they spoke, the other guests around the room found their way to their seats, and Liv wasted no time in getting into conversation with those that had joined them, which Jackson loved to see. He was so grateful that she'd refused to let him walk away from her and being with her felt like the most natural thing in the world. It wasn't forced, it wasn't hard work, it was everything he'd been missing for all these years he'd been messing around.

The night went on the celebrities kept coming which meant Liv was in her element. She didn't think she'd ever get the chance to eat somewhere as fancy as Vines, but since she'd arrived, she'd had nothing but invitations to visit other restaurants and she'd agreed to every single one, without even conferring with Jackson. She was just so excited to be eating the same foods she'd been watching on TV for years, and as the starters arrived, she audibly squealed.

It was a classic, but she expected nothing less. Tim Vine had made his name on TV by bringing a modern twist to classic English and French cooking. He'd taken the crown with the exact dish that was being presented to the table to start with and Liv was having another fangirl moment.

Pan fried scallops with pancetta, with various gels and purees. Hints of sharp apple came through, and sweet pea flavours that danced on her tongue and had her wishing the dish was bigger. There were different textures running through and Liv completely understood why the dish had won. Not that she had ever had anything remotely close to compare it to.

As the dishes kept coming, Liv kept falling in love, over and over again. Spiced monkfish with croutons, duck with orange and fondant potatoes, finished with a chocolate dessert that Liv thought was going to melt her heart. She spoke about each of the dishes with those at the table, who were all used to this kind of fine dining experience, even though she wasn't. Jackson seemed to be just as interested as she was, commenting on the presentation, the tastes, and the textures, and Liv was happy to find out just how passionate he was about food too.

By the end of the 4 courses, she was satisfyingly full, but almost wanted all 4 dishes again. She was so grateful that Jackson had given her the opportunity, and even happier that he seemed to be enjoying himself. They'd finished eating, but they were still sipping their drinks and chatting when Tim finally left the kitchen to meet and greet people.

There was a round of applause and people getting to their feet as he arrived at the front of house which was the least he deserved. He stood in his black chef apron, tall and proud of the work he'd just produced, and everyone seemed to agree. As the applause died down and people took their seat again, Tim said a few words.

"Thank you to each and every person who came out tonight to support the restaurant prior to our official opening. I'm not great with words as you know, but I appreciate all the hard work that's gone into getting the restaurant ready to go, all of my chefs in the kitchen who have been working consistently for the past 12 hours, the front of house staff who have been amazing too. To the designers including Mr Cotts who is here tonight, who not only designed the menus and website, but also played a hand in designing the restaurant itself"

There was another round of applause from everyone in the restaurant, and Liv squeezed Jackson's arm. He hadn't told her that he'd worked so closely with Tim and helped with the design of the restaurant, but it didn't surprise her. She knew that he'd wanted to expand the company because he had an interest in interior design, but knowing he played a role in the restaurant she now loved so much, made her love it even more, and him.

Jackson had no intention of sharing the extent to his input in the restaurant, but not because he wasn't proud. The interior design side of the company wasn't up and running yet, and this had been something he had done on the side to see if he had it in him. He was over the moon about how the final product had turned out, and he was really interested in pursuing more interior design commissions, which was lucky since following the speech, he had multiple enquiries for his services.

He was thankful that Liv was understanding, because whilst he shook hands and discussed new potential clients and their ventures, she busied herself with conversations around the room. She did so with a smile on her face the whole time and didn't once seem fussed that he wasn't by her side. He figured it was partly to do with the fact that she was in her element surrounded by some of the most adventurous cooking minds in the country.

Jackson found his way back to Liv who was stood talking to the man of the hour, and he welcomed Jackson with a firm handshake.

"We were just talking about you" Liv said, leaning up to kiss him, reminding Jackson was more than ready to go back to the hotel.

"All good things I hope?"

"Great things" Tim said, patting him on the shoulder. He was a tall and stocky guy, with dark blonde hair and a beard to match. His arms were covered in tattoos and there were discs in his ears, that you could see straight through. He radiated confidence when he spoke, and you could tell just how passionate he was about what he did, with every word that came out of his mouth. "I honestly can't thank you enough Jackson, the whole place is amazing, and I haven't stopped getting compliments from everyone. It's everything I wanted and more".

"It was a pleasure, and I'm grateful you gave me the opportunity" Jackson replied, "I'm sure Liv will be one of your most loyal customers based on her reaction tonight. It was genuinely lovely, and we feel privileged for the invite".

"Well after listening to your wife's critique of my menu, I'd be more than happy to get you back regularly. She's about to become my new chief taster!" he laughed, "I don't think I've ever met a fan of mine who followed me so closely through MasterChef, I feel privileged to have cooked for you both".

Jackson didn't bat an eyelid at Liv being referred to as his wife and didn't feel the need to correct Tim either. They spoke for a few more minutes before Tim took his leave, and Jackson finally got Liv back to himself.

"I'm sorry I've been disappearing all night" he said as she wrapped her arms around his waist and looked up to him. As much as he'd loved the dinner with her, and spending time socialising as a couple, all he wanted when he looked at her, was to take her back to the room and fall asleep next to her.

"You can make it up to me" she said, kissing him again, "and I've got a surprise for you too" she winked, and with that, they said their goodbyes and headed back to the hotel.

53.

Jackson loosened his cufflinks on the bed, whilst Liv dropped her dress, directly in front of him. She stood there in nothing, but her lacey underwear and heels and Jackson ran his gaze up and down her body. As he did, Liv slid her knickers over her hips and dropped them to her ankles before stepping out of them and straddling him on the bed. Liv kissed his neck as he ran his hands over her ass and up her back. He had no intention of calling it on after such a long night, but Liv had other ideas.

Liv fumbled with his bow tie, and then got to work on his buttons whist he continued to run his hands over her body. He relaxed as she eased his shirt off his shoulders and began to kiss them softly whilst she got to work on his sleeves, leaving him topless. Jackson took hold of her neck and tilted her towards him so he could kiss her properly. His tongue met hers, as he circled her clit with his thumb and Liv gyrated her hips.

He listened to the noises she made each time he stroked her and knew how much she wanted him.

"Are you planning on staying in your trousers all night?!" She asked, pulling away from him as he slowed down the movements between her legs and played with her nipples.

"Depends, what you have planned for me?"

"Well, take them off and you'll see won't you".

Liv hopped up from his lap and Jackson got up from the bed. She reached down to unbuckle her heels, but Jackson had other ideas and instructed her to leave them on. Liv laid back against the headboard and watched as Jackson undid his belt and worked his way out of his trousers.

He watched as she parted her legs and ran her hand down her stomach towards her pussy, sliding a finger between her folds and biting her lip as she did. Jackson was in no rush to get her to stop and started to stroke his cock as he watched her watch him, getting harder by the second.

"You finished?" She asked, gesturing him to come to her on the bed which he did.

He made his way between her legs and kissed from her thighs down to her ankles before releasing the straps on her shoes and running his tongue over her toes. Liv laughed and asked what he was doing, but Jackson told her he was doing what he wanted so she should let him.

He did the same down the other leg, smiling every time Liv let out a laugh and asked him to stop, but he couldn't help it. She'd had a pedicure, her toes looked perfect, and Jackson wanted to taste every inch of her tonight. He wanted to spend hours making her feel good, and getting everything, he could out of her until they were both too tired to do anything else. If that meant licking her from head to toe, then that's what he planned to do.

"Get on your back" she said, propping herself up on to her elbows and pulling herself back up towards the pillows.

"Why?" He said, lifting his head from between her legs, pissed that she planned on interrupting him in the flow of things.

"Because I'm going to fuck you" she said working her legs round him and easing him back on to the bed. Jackson obliged and laid flat on his back whilst Liv kissed his neck, his chest, and his torso.

He watched as she stroked her hand up and down his dick, cupping his balls, then ran her tongue from base to tip making him groan. She took him in her mouth and slowly eased her way down as she held him tight in one hand and ran the other over his stomach. Jackson watched Liv readjust her hair as her head rose and fell whilst she worked on his erection. She looked up at him as she did, and Jackson wanted to take her there and then.

Liv pulled away from him and climbed up the bed, where he expected her to straddle his lap. Instead, she climbed higher than he thought and straddled his shoulders, encouraging him to replay the favour, which he was more than happy to oblige to. Jackson ran his tongue over her clit, whilst Liv ran her fingers through his hair and gripped the headboard. He reached up and cupped her tits whilst she moved against him, and Jackson loved each and every noise she made.

Liv gripped his hair tighter as he forced his tongue inside of her and held her ass cheek firmly. He felt her try to leave, but he wasn't ready for that, and continued with his strokes until he felt her cumming whist screaming his name. Liv's body relaxed and she panted with relief whilst she eased her way back down his body slowly, kissing him as she did.

Jackson held his cock, whilst Liv slowly lowered herself on top of him, moaning as her pussy stretched over his helmet. He groped her thighs as she slid herself back and forward on top of him, and watched her body move as she took every inch of him. Jackson loved to be in control, to bring her to the brink of orgasm and to watch her body react to him, but that was before he knew how good it felt when she was the one calling the shots.

The wine had flowed far too easily all night, as had the conversations. Liv had watched how Jackson had interacted with everyone at the restaurant, but more importantly she watched how he watched her. He was always looking for her in the crowded room, and always trying to steer away from conversations to get back to her. She loved how he'd try to make her feel comfortable in front of every person he spoke to, and appreciated the fact that he didn't dampen her personality. He let her be herself and encouraged her to be too. Liv wasn't ready to tell him she loved him yet, but she was more than ready to show him.

She ran her hands up his body as she lifted herself up and lowered herself back down again rhythmically. Liv wanted Jackson to enjoy himself, but she didn't know whether she was any good at this stuff. He was always the one in control, setting the pace and changing positions, but she wanted to surprise him tonight. She wanted to be the one to make him cum and make him want her even more.

As she watched him, he smiled up at her and held her waist firmly. Liv readjusted herself so she was upright and quickened her pace back and forward. Her intentions were to make him enjoy himself, but as she sped up and realised how good it felt to ride him, she forgot all about it. She wasn't concentrating on his orgasm although it sounded like it was coming and was completely overwhelmed by how good it felt to grind against him whilst he was deep inside of her.

Liv threw her head back whilst Jackson joined in with her movements and helped her along with his hands either side of her, forcing her back and forth quicker than she could manage alone. He moaned her name loudly, but Liv was oblivious to everything other that the feeling of him inside of her again.

"Liv, I'm gonna cum" he moaned as she quickened her pace again, so close to reaching her own orgasm. She wasn't ready for it to all be over, but there was no way she ready to stop either. Instead, she carried on, whilst Jackson muttered curse words over and over, and she felt his cock pulse, whilst she tightened around him and found her own release.

"Ah FUCK!" she screamed, ruining the moment and immediately jumping off of him. Jackson moved instinctively wondering what had happened whilst Liv laid curled up on the bed grabbing her leg.

"What did I do?!" he asked panicking.

"I've got cramp!" she laughed pushing him away from her and trying to stretch her leg out across the giant bed. Jackson sighed with relief and helped to massage her calf whilst Liv hid her face with a pillow embarrassed that she was laying stark naked crying about cramp. She was reconsidering her decision to take control and go on top after all, even when her cramp subsided, and they were both left laughing on the bed about her dramatic exit.

"Thank you for tonight" she said as Jackson laid next to and running his fingers over her stomach.

"Did you enjoy it?" he asked, sounding genuine, but Liv didn't feel like he even need to. She'd absolutely loved the whole day with him, and she didn't want to go home and burst the little bubble they'd been living in for the past 24 hours.

"Honestly, it's been one of the best days of my life" she said excitedly, "I would never have got an opportunity like this before and I'm so grateful you brought me with you".

"It was my pleasure, thank you for coming, and thank you for being so understanding whilst I was collared by everyone" he said kissing her shoulder.

"You don't have to thank me Jax, you're talented, it's no wonder you're in such high demand. The restaurant is beautiful, I didn't realise you'd helped with all of that too! You really are a man on many talents aren't you".

"It was a nice job to work on, and now I know just how interested you are in modern British chefs, I might have to agree to some of the proposals I got tonight".

"I appreciate your support in pursuing my interests, but you have to promise not to leave me if I become high maintenance and expect to be fed at top restaurants regularly. You can't give me a taste of the good life and not expect me to take advantage of that. There's a lot of things I will stand for Mr. Cotts, but you depriving me of good food when I'm now aware of the contacts you have in your phone book is not one of them"

Jackson roared with laughter and climbed between her legs again, whilst she smiled up at him.

"Only the best for my wife" he winked, before he kissed her, and slid himself inside of her again.

54.

Liv was grateful for the lie in, but there was nothing else about her suspension that she was enjoying. She hadn't heard from the school about what was happening, but she had spoken to Dianne who told her that she wasn't going to stand for her being bullied and would be asking plenty of questions. Liv told her not to worry and she didn't want to get her in trouble by being in communication, but she appreciated how she always looked out for her.

Rather than mope about, Liv decided she was going to use her time to be productive. She was going to visit her mum, speak to the solicitor Jackson had put her in touch with, and after visiting Vines, she was keen to try her hand in the kitchen too. She needed to keep busy, because between missing work, and missing Jackson, she didn't know what to do with herself.

The weekend alone with him had been magical, but he was crazy busy with work, and she didn't want to intrude on him spending quality time with Clayton either. Even though neither of them had sat Clayton down and spoken to him yet, they both got the impression that he knew. He wasn't stupid, and Jackson and Liv found it hard to pretend that they weren't besotted with each other when it came to Clayton's tuition, which she was planning to continue despite her suspension.

Liv also had to organise something for Jackson's birthday which was only 2 weeks away but had no idea what she was going to do for him. She wanted to do something special, but she was mindful that he also shared his birthday with Joe which meant that they might do something together, or with his family. Liv was going to have to do some digging, but in the meantime, she figured it was about time she updated her mum on the new man in her life.

...

Business was booming and Jackson felt like he hadn't got a minute to himself after the addition of the interior design department. He'd shared his details over the weekend at Vines, and by Monday afternoon his inbox was filling up with enquiries from chefs up and down the country. His books were full for the next 2 weeks, and then he had annual leave, although it looked as though that was going to have to be rearranged. He loved being busy, always had, but now he was with Liv, he kind of wanted to take a step back.

He missed her the minute he left her over the weekend, and although she'd come to the house to teach Clayton, it wasn't the same. He wanted to take her to bed, make love to her and fall into a peaceful sleep, something that had been avoiding him every night he didn't sleep next to her. He didn't know how he was meant to do to help it, he couldn't expect Liv to stay with him every night, even though it's what he wanted, but he also didn't want the lack of sleep to affect his mood or his condition which eventually it would. More than anything, he needed to tell Clayton, then at least seeing her in the week might be more manageable.

The new recruits had started work, and Jackson had briefed them on the current jobs that they had lined up, which they were all excited about. Over the past few weeks, he'd tied up all the current projects he had been working on so that he could dedicate time to the new ventures and get them underway. Brad's productivity went into overdrive once he knew his work was going to be commended, and Jackson was impressed by how dedicated and focused he was in his role. In the end, they had hired all 3 of the shortlisted candidates they had, when they realised just how sought after their services were going to be.

He was counting down the minutes until the end of the week because he was exhausted and if he had to wait much longer to spend the night with Liv, he was bound to have an emotional crash soon. Whilst the staff took lunch, Harry and Jackson tried to organise each and every enquiry they'd had through, whilst Alice sat and took notes.

"I hate to be the bearer of bad news," she said when they finally finished organising everything, "but what about Ben and the gym site? I don't want Rachael rearing her ugly head again"

"I've got that sorted" Jackson said, which might have been the only benefit to not sleeping. "I finished the website, designed the new logo for merchandise, and I've offloaded it to someone for maintenance. I don't want anything to do with it, or give her any excuse to start again"

"When on earth did you find the time to design all of that" Harry asked looking concerned.

"Haven't been sleeping great," Jackson shrugged.

"Should we be worried?" he replied, raising an eyebrow, but Jackson didn't know.

He felt like he was still in a good place, and still level-headed, but the lack of sleep was starting to take its toll. He'd felt okay for a time, but his addictive personality was coming to the forefront, and his latest addiction seemed to be Liv. Before he could answer, his phone buzzed across the side, and he saw Clayton's name flash up.

> *"Clayt? Why aren't you in lesson?"*
>
> *"I'm on my way back to lesson now, but the school are going to call you. I think I've just got Liv in trouble, but they said Mum come to the school and put in a complaint about her and photos she found on my phone or something, but none of it's true!"*

Clayton rambled down the phone not making any sense and started crying. Jackson was confused and tried to console him, but he had no idea what he was talking about, so it wasn't easy.

"Clayt, calm down, and tell me what's happened"

"The headteacher called me into his office and there were police there and they asked if I had photos of Miss Turnell. They said that they were waiting for Mum to arrive but when they called her, she said she was running late, and she was happy for them to speak to me without her. They said that she had told them not to get you involved because the stress and your condition or something? But I promise I haven't done anything" he sobbed.

"Clayt, I know you haven't done anything, don't worry. Go clean yourself up and get back to lesson and I'll collect you from school tonight" he said trying to stay calm, but inside he was raging, "have you spoken to your mum?"

"I tried to ring her but she didn't answer. But dad, please don't shout at her. I don't understand what she is going on about because she doesn't even know who Muss Turnell is and she's never been to the school either"

"I'll sort it Clayton okay?"

"I'm sorry dad"

"Don't be silly, I'll see you in a couple of hours, I'm coming to the school now"

Jackson picked up a mug and threw it across the room where it shattered against the brick, then paced for a minute whilst Alice and Harry watched him. They knew better than to speak to him until he was ready, and after a few a few minutes, he exhaled.

"H, call Holly and ask her if she's been to Clayt's school at all" he said massaging his temples. He had a bad feeling about what was going on, and this didn't sound like Holly. Clayton was right, she had never been to the school, and she didn't have that much to do with his education or his upbringing. Up until recently, she never even had Clayton overnight and there was no way she was likely to get involved in something at school without telling. He waited whilst Harry made the call and was thankful that he'd known Holly for years. He didn't think he'd be able to keep a level head if the answer was yes, and he didn't want to disappoint Clayton if he lost his temper. He paced impatiently as he heard Harry ask her questions over the phone, then stared at him as he ended the call and put his phone back down on the table

"She said she's never been at the school Jax" Harry said shrugging his shoulders and glancing at Alice whose eyes were wide with concern. He watched whilst Jackson tried to compose himself, but he was struggling to understand what was happening.

"Hold my calls Alice, I'll be in tomorrow morning" he said grabbing his keys and heading for the door.

55.

Liv had always been close to her mum, but she didn't visit as often as she should. She always blamed it on work, but now she'd been suspended she had no excuse. Liv pulled up to her childhood home and walked her way over the drive. As a kid she remembered playing on the grass in the front garden, but as they grew up and got their licenses, her mum and dad sacrificed their lawn for a place for them to park their cars safely instead.

The house wasn't big, but it had been big enough to raise Owen and Olivia until they were old enough to move on. They'd made plenty of happy memories there, and Liv was grateful that her mum hadn't decided to downsize or move out. She'd always say that the house was their home, and nothing would ever change that. It had been through some upgrades over the years, Olivia's Groovy Chick and Owens Spiderman wallpaper borders had thankfully been redecorated when they went to secondary school, and their mum had always given them the best of what she could.

After letting herself in, Liv found her mum in the kitchen folding up the washing from the drier whilst the radio played in the background. Carrie was a short plump woman with a big heart, and a big personality. Liv had inherited her looks from her and they shared the same big brown eyes and freckles. She had short hair, a kind smile and a soft voice that could calm even the most hostile of people, which was lucky given her dads mood swings.

"Hey mum" she said, kissing her on the cheek and joining in with folding the washing.
"Well, this is a lovely surprise, what's going on? Why are you here?"
"It's a long story, thought I'd come over for a cup of tea and a chat" she shrugged.
"Well, you get the kettle on my darling and tell me all about it"
Liv did as she was told and explained to her mum that she'd been suspended from work. Carrie was outraged, but Liv couldn't

give her a reason as to why she'd been let off or what was going on. She said that she was still waiting for someone to get in touch with her, but she heard nothing over the weekend and when she'd called they said that there was nothing they could tell her.

"So have you done anything wrong?" her mum asked, accepting her cup of tea and taking a seat at the table, but Liv couldn't think of anything, other than the fact she was dating her student's dad.

"Well, no? Not at school anyway, nothing that would warrant them suspending me"

"If that's the case darling, I'm sure everything will work itself out and you'll be back to work in no time" she said, giving her a reassuring rub on the arm, and Liv smiled, "so what else is new?"

Liv could tell that she was waiting for her to talk about Jackson and was sure that Owen had been opening his trap, like he always did. Her mum smiled over at her whilst she blushed and sipped her tea, wondering where to begin.

"What's Owen been saying?" she asked, but her mum just told her that he'd said she seemed happy, and that's all she cared about.

"He makes me really happy" she said, remembering just how happy he made her anytime they were together, and reeled off how they'd met and how they'd got together to her mum who listened intensely. She told her about Clayton, about Jax's bipolar too, and although she knew Jackson wouldn't like it to be common knowledge, she knew her mum would understand better than most.

"And how do you feel about him having kids and having the same as your dad?" she asked, sounding genuine, but Liv hadn't ever thought about it. She didn't define him by the fact he was a father, or the fact he had bipolar, because when she was with him, he was just Jackson. She thought she'd accept him flaws and all, but she realised that she hadn't actually seen his flaws yet.

"I don't know Mum; I feel safe when I'm with him and he makes me feel like I'm the only one in the room when we're together. It's just hard because he doesn't want to disappoint Clayton, or have Clayton feel like he's not his priority which I understand"

"Well do you know what darling, even hearing you talk about him lets me know just how much you love him, and if you're happy, I'm happy. If you love him, and he loves you, he will manage his condition and you'll find a balance. I'm not saying there won't be bad days, but they are far outnumbered by the good, okay?" she said putting her hand on Liv's, "Now, most importantly, are you going to show me what he looks like?"

Liv laughed and dug her phone out, where she flicked through her photos and found one of them from the weekend. Her mum found her glasses and looked down her nose raising her eyebrows in approval. "Well, I say, he looks like James Bond!"

Liv felt better knowing that her mum supported her decision, even though she knew how hard it could be to love someone who didn't love themselves, and as they continued to talk, Liv was reminded just why she loved him.

56.

Jackson was angry and he needed to know what the hell was going on soon before he lost it. As he pulled into Clayton's school, he took a deep breath and tried to compose himself, which did nothing to calm his temper. The police were still parked outside, which he wasn't ideal, because if what he thought was happening was correct, he would be in handcuffs before long he imagined.

Jackson smartened his tie and head over to the reception desk where Liz was sat tapping away at her keyboard. As he approached, she glanced up and smiled widely, looking him up and down with approval.

"Can I help?" she asked sweetly, putting her keyboard to one side.

"My name is Mr. Cotts, and I'm here to see the headteacher, immediately" he said as calmly as he could.

"Mr Cotts! Certainly Sir, bear with me two moments and I'll dial for him to come out"

Jackson waited as she dialled the extension and explained that he was at the desk. She did some quick agreeing on the phone, and then put it back down before gesturing for him to follow her down the corridor. It was only a short walk down to his office, and she knocked softly before they were called in.

"I'll leave you to it," she said leaving the room and leaving Jackson standing face to face with Mr. Turn, and another woman who he assumed was a police officer.

"Mr. Cotts, please take a seat sir so we can get this matter resolved as quickly and amicably as possible" he said getting from his seat and gesturing to the chair opposite him, "we weren't expecting to see you, but I can only apologise for the chain of events we are currently involved in"

"Do you mind telling me why my son was being interviewed by a police officer without me present, and what the fuck is going on?!"

"Now, now, Mr. Cotts, there's no need for that language. Clayton's mother made it quite clear that informing you could be detrimental to your mental well-being" the officer explained, but Jackson didn't want to know. She was an older woman, with greying hair pulled pack into a bun and blue eyes. She was dressed smart, but wasn't in a uniform, which made Jackson wonder why there was a police car outside.

"Let's start by explaining what we know" Mr Turn said, readjusting some paperwork on his desk. "On Friday morning of last week, Jackson's mother called and requested a meeting immediately about a concern she had. When we met, she explained that she was growing increasingly concerned about messages she had found on his mobile phone. These messages were about one of our members of staff where he expressed sexual attraction towards her, which isn't abnormal for boys at this age, however following this, there were messages disclosing that they had met in person outside of school hours and, well…" The fat little man in front of him was nervous and hesitant to tell him something that he figured was going to cause him to lose his temper, which Jackson could feel was brewing.

"And what?" he demanded, not in the mood to be messed around, but the officer took over and got to the real issue.

"Mr Cotts, we have reason to believe that your son may have been in a sexual relationship with a member of staff"

"WHAT ARE YOU TALKING ABOUT?!"

"Please bear with us as we are still investigating the situation, and a few things aren't adding up. Clayton's mother was able to produce evidence that suggests that Clayton has been in communication with Miss. Turnell in more than a professional manner, including indecent photographs of this member of staff partially naked" she went on, and immediately Jackson's heart stopped. He knew exactly what photo's they had been shown, because he'd been the one that took them, but he had no idea how they'd ended up almost losing Liv her job.

"Are you all fucking idiots?" he steamed, pacing the room "Clayton's mum has never set foot in this school, and Clayton has never been sexually inappropriate with Olivia!"

"I'm sorry?"

"Did Clayton see the woman who was posing as his mother? How on earth did you let something like this happen? How did you let a stranger come into this school and pose as my son's mother, put in an allegation of inappropriate sexual behaviour, and not think to inform me, his primary guardian and sole carer! What kind of ship are you running here? And how *DARE* you interview him without me being here?"

"Mr. Cotts, your ex-partner has made us more than aware of your mental health condition and I'm concerned that you may be in denial. I know this is a lot to take in but…"

"But nothing! This has nothing to do with my disorder, or my mental state, and everything to do with how poorly you have handled this situation. I know the exact photos you're talking about, because I took them! Olivia and I have been seeing each other for weeks, and the woman who was here, is the same woman you are supposed to be keeping away from me!" he said pointing at the officer who looked shocked and confused. "The same woman who tried to set Liv alight, has turned up at my house, and at my work, and the same woman who has the exact same 'mental health condition as me, but also includes psychotic breaks, which you're lucky I don't suffer from! How dare you speak to my son about something he had no idea about. He left here crying that not only had he disappointed me, but he'd lost Liv her job too!"

Mr. Turn looked beetroot and the officer who was now introducing herself as a detective looked utterly appalled.
"Mr. Cotts, I am deeply sorry for how this has happened, it is unforgiveable, and I must apologise on behalf of the police service and the school. A full investigation into this matter will be carried out but we do still have questions".

"Such as what?!" he said glaring at her.

"When Clayton was asked if he had seen Miss. Turnell outside of school hours, he confirmed that he had. Are you aware of this?"

"Are you taking the piss? I literally just told you that Liv and I are together, of course he's seen her outside of school. Clayton doesn't know we're together; we didn't want it to make it awkward for him here, but she tutors him at home twice a week in preparation for his exams. I'm not answering anymore of your pointless questions, so I suggest you call reception and tell them to get my son out of lesson before I lose my temper and you lose your jaw" he spat.

With that he left the room, slamming the door behind him and went to get some air before he had to face Clayton, and face the music too. Rachael had gone too far, and he owed Clayton an apology and an explanation, as well as Liv. He needed to see her, because he was having to work to keep himself together, and he hadn't had to do this in such a long time.

Jackson tapped out a text to Liv whilst he waited for Clayton and tried to string together a way to explain what had gone on, but nothing he typed to Liv made sense and he rang her instead.

"I was just talking about you" she said chirpily, and even hearing her voice helped to calm him down.

"Were you now? All good things I hope"

"Of course, Mum says hi and she wants to meet you"

"Well, I'd love to meet her too"

"What's up? You not at work?"

"No, something came up at school. Can you come over a bit earlier tonight, I really need to see you"

"Is everything okay?" she asked sounding concerned, and Jackson could hear in her voice that she was worried.

"Nothing I can't fix" he promised. He didn't want to burden Liv, but he couldn't pretend that nothing was going on. He was surprised how far Rachael had gone, and he was scared how far she was willing to go too.

"I'll be over in half hour. Jackson are you okay?" she said, and he refused to lie to her.

"I don't know right now"

"I won't be long, okay?"

"Okay"

Jackson watched as Mr. Turn and the officer walked Clayton over to his car, and Jackson gestured for him to get in. He joined him in the front seat, and spun off out of the car park, leaving them both behind in the rear view.

"You okay Clayt?" he asked as he fiddled with the straps of his bag on his lap.

"I just feel like I've got Miss, in trouble and I haven't done anything. I promise nothing of what they've said is true Dad and I spoke to Mum, and she hasn't got a clue what I'm going on about"

"Clayt this is my fault, and you don't have to beat yourself up about it. Liv is gonna meet us at home so we can talk to her, but I wanted to talk to you first"

"About?"

"So, we wanted to wait until you'd finished this year, so it wasn't awkward for you, but Liv and I have been kind of seeing each other for a while" he said, hating the fact that he'd hidden it from him so long.

"Yeah, no shit" he replied, rolling his eyes like he'd just told him the most obvious thing in the world.

"What?"

"It's kind of obvious that you and her are sleeping together dad, you don't really hide it very well, no offence" Clayton shrugged.

"Oh" Jackson said, feeling relieved that he wasn't angry.

"But also, Uncle Joe told me about a month ago"

"Well, that was nice of him!" Jackson replied, not surprised that Joe had opened his fat trap again.

"He didn't mean to; I was talking about your birthday and he said that you'd probably want to do something with Miss without thinking and then told me not to say anything until you were ready to tell me. You know, I don't care that you have a girlfriend dad?"

"I know Clayt, just don't want you to think I'm not going to put you first because I will"

"I know. Are you mad about what happened at school?" he mumbled.

"I'm not mad at you. I'm mad at myself for being an idiot. The photo they're talking about is one that I took, but I don't know how it ended up at school. I probably have a good guess, but I now need to go and explain to Liv how I might have lost her her job"

"Dad, do you love her?" he asked, looking at him as they pulled up onto the driveway and Jackson parked the car. Jackson laughed and rested his head back on the seat before exhaling.

"I think so mate, but she might hate me after today"

57.

Liv pulled up not long after Jackson and let herself into the house since the doors were ajar. She kicked off her shoes and walked to the kitchen where Jackson was sat with his hands in his head.

"What's happened?" she said taking his hands and wrapping them around her waist. Jackson rested his head on her chest whilst she stroked his head, but wouldn't look at her.

"I really fucked up Liv" he said, and Liv's heart dropped. She pulled away a little and lifted his chin so she could see him properly, but she didn't know if she wanted to know what come next.

"Jax, what did you do?" she asked, dreading the answer. A million things were running through her head, but the way he was talking sounded like the inevitable had happened. He'd gone elsewhere, just when she was ready to admit that she was in love with him, he'd found someone else. He might have regretted it, but he was unhappy enough to stray in the first place which proved that maybe she wasn't the one for him.

"Is it someone else?" she asked as tears pooled in her eyes, and she was helpless to stop them falling.

"Liv? What?!" he said getting to his feet and cupping her face. He kissed her, whilst she cried, and Liv couldn't imagine having to leave heartbroken "Liv, I would never cheat on you! I love you. I just can't fucking believe I dragged you into this shit life. You deserve so much better than me and better than all the shit you've had to put up with just because I fell in love with you, and want to be with you"

"What's happened then, just tell me?!" she said, wiping her face still filled with dread and panic.

"I was at school today because Clayton rang me crying. He said he'd been questioned by the head and the police about having inappropriate sexual relationship... with you".

"What?!" she screamed, sounding confused, "Jackson you know that's not true, that's fucking disgusting! Who would make that up?!"

"Let me explain," he said pulling up a chair and getting a bottle of wine from the fridge.

"I can't drink, I'm driving".

"No, you're staying here tonight".

Liv began to protest but Jackson's eyes grew sad, and he looked too tired to argue, "please Liv, I can't sleep without you and I really, really need it. I need you tonight".

She exhaled and pushed her glass forward for Jackson to pour, then drank whilst he started reeling off the events of the day. He explained what Clayton had said on the phone, told her about what Mr. Turn and the officer had said, and then told her that he thought that Rachael had somehow got hold of his passwords and onto his drive account.

Liv listened but didn't know what to reply. She wasn't annoyed at Jackson, but she was annoyed at the situation and at how malicious she was. Liv couldn't show her face in school again, that was for certain, and Jackson was struggling to keep it together, which was the last thing she wanted.

"I'm so sorry Liv," he pleaded running his hands over his face again and looking exhausted, "I never meant for the photo to go anywhere, it was just for me. You looked beautiful and I wanted to remember it, but now I feel like the biggest idiot"

"Jax I don't care that you took the photo, it's not your fault your ex is a psychopath. Well, actually it is your fault that you slept with her in the first place, but not how she is reacting now" she said gesturing for a top up on her wine which Jackson provided. "First things first, how's Clayton?" she asked, trying to process the mess that today had brought with it.

"He's okay, he's upstairs" which made Liv lower her voice and ask why he wasn't at school still.

"He knows Liv, he's known for weeks"

"About us?" she asked, confused.

"Apparently, we make it obvious that we are sleeping together, and then Joe kind of let it slip but told him not to say anything. He seems happy though, he wasn't upset when I told him which is a relief, I guess. I don't think I could have handled that as well"

"Well, that's one less thing to worry about. Kids are more resilient than you think Jax. Now, how are you?"

Liv took his hand in hers and watched as his shoulders relaxed and he exhaled deeply. He wasn't himself, and he had every reason to be angry, but she didn't want that to send him into a downward spiral, not that she'd blame him. She could see how hard he was trying, and she felt like she was out of her depth, but all she could do was try.

"Jax, talk to me"

"I'm angry, and I'm tired. I feel like I'm going to do something stupid, but I don't want to lose either or you, and I'm trying to keep it together but I'm struggling, so bad"

"You're not going to lose us Jax, shit happens, and we will deal with it" she said, and she kissed him before he got the chance to reply. Jackson kissed her back, but it was different, it was desperate, like he never wanted to stop, and he lifted Liv up and around his waist.

"Jax," she said as he kissed her neck, lifted her top, and went for his trousers, "stop, Clayton's home"

But he seemed desperate, and Liv was too. He wasn't forceful, and she could have easily pushed him away, but she didn't want to.

"Jax we can't do this here!" she said as he put her down on the side and worked on the button of her jeans, but she wasn't putting up much of a fight and she felt like she needed this as much as he did.

Jackson knew why she was protesting, but at that moment in time, he didn't care. All he could think about was that being inside of her would make him feel better, and he needed that more than anything.

"Do you not want it Liv," he asked, but she wasn't doing much to stop him.

"Of course, I do, but Clayton's home and I'm not exactly quiet Jax, wait until tonight" she said, but by the time he'd worked his way into her underwear and slid his fingers inside of her, she gave up even suggesting that he stop.

Liv opened her legs wider and Jackson smiled against her lips as she did, grateful she'd given in to her instincts, and was ready to let him play with her. He felt her nails dig into his back as she moved her hips towards him and moaned against his mouth.

"Not in the kitchen Jax" she managed to get out as he lifted his hands out of her trousers, and over her clit making her eyes roll back and a moan escape her again.

"I don't want to wait until later" he said, as she ran her fingers over his helmet and kissed his neck.

"And I don't want your son to walk in on his dad fucking his teacher" she laughed, and Jackson sighed.

"What about the bathroom?" he begged, but Liv was going to make him wait, and Jackson was going to take full advantage of it.

"Fine" he huffed, as he rebuttoned his trousers and gave Liv another kiss, "but just so you know, I plan on waking you up multiple times throughout the night to fuck you, and I have work, so you won't get a lie in either"

"Just so you know, I look forward to it, so don't talk to me like it's a punishment" she said, jumping down from the island. "And if you're as tired as you look Jax, you'll be sleeping through the night and it will be me waking you up".

"Yeah, we'll see" he laughed.

58.

After Ben had walked out on her last week, Rachael pulled herself together and thought about everything he said. Jackson was many things, but forgiving wasn't one of them, and there was no way he was ever going to take her back after what she'd done. She knew that deep down, but that didn't mean she was willing to accept it. He'd hurt her worse that anyone in her past, and that was saying something. She'd been hurt by plenty of people, almost everyone she'd ever met, but Jackson was different.

Jackson had been there for her when she felt like her world was falling apart, and as more than just a friend. Despite trying to make things work with other people, she always ran back to him, and the last time had felt so different. He'd let his guard down, taken her out, and he'd even let her stay at the house which had always been off limits. Previous times, he'd never shown so much commitment, and that's why it hurt so bad now.

Rachael had stewed over her options for hours, but it done nothing but make her mania worse. She could put on a brave face, but everything was coming to a head, and she wanted to make him hurt the way she did. She wanted him to lose everything, and she knew exactly how to hit him hardest, by getting to Liv, and getting to Clayton.

Rachael accessed his personal cloud account, which wasn't nearly as exciting as she thought it would be. She wanted something to use against him. His password was easy enough to guess, but he used his work phone so much, she didn't know whether she'd find anything at all. She knew his work account was completely professional, and that didn't interest her, but she was able to get something. His phone automatically backed up his photo's so she flicked through his album looking for anything she could use and found them.

Photos of Liv sprawled across the bed, completely naked with a quilt covering her partially, but a full view of her breasts. Her blood boiled at the sight, and she launched a cup across the room in anger.

Raising the complaint with the school on Friday had been easy, and she knew he would lose it when he found out. She wasn't sure what that meant for her, but she had nothing to lose anymore. Jackson might have been a closed book to everyone else, but he seemed to forget how much he'd shared with her when they were together. She knew that Holly had nothing to do with Clayton and so posing as her was easy. She'd made sure to exaggerate his condition, told them it was volatile and stressed how important it was that he didn't find out she was there, not yet anyway.

Rachael had put on the waterworks when she asked that they wait to speak to Clayton until the police were involved because he was upset and embarrassed. She told them that if he knew she was there, he would feel even worse, which was the last thing she wanted, given the fact that he had been exploited by his teacher. She said how disgusted she was with what had happened, and how she couldn't believe her son had been taken advantage of.

Mr. Turn had been understanding and told her that he would get to the bottom of everything. He was apologetic and assured her that Miss. Turnell would be suspended with immediate effect whilst an investigation was carried out. He'd seen Rachael to the door, and she knew that she'd just opened a can of worms of momentous proportions, not just for herself, but for everyone Jackson loved too.

59.

Liv had thought that it would feel weird being at the house as Jackson's girlfriend instead of Clayton's teacher when he was around, but it wasn't. They ordered food, sat and laughed, and Liv felt more comfortable than ever. It was a weight off her shoulders now they didn't have to hide it from him, and Clayton seemed happy that things were out in the open.

Liv shared stories of Clayton's classroom antics, and Clayton shared stories of his dad over the years. Jackson seemed relaxed, as he always did in front of Clayton, and Liv was hoping that after the night they'd all spent together, they could put all the drama behind them.

She didn't want Jackson beating himself up about something that wasn't in his control, but she knew herself, and she knew she wasn't the kind of person to let it slide. She knew Jackson would try and stop her, but she had every intention of approaching Rachael herself, and asking her to back off. She didn't want her coming in between her and Jackson for sure, but more importantly, she didn't want Clayton getting hurt, or Jackson spiralling out of control.

Clayton settled for the night not long after they'd finished eating, and Jackson told him that she was staying, not that he minded. Liv was apprehensive, but she wanted this with Jackson, and becoming comfortable with Clayton was something she was going to have to get used to if she wanted a proper future with him, which she did.

"You wanna go to bed?" he asked, kissing her neck once Clayton had disappeared, and Liv felt like she'd been waiting for an age to kiss him.

"I do" she smiled.

...

In the past Jackson had used sex and alcohol to help him feel better, but that's the last thing he wanted to do now. He wanted to be with Liv, and relive everything they did over the weekend, but he didn't want to do it for the wrong reasons, and he knew that if he went all the way with her that night it would be just that. He'd enjoy it, but only because it would stop his mind from going into overdrive and spiralling out of control.

He still couldn't believe what Rachael had done, and there was no way he was going to let it slide. It was one thing to try and hurt him, but to bring Clayton into it, and Liv too? That was a step too far. Jackson was going to see her and set things straight once and for all. Or so he thought.

Liv had climbed into bed whilst Jackson got himself undressed clumsily, angry at everything. She watched as he stressed about his belt being difficult to unbuckle and his trousers getting stuck on his foot, and it seemed like every minor thing was getting his back up.

"You wanna talk about it?" she said, drawing her legs up to her chest and wrapping her arms around them, but Jackson didn't know if he did. He didn't want Liv to know how angry he was or let on to how close he was to losing it, but he also didn't want to lie to her.

"All I want tonight, is to get in bed with you and sleep" he said, climbing in next to her and watching as she made herself comfortable on his chest.

"It's not something we can just ignore Jax" Liv told him as she traced her fingers up and down his stomach, and Jackson agreed with her. Rachael wasn't just going to go away, unless he made her, but he didn't know what that would mean for him and Liv.

"I'm going to see her, and tell her to back off" he said kissing her forehead, but Liv rolled her eyes, which suggested that she wasn't keen on the idea, "what do you suggest I do then?"

"I'll go and see her".

"Over my fucking dead body" he spat, not even considering the suggestion. There was no way he was letting her anywhere near Rachael after last time, and he had no idea what state she was in now. If he had to guess, she was going for blood, and he had no doubt that she'd stopped with her meds, because the way she was acting was irrational and out of hand. It was one thing turning up to throw abuse at him at work, but this was different.

"Jax, I'm a big girl, I can handle myself, and to be fair I wasn't asking for your permission" she said, lifting her head from his chest and looking up at him.

"I don't doubt it, but can we please remember that last time you two met she tried to set you alight" he said calmly, but inside he was screaming. He didn't want Rachael to get the better of Liv or to manipulate her in any way. He wanted to fix it, and he wanted to do that without Liv being involved.

"I appreciate that, but I don't want you seeing her, losing your head, and spiralling out of control. I don't want her to cause a rift between us, because you want to protect me and Clayton" she said, losing her patience.

"Liv, I'm not prepared to argue with you about it. Our first argument isn't going to be because of Rachael and her stupid little games. I'm not prepared to let her come between us, but you tried speaking to her once, and you saw how irrational she was. She's obviously doing this to get back at me, and so I'll be the only one who's able to sort this mess out".

Liv was silent and didn't speak, just listened as Jackson reeled off the reasons why he didn't want her going there. He told her that he didn't think Rachael was taking her antipsychotics, and she was quite clearly hell bent on ruining his life, along with Liv's too which he wasn't prepared to let that happen.

"You're not saying anything?" he said, when she stayed silent, even when he'd finished.

"What's there to say? You said you didn't want to argue, so be it"

"But now you're in a bad mood with me?"

"I'm not in a mood with you Jax, I'm just worried. If you think that it will be better for you to see her, then by all means do it, I can't stop you can I? I'll still be here after it all, I just hope you can convince her to stop, so we can get on with our lives and live happily ever after" she muttered, leaning up to kiss him.

"I love you?" he said, not knowing whether he'd get the reply he wanted or not. When he'd told her he'd fallen in love with her earlier, she'd been too caught up in trying to work out whether he'd cheated, that he didn't think she even heard him. He didn't know if she loved him, but he wanted her too. He wanted to give her the world and more, but he felt like he was failing her.

Liv kissed him but didn't say the words. She climbed on top of him with her legs straddling his lap, then laid her head on his chest whilst he tickled her back.

"Promise me that you'll get this sorted, without losing your head, and come home to me, so I can say it too" she said.

60.

Jackson slept better than he had all week and was thankful that Liv agreed to stay the night, because sleep was exactly what he needed. His alarm started buzzing at 6:00am, but there was no way he was getting out of bed and leaving her there. She was still snoring next to him and didn't even stir at the alarm which he figured had something to do with the fact she had other ideas than sleeping last night, not that he was complaining.

He laid there for a few minutes, watching her as she slept and wondering how he'd got to this point in his life. 6 months ago, when he met her, he couldn't wait to get rid of her, but now, he never wanted to leave her. He meant what he had said when he told her he didn't stop thinking about her, it took weeks, and even then he never forgot her completely. Then, when he walked into her classroom he had this overwhelming sense of déjà vu, and it felt as though he was meant to find her, some way or another.

Now he was in a good place, Rachael was putting all of that at risk, and he didn't know what he was meant to do to resolve it all. He needed to see her, that much was obvious, but he didn't know what the best way to approach her. He wasn't scared, but he was cautious. He knew her history, and he didn't want to be on the receiving end of any of her silly games.

The more he thought about it, the more frustrated he got, and in the end, he had to get out of bed. He was tossing and turning so much that he thought he'd wake Liv, and he didn't want her to know that he was anxious, because he didn't want her to worry. He grabbed his phone and headed downstairs to the kitchen, tapping a message out to Rachael as he did telling her they needed to talk. He didn't expect a reply anytime soon, but he was mistaken, and his reply came in the form of a cold, broken voice behind him.

Rachael had made plans to get revenge on Jackson, but after the police came knocking on her door, she had to change them rapidly. She thought she'd have more time, but it turned out they took the complaint more seriously that she thought they would, and time wasn't something it looked like she had. She still had things in the works, but when she did her usual drive by of his house and saw them all sat in the lounge laughing and joking at her expense, she knew that what she had planned wasn't working as she thought it would.

She watched for a while. Watched them laugh, but Jackson and Liv weren't intimate until Clayton left. As soon as he left the room Jackson and Liv held hands and kissed without any idea that they were being watched. They were taunting her, putting on a show, and she wasn't going to let him do that to her, or himself. Rachael knew that Jackson and her belonged together, and it looked like she was going to have to make him see that the hard way.

She'd gone home and paced for hours trying to think of a way to get him to see sense, but she couldn't. She needed to see him, and she was going to be calm and collected. She couldn't be rash about this, and she would apologise for everything she had done because she didn't want him to hate her. She didn't think it was too late for them, but she needed to wait until he was alone, and Liv wasn't in the picture.

By the time it was 4:00 she knew she had one shot to make him see sense. The more time he spent with Liv the less likely he was to forgive her. Rachael knew that he would never lose his temper in front of Clayton and so, she planned on being there when he woke up so she could apologise over and over, and he would have to listen because he wouldn't lose his cool whilst Clayton was in the house.

What she didn't expect was for Liv's car to still be there when she pulled up at stupid o'clock, and what it would do to her. Up until that point she'd felt like she'd kept a level head, but now she didn't care. She let herself in with the key round the back, one that she had acquired in the past and never gave back.

She'd watched as they slept, wrapped up in each other's arms and wanted to smother the woman in front of her with a pillow. Instead, she did nothing, just took herself back down the stairs and waited until one of them woke up, and she didn't care which one. Minutes felt like hours, but eventually she heard his alarm go upstairs, and his footsteps came not long after.

She was sat at the table looking out at the garden and her phone buzzed in her pocket before he even set foot in the kitchen. When he did, she didn't hesitate in making herself known, and watched as his face turned to pure anger.

"Talk about what?" she said, fighting back tears. She didn't know if she was sad, tired, angry, hurt, or what was causing them. But they were going to come regardless.

"What the fuck are you doing in my house," he hissed through gritted teeth, shutting the door behind him to the hallway and trying to keep his voice down, "and how the fuck did you get in?!"

"You wanted to talk, so did I" she said shrugging, but it was taking everything she had to not scream that she loved him and needed him, but he wasn't making it easy.

"You don't do talking Rachael, you do manipulation" he said approaching her at the table, "now get the fuck out of my house before I chuck you out"

"Temper, temper" she laughed , but Jackson didn't look like he was in the mood to play, instead he took her wrist and pulled her from the chair, towards the door,

"Don't fucking touch me!" she shouted, not caring that she was going to wake the others.

I've had enough of you trying to ruin my fucking life Rach, now get your fucking bag and get out of my fucking house" he shouted back, knowing full well Liv and Clayton weren't going to sleep through the commotion.
"I'm trying to help you! She's using you Jackson and you're too fucking blind to see it!"
"Using me for what?! I don't have anything to give her? She's too good for me, and she doesn't ask for anything! Why can't you just let me be happy?"
"BECAUSE I MADE YOU HAPPY! I WAS WHO YOU COME BACK TO ALL THEM TIMES THE OTHERS DIDN'T CUT IT, I'M THE ONE YOU TOLD HOW YOU FEEL, I WAS THERE TO PICK YOU UP AS MUCH AS YOU DID WITH ME AND NOW YOU WANT TO ACT LIKE IT NEVER HAPPENED"

Rachael gripped at her hair and Jackson watched as her face turned red. He heard her voice break as she shouted at him and felt nothing but pity for her, because she was wrong, she hadn't done that for him, because he hadn't let her. She was confused and in a state of manic that not even he could pull her out of. Jackson had always been careful not to get too attached to her, but it was obvious she didn't share that opinion.

She began pacing and muttering to herself whilst Jackson asked her over and over to leave, but she wouldn't. He watched her frantically look around the room, desperate for something, but nothing came and then everything came all at once.

Rachael had gone too far and it was obvious that she'd been going without meds for too long to, which Jackson was all too familiar with. He'd watched the breakdowns before, but back then he could comfort her until she come down, now he felt nothing but disgust and pity, that wasn't possible.

"I'm calling the police" he said, getting his phone out of his pocket, but Rachael didn't want that. She took his phone from his hand and threw it hard to the floor before Jackson even had a chance to unlock it.

"I'm sorry" she begged, touching his face and trying to wrap his arms around her, "I promise I'll do better, and I'll be better, and I'll do anything you want Jax I promise"

But Jax had had enough, and he needed to keep Liv away because he was worried about what was coming next. He pushed her away from him and could hear Liv calming Clayton at the top of the stairs whilst he called for him. Jackson didn't want either of them to be anywhere near Rachael whilst she was like this, but it was too late because she'd heard it too.

61.

Rachael ran towards the door before Jackson had time to stop her, throwing things behind her on the way to slow him down. He caught up with her as she reached the handle, and kicked the door shut before she had a chance to get it open again, but Rachael wasn't stopping, and Jackson didn't want to hurt her. He could have, and it was taking everything in his power not too, but Liv and Clayton were in the house, and he didn't want them to think he was capable of that.

"Liv! Take Clayton and get in the car!" he shouted, watching her eyes turn feral, but Rachael was screaming so loud he had no idea if she could hear him. He looked round to the door leading on to the lounge, but Rachael blindsided him with chopping board she found on the side and the next thing he knew pain was radiating through his head, and the room was spinning.

He watched as Rachael made for the knife block, and headed for the doors, but his head was pounding as he wasn't thinking straight. Jackson went back into the hallway, trying to cut her off, and saw Liv halfway down the stairs.

"Jax you're bleeding!" she said, running down the remainder of the stairs, but he pushed her away as Rachael appeared, wielding a knife and screaming.

"Liv, go back upstairs" he pleaded, but she had frozen.

"She's ruined our lives Jackson!" she shouted, as her knuckles gripped the handle so tight they went white and Jackson stood protecting Liv. He was trying to stay focused, but the walls were spinning and blood had made its way into his eye whilst he tried to shake the confusion away.

"JAX! MOVE!" she screamed, and he could see just how desperate she was.

"Rach, leave Liv alone and I promise we will talk" he said, wiping what he could out of his eye and holding his hand out. He could feel Liv pulling him towards her, and knew that she wanted him to back off, but there was no way Jackson was moving from between them.

"Jax please? Please come back to me, I don't want to do this anymore, I need you. You won't come back to me whilst she's here, will you?" she pleaded, but the more she spoke, the more she worked herself up, and nothing Jackson said seemed to be helping calm her.

"I've promised I'll talk Rach; you don't want to hurt me?" he said, pushing Liv back up the stairs, "you're right, I probably did love you, but we grew apart, and I thought we were both moving on. We will talk okay? Just let Liv go and get her stuff and get Clayton out of here?"

"Jax?" Liv whispered, not wanting to leave him, but he shrugged her off. He just wanted her safe, and that meant her not being there, whatever that might mean for him.

"Liv leave us alone" he begged, but it wasn't enough for Rachael.
"YOU'RE LYING!" she screamed, and Jackson instinctively pushed Liv away as Rachael lunged towards them, holding the knife high and trying desperately to hurt her.

Liv had woken to the commotion and managed to get to the stairs before Clayton did. He was a mess, crying and begging her to move so he could get to his dad, but Liv knew he'd never forgive her if she let him get hurt. She told Clayton to call Joe, and call the police, and not to come out of his room until someone he trusted came to him. Liv had no idea what was going on in the kitchen, but she'd never heard Jackson lose his temper.
When she finally managed to convince Clayton to lock himself away and headed for the stairs, the door was flung open again and

Jackson had stumbled out, bleeding from his head, and looking frantic at the sight of her, but she wasn't expecting to see Rachael wielding a knife, and looking like she did.

Her eyes were dark and sunk in, like she hadn't slept in days, but it was the look in them that was scariest of all. Liv had never seen her not made up, but she had no doubt that this was what her psychotic break looked like. Her hair was greasy, and unkempt, tied in a rough knot at the back of her head, and her clothes looked like something found on the bedroom floor.

Rachael was livid, and Olivia was scared, scared for herself and scared for Jackson too. She wanted to do something to help, wanted to see to his head, but he wouldn't let her. As she stood behind his back, and he shielded her from Rachael's sight, he squeezed her hand tight and pushed her towards the stairs, signalling that he wanted her to leave.

Then everything past that point happened in a split second.

Rachael screamed at Jackson after he'd tried to calm her, and when Liv tried to move, she lunged towards them angrily. Jackson lifted his foot hitting her square in the chest, sending her backwards into the doorframe and begged Liv to leave, find Clayton and lock the door. But his head was getting worse, and he fell on to the stairs. Liv couldn't leave him with Rachael, and made for the knife, but she was too slow and before she knew it, there was an impact that felt like she'd been hit by a truck, and her body was numb.

She wanted to scream, but it wouldn't come out. Instead, her breaths became panicked, and she didn't know what to do. The pain wasn't immediate, but when it started, it radiated through every inch of her body like something she'd never experienced before.

Rachael's face went white, and she stepped back with the realisation of what she just done. Her hands were red, and the white shirt the Liv was wearing was slowly turning red too. Adrenalin took over and Jackson went to her, whilst Rachael stood there staring at the knife protruding from Liv's abdomen.

"CALL A FUCKING AMBULANCE!" he shouted, reaching for his phone, and realising it had been one of the many things she destroyed on her rampage.

Liv screamed as he lowered her to the floor and she drew in shallow, scared, breaths. He supported her head and tried to assess the damage, whilst Rachael panicked and ran out the front door leaving him there alone.

"CLAYTON! CALL AN AMBULANCE!" he called up the stairs, fighting back tears that were gradually pooling in his eyes. Jackson stripped his shirt and wrapped it around the knife. He didn't want to move it, but he knew needed to apply pressure and he didn't know how he was supposed to both.

"Liv, I'm so sorry, stay with me" he begged, as tears rolled down the side of her face and into her hair. Her bronze skin looked pale, and Jackson was desperate to get her help.

"DAD?! What's happened?!" Clayton cried, crashing down the stairs in panic. It was something he didn't want his son to see, but right now he didn't have a choice. Liv was deteriorating by the second and she needed medical attention.

"Clayt, I need your phone to call an ambulance and get Liv a pillow" he said with his voice breaking as he did. He wanted to be strong for them both, but he couldn't. This was his fault, and there was no way he could fix it. Clayton shakily handed his phone to Jackson after calling 999. He grabbed a cushion for Liv's head whilst Jackson tried his best to give over the information that the emergency services operator was asking for.

"Clayt, can you wait by the door so the ambulance know where we are ok?" he said, when the operator asked, and he did as he was told. Jax spoke to Liv over and over, trying to calm her, and begged her to stay still but she was in pain, and it was getting worse.

"The paramedics are 3 minutes out ok? Just try and keep calm and continue to apply pressure" the woman said down the phone, but that wasn't helping. 3 minutes was too long, and he needed them to get there now.

Jax heard a car screech outside and panicked. He thought Rachael had returned, and Clayton was out there alone, but he couldn't leave Liv unattended.

"Jax?" Liv managed to force out, and she looked as scared as he felt.

"Clayton!" he shouted, panicking all over again, but his panic was short lived, when Joe's voice came booming in from outside the house, comforting Clayton who was a mess.

"What the fuck has happened Jax" he said, bounding through the door and looking at the scene surrounding him. Jax's head was still bleeding, trickling down his head and his shoulder. He was knelt beside Liv with his hands pressed either side of the knife that was still inside of her, and both of them were covered in blood. Liv looked pale, and she was trying as much as she could to stifle her screams, whilst Jax promised she'd be okay over and over.

"What can I do?" Joe asked, taking off his Jacket and kneeling beside them both and with that, the tears began falling thick and fast.

Joe kept his voice low and calm when he replied and squeezed his shoulder "Jax she's going to be fine okay. You don't realise because you're in shock, but I promise you it looks worse that it is.

The fact she's in pain enough to scream is a good sign and even though there looks like there's a lot of blood, if it was a major organ or artery, she'd be unconscious by now. You've done everything right okay?"

There were times when Jackson loved how straight-talking Joe was, and others where it didn't help a situation. Whilst he was holding on to the woman he loved, scared that he was going to lose her forever, Joe's pep talk was comforting, and was exactly what he needed to keep him together. Even in a panic, he was level-headed, and Jax was grateful for him more than ever in that moment.

Liv's screams were getting louder when Clayton ran in to say that the ambulance had arrived. She was sobbing uncontrollably and telling Jax it was hurting, and she was sorry, but everything she said broke his heart more. The paramedics wanted to take over, but Jackson didn't want to let her go because he was scared that he wouldn't get her back.

"Jax, let her go and let them work" Joe said, squeezing his shoulder reassuringly, and although it went against every fibre of his being, he released his hold on Liv and left the paramedics begin to apply pressure to her abdomen, rustle in their kits, and prepare the stretcher. Seconds felt like hours, and whilst Joe ran to fetch him a t-shirt, Jax comforted Clayton who was still a wreck.

He held Liv's hand, and wrapped his arm round Clayton as he did so, wanting to be close to both of them, and not wanting to have to choose one or the other. He needed to go with Liv to the hospital, but he needed to be there for Clayton. He never should have witnessed something like this, and Jackson felt like he'd let them both down as he listened to Liv sob through the oxygen mask they'd placed on her face and told her he was sorry.

"Dad is she going to be okay?" he cried into his shoulder, but Jax didn't know. He was just as scared as Clayton was, and he couldn't give him the answers he wanted. Liv squeezed his hand as he held it, and comforted Clayton, but her hand went limp, and her screaming stopped before they lifted her on to the stretcher. Joe threw his top to him and Jackson dressed whilst they lifted Liv on the stretcher.

"We'll meet you at the hospital" Joe said, and Jax was thankful that he left him without having to make a decision, because although hearing the screams escaping Liv's lungs was scary, hearing nothing but silence was even scarier.

62.

Jax had planned on his first formal meeting with Liv's family to be under different circumstances, but right now he had no choice. Joe was sat comforting Clayton in one corner of the waiting room and although he'd asked him to take him home, neither of them wanted to leave. He'd been pacing the waiting room since they'd taken Liv down to surgery, and the police had tried to question him the whole time. The nurse had attempted to see to his head, but Jax couldn't stay still. Instead, he promised that he'd keep an ice pack on it, but Joe had made them glue the cut and dress it, much to Jackson's dismay. Joe had managed to get hold of Harry, who in turn got hold of Jade, and she went on to contact Owen as well as Liv's mum and dad.

Half an hour later, Jade arrived along with Harry demanding to know what had happened, and why her best friend was in surgery. Jax explained for the second time what had happened with the complaint at school, and with Rachael, and what the medics had said enroute to the hospital too. Thankfully, the knife was still in place and so although she was bleeding, they were guessing it had helped to prevent at least some the damage. He said that they wouldn't know more until they got her into theatre, but that given the circumstances, the position of the knife was the best they could hope for and had missed her vital organs. She had lost blood, and lost consciousness, but they were pumping fluids and monitoring her vitals and there wasn't much more they could do to support her until the surgeons removed the knife.

Jade looked like she could kill someone as tears streamed down her cheeks, and Harry took over in giving the details to the police about Rachael and their history in a separate room, away from Clayton. As they left the room, Jade pulled Jax to one side, and he tried to engage but he couldn't think straight.

"Owen, Carrie and Dave are on their way up Jax" she said, keeping her shaky voice low "I'd get Clayton out of here, because I imagine you and Dave will come to blows and I don't think it will take long"

"I don't blame him"

"Nobody is asking you to leave Jax but be prepared for sparks to fly. Dave can fly off of the rails quickly, and Owen isn't the calmest of people either. She loves you, I know that, and she will want you here when she wakes up" she said rubbing the tears from her eyes, which were closely followed by Jackson's.

He wouldn't blame any of them for hating him after what he'd allowed to happen, but the only thing he cared about was that Liv pulled through. Even if she never forgave him, he'd do anything just to see her again, and tell her how sorry he was for everything he put her through. He wished he'd committed sooner, never considered calling things off, told her he loved her more, and all he kept thinking about was whether he'd ever get to tell her again.

He turned to Joe and told him he needed to leave with Clayton, but neither of them wanted to. After some protesting, Clayton finally agreed and Jax told him he'd keep him updated, promised he'd be home as soon as he could, then hugged him tight before they left. For now, it was just him and Jade, and the silence in the room was deafening. Other than the sound of them both sniffling back tears, the room was quiet.

Jackson sat on the floor with his head between his legs and his arms draped over his knees, waiting for something. At that moment, he didn't care what it was, but sitting in silence was making his mind go into overdrive. He wanted to scream, he wanted to smash something, he just needed something to take his mind off the torment going on in his head.

Fortunately, he didn't have to wait long, because Harry returned, followed by Liv's family, and the tension in the room became suffocating.

"You've got 30 seconds to tell me exactly what the fuck happened to my daughter, and then you can get the fuck out of here" came the gravelly voice of Liv's dad.

Evidently, he wasn't wasting time on introductions and Jax didn't even bother getting to his feet. It was taking all he had not to blow up in response, and now wasn't the time. Her dad had every right to be furious, and thankfully Jade was there to explain everything he'd told her. Jackson wasn't about to put on a brave face, and pretend like he was tough, because the pain he was in was written all over his face.

"Take a walk with Dave" Carrie told Jade, and though he tried to protest, one glare from Carrie had Dave leaving the room, knowing all too well what that tone of voice meant, "You two too" she said tilting her head at Harry and Owen, and they followed suit leaving the room, and leaving Jax and Carrie alone.

He didn't move when she sat down beside him, and he didn't think he could face looking at her. She took his hand in hers and patted it reassuringly as she spoke to him, in a much kinder way that he was expecting.

"When Dave and I first got together, he was well known for being a hot head. He'd fly off the rails at the smallest things and we'd argue over stupid stuff before he'd leave for days at a time. Each time he came back, he'd come back a broken man. He'd cry, and apologise, promise he would change, but it would repeat over and over again, I knew something wasn't right, but Dave wasn't having any of it and so it continued. Then, I had Owen and I kind of settled for what it was. He was a great dad, but he was a difficult husband, and I put up with it because I loved him, more than anything in this world. Sometimes, I didn't like him, but I always loved him even when he had disappeared. I knew this was how he coped, and I accepted that, even though it was hard"

"Anyway, fast forward 3 years, Olivia came along, and things changed. You see, it wasn't until I had a daughter, and imagined her growing up and falling in love did I think to myself, I wouldn't want this for her, so why am I settling? I never wanted my kids to grow up aspiring to settle for relationships like ours, so I sat Dave down, and I told him my worries, and my fears about how I didn't want my daughter to ever be with someone who walked out when thing got hard, or flew off the rails at the tiniest things, and after 6 years together, he finally got help"

"Olivia came to me yesterday and she was glowing. I've never seen her look so happy in all of her adult life and that's all because of you Jackson. Life isn't perfect, and I know that you're scared, but this isn't your fault, and I know all too well how fragile the mind of someone sick can be, I've got the scars to prove it. You need to pull yourself out of this black hole you're putting yourself in, because when she wakes up, she needs to see the version of you that she loves, not the person you're scared of" Jackson let the tears come and sobbed for what felt like hours whilst Carrie comforted him.

He hadn't expected her to be understanding, he'd expected screaming and shouting, and although she was crying with him, she seemed to be holding it together a lot better than he was. Carrie wrapped her arm around his shoulder and patted his arm as the tears finally began to stop and Jackson finally plucked up the courage to speak.

"I'm so sorry, I never meant for this to happen" he said, finally facing her, with puffy eyes.

Liv looked like her mum. They had the same big brown eyes and welcoming smile, and it made him miss her even more.

"I know you didn't sweetheart, she will know that too. Now pick yourself up, you need to be ready for when they say she's stable" she said, getting to her feet and offering her hand to lift him from the floor.

Carrie walked her way over to the door and poked her head out, where all 4 of the people she'd sent on their travels were wating. Jade was crying into Harry's shoulder, Owen was sat on a chair with his head in his hands, and Liv's Dad was pacing back and forward past the vending machine over and over.

"You 3, go and see to Jackson" she said to Owen, Jade and Harry before targeting Dave with a finger, and lowering her voice "You, sort yourself out and pull yourself together. Liv loves this man, and let's not forget some of the stupid shit you did during some of your worst times. Jackson didn't do this, and I can promise you now, if you're not willing to accept this man, you're going to lose your daughter. You don't have to love him, but today you *will* be civil to him. His heart is breaking in there, and you are not helping!" she hissed.

With that, she wiped the tears from her face once again, and waltzed back into the waiting room with Dave in tow, who nodded to acknowledge Jackson, and joined him in pacing back and forward with worry. Though they didn't say a word to each other, it was clear that they were both feeling the same way about the woman they loved.

63.

It felt like eternity had passed, but after almost 3 hours the doctors finally arrived in the waiting room. Everyone stood, waiting apprehensively for news, but Jade was the first to speak.

"Is she okay?!" she asked, squeezing on to Harry, who hadn't left her side since he'd returned from speaking to the police.

"Who is her next of kin?" he asked, noting the amount of people in the room.

"I am, but we're a very close family, and we really need to know if she's okay" Carrie said, eager to hear the news.

"Husband?"

"I'm her partner" Jackson said, stepping forward "I agree. I think we all need to know"

"As you wish. Miss Turnell is out of theatre and is stable. Surgery went as well as could be expected. Thankfully the knife was located in the left lower quadrant of her abdomen and so all of her vital organs are intact. The knife had pierced her bowel, but due to it remaining inside of her, the damage was able to be rectified quickly without too much damage. I don't know if it was sheer luck or a miracle, but the knife completely missed her womb and ovaries, and mum and baby are well. She can have visit-"

"Baby?!" Jade squealed, "What are you talking about?"

The doctor looked around the room at the shocked expressions, as the colour drained from multiple faces, including Jackson's.

"I'm deeply sorry for sharing the news in this way, I assumed since you were close you would all have known. I've been working all night and it was a complete error in judgement I can only apologise for"

"Liv's pregnant?!" Jade squealed, almost crying with excitement.

"It's very early days, but I shouldn't say too much else until she's awake. I hope you'll forgive my mistake, but congratulations to you all, and I'll catch up with you during the week. Liv can have visitors, but it's probably best to minimise it to one, maybe two at a time. The doctors for the day will update you, but ensure she gets plenty of rest"

With that, he left and a nurse entered ready to show them too her bed. Jade was hugging Carrie and Owen and Dave were hugging with relief. Harry had joined Jackson to pat him on the back and hug him too, and it seemed like there wasn't a dry eye in the room.

"She's asked to see Dad" the nurse smiled, and Jackson knew he needed this even though he didn't know what to say. He left the room with Carrie hugging her boys, and Jade hugging Harry with excitement, but he was in complete shock. Not only had the woman of his dreams pulled through, she was carrying his baby, and he was going to be a dad all over again. He tried to put words together in his head, tried to think of something to say to her, but the minute he saw her lying there, words escaped him, and the tears came again.

He pulled the chair as close to the bed as he could and sat beside her, taking her hand and kissing it over and over again. He was too scared to touch anywhere else, to kiss her face, or lay beside her, and even though he wanted to be close, it was all he could manage.

"I'm sorry Liv," he sobbed as her thumb ran over his knuckles, and she mustered a smile through her oxygen mask, "I'm so, so sorry"

Despite what she'd been through, Liv looked more beautiful than ever to him, and in that moment, he knew that he wanted to spend every day of the rest of his life with her. Liv tried to talk, but her sounds were muffled through the mask she was wearing, and he couldn't understand. She lifted it off her head in frustration and panted a little at how much energy she used before she tried to speak again.

"I love you" she croaked through her dry lips, and Jackson felt like he'd been waiting a lifetime to hear those words. He leaned in to kiss her and felt her smile against his mouth whilst tears fell down her cheeks.

"How are you feeling?" he asked, wiping them away and tracing his thumb over her face.

"Like shit" she laughed, but the movement sent pain through her body making her wince.

"I'm so sorry Liv" he repeated, not thinking it would ever be enough. He wanted to get her home so he could keep her safe, but in the back of his mind he was worried about Rachael and just how far she'd gone this time. Liv said nothing, just laid there staring at him, whilst he kissed her hand and the tears kept falling.

"Did you know?" he asked, placing his hand gently on the safe side of her stomach and watching her face as she smiled and shook her head tiredly. Jackson didn't think that this would be something she'd hide from him, but he couldn't hide how happy he was as he beamed over how beautiful she was, and thought about how she would make the perfect mum.

...

Liv was tired, but she was scared to close her eyes. She'd had to beg Jackson to leave to see Clayton, because even though she wanted him near, she also wanted a chance to cry, and a chance to talk about what had happened. She didn't understand how everything had gone so wrong, or how she had ended up in a hospital with a knife wound, and a baby. She didn't think she could burden him with everything going through her mind, because she knew if hers was full, his must have been on overload.

Her mum and dad had cooed over her, telling them how much they loved her and how they couldn't believe they were going to be grandparents, but Owen hadn't been able to face her.

It wasn't until Liv had finally managed to convince her mum and dad to let Jade in, that she felt like she could let her guard down, and finally explain how she felt. Jade wouldn't entertain Liv saying she was fine, because it was obvious that she wasn't. Liv was in pain physically, and mentally visions of the commotion with Rachael kept repeating over and over again.

"Liv, you don't have to pretend you're fine, and you don't have to be strong for everyone else. You're allowed to be selfish for once, especially when it's about your health. There's two of you to look after now remember!" she said, climbing in bed with her and Liv sobbed into Jade's shoulder for what seemed like forever.

"Thanks Jay" she croaked when the tears had stopped falling, and she was grateful that she'd saved her until last.

"You don't have to thank me, you're my best friend, I just wish this had never happened to you"

"I don't even know how it did, everything happened so quick and I just didn't want Jackson getting any more hurt" she said, "I don't know what I was thinking"

"Well, love makes you crazy they say" Jade replied, resting her head on Liv's for a few minutes in silence. Liv didn't know what to respond, she thought Jade would take the words out of her mouth or ask her all the questions she was sat worrying about, but she didn't.

"So, are you not going to ask about the baby?" she finally asked, adjusting herself on the bed whilst Jade moved over. Evidently Jade had been dying to ask her because she started clapping excitedly as soon as she mentioned it.

"I know you're probably scared and nervous and worried and all over the place Liv, but honestly I'm so happy for you!"

"Really?"

"Honestly, it's shit how you found out, and it's shit that this is all happening at once, but you really do love him and he would do anything for you" she said, "nobody can tell you what to do Liv, but I know you, and I think everything happens for a reason, no matter how hard they are to understand".

Liv really did love him, there was no denying that, but she didn't know if she was ready to bring a baby in to the crazy life they were currently living. In the past few weeks, she'd lost her job, been introduced as Jackson's girlfriend, been impaled with a knife, and learned that she was pregnant. It was a lot to take in over a lifetime, and Liv didn't understand how everything had gone so wrong, so quickly.

"What if we're not ready for a baby Jade?" Liv asked as she fidgeted her fingers between the blankets nervously, "We've only known each other a few months, and I never planned on things happening this quickly".

Jade looked at her with a kind smile and held her hand. The years they'd spent together as friends had put them in all kinds of positions, but none like this one. Liv was always so confident and outspoken, to see her sat hurt and worried was surreal for Jade, surreal because it sounded like she'd already planned it out in her head for the future.

"Of course it wasn't planned Liv, and maybe it is too soon, but do you know what?" she said, matter-of-factly.

"What?"

"You will never, ever regret keeping this baby. Never. But there's a chance that you will regret it if you make the other decision. Jackson is an amazing dad, and even if things get rocky for you two, he will never abandon this baby, and neither would you. I know you Liv. I know you hated the fact that Tommy never commit, and maybe this is exactly why? Maybe this is exactly where you were meant to end up. I've never seen you so happy, well, obviously not right this second" she laughed as Liv furrowed her brows and tilted her head. "Tell me, before all of this happened, did you imagine yourself settling down with Jackson? Kids, marriage, house, holidays?"

"Well yeah, of course" she said, as tears began to roll down her face again.

"Then stop worrying, because everything you've ever wanted with him is on its way and everyone with eyes can see how much you love each other. If you love this baby even half as much as I can see you love Jackson, then you have nothing to worry about. Besides, if he dumps yo' ass, I can move in and be the best nanny ever!"

Liv exhaled playfully, trying to avoid laughing, and was happy that she had Jade to talk sense into her. She couldn't have spoken to Jackson about her worries, and her mum and dad were so over the moon that she didn't want to let them down, but she knew Jade would tell her straight, and Jade was right. She loved Jackson, more than she liked to admit, and she had spent every day imagining the rest of her life with him. A baby wasn't going to change that, and whilst it was sudden and she was shocked, she couldn't deny that the thought of watching him be a dad all over again made her beam.

"I'm gonna be a mum" Liv smiled, rubbing her stomach despite their being nothing to suggest there was a baby in there.

"The *best* mum" Jade said, kissing her head.

...

Jackson hadn't wanted to leave Liv, but she'd insisted he go and see Clayton. She wanted him to check that he was okay, and that was just one of the many reasons he loved her. She was always selfless, and she genuinely cared about his son, which she'd made clear from the minute he walked into her classroom.

Joe was waiting outside for him, when he finally tore himself away from the hospital bed, and he didn't hold back in letting Jackson know exactly what he was thinking.

"What the fuck happened this morning Jax and what the fuck is going on with Rachael? When you said she was psycho I didn't think you meant fucking literally! I'm glad Liv's fine, but Clayton was there as well today! Why the fuck would you involve someone like that in your life?!" he rambled on as they drove down the road.

Joe was protective over Jackson, but not nearly as much as he was over Clayton. When Jax had got out of rehab Joe had practically lived with them to make sure that he was taking his tablets, and was looking after Clayton properly, although he didn't know why. Jax had never had an issue in caring for Clayton, it was only ever when he wasn't around that he would fly off the rails, but Joe insisted on doing it anyway. Back then Jax had felt suffocated, because if it wasn't Joe, it was his mum and, in the end, he had to tell them both to stop smothering him and trust him.

Jackson had never been forthcoming about where he met Rachael to anyone other than Harry, so Joe didn't know that when he said she was psycho, he was talking literally, not figuratively.

"I know Joe" he said, as the onslaught continued.

"Do you though? What were you thinking getting with someone like that when your moods are so volatile anyway!"

"Liv's pregnant" he said, cutting him off. He didn't need Joe to tell him he was an idiot, but he did need his advice. It was the first time he'd said it out loud, and now he'd said it, he felt sick.

"What?!"

"Yeah"

It wasn't the thought of having a baby wasn't making him feel sick, but everything that had happened was running round and round in circles in his head, and he kept asking himself what if?

What if Liv hadn't made it? What if Clayton had got hurt? What if they'd lost the baby?

He could feel himself spiralling downwards, and all he could think was that he wanted to get hold of Rachael and make her pay. He wanted her to hurt, like she'd hurt Liv, and he genuinely thought he was capable of it in that given moment. His hands were shaking which he tried to hide, but Joe had already noticed by the time the tears started to fall again and pulled the car over.

"Tell me what's going on Jax"

"I can't believe I let this happen. I brought her into my fucked up life and now she's laying in a hospital bed! How am I supposed to step up and be there for her and this baby, when I can't even keep her safe Joe!" he said, his voice breaking as he did. Jackson put his head in his hands and let out everything he'd been holding in for the past 12 hours. He felt weak, and he felt unworthy of everything she gave him, and was yet to give him.

"Jax, you love this girl, right?"

"More than anything"

"Then you'll spend the rest of your life making it up to her. What happened today was shit, and yes, you're an idiot for ever entertaining that psycho bitch, but now you're gonna pick yourself up, like you always do, and you're going to go and tell my nephew that he's going to be a big brother. I promise you Jax, you will get through the shit and out of the other side with a life I can only envy. You're an amazing Dad, and I don't expect anything less for this new addition" he said squeezing his neck, "You know I always got you right?"

Jackson nodded and wiped the rest of the tears from his face whilst Joe pulled off again. He was right, he couldn't change what had happened, but he had the rest of his life to make up for it, and he planned on starting right away. The last thing he wanted was to repeat the mistakes he'd made when Clayton was young, and with that in mind, he pulled himself back together and headed back to tell his family they were about to get bigger.

Printed in Great Britain
by Amazon